THE POINT OF LIGHT

A NOVEL

JOHN ELLSWORTH

D1051894

AUTHOR'S NOTE

In this work, the Nationalsozialistische Deutsche Arbeiterpartei (the National Socialist German Workers' Party), has been abbreviated as "NSDAP" or referred to as "the Party" or "the Nazi Party." The Schutzstaffel (a paramilitary organization under the NSDAP) is usually abbreviated to "SS." Certain factual elements, including the timing of some events, have been altered for the sake of storytelling.

Much of the Auschwitz testimony is taken from the Nuremberg testimony of survivors.

This is a work of fiction. Names, characters, places, and incidents are the product of the author's imagination or are used fictitiously.

PROLOGUE

Paris-Soir Newspaper
Article dated 1/21/1946
By: Claire Vallant

In exactly one week, I will testify at the war crimes tribunal in Nuremberg, Germany. One Nazi who committed some of those crimes hasn't been found by the authorities. His name is Sigmund Schlösser (Waffen-SS), and he committed millions of war crimes by sending millions of Jews to their deaths at Auschwitz. He also committed a war crime against my family by sending one to her death.

The purpose of this newspaper article is to plead for help in finding this criminal. I will see him hang for his crimes before I am done, but I need your help. He cannot be executed if we can't find him, and so far, we can't. We have heard reports he fled to Argentina. Others say he's hiding in a villa in Spain by the ocean. A confidential informer says that's all nonsense, and he's hiding back in Austria, just outside his birthplace. My husband and I have spent much of our own money searching for him, hiring agents and investigators in our effort to bring to trial the man who scarred our lives so deeply.

The family member I lost was perhaps like the family member you lost. She was young, full of spirit, and had her entire life ahead of her. She had yet to experience her first love. She'd known none of the magic the world can offer.

When I woke up this morning, my arms ached to hold her again. When we were last together late one night, she crept into my bed when she was tired and scared. I held her until she fell asleep. Finally, I moved her into her own bed, but then I lay awake listening to the echoes of the city outside my window. Before her next birthday, she was dead.

So I write this plea to you. If you have seen this Sigmund Schlösser of the SS, please notify this newspaper. If you have information about him, please notify this newspaper. Your name will be held in complete confidence, I personally promise you.

Paris-Soir, Paris, France

1

Paris 1939

A new German 35 mm camera, the Exakta, was her grandparents' birthday gift to Claire Merie Vallant when she turned seventeen. "Go," her grandfather had whispered to her, "make yourself a star."

Claire's mother, the physician and surgeon, and her father, a design engineer for Delahaye Motors, had encouraged their daughters and sons to be something other than a star. They had always encouraged them to ignore convention, to be their own person. Moreover, they had always challenged Claire and her younger sister, Esmée, to make their life as a woman stand for something. This was in a Paris of 1939 where *filles* rarely were able to access a life that "stood for something." More often than not, their lives stood for early marriage and childbearing.

When it came Esmée's time to make *her* life stand for something, she had snuck out of the house late at night and gone carousing with an unsavory crowd from school. When her nocturnal travels were discovered by their parents, she allowed that her only complaint was she hadn't yet seduced a certain boy two years her senior. Time and opportunity had run out for her, and Esmée's leash had been tightened.

But Claire, inspired by her parents' challenge, gathered herself up and visited the Levy Jewish Hospital. Her mother served the hospital as a surgeon and had told Claire it might be a good place to begin her search for her life's meaning. Claire dutifully went and observed the patients with their families. She felt quite intrusive in the hospital; she didn't want to encroach. She found a nurse taking her cigarette break on a small patio. Outside Claire ventured, out through the glass door, onto the patio where she took the table beside the nurse's and placed her camera case in front of her on the table in plain view.

"Oh," Claire muttered, "please don't do that." She was speaking to her camera as she'd lifted it out and was fiddling with the viewfinder.

The nurse peered up from her reverie. "Broken?"

"I don't think so, but I'm not sure if I'm using the camera right."

"Are you here to take pictures?"

Claire indulged a quizzical look on her face. "I am, but I'm quite new at it, and I don't know what subject to try."

"Here," said the nurse, "you may try with me. Take my picture."

"Really? You would allow me?"

"Yes. It's nothing."

Claire wound the film, readying the camera. She leveled the viewfinder and sought out the nurse's visage. Deftly and without hesitation, she clicked the shutter button. Without asking, she wound the film and snapped another. Then another.

"There, surely that's enough," the nurse jokingly scolded. "I have to get back." She stood to leave.

"Do you want me to come back and show you the results?"

"I work on maternity. You may find me there. I would like very much to see my picture."

"I will find you. I promise."

Claire sat back in her chair. A certain feeling had started in her chest and ballooned until she thought she would explode. It was excitement! How thrilling to take another's picture and have them want to see your work! She had said she would return and seek out the nurse, and she would. In fact, she could hardly wait.

Her father kept his chemicals and printer in the basement of the family home. She had been warned to always ask him before going there to develop her pictures because the chemicals were dangerous. As she skipped along toward home that day she knew she should have asked him before she promised the nurse a finished photograph. Her skipping slowed. Why hadn't she remembered that? Should she go back, find the nurse, and tell her she'd made a dreadful mistake and didn't have the chemicals to develop and print her picture? She decided to push on, to take her chances and see what her father said.

Surprisingly, he didn't resist. Especially not after she'd told him about the nurse and the look on the woman's face when Claire had told her there would be a picture for her. So the next day she developed the nurse's three pictures and printed them. She studied all three until she had a favorite, then returned with it to the hospital.

Up to the fourth floor, maternity ward, she rode the lift. After making her way through the lift's accordion door, she turned right and hurried toward the nurses' station. But her nurse wasn't to be found. And she didn't know her name, so the attendant was unable to help locate the woman.

Claire decided to visit the nursery on the off-chance her subject was there. Back down she went, retracing her earlier steps, this time making her way beyond the lift, all the way to the glass wall of the nursery. Sure enough, the nurse's giveaway dark, sultry eyes peered back at her. Claire pulled the photo from her handbag and held it up against the glass. The nurse, holding a newborn against her shoulder, widened her eyes. She came to the glass and took a closer look. Then she threw back her head, laughing with happiness. She liked it! Claire had produced a photograph that the subject liked. It was an exhilarating moment, and the same bubble of excitement pressed on her chest as before. The nurse held up one finger, placed the newborn back inside its tiny bed, and came out of the nursery through a side door.

"*Mon Dieu!*" she exclaimed. "Let me hold it, please."

She passed the nurse the picture. "It's a good likeness," Claire suggested.

"Oh, it's the best ever likeness. I want this picture for my beau. Can I pay you?"

"Absolutely not. Take it. It's yours."

"*Mon Dieu.* I'm so happy. So happy."

"Do you have a baby I could photograph?"

"Yes, there is one. He is the son of my beau's sister. Let me get him." She returned moments later with a wrinkled newborn whose contorted face looked eighty years old.

"Oh," whispered Claire. "Is he in pain?"

The nurse laughed. "He's very gassy, that's all. Let me see if I can tickle his cheek and get him to smile."

Claire readied her camera and adjusted her focus. Now, if the boy would only favor them with a smile... Then he did, and Claire snapped the picture. She took another dozen. She had an idea. What if she returned with the pictures, and the new parents liked them enough to give her name to other new parents, people who might pay her? It was a long shot, but Claire was hoping against hope that something like this might happen. That she might be saved from the next step in the usual Parisian girl's life: marriage, then children. Just then, she determined she would establish a picture business for babies. It would be the first step toward earning her own money.

She all but ran home to develop and print the baby pictures.

Six hours later she was back with one dozen good pictures of the newborn. In fact, they were excellent pictures, she knew. All of her experimenting had paid off: how to work with light, with expression, with lens speeds and exposure. She thought she might even have a product valuable enough to trade for money.

The same nurse was at the nurses' station this time. Claire walked up and, without a word, spread the photographs in front of the stunned worker. The pictures were beautiful. They looked like they were the result of long hours of posing and coaxing in a photographer's studio. But they weren't—they were even better. They were the candid shots of a new life in progress.

"Leave them with me," said the nurse. "Come back in the morning."

"All right."

"Hey, how much do they cost?"

"Lunch. They can buy my lunch."

"I'll tell them."

At eight o'clock the next morning, Claire walked off the lift. This time there were wings on her feet as she made her way back down to the nurses' station. Her friend smiled as she approached. She pulled open a drawer in the desk where she sat. "Is four hundred francs enough?"

Claire didn't wait. It wasn't much, but it was a start. "I would be quite happy with four hundred."

The nurse spread the francs before her. "Now, enjoy your lunch. Oh, yes, and I have two more new mothers who also want pictures. Even the hospital is interested in talking to you."

Adrenaline pumped through Claire's veins. What was this about the hospital wanting to talk? Might they even be interested? Surely not. She wasn't even a real photographer. She was a nobody with a camera who, until a few days ago, had never taken any photographs other than models, classmates, and family members. And now someone was going to pay for her work? Was that even possible? She opened her handbag and stuffed the francs inside. Yes, it was possible. In fact, it had even happened.

When she did talk to the hospital, they came to an agreement that Claire would visit the nursery three days a week and offer to take pictures of newborns. Claire was also free to look around for other patients and families who might want pictures.

Claire investigated the hospital for other opportunities. One day, she visited the old people, where she was warmly received. So she stayed and watched the elderly interact with their family members. She was delighted by what she observed. Those family moments touched her soul profoundly. Armed with her camera, she visited the geriatric wards and traveled room to room, snapping pictures. Later, she distributed the finished prints to patients and their loved ones. Before long, the established veterans around the ward would smile to see the young woman coming. Everyone loved the pictures; everyone wanted new ones. As for Claire, she came to love the old Jewish people and would sit in their rooms for hours, never noticing the time, while this one or that one imparted their life story.

In one of her favorite photographs, she had captured three beds, three elderly patients, two women and a man. One woman had fallen and broken her hip. They had admitted the man with pneumonia. The third woman, younger than the first two patients, was suffering a wasting disease, TB, and was gasping for every breath. One body was fawn colored, one yellow jaundiced, and one white. The sheets covering them were white, starched, and the pillows too soft so they'd been doubled in number.

Photograph:

camera - Kine Exakta

Plano-convex magnification

Xenar 1:2 f = 5cm fast lens

film - monochrome

3 beds, starched white sheets

patient #1: 82-year-old female, fractured hip in traction

patient #2: 84-year-old male, pneumonia, on oxygen

patient #3: 75-year-old female, Tuberculosis

family members/friends on each side of beds

Descriptor: "From each side of each bed, the hands of family reach out to soothe, to touch, to let the patient know family and love is nearby. But their faces tell a different story: full of sorrow and sadness as their loved ones languish."

Title: "Heartache"

Tears flowed and hands withdrew as the patients slipped away until, one day, Claire would return, and the bed would be empty.

2

Old Rissa Nussbaum captivated her with stories of her youth and her dream of becoming an artist. She described how, as a child, she would sit and watch the sunlight walk across her family's backyard as she studied the shape and form and color of her world. How Claire could relate, having practiced the same with sunlight with her bedroom skylights. The old lady's feelings further inspired her so that she snapped photographs by the hundreds of the grounds, the machines, even pictures of her own mother, the eye surgeon, restoring vision in the operating room, helping the blind see. The patients would clamor for Claire to come to their rooms whenever they had visitors. They were always disappointed to find she wasn't an employee with regular hours.

Prematurely hopeful, Rissa called her son of eighteen years and made certain he was in her room when Claire made one of her appearances. Claire was so shy she all but ignored the young man except to pose him this way and that with his grandmother. He said he played violin. Claire turned him a quarter-turn so he was more directly facing the Exakta. His wrist was thin like his grandmother's and his skin sallow, silvery, as if he didn't get outside much. He saw her looking at his wrist and guessed what she was thinking. "I am told I'll one day play for the Philharmonie de Paris," he offered. Claire told him that was nice and wished him well.

One thing was certain, neither of Claire's parents encouraged romance. Was romance anathema to their blood? Did it always wait second in line to one's purpose? Other girls had had the family talk with their mothers, so why hadn't they? Was it because their mother, the physician and surgeon, had waited so long to start a family of her own, a family that came only after medical college and internship and residency? Plus, their mother was one-hundred percent German, a Berliner by birth, suffused with intense Germanic purpose that left no room for romantic idylls. She had long insisted that all household conversations be held in German, making Claire and Esmée conversant in the language with a whisper of a Berlin accent. Was the mother's science why she had never once engaged with Claire about family, about falling in love and having children someday? Or perhaps her no-nonsense German upbringing made her cold, almost icy? The girls' father would never be a part of such talk. M. Vallant was a vice president at Delahaye, the maker of France's most desired automobile of 1939. A vice president in charge of the cabriolet design might think of his family twice, maybe three times, on a family day like Sunday. Any other day of the week it was unlikely he would consider his family even once. If there was to be any family talk, it would not flow from him.

It was against the hospital backdrop that Claire had first felt a yearning for romance. The yearning was an unexpected by-product of witnessing the deaths of geriatrics at the hospital. Episodes of lying in bed late at night and feeling terrified to be, as she perceived it, alone in the universe, had left her open to the idea that maybe she'd be happier with a beau.

Her thoughts flowed to Remy Schildmann, the boy she knew best.

Her feelings for him had altered throughout the years. Originally, she felt as though Remy was like a brother. When she was younger and let her mind roam among her classmates in search of the ideal beau—a partner in the kind of love she thought would be appropriate for someone her age—Remy's name had never before been on her list.

At twelve, Remy had been very handsome or very homely, she was never sure, with his shock of black hair, his playful blue eyes, and his solid jaw and straight, even teeth. But his physique had reminded her of the old men around the parks, the men with the sunken chests and spindly arms. Would he ever grow into a body like that of other boys his age, the boys who fenced and rowed? Certainly not by twelve; so far, she had thought him all thorax and pincers—her mother's casual observation one evening after a visit from Remy. Still, from that tender age, she had nursed a fondness for Remy, which on rare occasions had steered into the realm of romance.

At the end of that sixth school year, as she packed up her lunch bag and cleared out her locker to go home for the summer, Remy had given her a 78, a record, a *chanson d'amour* entitled "*J'attendrai*," sung by Rina Ketty. He instructed her to play it every day over the summer and try not to think of him as she listened to the words, "*I will wait day and the night. I will always wait your return.*"

In September, on the first day back to school, he'd caught her at her locker and asked her what she thought of the song. They'd seen each other just about every day over the summer, taking an advanced summer class together, field trips to the countryside, and church on Sundays. They talked and laughed, but never once did he ask her about the 78 record and its song. Never once did they touch, either, much to Remy's dismay. Now, back in school for the fall term, he leaned against her locker so she couldn't pull it open and said, "Well, what about the song I gave you?"

She was shy and thought herself beyond unattractive. She was naïve in the ways of love, and couldn't imagine what Remy wanted from her. "I honestly didn't listen to it." It was a bald-faced lie, a lie straight out of Hell as Pastor Berger would've had it. Guilty, yes. But she proceeded with her lie because she couldn't stand to hurt Remy's feelings, so in love was he, so launched into another world that didn't exist, the world where she loved him back. That world couldn't exist for her because she wasn't worthy. It was too difficult —impossible, really—to return his love, so she fought it away. Had she been able to look deeper into her heart, she might have realized she was in love with Remy, but she couldn't bring herself to look there. Not only did she consider her ears an embarrassment, she thought her whole, awkward self an embarrassment, too. So she said the record meant nothing to her. It was safer that way.

"Didn't you listen to it? I should have reminded you. How could you forget?"

"Between school and work and piano, I just forgot, that's all. Why's it so important to you that I listen to a dumb record anyway?" True, she meant to back him off, and those mean words would do just that.

"Not dumb, expressive. That record contains my feelings for you, Claire. Do you understand what I'm saying?"

She understood. She understood his feelings. However, they weren't her feelings—they couldn't be. What did she understand of love?

"You care for me. And I care for you, too, Remy. But I don't care in the same way as you. I think it's best if we don't see each other until this semester ends. I need some distance from you."

Tears clouded his eyes. He rubbed the sleeve of his shirt across his face and looked away. His chin was shaking, and now tears were forming on his cheeks and giving him away. "I'm sorry," he whispered and walked off down the hallway, head hung forward, looking neither right nor left at the other students who greeted this popular young man. She could've died right on the spot, it hurt so much to upset him.

Then one night, when they were fourteen years, there had been a birthday party. The girls-only sleeping party had been in full swing when the door had flown open, revealing Remy and four desperate-looking male classmates. Clearly torn between staying and running away, they had looked around nervously for fathers or big brothers, only to hear the voice of the birthday girl's father booming downstairs, sounding like God himself inventorying his parlor, "Who's down there and why?"

Four of the interlopers had turned and fled, leaving Remy Schildmann standing frozen with fear, too frightened to follow his mates out the door. He had been hyperventilating when, almost dreamily, Claire got up off her pallet, sidled up to Remy, and whispered, "I'm glad you came." Her bravado and her lack of inhibitions had shocked her, but she didn't leave his side. When their hands brushed, ever so slowly, they reached and interlocked their fingers and, for the first time, they had held hands with someone besides a family member. It had gone on all night, the closeness. At last, when the birthday girl's mother had come and sent Remy away hours later, Claire had followed him out onto the porch. There, as he turned to go, she had thrown her arms around his neck, pulled him down, and kissed him sloppily upon the mouth. He had jerked away for a moment, then returned the kiss, this time not so wet and with much less ticking of teeth against teeth.

She had before thought him a brother—not a beau. But their kiss had changed all that. From then on, she carried him in her heart everywhere she went.

3

Claire had matriculated at the *École Supérieure de Journalisme* in Paris. This was the self-proclaimed Superior School of Journalism that most journalists agreed was aptly named.

They based admission on a competitive process: students took preparatory study, a national written exam, and an oral exam, resulting in the students being ranked nationally. Without her national rank ever being revealed, Claire had received her letter of admission and congratulations on June 25, 1939 and began her studies that September.

She loved everything about ESJ and was soon heavily involved in the photojournalism core courses.

The Exakta model with the 35 mm lens that her grandparents had acquired for her in Marseilles became known as the Kine Exakta —a waist-level viewfinder camera capable of firing off flash in low-light conditions. The anonymity that the small camera gave her in a crowd of people or during an intimate moment was essential in overcoming the formal and unnatural behavior of those who knew they were being photographed.

She enhanced her anonymity by painting all the shiny parts of the Exakta in black. The Exakta opened new possibilities in photography—the ability to capture the world in its actual state of movement and transformation. It became her spiritual twin. The irony it was German-made but would be used to record German war crimes wouldn't be lost on her in times to come.

Six months after enrolling in photography school, the drums of war sounded in the distance, prompting Claire to seek a job as a photojournalist with *Paris-Soir*. She was earning a few thousand francs each week from her hospital babies, but it wasn't enough to support a career. The photojournalism attraction was strong in her. Come wartime, she intended to be on the front lines, if not even behind enemy lines. With her camera, her command of German, and her ability to look ambiguous—of German, French, or Swiss origin—it was all within easy grasp for her.

A help-wanted advertisement for an entry-level photojournalist appeared in the *Paris-Soir* in February 1940. The advertisement was running a third day when Claire dropped by the newspaper offices and left her résumé with the receptionist. She then told the receptionist she would wait while the document made its way to the hiring office.

"It might be two days before Monsieur Marseille actually views your résumé," the baffled receptionist told Claire. "Don't you want to leave and let us call you if there's interest?"

"I can wait. This job is very important to me," Claire replied.

With a sigh and a shake of her head, the receptionist stood and explained that she would be taking the résumé directly to M. Marseille as a favor to Claire. After all, she couldn't see the young woman waiting for days in the reception area of the giant newspaper. It just wouldn't look right, for one thing.

Two hours later, word came back. The hiring manager who'd placed the advertisement would see her at one o'clock that afternoon. So Claire worked the crossword puzzle in the latest edition and waited.

Her employment interview was with a young, assistant editor by the name of Jacques Marseille. He was two years out of ESJ himself and was eager to speak to the school's *corps de caméra*—his words—as the buildup got underway for the massive journalism campaign the coming war would demand. Claire was shown into his office just after lunchtime that day. M. Marseille had downed maybe one chardonnay too many with his meal and, when he came face to face with Claire across his desk, his mood was expansive, his breath fragrant with grape.

Jacques Marseille was a handsome young man who was more aesthete than soldier. True, he had served in the French Army in peacetime until a practice grenade took off his left hand. After that, he showed his superior officers he could still shoot, but they dismissed him. When he met with Claire three months before the German invasion of France, Marseille was in his mid-twenties, dark skinned with dark eyes that peered out from beneath sharply etched eyebrows. Marseille's appearance was almost pretty, but he was a serious newsman with a religious fervor in his preparation for reporting his slice of the French press before the rumored German invasion.

"*Paris-Soir*," Jacques Marseille said of the newspaper, "needs adventuresome, young photojournalists. We must record the coming invasion for the terrible crimes these Nazis are sure to commit. Please tell me about yourself."

"Well, I'm seventeen and have another year of school left to complete."

"I didn't realize. That's not good."

"But I already have my own small photography business. I'm quite experienced."

"Tell me about that, please."

"I take pictures of newborns at Levy Jewish Hospital. I don't make much money, but the experience has been invaluable."

"Any experience with action photography? Sporting events? Fires and floods? Anything outside the hospital?"

"No, I'm sorry."

"I was hoping for more experience. And when do you graduate?"

"In May of 1941."

"Don't you think we should wait until then? Why should I hire you before you have your degree?"

"Because I am sincere, hard-working, and I will work long hours and do whatever it takes to get the photographs you want. I won't let you down, monsieur."

"We're all hearing the same thing. Hitler is poised on our border, just waiting to invade. How would you feel about taking photographs of wartime casualties, twisted, bleeding bodies, that sort of thing?"

"How would I feel? Like anyone would feel, I'm certain. It would be very difficult to see my countrymen injured and dying, but their stories all deserve to be told. It is what will give them existence beyond the grave, having their stories told."

"Ms. Vallant, exactly what I wanted to hear. I want you there."

"I won't let you down, I promise." She was in high spirits, some of it perhaps from his wine-flavored breath that rather reeked in the confines of his shared small office.

"Someone must do it and why not you?"

Claire looked beyond the wall of windows opening onto the main reporters' room and its 100 desks. *Paris-Soir* lacked any political agenda, which she was happy to note. They were dedicated to providing sensational stories and reports to its news-hungry crowd of some 1.7 million circulation, double that of its nearest rival, *Le Petit Parisien*. "Yes," she said, "I think, why not me? I will accept whatever the job pays and can start Monday next."

"Who said anything about pay?" wafted the winey voice. But then he laughed at his own humor. "Pay is one-thousand francs. That's two-hundred above *Le Petit Parisien*."

"Why, that's almost enough to move out of my mother's basement up to my old room on the first floor," Claire replied, matching wit for wit. "But I'll take it. Is Monday next all right?"

"Perfect. You'll be issued a camera and gear that morning, followed by a two-day photo course we require all new photo hires to attend."

"I have my own Exakta 35 millimeter. Am I allowed to use that in place of the newspaper's choice?"

"That's an even better camera, perhaps, for the candid shots we're pursuing. Small and easily hidden in your hands, it's perfect."

They shook hands on the deal, and with a light step, she left the building and headed south on avenue de l'Opera toward the Seine. Claire was scheduled for a late lunch with Remy. At two o'clock, they were to meet at La Café Marly, a small eatery in the shadow of the Louvre, featuring a small menu but the freshest seafood in Paris, her treat, as she had promised, if she landed the job.

She was wearing her gray suit with a red necktie and Remy came casual, wearing slacks and an open-throat linen shirt. Into the small restaurant they went.

The air inside was warm on the skin, especially for March in Paris. She decided the owner was keeping the two rooms extra warm to soothe the nerve-wracked citizens who dined there, distraught at what the Germans might have in store for them.

When they'd been seated and drink orders placed, Remy reached and took her hand. "Tell me everything from the beginning," he said.

"He was nice, and he was all-business. Well, not all business. He made a joke or two, but I would ascribe that to the wine he'd downed with his lunch."

"Sounds like our kind of man," Remy said, studying her for any signs of fondness for her new boss beyond what the accord of an employee, at the outset of any job, might hold for the person who'd just trusted her enough to hire her on.

"He is our kind of man. You'd like him, Remy. He's young and passionate."

"Is he married?"

"Who could say? There was no ring on his remaining hand."

"That means nothing anymore. He could still be in the market even if he were wearing one."

"But there was a common dreariness in the newspaper proper. Everyone is sick with the war news. I could feel it there."

"It's definitely coming," Remy said. "I hear they're massing Germans on the Belgian side of the Ardennes."

"There's been no German declaration of war on Belgium. How could German troops already be inside Belgian borders?"

Remy spread his hands. "You'd have to ask one of your reporter friends from *Paris-Soir* that question. I'm sure I don't know. But I do know," he said, leaning forward conspiratorially, "the French Resistance is strong. Almost everyone we know is ready to engage and make the Germans' lives a living hell when they touch French soil."

Their wine arrived, a *Château Haut Brion*. The sommelier waited while they tasted his offering and only left their table when they'd indicated their satisfaction.

"You're still with us?" Remy asked when the man had left them. Remy was speaking of *La Résistance*, the Resistance.

She brushed a wisp of hair away from her forehead. "You never have to ask me that question again. I'm with you. With us, I mean. I'm ready to do whatever I can."

The waiter served Trout Meunière Amandine. The diners busied themselves with the late lunch. They spoke little between bites, a sign of the comfort between them.

Again leaning across the table for privacy, Remy spoke up. "Some of us will train this weekend. It would be a good chance for you to learn to operate a gun and shoot."

Without hesitation, Claire said, "Count me in. I hate guns, but I'm in."

"Understood. You'll find many of us in the same mindset. No one wants to shoot anyone, but if it has to be done, make it Germans on French soil."

"*On ne passe pas!*"

"One does not pass!"

"How many in our group?"

"Not enough. Not yet."

4

Claire accompanied early Resistance spies on reconnaissance missions where the goal was to observe enemy positions and put them to maps. This was before Germany invaded France, but German probes—small groups of soldiers—were already inside France mapping routes and pockets of French troops. Claire's mother railed against her daughter photographing guns and killing, but Claire had stood her ground. She was going with the fighters, many of whom were her childhood friends, and that was the end of it.

But the parents went into a full-blown resistance movement of their own when Claire's younger sister, Esmée, insisted she would go along, too. The parents said flatly no and threatened both young women if Esmée disobeyed.

Claire was mature for her age, but Esmée was naïve and often found herself in trouble, which the parents used to make their point. She was still in their control, they reminded her, and she was not, under any circumstances, to disobey by accompanying her older sister and the fighters.

Esmée went anyway, departing town, one morning, ten minutes later than her sister and that crowd. At seventeen, she was advanced emotionally and highly intelligent. She had her politics and her economics and her social studies and she knew exactly where she came down on all three. She was excited to go; she insisted on joining.

The fighters traveled openly on their bicycles, posing as French youth out for a frolic on a Saturday morning. Four kilometers outside the Paris city limits, they were signaled to a halt by Jaccan Pierzelof, a baker from the West Bank who had been bringing up the rear but now shot forward past the other riders. Pierzelof wheeled his bike up to Claire, leading the group on its journey.

"Claire," said Pierzelof, "you won't like this, but I believe that's your sister back there."

Claire shaded her eyes with her hand and peered back along the road, all the way back to the horizon. Sure enough, there pedaled a lone figure, indiscernible to Claire except for one thing. The figure was wearing the exact black-and-red checked scarf Claire had presented to Esmée on her birthday last winter. "That little—"

"Easy Claire," said Pierzelof, "I believe you mean that's your sister coming."

Claire dropped her hand from her eyes. "I do. It is. All right. Thanks, Jaccan."

Claire and the others pulled their bicycles off the roadway and laid them against the hillock running alongside. They sat down in the dewy grass and lapsed into small talk while they waited for Esmée. Several minutes later, huffing and puffing at the extra effort it had taken to catch up, Esmée pulled her bike off the road and collapsed alongside Claire's bicycle. "Oh," she groaned. "Why are you stopped?"

Claire's eyes burned holes into the girl. "Why are we stopped? So we don't lose a family member out here? Would that be why, perhaps?"

"Look, they wouldn't let me come. I had to wait until I could get away. The last thing I want is to hold anyone up. Let's just go now."

Claire sat up in the matted grass. Nasturtiums grew wild along the ditch where they waited. If Claire closed her eyes, the smell of the flowers and summer earth could conjure up a summer in peacetime when all was well and bike rides on Saturday mornings were common. Esmée clasped her sister's shoulder.

"This doesn't work for me," Claire scolded. "Maman and Papa will send you to your room for the rest of the school year. And they will take away your allowance and prevent you from going to dances and movies. You will be a captive held in your own house. Me, they'll just skin alive for letting you come."

"I'm coming anyway," Esmée snapped. "It's my war, too. If they're too old to understand, that's not my fault. They need to come to grips with how French youth feel. We'll all be fighting before it's over."

"That's not my point. I'm talking about today, right here and now. The Germans are everywhere. Your parents—"

"Our parents—"

"Our parents are still denying what's happening all around them. Already Hitler is taking the Jews of Germany and sending them off to Poland and death. For you, you're too young for all this. Go home now!"

Esmée pointedly ignored her sister.

"And Hitler will send us away to the camps if he suspects

anything," Esmée added. "You just made my case for resisting him with everything we have. We cannot stand idly by—I cannot—when he invades and creates genocide camps and murders our citizens. It's unacceptable."

A Resistance fighter named Zar Chomill added, "Let her come, Claire. Your sister's heart is in the right place. There are no age requirements for killing Germans."

"See?" sniffed Esmée. "Even your group knows I should get to come and fight. All of us are needed. Mount up on your bicycle, Claire, two sisters off to fight together. The Vallants are on their way. Hitler be damned."

Claire touched the camera inside its case inside her bicycle basket. "I don't go with guns. I go with this," she said meaning her camera. "Reporting the war is a much bigger job than fighting it."

A silence fell over the group just then because Claire was all but yelling these things at her sister.

"Claire, your camera is more important than our guns? Did you really just say that?" said the voice of another young woman from the middle of the bike riders. "Maybe you're the one who doesn't belong here. Maybe you should be the one sent home while your sister stays."

"Marietta," said Claire to the speaker, "you know what I'm trying to say. There is more than one way to fight the war. Yes, guns are required. But so is truth, the truth about Hitler's evil. That's why I'm here, and it's every bit as legitimate as your Lebel rifle."

"Still, your sister is right. We do need her and want her here. Have you forgotten that I'm her age?"

Claire could only shrug. Without agreeing with her sister's desire, she couldn't resist her words. So, she re-mounted her bike and rolled on down the narrow highway. Esmée and the rest followed close behind. The point had been made. The fight wasn't Claire's fight, and neither did it belong to her parents. It was a fight for all French people. Esmée couldn't be denied. Moreover, it was clear there would be thousands more just like Esmée, ages sixteen, seventeen, maybe even younger. It was only just beginning.

Five kilometers further down the road, Esmée pulled over at a roadside market to load her knapsack with wine, bread, cheese, and sausage enough for the eight friends comprising the cell. The rest of the group stopped, some wandering the aisles of the store, some outside at the bicycles, smoking and drinking water they brought along in army canteens.

Esmée reappeared back outside. She walked up to the group and announced that she would like a gun of her own to learn, to maintain, and to arm herself with so that she, too, might kill the invading soldiers. No one replied. Not one of them was about to give Esmée Vallant a firearm and risk the wrath of her mother, Dr. Vallant, whom all knew or knew of, being the outspoken, quick-to-anger woman she was.

Finally, it was Claire—lo-and-behold—who answered her sister's demands.

"I have a gun hidden away with the others," said Claire. "You can learn on it. I'll teach you."

"What is it?" asked Esmée.

"It's from Italy and it's brand new. I took it from father's drawer. He would kill me if he knew I was giving it to you."

"Then why did you steal it?"

"I brought it for the fighters. Our cell needs every gun and grenade we can find."

"But I thought you've been saying you're against all this," Esmée protested. "You don't believe in killing, so how can you steal a gun and bring it?"

"I personally don't want to kill anyone, but that doesn't mean I don't believe in what others in the Resistance need to do if France is to be free," Claire said to her sister. "I've got a thousand bullets for it. Today, we'll practice. You'll shoot hundreds of times until you don't flinch and you don't hesitate to pull the trigger."

"I want a machine gun of my own, as well."

Claire only looked at her sister, dumbfounded. Where was this coming from?

"That can possibly be arranged," said the leader of the Resistance cell, a man named Marceau. "Thousands of firearms are finding their way into France every day. The citizens of France have taken up guns and rifles. Even clubs and axes. We will not go quietly under the Nazi heel. Yes, I'll make certain you are provided with your own machine gun, Esmée. You deserve it."

Claire shook her head but couldn't help smiling at her sister. "There's your answer. Welcome aboard, little sister."

Pushing ten kilometers beyond the city limits, they rode north and east and soon found themselves pedaling past fields of barley, green waves in the early morning sunshine, heartily welcoming the sunlight and cool, caressing breezes sweeping their stalks, rippling the rolling fields. Apple orchards and vineyards passed by as well, with shepherds tending watch and school children here and there with fishing poles and bikes out for a frolic. The war could have been a million kilometers away. But there was a quickness in the air, too. People knew there could be a German hiding behind every bush. Scouting reports had the Germans everywhere across the countryside now.

At last, they turned east on a long, gravel road until the road dipped down and trailed off to become a dirt road. There, they encountered a natural depression with hills rising up from the belly of the lowest reaches—a perfect backdrop for target practice and well enough away from other people that they likely wouldn't be discovered as they practiced with targets and tin cans and wine bottles. Target practice was a ritual on these scouting runs.

Two men retrieved the guns from a cache dug into the ground and hidden away by a hedgerow. The group set up targets, loaded their weapons, and started shooting.

Marceau, meanwhile, took Esmée aside and instructed her in the use of the various weapons she would come into contact with as a member of the Resistance. The firearms were broken down, the parts examined, and the shooting process explained. They reviewed ammunition calibers and loads as well as the manner of choosing the best weapon for the job at hand. Only then did the younger sister begin loading and firing the others' weapons at the paper targets.

An hour passed by while gunshots rang out. Then two hours, and ears were ringing.

Two Resistance fighters, Zar Chomill and Natan Luscenne volunteered to scout up ahead several kilometers and investigate strategic routes where Germans might lurk. So off they went, Chomill and Luscenne, on foot, jogging northeast while keeping all senses on high alert. An hour later they had easily covered six kilometers when, without warning, Chomill—in the lead—froze. He indicated with a hand signal that Luscenne should remain perfectly still as well. Then Chomill slowly lowered himself down onto all fours and crawled northeast, away from the path, into a stand of birch trees. Luscenne followed soundlessly. Once they were safely hidden away in the underbrush, Natan Luscenne could raise his eyes to the far side of the field, looking for what had alerted his partner. Then, there it was. Three men wearing the distinctly dark-gray-with-black-collar uniforms of the German SS. The lightning bolts were even visible. Luscenne withdrew farther into the underbrush.

The Germans were sitting on the bank of a small creek, a map spread before them. They were but seventy meters away, and the Resistance fighters could easily discern what was happening. "Scouts," Chomill whispered to Luscenne.

Luscenne nodded his agreement. "Just like us," he whispered in reply.

"We wait here," Chomill whispered.

"Are they headed to Paris, do you think?" whispered Luscenne.

Chomill put a finger to his lips to silence Luscenne. The French fighters could neither proceed nor retreat, close as they were to the Germans. They hunkered down on their bellies in the dense underbrush and waited.

The Germans, meanwhile, studied their map. Two of the soldiers observed by Chomill and Luscenne were answering to the older, heavier SS officer. While their uniforms were unbuttoned at the throat, his was not. He maintained a perfectly regal posture and visage the entire time the Frenchmen watched.

His name was Sigmund Schlösser.

5

Sigmund Schlösser was born in Austria in 1908 and, when he was spied that day in France, with two other SS soldiers, by French Resistance scouts Chomill and Luscenne, Sigmund held the rank of SS-Obersturmbannführer in the Waffen-SS. He was tall and heavy and maintained a stern, regal bearing day and night like all good SS officers, especially the combat officers in the Waffen-SS. His broad nose and low forehead, with piercing blue eyes and Hitler mustache gave him a decidedly nationalistic look, a look he strived for, cultivated in the image of the Führer when Hitler began blowing up borders that separated Germany from Poland, Hungary, Luxembourg, France, and Russia.

The Führer's plan had become the prime ambition of all good German males, and Schlösser was like all the rest. On the afternoon Chomill and Luscenne spied him beside the small creek in France, Schlösser would have gladly died there on the spot for the SS, for the Fatherland, and for Adolf Hitler. He was one of Hitler's top field officers, but he was unaware, that day in France, that he and his two soldiers were being observed.

75 meters away, Chomill and Luscenne held their breath every time one of the Germans looked in their direction. While they appeared to be looking directly at them, the Germans were actually pointing out the direction each thought they should move next as they closed on the main road leading from the north into Paris.

As the Frenchmen watched, they saw how the two German soldiers with the open throat tunics would move away from their machine guns as they struggled with their map, moving it this way and that, rotating it from 0° to 90° to 180° and back as they deduced their location. Chomill turned and looked at Luscenne, who smiled and nodded. They both saw the same thing, how the weapons were over one step away from their owners again and again.

With the officer in the buttoned tunic, however, it was a different situation altogether. The same machine gun as his underlings carelessly left propped against a tree and a large stone, Schlösser kept his own always in his hands, the strap up and over his right shoulder. If they were to attack and kill the intruders, the officer would be the primary target. The armed man would have to go down first.

Chomill turned and shrugged at Luscenne. Luscenne replied with a thumbs-up. He indeed wanted to attack. Ever so quietly, ever so slowly, Chomill crawled forward on his belly. Luscenne followed. At first, Luscenne thought he might go the opposite direction so the two Frenchmen could attack from both sides simultaneously, but then he remembered their field training. If he went with his instincts, and circled from the other side, there was a good chance he and Chomill, firing at the Germans from either side, would also be firing directly at each other. Bullets that missed the first line of flesh might, indeed, hit flesh in the second line—friendly flesh. So

Luscenne followed on the heels of Chomill. They would attack simultaneously, but side-by-side.

Halfway around, the French saw the German officer suddenly stand and slide the charging handle on his machine gun. He was ready to shoot at whatever his eyes and ears could locate, for he'd heard a twig snap. "I see you!" he cried sharply and swept the muzzle of his gun right at the French without firing a shot. Chomill and Luscenne, imagining he was set to fire on them, froze. Then Luscenne, the most inexperienced at armed confrontation, suddenly stood and raised his Lebel carbine as if to drop it. Schlösser instantly pointed his weapon at Luscenne. Chomill, who hadn't moved, took careful aim down the barrel of his Lebel bolt-action carbine. He had it aimed dead-center on the SS officer's cap when, off to the left, a female voice called out.

"Chuey," she cried, using Chomill's nickname, "Frankie, where are you guys? I've looked and looked!" Chomill could see the girl was oblivious to the German officer and to the gun he had pointed at her chest. Chomill looked closer. "Oh, my God," he whispered up at Luscenne. "It's Esmée, Claire's sister!

Now the German was dancing the muzzle of his gun from the girl to Luscenne and back again. Maybe it was a smart thing to do and maybe it wasn't, but Luscenne chose that instant to drop his rifle to the ground, indicating he didn't want to engage. He wouldn't risk Esmée's safety by starting a shooting war with a man she hadn't even seen aiming at her yet. But then, as his weapon hit the earth, Esmée's head whipped around and she saw Luscenne.

"There you are," she cried with glee. "You are bad men and we've been calling you for lunch!" She was all of maybe sixteen, thought Luscenne. And she sounded just about that age. But then, two steps ahead of the French, the German officer pointed at the girl and, in perfect French, commanded her to come to him. Esmée looked to Luscenne for an answer. He nodded and brushed at her as if to say, "Go, do as he says."

By this time, the two German soldiers were in possession of their guns and were pointing one of them at Esmée and one of them at Luscenne. The officer then strode up to the girl and took her roughly by the forearm. He turned and dragged her stumbling step over step behind him. She had been taken prisoner, he was saying now in German, and she was tossing anxious glances at Luscenne, who remained standing helplessly by as his comrade's sister was taken away by the three Germans who, with Esmée in tow, now disappeared back into the dark woods.

"Holy shit," said Luscenne.

"What have we allowed?" cried Chomill. "We did nothing to stop it!"

"Easy," said Luscenne. "We had no options. They had her and were dragging her off before we could even think."

"Do we follow?" Chomill wondered rather than asked.

"We do not," Luscenne insisted. "There are three of them and but two of us. Plus, if they see us again, surely they will kill Esmée on the spot. We must run back and tell the others. Marceau will know what to do."

With that, the men stood and, their weapons held at the ready, jogged southwest for their cadre. With each step, the men knew they were doubling the distance back to Esmée and, as they ran, they came to understand they would probably never see the girl alive again. Without any words passing between them, their pace soon slowed and then slowed some more until, weary with their runs for the day, they were merely walking. Even so, they kept up a good pace and wondered which of them should break the news to

Claire. They decided they both would talk at the same time. They both would tell the story of Esmée and the Germans.

It was nearly nightfall when they located their group. To say Claire was beside herself with worry as the men entered the temporary camp would be to grossly understated. Luscenne explained what had happened. His description didn't attempt to make anything hopeful out of what had happened. Claire was at once terrified and in a rage at her sister for creeping away to call the two scouts for lunch. With Esmée's naiveté of what scouts did, it must have seemed a small task to her to find Chomill and Luscenne and bring them in to join the others for cheese and sausage.

"Esmée ran right into the arms of the German scouts," Luscenne and Chomill said almost word-for-word. "She was taken captive and dragged away. We watched the whole thing!"

"Why didn't you stop them!" cried Claire. "There were two of you, and you were armed. You had guns!"

"There were three of them and they had machine guns. We've got World War One Lebels. We would have all died immediately had we fired on them. By holding our fire, we actually helped keep your sister alive. They took her and ignored us."

"*Mon Dieu*! My mother is going to die!" Claire broke down in tears and covered her face with her hands. Remy went to her then and put his arm around her.

"We'll all go in with you," Remy promised. "When we reach your house, we'll all go inside and explain the mistake."

"She is going to kill us all," sobbed Claire.

In the end, Dr. Vallant made a dozen telephone calls in a wasted effort to locate a highly-placed German who might help free Esmée. "She's just a child. It's all a big mistake," Esmée's mother repeated several times that night. "We want her home, away from the war. No, we're not taking sides. My medical practice remains open to treat all comers whether French or German. I'm a physician, not a partisan."

But nothing came from all their calls and pleas. Dr. Vallant hired armed men to go into the hills and scour them for her daughter. They all returned with downcast faces and sad looks. "She's nowhere. No one has heard or seen anything. We have no place left to look."

Finally, there was nothing left to do but wait. But first, Claire promised her parents she would find Esmée and return her home safe and sound. She didn't know how—had no idea whatsoever—but she felt like the whole episode was her fault.

So she promised her sister's return.

6

J acques Marseille—Claire's editor-in-chief—called an all-
hands meeting at the newspaper. Present were not only
Claire and the other wartime *Paris-Soir* newspaper staff but
also *Look* and *Life*, *the Daily Mail*, *Wireless Times*, *New York Times*,
and *Pravda*. This was in early May, and all-told there were eleven
journalists present, most of whom were self-invited once the word
got out that *Paris-Soir* might be shut down by the Nazis and that
other news organizations were desperately needed to suit up and
get the war news out of France. It was also a time for local journalists and photojournalists like Claire to establish contacts inside
the other news organizations in order to keep their reportage and
photographs flowing to the outside world. The meeting was unan-
nounced, definitely unpublicized, and would be on no news
organ's official books or records. An hour into the meeting, during
questions and answers, Claire raised her hand.

"Yes?" said Marseille, giving her the floor.

"What about people like me? I know the Resistance as well as anyone here. Is my best use to record their activities with my camera and stay underground?"

"What do you say, everyone?" asked Marseille, "Does she stay underground now?"

Look said underground. *Life* said underground. *Pravda* said she belonged on the Eastern Front. Marseille himself weighed in for *Paris-Soir* and suggested she was at great risk—as was all reporting staff. The paper preferred she work the system they had set up for getting photographs and reports into the hands of the editorial staff by means of the systems of dead drops set up around the country. For Claire, this meant knowing the dead drop system in the city of Paris, because it was her beat. She reviewed the system with them for the third time that afternoon and, when she was satisfied she knew the where and when of making her deposits, she sat back down. "Thanks, everyone," she said. "See you after the war."

Jacques Marseille asked her to remain after the meeting broke up, which she did. When the room had cleared out, he took her back into his private office and shut the door.

"Sit down, please," he told Claire. Now they were alone. He stepped behind her and pulled the blinds that normally opened onto the reporting pool outside his office.

"Now," he said, taking a seat at his desk. "I want to ask you about an assignment."

She sat ramrod straight, seventeen years old and ready—as her mother put it—to save the world. That wasn't how she viewed herself, she was much beyond that, but her mother had a way of sometimes holding her down with such remarks. Now, today, just might come a chance to erase those comments, those maternal bylines.

"Please ask," she said.

"We're getting horrible reports out of Poland. We have no reason to believe they're anything but accurate."

"The camps?"

"That's right. They are a reality, Claire."

"I had no doubts about that. We've talked to a few who escaped all that by being in the right place at the right time. The lucky ticket on the last train to leave Warsaw. The inherited automobile packed with an entire family that drove two days and two nights to escape to France. There's more."

"Exactly. But we're afraid there are some horrible numbers of those who haven't been lucky. We're hearing the Nazis are murdering thousands of people every day. In Poland. In Germany. In Russia."

"In France?"

"That's what I want to speak to you about. Claire, if it happens here, I need you there, in the camp. I need that story. It will be the biggest story of the war for France."

Claire felt her heart jump in her chest. She hadn't expected such a sudden and total immersion into Hell, and she immediately knew she wasn't the one. She had expected she'd tag along with the Resistance and report on their exploits. But this was overwhelming. Her hands began shaking and her lips quivered. She needed to know more.

"I'm to infiltrate a German concentration camp?

"You are to do whatever it takes to report if any such thing happens in France. That is your assignment."

"But how will I do it short of allowing myself to be taken captive?"

"You wouldn't be a prisoner. I'm thinking there must be some skill, some knowledge you have that the Germans might find useful. If you could entice them to take you in and use that skill. To be honest, I'm thinking your German language skills."

"German skills aren't that unusual. Why me?"

"Combined with your ability to take photographs of the horror of the camps and your ability to get your work into the hands of the right people, your German skills become unique. Do you see where I'm going with this?"

"You want me to go into a concentration camp. At least I think that's what I'm hearing. But it's wrong. The Germans wouldn't allow pictures to be taken in the camps. How does that get done, anyway?"

He sidestepped her question. "I'd like to think of you more as a clerk, an office worker. Someone who knows Paris and knows the German language that would be useful in a setting close by the Nazi horror show. Maybe there is some way to sneak pictures from such a post."

"I think I see. It's terrifying, Jacques."

"It is. But I don't have anyone else to ask."

"Why not? I can name a half dozen other photojournalists who have German. Why me?"

"Because you have the gift. Your photographs are worlds away from theirs."

Her mind was racing now. She desperately wanted to throw open the window and fly away like the starlings outside, like a bird, just soar into the heavens and disappear.

"You need to find someone else, Jacques."

"Let me get you a drink. Wine? Water?"

"A tall glass of wine, please."

"Did you say tall glass?"

"Yes, tall. Jacques, I'm scared to death of what you're asking."

"So am I. Let's pour two. For now, forget I even asked about the camps and helping there."

After placing a glass in front of Claire, Jacques said, "One other thing. Word is, you're capturing so many successful raids on film the Germans are looking for you now. I know you know this, but be advised."

"I'm aware. I'm very careful."

"I don't ever want your name out there. From now on, my paper will refer to your code name only."

"Oh?"

"We've decided. Lumière. Your code name is Lumière."

She laughed. "Light. I think I can remember."

"It's the only name we will use in-house when discussing publication of your work. You no longer work here, Claire. Someone named Lumière has taken your place."

7

I n mid-May the Germans were everywhere, likened, by one grizzled soldier who had served in World War I, to "a bloody scythe." In those days, as the Nazis invaded the Netherlands, Luxembourg and Belgium, Lieutenant Colonel Schlösser was preparing his tanks and his soldiers to invade France at Sedan. On 12-15 May 1940, his German tanks advanced into France. The Netherlands surrendered. Five days later, Schlösser's tanks reached Abbeville and cut off Allied forces in the north of France.

While the SS ground soldiers punched south, Esmée was held behind, at a quickly improvised medical camp the Germans were readying in anticipation of the invasion. Everyone there had a role —some were cooks, some were medics, some were construction workers charged with fencing and clearing, some were office workers, but all of them answered to German SS officers whose specialty was the administration of the Reich. Hitler had known that information was everything and during the latter part of the 1930s, he had spent eighteen months restructuring how Germany did business and how records were kept and cross-filed between different arms of the Reich.

Esmée's daily first job in the war effort was unskilled. She was tasked with making bandages from the bedsheets and pillowcases forcibly removed by the Germans from the homes of villagers and farmers. The tank crews were the main marauders as their machines wouldn't be proceeding any further west for at least a week while the main battle raged north in Belgium and the Netherlands. The tankers, held with their tanks in reserve, spent their time productively, scavenging the countryside, demanding foods and wines be turned over for the army's use, slaughtering cows and pigs for the troops' meals, and stealing anything else of value on the whimsy of the soldiers who were going door-to-door with strict orders to take only food, wine, and bedclothes. At the other end of the supply chain were Esmée and a houseful of other young women tasked with making bandages and precooking meals for the SS officers so there would be hot food waiting when they returned from the field.

LESS THAN 100 KILOMETERS SOUTHEAST OF ESMÉE, CLAIRE WAS starring in the Paris Cafe Theatre's play. Claire had found a flat on the north side of the river on rue des Amis. It was very small and expensive and would take over half of her salary as a photojournalist. But it was furnished and had wonderful morning light on the small porch with a view of the Sacré-Coeur Basilica. The Parisian home offered a mix of old and new, flea market finds like a vintage clock and a lamp, paired with a simple modern sofa. Her parents gave her two white chairs. The walls were white to maximize natural light and, in Parisian style, the colors used on the other furniture were darker and richer to create a stark contrast. A central rug was patterned and featured a bold color to contrast the white walls.

As much as possible, she was maintaining a consistent, normal profile in her life and her comings and goings. The busier she remained, the less she thought of her sister in the hands of the Nazis. Esmée was tough and spirited, and her tenacity would either help her or get her killed. Clair could only hope that she was still alive.

Claire was playing Joan of Arc. Three other Resistance warriors had likewise joined the troupe as a way to maintain the freedom to move around Paris at will. Their movements looked legitimate— for the play—at night. The players had a ready-made excuse for being out and about after curfew. Such nighttime freedom of movement was priceless. Buildings exploded and small supply convoys were intercepted thanks, in part, to the troupe.

The towns in and around northern France continued to fall to German ground troops. Considering the core of brutality that accompanied all troop movements, resistance to the sweeping tide of gray-clad Reich soldiers was brief and, for the most part, blood-less. Orders were out to the Resistance: it made no sense to resist in the face of such insurmountable odds. The Resistance's true pushback would occur mostly at night and would look to be random events. This just wasn't the time to risk one's secret, not in the face of an invasion that delighted in discovering and torturing freedom fighters. Claire, Remy, Chomill, Luscenne, and the rest of them stayed home and let France's occupation happen around them.

Their time would come.

Then, on May 28th, Belgium surrendered. On that day, Claire's troupe played a matinee and an evening performance of the troupe's adaptation of George Bernard Shaw's *Saint Joan*. The adaptation essentially shortened the Shaw offering, edited-out his British embellishments, and added a fantastical love interest. The new piece was co-written by Claire and a classmate named Jean Renoz, a slight young woman with close-cropped hair who could drill a scarecrow dead-center at one hundred meters with her Thompson M 1928 submachine gun. The show closed its doors that night, prematurely, in the face of the gathering of German forces at the Somme in what was plainly a coming full-scale attack against France. All able-bodied men and young men were conscripted on the spot and sent to shore up French defenses. Claire's drama troupe was decimated by the loss of older boys and the young men in her school who had been playing parts in the sainthood of Jeanne d'Arc.

Claire's new role was to find her way into the German war machine—on orders from her editor. From there, she was to undertake her photojournalism efforts in earnest by sending home dispatches of Nazi cruelty and greed and nationalism. How move from her present circumstances of local journalist and member of the community theater to the undercover hero of French journalism?

Then came Feast Day on May 30, the French national holiday honoring Jeanne d'Arc, a day of soul-searching for the very young playwright, Claire Vallant, for it was on that day that she decided she was going to collaborate. Greater sacrifice was demanded of everyone. Claire determined that she would do more.

100 Kilometers northeast, Esmée and the SS work staff were herded together before dawn. There were a dozen French women who had been kidnapped and enfolded into the German army as

maids and servants. They spent their days in manacles, for the most part, as they went about their chores.

One early morning, the SS soldiers placed black hoods over the heads of the young women and bound them tightly at the throat. An order to proceed was given in German, and Esmée was roughly yanked ahead. Her next sensation was of being blind and being dragged over rough ground. She proceeded to pass out with fear. In a dream, she was yanked to her feet, and then ordered in German to hurry alongside Schlösser as they fled through the woods.

French scouts had been spotted. The French had evidently been observing the Germans and their captives from a distance. Schlösser had immediately made the considered judgment that, where there were two Frenchmen, there would be more. He and his comrades were but a few hours ahead of the advancing German army. They were sitting ducks for the French, who'd probably learned that a handful of German SS was headed south with the captured French girls. That information in and of itself would have galvanized French soldiers and freedom fighters. As Schlösser's brigade dashed for the main road to join up with the German Army, they found French roadblocks manned by French soldiers, patrols out in the Ardennes and lesser woods, valleys being scoured and hills being trampled by the great outpouring of men bent on locating the captives. Esmée was aware of none of this call-to-arms. Her head enshrouded in canvas and her hands shackled to her waist, she knew only that she wasn't moving fast enough for her captors, who prodded them with batons. When she would gasp and beg for water, her requests went unheeded. It seemed to her that the men who forced her to march needed neither drink nor food—north and north again was all they had to offer as the Schlösser advanced army jockeyed to join with the main German army.

Then they laid up against a hill for the night. There were no fires, no lights, not even French Gauloises—the cigarette prized by the Germans—were allowed.

"You'll be relieved to know," Schlösser told his young captives in his sarcastic way, "French troops are fleeing Paris by the trainload."

Esmée drew herself upright where she stood, exhausted. "France will never surrender. It must be a military tactic, sir."

While she could hope it was only a tactic, less than three days later, German troops entered Paris. Esmée was dismayed when, a week later, Schlösser returned to his new command center just north of the city—where Esmée was being held under house arrest—and advised his young captive that Pétain broadcasted to the French people urging them to stop fighting. Pétain also asked the Germans for the terms of an armistice.

8

Claire was running an errand for her mother the day Germans poured into France, and Claire was unimpressed when, at La Parisian Fleurs, she heard news of the invasion. She was unimpressed because it was her eighteenth birthday and nothing—not even a full-scale German invasion—would derail that night's birthday party.

Remy Schildmann had RSVP'd that he would attend; Claire's heart beat faster thinking about getting Remy alone. She had decided tonight would be the night they would make love. After losing Esmée, she would not lose Remy, too. And he would fill the hole that her sister had left.

The flower shop was an important one, her mother said. She should go inside expecting the unexpected. When Claire passed through the tinkling door, the first thing she felt was a ten degree temperature differential. The large shop was cool, which soothed her skin, hot as the sun was that twelfth day of May. And it was well-lit, like noon, causing her to look overhead, where she saw a long glass tunnel of clerestory windows dousing the flowers below with long planes of light.

Her face upturned, the light penetrating and glowing beneath her skin, her perfect alabaster face caused the old Jew behind the cash register to be transported backward in time fifty years to when his Imelda was eighteen and unflawed. He fell in love for the tenth time that day as old men fall in the presence of beauty they can no longer seize, nor even pursue. The young woman knew none of this. She knew only white zinnias.

Claire was an inveterate fan of the wireless. Last week, a program note had stated Gypsies thought white zinnias a herald of wondrous times. Most parents scorned Gypsies, so Claire, in a hint of rebellious pique, was attracted, not so much to the Gypsies but to the disdain her parents held for them. If the Gypsies believed white zinnias a herald of wondrous times, then white Zinnias it was. So Claire ambled the aisles, looking for white zinnias—or any other amulet—that might stop the Germans and replace them with beauty and light. The young woman wasn't ready, yet, to turn loose her remaining girlhood. The damnable Germans could just go invade some place other than France.

She was a tall, slender reed with straight black hair she groomed to cover ears she thought too big. Her face most often countenanced a positive optimism, eyes that looked at the world with a hope that hadn't yet surrendered. Her top front teeth were gapped, but she smiled and made friends easily. Remy, the putative beau, said this was a trait that would stand her in good stead when the Resistance needed collaborators to spy.

The aisles in the florist shop were all but impenetrable, flanked with bright orange nasturtiums, zinnias, dahlias and asters, flowers still reaching for the heavens before the springtime skies over

France buckled beneath the far-off bombardments along the Maginot Line. As she listened to updates on the florist's wireless, Claire's step quickened on the stone floor. A clutch of flowers then caught her eye, and she paused to study the rarest of the rare: white zinnias. They were priced twice what other flowers cost in a comparable bunch. She reached for the leather case that lay against her side. A picture would be nice, but she remembered she hadn't brought along her camera that day. The trip was to be a quick one with no need for her tools as a photojournalist. So, she chose the white zinnias and backed away from the flower rack. Her canvas shoes squished from the watering system, but she had her zinnias.

The wireless rambled on. After months of nervous speculation among the French people, German bombers were now hitting air bases in France, Belgium, Luxembourg, and the Netherlands, destroying large numbers of Allied planes on the ground and crippling Allied air defenses. German paratroopers floated down out of the skies across the French countryside into fortified Allied points along the front, which they easily overran.

"Goodness," whispered Claire, "were we not ready for all that?"

She thought of Remy. He had confided to Claire that he was helping form up a French underground for this day. He was the youngest son of the German foreign minister to Paris. Remy and Claire thought the minister was a spy for the Führer. Remy had even told Claire his father had promised him to Hitler. When the Axis armies reached Paris, they would conscript him into the German Army. A future career in the foreign service also awaited him in Berlin—all of this despite his sworn oath to fight for the other side, his adopted France, the land he called home.

The wireless continued blaring. On the ground, German forces were advancing through the Netherlands and northern Belgium. But those fronts were a decoy because, to the south, the Germans had sent their main forces through Luxembourg and into the Ardennes Forest on a path that led unwaveringly into the French heartland. Unaware of the German advance to the south, Britain and France had sent the bulk of their troops to Belgium. Claire straightaway understood: the Germans would meet no resistance as they marched the 200 kilometers into Paris. Her look soured as she wondered, would her birthday party be over and done before the first Nazis came hammering at her parents' door? She shook her head at her juvenile thoughts. How could she possibly be thinking like that even as her beloved France was under invasion? Her youth, once wonderful and prone to the selfishness of younger years, was over.

Claire completed her selections and proceeded numbly to the cash register. M. Boulanger rubbed his hands together as she approached. Even from a distance he counted her several bunches of flowers and rang them up. He punched the largest key on his machine, and the drawer shot open with a loud ring.

"Your birthday party?" he said as Claire plunked down her colorful bundle on the counter and reached for her purse.

"Yes. Don't ask, eighteen."

"Your mother told me last Saturday about your new camera. She knows I love to take pictures like her daughter."

"She told you about my new Exakta? It's my second one. This one's for work, Monsieur Boulanger, not for flowers."

He struck a hurt pose, but only for a second. Then he laughed. "You're the photojournalist. I'm just a dilettante, it's true. Have you taken any strategic photos with it yet?" He said this with a twisted smile. She felt he might be making fun of her inexperience. Or did he know that she, like Remy, wanted to help the Resistance? Maybe he was even asking, so he had something to trade to the

Nazis in return for not closing his business. M. Boulanger was a frightened Jew. Her mother said so.

"Have I taken any strategic photos yet? I'm not sure what you consider strategic, monsieur, but I'm thinking about going out to greet the Germans with my Exakta. It sounds like the French army is leaving it to me."

"The French army went north into Belgium. It's a lost cause now," said the proprietor.

She played along. "But the French army is larger than the German army. Surely, the French will hold the Maginot Line?"

"Yes, but we're fighting Germans."

"And the French are more technologically advanced," she added. "Who hasn't been reading the newspapers?"

"Yes, but they're Germans. Never forget that when you're fighting the Germans, you must multiply times two."

"Two it is," Claire mumbled. The wireless went on a commercial break, and her thoughts drifted far away from the store as she was checking out. Her attention settled on Remy and what the war might do to him. And what it might do to her. Might she one day fight at his side? Her France, her family, her home, and she herself would not go down easily when the Germans came. She received her change from the cash drawer, it banged shut, and she turned and left.

She hurried outside and turned south toward the Seine River. The day was glorious, bright and sunny but, far off in the distance, she heard the first explosion. The ground shook beneath her feet. *Mon Dieu*, they were going to blow up her entire country! Just then, as a sharp breeze tugged at the flowers in her hand, she knew she would be a freedom fighter, making a weapon of her camera. Her subject would be the Nazi lie of a genetic right to rule the world. She'd read her mother's German language newspaper.

But then she remembered. She was a nobody who'd never even met a Nazi. How could she expect to get close enough to snap a famous photograph? The ground shook again, more powerful this time. Her mind raced; there was much to do before the Germans arrived. A thought came to her then: *Beware the man wearing the disguise. He will be your subject.* How did she know this? She knew it because she had studied picture books for years and learned that the great photographs, the photographs that changed the world, always started out as less than what they would become. They appeared in full disguise.

She drew a deep breath as she walked onto the Pont des Arts, the wonderful bridge over the Seine everyone came to Paris to see. As the bridge and river drew her nearer to Paris than ever before, she had a sensation of entering a time that would enlarge her without effort. She loved her Paris, loved the life that floated in the air. Never mind she saw no path to capture the Nazis on film at their brutal worst. She would be ready when her composition appeared in whatever disguise it might wear.

A third explosion startled a family of geese floating down in the water below. They took flight, flapping their long, powerful wings as they moved away from the sound. The Germans were coming and there was no time to spare. It was what gave her time with Remy tonight its special urgency. Before the army arrived, she planned to save him from his patriotism.

Even if only for an hour.

9

France was officially at war. By June 12, German tanks had pierced the key fronts along the Somme River and the heavily fortified Maginot Line. Nothing stood between Hitler and Paris now. The French government decided to preserve Paris and the countryside. On June 22, 1940, France signed an Armistice with Germany. Hitler insisted that it be done in the same railway car in which Germany had surrendered to France in 1918 at the end of World War I. On June 23, Hitler flew to Paris for a brief sightseeing tour of the occupied city, during which a widely published photo was taken of Hitler standing against the backdrop of the Eiffel Tower.

The surrender of France was a major blow to French pride. Many believed that the government had let the people down. The creation of a Nazi-approved Vichy government, primarily in the center and south of the country, was further proof that politicians had sold out.

The Chief of State of the Vichy regime, Marshal Philippe Pétain, was still favorable to the French public, and in the early days of

Vichy regime, his leadership gave it some stability. Therefore, there was no immediate drive to create a resistance movement *en masse* in central and southern France.

Paris was a wholly different matter when it came to the Resistance.

Paris wouldn't wait, wouldn't sleep, wouldn't pass peacefully beneath the German boot heel.

Remy clipped the photograph and brought it to Claire. "It's time to move against the Germans," he told her the night of the Armistice. "Are you with me?"

Claire's mind was made up. She would stand by the man she loved and by her country forever, regardless of the personal cost to her.

"I'm with you," she replied.

"Good. I have a gun."

"And I, a camera."

Days later, Remy was conscripted into the German army. He disappeared in the middle of the night without a trace. In early July, after they signed the German-French armistice, Remy was all but abducted by his own father and driven to Nazi headquarters in Paris.

Wilhoite A. Schildmann, the German foreign minister to Paris and Remy's father, wore his reserve officer's SS uniform, where he held the rank of Generalleutnant der Waffen-SS, or general lieutenant of the Waffen-SS.

The city had just been visited by Adolf Hitler, and spirits were high as the German army enjoyed its new conquest and rapidly went about creating the administrative and military hierarchies required to prosecute the war. "Today we're off to join the army for you," said the elder Schildmann.

"We've been over this, father. My loyalties are with France. I cannot fight for Germany against the country that raised me." It was true; he had grown up in France while his father served his diplomatic career in Paris.

"An officer's academy has been established on the north outskirts of the city. We're going there, as you're already enrolled. You will be sworn into the army, and we'll hear no more of such talk. You're German; you are not French. Now swallow that down and stiffen your backbone, Officer Candidate Remington Schildmann."

Remy was half-afraid of his father. Though it hadn't happened in the past year, the huge man was quick to beat Remy for any "infractions"—his father's words. Plus, an idea was forming in his mind: what if he was to pretend allegiance to the Reich while serving as an army officer, but at that same time he would share all information with the French Resistance? Would he dare to be that brazen? He decided, riding along, that he was going to find out.

His father continued, oblivious to his son's true thoughts. "Plus, if you complete a successful military career, a future career in the foreign service also awaits you in Berlin."

He was still in shock two days later. He had been stripped of his civilian clothes, the garments of a student, and outfitted with the uniform of a Schutzstaffel—SS—soldier without the SS lightning bolts—unearned and un-bestowed. As yet.

Then, Captain Schlossmaier confronted him his third day at the college. "Candidate, Schildmann, how do you view the Jewish problem?"

"I hadn't thought there was a problem, sir."

Long silence with an amazed look on the captain's long, thin-lipped face. Then, "You've heard what the Führer has to say about this?"

"I've heard he believes the Jews are the problem with everything. I don't agree with that."

Ordinarily, the candidate would be failed over such a statement. But this man's father held a high office inside and outside the SS. Schlossmaier backed up and tried it again.

"Regardless of your beliefs, can you do your job and root the vermin out of our society?"

Remy knew better than to argue the point. Absolute acquiescence was required or he, too, would end up locked away in a camp, and then he could do the Resistance no good at all, for he'd already decided that his entire German service would be in sabotage of the German war effort. So he said, "I can root the vermin out, Herr Captain."

"Your job will be to send them out of Paris to a camp. Then you will search out their property and make it become the property of the German government. Do you understand this?"

"I understand."

"And you are able to do this work?"

"Absolutely. The Jews have property they've taken by deceit and fraud. It is the job of the German officer to help repatriate that property with the Fatherland."

"Very good, Candidate Schildmann. You are a quick study."

Completing officers' college in ninety days, Remy was commissioned an SS-Untersturmführer, or lieutenant, and assigned to a company of SS whose primary function was to round up Paris Jews and separate them out of the community. These people were sent first to Nazi camps north of the city where they would spend two months before being loaded onto railroad cattle cars and sent to Auschwitz and Treblinka in Poland. The long and short of it was, once Remy and his squad rousted a Jewish family from their home, they were as good as dead. From that point on, it was simply a matter of processing, which consisted primarily of locating and boxing up the physical assets to be sent to Germany and transferring the intangible assets—stocks and bonds and money accounts—to Third Reich accounts.

Remy reported for duty under Captain Daniel Schlossmaier, a severe, dangerous man who wasted no time letting Remy know he didn't think the recruit had what it took to be an SS officer. He assigned Remy to the role of rouster—a member of a German team that, at night, went house to house, rousting Jews from their slumbers in the middle of the night, separating some for the concentration camps and some for the citywide work details and, in all cases, robbing them of everything of value. Remy was cut deeply by the enforced servitude; his heart ached for the Parisians he rousted, beat, sent to their deaths, and robbed blind. In the early morning hours, back in his bunk at headquarters, he would pull his pillow over his head in those early days and cry himself to sleep.

But before long, his skin thickened. In his mind, he plotted how he would use his position to undermine the German war effort and the German occupation effort however possible. The victim was quickly becoming a traitor to Germany and a French loyalist with tendencies and strong intentions that went way beyond what he had known before they conscripted him. His feelings were now the feelings of a man. His plans for launching his own counter-offensive were the plans of a man soldier, no longer a student playing at war.

He learned everything he could about the modern German guns and armaments. He took a course in explosives and volunteered for training as an infiltrator, a forward scout who would enter countries before Germany declared war. The day came when he could no longer be denied. Captain Schlossmaier himself pinned the SS lightning bolts onto Remy's collar one freezing morning in November when the snowflakes fell across the camp and the coal-fired furnaces of what was once a Paris electric substation, now commandeered to serve as one of the Nazi headquarters, blazed industriously and warmed the freezing German administrative buildings.

ON HIS FIRST WEEKEND PASS, REMY HAD WASTED NO TIME disappearing underground in Paris in his civilian clothes and searching out Claire and the Resistance.

Her first words to him were, "I've been playing our record every day."

She was alluding to the day six years earlier when they had left school for summer vacation. She'd been listening to the record ever since he'd left for the German army and wanted him to know she'd been thinking of him.

He smiled and took her hand. "Let's walk."

Remy wanted to discuss the Resistance, so they went sneaking along late afternoon streets toward a favorite cafe, a place that would be crowded where they could meld with the customers and perhaps grab a small table and say what needed to be said.

They lucked out and found a table away from the front windows of the cafe. The balance between them fit with what each had determined was right for them. For Claire, she viewed Remy's new position as an entrée into the world of the German military. Who knew what she might access once she had her foot in the door there? And for Remy, if he could help expedite the intelligence for strikes by the Resistance against vulnerable German targets, then he had the resource he required to wage his own private war.

They were seated at the rear of the cafe, the table next to the kitchen's swinging doors. Waitstaff banged in and out and busboys came and went with their clashing trays and jitters of flatware, the noise and clattering masking the words of the two who had gathered there to plot. And maybe more, maybe exchange feelings, though neither one had a feelings agenda in mind upon arrival. But even vague feelings and ambiguous longings could coalesce and become expressed needs in a twinkling, and the lifelong friends knew this. A certain care would have to be taken, a certain guard against the vulnerability that had all but destroyed Remy in the past. They were both much older now, years older, than they had been just six months earlier. Their emotional growth had far exceeded in sophistication what few months they had had to germinate. This time, the duo was ready on more than one front.

"So," said Remy, removing the black leather gloves he'd snatched out of his pockets. "You've been playing our song. And what do you think about it? What feelings do you have?"

She was shocked. He had become emboldened almost overnight. She studied his face. Good Lord, he was even shaving regularly now. Here, toward the end of the afternoon, a heavy black shadow was appearing where a half-year ago there had only been a mild case of rosacea, pink cheeks and all. Now that was all gone. At least in the cafe's dim light and the afternoon's wintry gloom. Her beau had become a man. Her blood stirred. This was already more than she had bargained for.

He reached inside his coat and produced his official army photograph, taken the day he received his SS collar pins.

"You look magnificent," she said, all but breathless. And her heart jumped, too, because it was the truth. He looked so clear-eyed, so crisp, so—malevolent?—that she almost got up and fled the company of this German soldier. But she resisted. She resisted because she kept reminding herself that here sat Remy, and he wanted to engage with the Resistance and do whatever he could to weaken his employer, the German war machine. And she stayed because she no longer feared death; she feared loss of life and the joy it could bring.

He circled back to his original question. "What feelings do you have?"

"You know I've always loved you, Remy," she said, her voice cracking as she spoke. She fought down a sob, so overwhelming was this new Remy. Twenty minutes ago, she would have denied these feelings would ever exist for Remy. Yet, here she was now, melting before him.

He reached across the small table and covered her hand with his own. "We should take a room. I've got forty-eight hours before I have to report back."

"We should do that," she said without hesitation. "We've no time to waste."

There, it was done. She was onboard with him one-hundred percent. Her birthday wish to make love to Remy Schildmann had been blown to smithereens, literally and figuratively, by the invasion of the Nazis. She would take that wish back. A Paris hotel, a quick holiday away from war and sorrow and pain, sounded perfect just then.

"Let's finish up our croissants and coffee, and we'll grab a taxi. I know just the place."

"Our song has made me cry. It has made me long for you. Is that what you want to hear?"

He smiled and touched the side of his head. "I already knew that, Claire. I've just been waiting for you to know it, too."

Back outside into the blustery Paris wind, Remy stepped off the curb and leaned into the oncoming traffic lane. He had a petrol-preserving bicycle-taxi pulling over to take their fare in just minutes.

She got in first, then he followed and closed the door. She gave the operator her address.

Without a word, Remy turned to her and she to him. There, in the closed compartment of the bicycle-taxi, her lips met his. She was swept away; the long kiss was a farewell to youth. They both knew it, and there was no turning back. A new era had begun, and when their lips separated and his hands brushed over her body, she was his.

Then the cab pulled into traffic and they were gone.

10

E smée spent her seventeenth birthday doing triage in a bombed-out farmhouse south of the Maginot Line near Roye, France. The work consisted of cleaning and inspecting wounds, then sorting those that needed surgery, those who wouldn't survive, and those who would be treated on the spot and then sent back to the front and the war. Esmée had the same command of German as her sister, Claire, so it was a simple matter for her to ask questions and fit right into the triage tent and wash and sterilize wounds with antiseptic. The hours were sunup to long after sundown, sleep for maybe three hours, then up and stirring around for a quick cup of coffee before running down the hill to triage and starting all over again. The faces were a blur, and the wounds became repetitive, but still Esmée persisted. She was the type of person whose mission was to help regardless of which side in the war she was helping. German or French, friend or foe, her heart was big enough to welcome and aid them all. However, she treated only Germans. The French dragged their wounded, dead and dying off in a completely opposite direction.

She reported to Schlösser every morning when he would return from a night at the front and demand a hot breakfast and a bath. Then she would leave triage and accompany him back up the hill. She heated and made his bath and scrubbed him with her eyes tightly shut while he sat back in the steaming tub with his eyes closed, luxuriating. He hadn't tried to force himself on her or seduce her; she was too close to him by now to try such a thing. Moreover, Esmée was off-limits to the entire German army, orders of Colonel Schlösser himself, unspoken orders though they were. In this manner, the girl was protected from the ravages the German foot soldiers were perpetrating in all other areas of France when girls and young women were located and confronted.

She had made a friend, a young man named Sven Godmundsen who had been pulled out of line at a Paris train station as he was attempting to make his way back to the coast and a boat ride home. Sven had no German, but he stayed close to Esmée and followed her instructions—in French—as she taught him how to assist with the wounded. Sven's job was the most difficult of all in the triage tents: collecting and packaging the personal articles from the dying soldiers for shipment back to their families. Without speaking—he knew only a few German phrases anyway —he would bend to the dying and apologize for what he was about to do, removing rings, crosses, military insignia and badges, watches and ribbons and placing them into reinforced shipping bags for transfer back to Germany. German soldiers at the time wore dog tags that cross-referenced to files leading back to family and home addresses. Sven knew enough about Germany and its main cities and towns within a few weeks of starting work that he had become very proficient in what he was doing. Best of all, to people like Schlösser and his underlings, Sven never complained and never left his job undone. It was thankless work, after all, but

Sven, like Esmée, didn't seem put off by the fact he was helping the same army threatening war against Norway. He went ahead and did what was in front of him without hesitation.

As the war shifted into second gear and raged across France for those first few weeks following the German invasion, a shift in the dynamics of Esmée and Sven's day-to-day occurred because now French and British POW's began appearing at the field hospital. The triage duo were dismayed to see the Allied soldiers always last in line for triage and treatment. They talked about the unfairness of the German system as they came and went before and after work and, during those times when there was an interlude in injured troops arriving for treatment, they would sneak away together and picnic—as it were—a few hundred meters from the growing footprint of the field hospital and its endless in and out of ambulances. Those times were rare; however, because they were rare, the youngsters found themselves saying things about themselves and about each other that, in peace time, would've taken months—maybe even years—to get said. On this end of that telescoped time they found they both had feelings for each other and they didn't hesitate to express them. The same month they met, then, they became lovers. For him, it was his second serious romance in his eighteen years; for Esmée, it was her first. Their first commitment to each other: that no one find out what was happening between them. Their second commitment: that no pregnancy occur. Pregnancy prevention was easy enough: roughly twenty percent of all injury and disease presentations at the field hospital was for venereal diseases. Following successful treatment, the cured soldiers returned to the field with a pocketful of condoms and a strict warning against failing to use them again. Easy access to the devices meant Esmée and Sven wouldn't—shouldn't—conceive. Their first commitment, that no one should find out about them, was even more important because Sven had a secret.

When he was pulled aside at a Paris train station and essentially conscripted into the German medical corps, Sven, a budding DJ back in Norway, had smuggled in his knapsack all the parts to make a short-wave wireless. He'd brought that along with him to the field hospital following his arrest and had it with him still. One thing led to another and soon, because he was helping with Allied soldiers, he was being asked to get word to loved ones that, even though captured, the POW was okay and being well-treated. This came up for the first time with a young British soldier named Angeman Kincaid, a soldier who'd been shot and left in No-man's-land when the Allied forces beat a retreat, leaving him behind. Taken prisoner, Kincaid soon found himself minus his left arm from the elbow down after the German army surgeons finished with him. Esmée had diagnosed him in triage and he had asked her to help get word to his mother that he was alive and safe. She'd told him she had no way to do that. She shared his story, that night, with Sven, who, for some odd reason, she thought, didn't see the situation as hopeless. In fact, he asked for the man's full name and military number—his dog tag information—which Esmée retrieved the next day.

That night, after a fifteen-hour shift at the hospital, Sven went on the air with his shortwave and broadcast news of Angeman Kincaid. All particulars were given and, when he was finished, no one seemed the wiser. This help put Corporal Kincaid's mind to rest and his recovery went well thereafter. Kincaid, two days later, referred a French POW to Esmée for the same help and again Sven jumped into action. Allied servicemen were being helped, and the Germans didn't seem to have even a hint of what was going on right under their noses.

Sven taught Esmée how to operate the shortwave wireless so that she could broadcast on the nights when he was held over. He knew—and she knew—that there were listeners somewhere out there that had taken to monitoring their broadcast frequency at about the same time around midnight and neither Sven nor Esmée wanted to let them down. They were determined there would be a nightly broadcast.

Sven took it upon himself to disguise his shortwave wireless. Using the frame of a portable camp heater, one that had seen better days and was now discarded, Sven turned the heater into a shortwave wireless with a potentiometer that operated from the heater's temperature knob and a frequency selector that operated from the heater's timer control. The whole thing was about the size of a soldier's backpack. The newly rebuilt heater was placed in an alcove just inside Sven's temporary quarters, where he could access it easily without worry of discovery. What prompted this makeover was the knowledge that, if the shortwave itself were ever discovered, its owner would be shot or hanged on the spot. Sven had no doubt that that was the case and had even been told as much, that he should never communicate with the enemy.

One night, as Sven was speaking in a whisper into his wireless, a sentry posted inside the sleeping hall heard what Sven was saying. The sentry spoke enough French to know Sven was just on the other side of a folding door, speaking to someone about a prisoner's status. The sentry went for his sergeant but while he was gone, Sven signed off and set the heater wireless back in its place. When the sergeant arrived and rousted Sven from his sleeping pallet, there was no one else around and Sven denied he had been speaking to anyone. The sergeant, a suspicious man of forty who had no use for youthful games and remonstrances, marched Sven outside, placed him up against a fir tree, and told him he wanted a name or he would be shot. Sven had no name. He raised his hands to protest, tried a smile, and the sergeant, without another word, shot the young medic in the head with his grease gun. Sven crumpled to his knees, toppled to his side, and fell over, dead.

Esmée begged off work sick over the next three days. Grief stricken, she couldn't even get up off her pallet. She had loved Sven and had committed to him. After the war there were plans to marry, settle down and have a family, but now that was gone. Now Sven was gone, too.

Except he had left behind the wireless.

And Esmée knew how and when to use it.

11

Jacques Marseilles called Claire into his office Wednesday morning. It was the day before Christmas, and the ice flowing along the Seine River ground together and moaned as if in pain. Germans were everywhere in the city—newly arrived and more arriving daily. Already condiments were scarce, and shop signs said the same thing throughout Paris: no cheese, no butter, no cooking oil, no beef, no poultry, no pork, no milk. Whatever people lived on had been emptied out of the stores by the Germans before the French ever had a chance in line. Ration cards —everyone had them, but they didn't magically produce goods to purchase, for the shelves were all but empty.

Claire's camera was capturing the shop signs and the long queues up and down the blocks where butcher stores and baker shops could be found.

She photographed the glum looks as eyes searched out the constant aircraft traffic and ears searched out the sounds of guns booming and explosions in the nearby countryside. Entwined with the other sounds of war was the ever-increasing rat-a-tat-tat of automatic weapons' fire inside the Paris city limits as intransi-gents were rooted out and dealt with—a city under siege, an occu-pied city, an age of untold repression all captured on 35 mm film.

Her pictures were not happy ones. But more and more they'd been appearing in transatlantic newspapers and newsmagazines, and her photo credits were earning her a name with increasing recognition.

She entered Jacques' office and continued standing, her camera slung across her shoulder, her handbag slung across the other. She was gnawing on a Christmas apple. "You wanted to see me?"

"There is a series of photos we need. I'd like to talk to you about doing some freelance work for us."

"I'm on my way. Where?"

"The train station where the Jews are shipped off to the camps."

Claire felt a chill up her spine. She knew Gare du Nord train station wasn't safe and said so. "The Gestapo rules that place. Guards and dogs every ten feet. They want no photos made. How did you think I might do this without getting myself shot?"

He rubbed his hands together. Then he pulled a bottle of brandy out of a drawer. "Care for some?" He was already pouring himself a small glass when he asked.

"Not right now. How do I avoid getting shot?"

"You're a smart girl, Claire. We thought we'd leave that to you."

"Who is this 'we'?"

"Associated Press and our paper. The Americans believe such pictures will soften their country's hardline against coming into the war. Roosevelt refuses. Maybe the right pictures will influence him."

"So it's a political shoot?"

He swallowed off half the glass of brandy and swiped a hand across his mouth. "Political, you ask? Aren't they all?"

"All right. I'll get your pictures. What's the publication deadline?"

"This is Friday. I would like to see them in Sunday's paper."

"If it can be done, that's no problem. But it's a big 'if.'"

"Agreed. Don't get yourself shot. Be smart. Kids, Claire."

"Shoot kids?"

"Get lots of pictures of kids. They sell papers."

"That's rather sanguine, Jacques. Have you been in the streets?"

"I know all about it. My neighbors were rounded up two nights ago. Middle of the night, kids crying, mother screaming, father begging and pleading. Horrible for them."

12

SS Lieutenant Remy Schildmann marched his soldiers along rue des Martyrs, scattering the few shopkeepers and workmen still out just before curfew that dark night. The German soldiers in France were oblivious to Paris and didn't care. They were oblivious to how the city's glorious, distinctive residential buildings were built in Haussmann's style, oblivious to the stealth of the falling snow, and oblivious to the terror they struck in the Parisians hidden by their blackout shades as the squad came in goose-step up their street.

At Schildmann's barked order, "Halt!" they jolted to a standstill before a large stone five-floor terrace building marked by the perfect alignment and symmetry of its balconies, windows, and mansard roofs. It was beautiful French architecture and would have bustled with occupants and visitors just six short months ago before the Germans came pouring into France, but that wasn't the case. Only a late-night visit by the German SS was underway.

At number 217 they entered the building with its cuprous awning and leering gargoyles, clomped inside and across the parquet floor, their jackboots leaving snow prints behind. They climbed the twisting staircase up four floors, Lieutenant Schildmann leading the way.

At the top of the landing, they turned right and pounded on the locked walnut door. When a peephole opened, Remy—Lieutenant Schildmann—shouted in French, "Open before we break this door down!" The door squeaked open, and the soldiers stormed inside. Remy's gaze swept around, taking it all in, understanding immediately who he was dealing with. The spacious apartment featured elegant architectural flourishes: high ceilings, parquet flooring, floor-length windows, and intricate wood and plaster-work. A young woman drew open the door then backed away until she pressed up against a white fireplace mantle with elegant gold fluting. Arms wrapped around her torso, she cowered, turning away.

To the woman's right, just entering the room, came a man a couple years older than Remy's 21 years. He was carrying a bottle of wine in his right hand and two stemmed glasses between the fingers of his left hand. A drink before bedtime was planned. He was still wearing suit pants and a white shirt from the day, but now donned a smoking jacket. The wife was dressed in a long, willowy robin's-egg blue lounging dress, her long arms and bare feet exposed and safe—up to now—in her own home.

"Do you know why we're here?" demanded Remy. At this point, he was feeling feverish, hating everything about himself for what he was about to do. But he shut off his feelings and commanded the inner German soldier clutching his heart to turn loose and step forward. It would take someone other than the old Remy to deal with this couple and, God forbid, their children if any were asleep in the bedrooms.

Luckily for Remy, unluckily for the couple, his inner German stormed forth and spoke. "We've come to take you to Gestapo headquarters. You must come and answer Captain Heiss's questions."

"But it's late and we aren't dressed. It's Christmas Eve. We have no one for our daughter—" protested the husband, the father. Whereupon, one soldier reversed his carbine and struck the man in the face with the butt end of the gun. He fell back, blood erupting in a spray from his nose and mouth.

"Take them downstairs," Remy ordered. He needn't have said a word; this was a nightly ritual, the rousting of Jews from their homes. They had already done a dozen others that night. The SS had started with a list of the most prominent among the Jewish population and was working its way through them, like shears pruning a thorny branch. The young man tonight, Nussbaum, was the reserve conductor of the Philharmonie de Paris, who also played second violin. Now he and his wife were headed for the camps outside Paris for processing, then off to Auschwitz or Treblinka in Poland. Remy knew they would likely die before New Year's.

"The bedrooms?" asked Corporal Friedrich. "He said there was a child?"

"*Nein*," said Remy, "I'll do the bedrooms. You help with the vermin."

With that, Remy strode toward the hallway and whatever bedrooms awaited. There were three: the master bedroom, now empty; a second bedroom along the hallway, filled with stringed musical instruments and four chairs; a third bedroom, lights off. Remy flicked the light switch and stared into the face of a sleeping girl of three or four with brown curls, clutching a rag doll to her chest, sound asleep. The image of her being trundled off to

Auschwitz and certain death caused him to stagger. He all but went down to his knees. Already that night he'd sent a dozen children away on the camp trains, and his heart was breaking. Could he stand to send away even one more? His job was to roust her and drive her downstairs to join her parents in the prisoner lorry. But instead, the twist of her lips, the curls on her head, the tiny hands —something, or everything, brought him to a standing halt. He had been death hurtling toward everyone in his path; and then, he was not. Instead of taking her downstairs, he lifted her from beneath her bedcovers and carried her to her armoire. Clutching the sleeping girl in his left arm, he pulled open the side door with his right hand. He jerked down a flurry of her clothes from their hangers and laid the sleeping child upon them. Just as quietly, he shut the door, slid the latch, turned, and flicked off the only light. He stole back into the living room.

"What?" said Corporal Friedrich. "Where are the children?"

Remy shook his head. Here he was at a crossroads. "No children. Musical instruments, that sort of thing."

Friedrich took a step toward the hallway. "Suppose I have a look, Lieutenant. Perhaps you missed something."

"Corporal, I'm ordering you to proceed downstairs and prepare the prisoners for transport."

"A quick look."

"Corporal! Are you disobeying my direct order? There is nothing to discuss here."

"Nothing, Lieutenant? Very well. But I'll be back later tonight with orders from the captain. I can promise you that, sir."

The "sir" was sarcastically emphasized. The man knew Remy all too well and had his ploy figured from the beginning. Friedrich would confront Remy's captain, as was his right, and ask to return here—also his right.

"Sir, yes, sir," Friedrich said at last, bowing to his lieutenant's command. "I only hope you've searched well, sir."

"I'll be down momentarily, Corporal. First, I must locate the safe and see about jewelry and francs." It was a standard procedure for the officer in charge of the detail to steal whatever valuables he might find lying around. Later, he would share with his troops if he wished, and Remy always did.

No sooner was Corporal Friedrich gone from the apartment than Remy dashed to the telephone and dialed the phone number belonging to Claire Vallant. She picked up on the second ring.

"Claire. Come to 217 rue des Martyrs immediately. Fourth floor, turn right. Third bedroom, armoire. A small girl is locked inside. Take her away from this madness. I'll talk to you in the morning."

Then he hung up without waiting for her reply.

But then what? He was suddenly dizzy as he considered his actions.

After sending Corporal Friedrich downstairs with the second-chair violinist and his wife, Remy found the wine bottle the husband had left on the fireplace mantle. It was open. Remy drank down a mouthful of the sparkling liquid. Then another. It was almost too much for him, and for just a moment he felt an urge to roust the sleeping child from the armoire and take her downstairs with her parents. It would be far safer for him to do so. As it was, he was in danger of being shot for dereliction of duty if caught hiding the child. But a third drink of the alcohol warmed his gut and his extremities, and his courage returned. To hell with the

German High Command and to hell with Friedrich and his returning here. He was saving the child, and that was the end of it.

He replaced the cork, set the bottle on the mantle, and headed for the door.

Pulling it closed behind him, he paused on the dimly lit landing, said a quick prayer for the girl, and clomped down the ancient stairs.

She now belonged to him.

13

Claire hung up the call with Remy. It had been over year since she'd seen him last. He was still held captive by the German army in a German army officer's uniform—an SS uniform—the result of his German father's conscription of his own son when Germany invaded France seven months earlier. His call told her that he'd sent another family of Jews, minus one, to the concentration camp at Auschwitz. The minus one represented the child he had somehow pulled aside and held back from the imposition of that death sentence. She knew Remy and understood what had happened.

It was just after two in the morning when she gave up trying to get back to sleep. The Paris curfew was in effect so going to pick up the child was out of the question until dawn. At that time, she would have to decide. Did she retrieve the child at great risk to herself, including instant death if she were caught helping a Jew to escape? Or did she ignore the whole thing and go about her day as a student at *Ecole Supérieure de Journalisme de Paris*? The one made her a criminal subject to the death penalty; the other meant she remained in school, studying photojournalism, where she was matriculated. For a young French woman with no real hope of ever having a career in 1941 Paris, the school was almost superfluous. It would amount to nothing in the end; it was folly. But it was her folly. She loved photography, loved her camera, and loved recording the world as seen through the eyes of an eighteen-year-old, unmarried, unengaged, female, the daughter of a physician mother and engineer father, who was financed by her parents while her dream—of amounting to something besides another housewife bearing children—played out. A little girl, a little Jewish girl in hiding, would turn her life upside-down. In the end, she decided against rushing to the rescue. Her life, her dream, would never survive if she did. Maybe she wouldn't survive, either.

She decided to telephone her mother. Her mother would guide her. So she dialed her up even though it was the middle of the night. It would be okay because, as a surgeon, her mother was called to the hospital on emergencies at all hours of the day or night anyway. As a surgeon she had a "24" stamped on her ID card, meaning she could move freely about the city 24 hours a day. It went with being in a critical field such as medicine. Paris police, electrical workers, and sanitation workers all had the same endorsement on their cards, as did many others.

The phone was answered on the third ring.

"Maman, I've received a call, never mind from who. A young girl's family has been rousted. A soldier hid her away in the apartment and has told me to go and pick her up. I have no resources for doing that. I feel horrible for the child."

"My goodness, say no more on the phone. I'll be over in thirty minutes."

Claire hung up and went into the kitchen. She put the kettle on for coffee. When it whistled, she poured boiling water over freeze-dried coffee in a single cup. Stirring in a small portion of milk, she turned the flame on low so the water would remain hot for her mother. The coffee and the milk were a luxury and were obtained by her father who, as an employee of Delahaye, knew the right people for acquiring luxury items outside the mainstream of daily French commerce. Normally, Claire limited her consumption to one cup a day, but today wasn't an ordinary day. Today called for coffee in the middle of the night. Today was a perilous time and required heightened senses and thoughts. The coffee could only help in that regard.

She walked quietly into the small living room and stood at the cold fireplace. Over the mantle was a small mirror and an oil painting, and arranged on the mantel itself was a small collection of Arabian statuary from an import store she frequented on avenue de la Bourdonnais, south of the Seine River. Books on end and three gold candles completed the composition—a composition pleasing to the eye of a photographer, such as she had become with her studies and in her life. She sipped her coffee and considered her predicament.

Then came the secret knock at her door: one knock, a rattle of the doorknob, then three soft raps.

Maman.

14

Dr. Constance Vallant—Maman—breezed into the room, wearing her surgical greens under a fur coat and hat. Black gloves and slip-on boots completed her early-Christmas-Day wear, the surgical scrubs worn to convince any inquiring Germans that she was, in fact, on her way to the hospital. She was a rosy-cheeked woman who, like Claire, was pale-skinned with jet black hair and gray eyes. The hair was stylishly short and coiffed, the makeup non-existent, and her eyes darted about the room when she entered as if she expected a small child to pop out of hiding at any moment.

But there was no small child. There was only the possibility, and that was the purpose of her visit.

"Here, let me get you coffee," offered Claire as her mother hung her coat at the door.

"While I build a fire. It's freezing in here, Claire. I don't know why you don't keep a fire going yourself."

Claire went into the kitchen and poured steaming water over

coffee crystals, this time finishing with a cube of sugar—another of her father's black market acquisitions—but no milk. She returned to the living room and set the cup beside one of the two white upholstered chairs, chosen by her mother, nearest the fireplace where kindling and newsprint ignited a hefty wooden log. Maman accepted the coffee, resting it in her lap and crossing her legs at the ankles. She was still wearing her fox coat. "Now," she began, "what's this about a child?"

"Remy called. His squad rousted a family of Jews. Evidently there was a young girl and Remy couldn't stand to send her to her death. You know Remy."

"I do. If ever a man was unsuited for the German army... Well, go on, what else?"

"Something about he'd locked her into an armoire.

"Locked her in? You're sure of that?"

"Yes, locked her in."

"Then something must be done for her."

"Why? What if she wasn't locked in?"

"Then in that case, she'd be none of your concern. But being locked in—that puts her in immediate danger. She might even suffocate. Or has already."

"Being a Jew also puts her in immediate danger. What do I do, Maman?"

"If he hadn't locked her away, she would have gone with her parents and her death assured. End of story. But since she's hidden away and in physical peril, she becomes someone else's concern. The fact that the Nazis don't have her yet means there's still hope for her. The question is, who holds the key to her hope? You, my dear Claire?"

"Who else, Maman? I'm the one he called."

"It's a terrible predicament. Go to her aid, and you risk your very life. I know you're young, and it might seem like something you would want to risk, but there's a terrible finality to death to one like your mother, the surgeon. Death is actually the end of things. Are you willing to risk your end for a child whose fate is sealed anyway? And what of the day after you bring her home? How hide her? If she's quite young, you must drop out of school to stay home with her and look after her. Plus, there's extra food, maybe special foods for her. Who can say? I'm thinking you must let this pass you by, Claire. As terribly hard as it is, I don't think this is your game."

"But she'll die without me. That's what I keep coming back to. Yes, death is final for me. But it's final for her, too. Balancing that against my schooling, what's the most important? I have no future of any kind. Women don't get hired for exciting photojournalism jobs—it's a man's world. So what am I actually giving up by dropping out of school and caring for this child? What?"

"Valid points. Your future is marriage and children in France. I was a lucky one, born to great wealth in Berlin and able to buy my way into medical school. My father's money. You don't have that same opportunity."

"Plus, I don't want to be a doctor."

"No, you want to take pictures. I'm not sure how there's a career in that. Not for a woman, Claire. So your point is valid as far as it goes."

Claire set aside her coffee cup. She stood and looked around, stepping across to the fireplace mantel and retrieving a cigarette from her seldom-used stash. She struck a match, and for a moment, her face was caught in its flare as she lit her cigarette. After she inhaled deeply, she blew out a long plume of smoke. It reached the glass mirror and swept off in an ever-widening ring. "Oh, my God. What to do?"

"Maman says you do nothing. Maman says you go in and take a hot bath and get ready for school. That's what you do."

Claire sat down in her chair. "I don't think I can. How can I comfortably sit around my classrooms and my apartment, knowing there's a child whose life I can save if only I will? She will die if I do nothing. My conscience won't allow that."

"Then borrow my conscience. Trust me in this, Claire. Stay away."

"I know all the truth about what you say. But my feelings are otherwise. When I put myself in her shoes, terrified as she is, especially locked away in a dark cabinet, I have no choice but to go and try to help. I'm sorry, Maman. I can't turn away. She could be suffocating right now!"

The physician-surgeon, who knew the true meaning of hopeless, bit her tongue. It wasn't her decision to make. While she disagreed, she believed in her daughter more than her own logic. She would back away now. "All right. How can I help?"

15

Just after seven the next morning, after her mother had departed for the hospital, Claire took a bike taxi to the address given to her by Remy. The taxi let her off on the corner. Then she walked a half a block to 217. It was early in the morning; the curfew had just lifted for the day. She ran up the four flights of stairs and turned right. The door was unlocked, so she went right in. First off, she heard crying coming from down the hall. She was alive! She turned left and followed her ears down to the third bedroom on the right. It had to be the armoire.

The door had been shut with the latch engaged. She slid the latch open to the armoire door. There stood a young girl, weeping, her face wet with tears, her head between two clothes hangers. She threw her arms around Claire's neck.

Whether the girl thought it was her mother or was just embracing her savior didn't matter: Claire was bear-hugged by a three-year-old, and that changed her on the spot. Here was one who needed someone. At that moment, more than any other since she was twelve, Claire realized she needed someone, too. What's more, she was right to come. The decision had been the correct one.

"Where did you go!" cried the little girl.

Claire understood; the child was speaking as if to her mother.

"Maman had to leave with Papa. I came to get you out. We're all terribly sorry this happened to you."

"Tell Maman I want her!"

"I'll try to do that."

"Where is she?"

"She had to leave with Papa. We'll have to wait and see. Are you hungry?"

"No. I want Maman."

Claire plunged ahead. There was nothing else to do since she had to leave the apartment with the little girl, and it was too risky for the child to be crying as it might draw attention. If that happened, the little girl, without papers, would be taken away. She'd probably never be seen alive again. Claire could just as easily be disappeared by the Nazis, too. There could be no tears when they left the apartment.

"We'll see about Maman. Hey, are you hungry?"

"Who are you?"

"I'm your new friend. I like you."

"We can be friends?"

"We will be great friends," she whispered to the child as she lifted her out of the armoire. "Are you hungry?"

"Jam," said the girl. "*Petit pain* and jam."

"We can do that. Let's go check the kitchen."

"Maman in the kitchen?"

"Not just now. Maman and papa had to go someplace."

The crying began. "No, no, no, I want *Maman*!"

"Well, yes, you do. We'll see what we can do about that, too. But first, let's have a breakfast roll. *Oui*?"

"*Oui*. Hungry tummy."

"Let's plop you down on the toilet, too. Do you use the toilet?"

"Potty. Let's go."

"Yes, let's go."

She placed the girl on the toilet with the potty attachment and stood in the doorway. When the child finished, she, without being told, got upon tiptoes and ran water in the sink. She washed up and pulled down the hand towel. A drying of the hands then she walked past Claire and led them into the kitchen.

"What's your name?"

"Lima."

"Well, Lima, my name is Claire. Nice to meet you."

"Where is Maman?"

"Maman had to leave for a while. We'll see what we can find out about that, okay? But first we'll have a muffin and jam."

She rummaged in the bread box and was rewarded with a stash of breakfast pastries. She cut one crosswise, pasted it over with strawberry jam, and handed it on a plate to Lima. The girl had parked herself on the end chair at the rectangular kitchen table and watched eagerly as her food approached. "Milk?"

"Of course."

Claire poured milk into a small glass and set that beside the breakfast pastry.

"Now, you gobble that down and then we will go shopping. Do you like to go shopping?"

"Yes. Butcher shopping?"

"I think we'll go coffee shopping. Some nice cafe where two girls can have a chat about this and that. Do you like cafes?"

"No."

Time was a matter of greatest importance. The longer they dallied in the apartment, the greater the odds of some German happening back to loot the place and catching them there. The pause for a snack was only to establish a sense of trust, no more than that. While the child munched, Claire returned to the girl's bedroom with a paper sack and loaded undies and two dresses and other middling child's wear. She needed little; Claire would replenish whatever they were short. A full wardrobe could come later. But she thought to add the rag doll from beside the child's pillow. That was a must, she was sure.

Claire coerced Lima downstairs with promises to read to her later and hurried her along to the corner, away from the apartment. They couldn't get away fast enough to suit Claire. The less opportunity the Germans had to find and trundle off the little girl, the better.

She hailed a bike taxi, and it drove them back to her own flat on rue des Amis. They unloaded at curbside.

"*Guten morgen, frau,*" said a voice from behind as soon as they had stepped onto the sidewalk. She turned. Two German soldiers in green uniforms, machine guns nestled in their arms.

"*Guten tag,*" she said.

"*Unterlagen?*"

He wanted to see her papers.

She opened her bag, drew out her documents, and passed them to the soldier. He was husky, and his wrists and hands were like hams. His face was wide, his nose flat, and his hat placed on his head at a jaunty angle. His partner was young, thin, and hung back while the older man scanned Claire's papers. Then he passed them back to her. "What about your daughter? Papers?"

Claire's worst fear had come true. She had no papers, and even if she had, they would reveal the child was a Jew, and they would take away her. She smiled her best smile at the man. He wasn't moved. "Documents for the child?" he continued in ill French.

She responded in German, "Her father had a seizure, and we went to hospital. We left behind her papers in her bag at the hospital. We thought we would come home, change clothes, and return to her father's bedside."

"What is wrong with the father?" he asked.

"Pneumonia. Too much cold winter air. He works outside."

"What is his name?"

"Remy Schildmann. He's in the army."

"German army? What hospital is he at?"

"Can I run her inside the house? She's dressed in this flimsy jacket, and it's freezing this morning. Now I'm worried about her."

The German took a step back. "What rank is her father?"

"Lieutenant, SS."

"Is he your husband?"

Obviously, their names were different.

"No, he's not."

"Give Lieutenant Schildmann our best wishes. Here's to a speedy recovery. Now take your child inside and warm her up, *frau*."

"I will, thank you."

The two soldiers sidestepped around her and continued down the sidewalk beyond Claire's front stoop. Claire's pulse was pounding, and she felt dizzy. The adrenaline was coursing through her body, and she felt a strong desire to run even though they'd just accepted her story. Instead, she took Lima's hand in her own, bit back her feelings, and forced herself to put one foot in front of the other as she walked up the remaining steps to her front entrance. There, they disappeared through the door.

She got Lima inside her flat and showed her where she'd sleep beside Claire in the twin bed until she could arrange a second bed. Next, Claire combined two drawers in her wardrobe into one drawer, emptying a lower drawer for Lima's things, which she had the little girl move from the paper sack into her drawer. Finally, they examined the rag doll who'd traveled with them.

They placed it on Claire's bed pillow, and she told Lima she'd be there waiting for her that night. Whereupon, the child became frightened and whimpered for her mommy.

"Maman is coming?" she asked.

"Maman is off seeing about some business. But we will try to locate her and see if we can help. That much I promise you."

Claire took an inventory of the situation. First, she had no idea what the child's last name was. There hadn't been time to rummage through mail or old papers and locate the family name. Second, she had no idea about the parents' whereabouts except they'd been taken into custody. If they were Jews—and she believed they were—then the chance of them ever returning to their daughter was next to nothing. Which was why Claire, in speaking with the girl, never said they'd find the parents or anything so positive. She tried to say only that they'd look, and she'd leave it at that. She didn't want to create false hope, although that was becoming increasingly difficult with the child's tears for her mother. Finally, she had zero idea what to do with Lima when she went to work. She was tasked with taking pictures of children at the train station, and she knew Lima couldn't accompany her there, so what to do with her? Helpless and no place to turn, she wished Esmée was there to help. She was needed more than ever, but Claire knew better than to involve her younger sister in hiding away a Jewess. That could mean Esmée's death, too.

Claire finally decided she would take Lima to her mother's house and find out if their nanny could help while Claire attempted the train station photo shoot. But even that solution wasn't really a solution because she didn't dare venture out again without papers for Lima. No papers meant the child was subject to being dragged off without further questions and sent to a camp. No papers meant the person was probably a Jew or a Gypsy. So, she was stuck. If only Remy would call again and help with the child. She was resenting him a little for getting her into such an impossible situation and then disappearing.

She spent the day making cut-out paper dollars with Lima, telling her imaginary stories, making scratch cookies. The attention span was short, but she was an easy child to be with and loved drawing on blank paper with a soft lead pencil. Now, if they only had colors, which were on Claire's next shopping list. At seven o'clock, Claire helped Lima with her bath, toweled her dry, and got her ready for bed. They then went in on the bed, where Claire regaled the child with stories of Sammy Squirrel—Claire's new make-believe character who, it was hoped, had more adventures than just that first night. Sammy would be requested over and over in the nights to come. Claire then switched off the bedroom light, cracked her door several inches, and crept into the living room.

She sat back on the couch and luxuriated for a few minutes, knowing that her new duties had been done. She fell asleep.

She awoke to the sound of a door rattle, then rap-rap-rap at her apartment door. She opened her eyes and rubbed them. What time was it? She glanced at her watch—who would call at midnight? She realized it could well be the Gestapo come for Lima.

Her heart jumped into action and, within seconds, blood was coursing through her veins as she prepared a plan to save Lima from whoever was on the other side. One thing: no one would take the little girl away from her. That much she knew.

She went to the door and pressed her ear up against it. "Yes?" she softly called.

"Open. Remy."

Her heart jumped. She couldn't pull it open fast enough. There he stood, splendid in his SS uniform, looking every bit like the rough German soldier he had become. She swept him inside and collapsed in his arms. "*Mon Dieu*."

Remy looked around Claire's flat just as soon as he'd come inside, out of the cold December air.

"You have her then?"

"I do. She's sleeping in my bed."

"How is she?"

"Terrified. I spent the entire day helping her think about anything other than her mother. It didn't work, but we made it through. What's it all about, Remy?"

He came on inside and sat heavily on her sofa. Leaning forward, hands on his knees, he looked totally out of place, the German soldier in the tasteful French flat. "She's one I couldn't stand to send away. It was one too many. So I hid her. Then I confined a soldier to his quarters so he couldn't return later and steal her away."

"What's her name?"

"Nussbaum was her father's name."

"Was?"

"Alas, he and the mother are bound for Auschwitz as we speak."

"Oh, my God. So what will become of her?"

Remy sat back and crossed his arms. "That's the question. If not for you, she'd be on a train herself."

"Bound for Auschwitz?"

"Bound for Auschwitz. I'm sorry I got you into it."

"Well, we can't let that happen. We must have a plan."

"You must keep her, Claire. There is no other plan. But know this, people are getting shot for harboring Jews. I don't have to tell you what it's like now."

"No, no, I'm aware. All right. The first thing she needs is papers. She needs papers with my name."

"That I can arrange. I have my friends at Gestapo Records. Who do we say is her father?"

"Her father is...Gustav, we can say. He is off fighting in Russia, we can say as well. That's all I know."

Remy nodded. "That works. Same last name as you?"

An idea then came to mind; forget Gustav, he'd been replaced.

"I've got an even better idea. Let us take your name. I am now Claire Schildmann, and she is Lima Schildmann. We're married, you and I."

"Oh, Claire, I don't know. People who know me know I'm not married."

"Nonsense, you've kept it a secret all along if they ask. Besides, who will ask? No one, I'm sure. But that will give Lima and me the German name and respectability we need. Married to a German soldier I can move about."

"I don't know if that will keep her safe..."

Claire then did something she'd never done in her life. She made an important decision about her life without consulting her mother. But it felt right. She had the little girl and so, really, she had no choice but to go all the way with it because no one else was going to come and take over with Lima. Claire felt she owed the little girl the absolute best chance she could give her. So she blurted it out.

"How about this, then? How about we marry, and we give Lima our married name?"

His eyes grew wide, clearly shocked. "You would do that?"

"For her? Of course I would."

Remy uncrossed his arms and settled back. She could see him relaxing inch-by-inch.

"Would you like wine?" she asked.

"I think I need a glass of wine. To celebrate."

"Celebrate our marriage?"

"Yes!"

"You mean what we are about to do?"

"Absolutely. I mean for it to be real in all respects. Claire, I've always loved you. Marrying you is easy for me. But for you, it only tells me how much you've become attached to Lima in just one day."

"That's not all. You must know my feelings for you."

"It's good to hear it, though. I'm in heaven."

Before Claire retrieved the wine from the kitchen, she sat briefly next to Remy on the arm of his chair, and they embraced. With a quick kiss, she left and returned with the bottle and two glasses. As much as she wanted to revel in the strength of Remy's arms, it wasn't the time. They needed to talk and plan.

Claire sat again in the other chair, the one her mother had only sat in twenty-four hours ago, and handed Remy a glass. "She is so vulnerable. We're all she has, Remy. We must do right by her."

"And we shall."

"I'm serious. No one will ever take her from me."

"Nor I. It was too much for me to lose her last night. I feel the same tonight."

"War does insane things. We would never marry if not for Lima."

She was testing him, waiting for his response. But he said nothing, pouring the wine instead. Then, "When is our wedding?" he asked.

"Tomorrow? Can you get time?"

"It would be unusual, but I will steal away for a few hours and make it happen. I'll go on sick call. We'll go to the town hall and get a license and let the deputy mayor marry us."

"What about the waiting period? The physical exam?"

He smiled. "Really? A waiting period for German officers? I don't think so, beautiful Claire. Nobody would dare to tell me no."

"Whatever works fastest. Surely, the Gestapo has no laws against marriage?"

"Even if they did, I'm SS. They wouldn't dare interfere. Not only that, I'm an officer, a lieutenant. I'll outrank anyone we come into contact with. Consider it done."

He drank down his wine in two gulps and abruptly took to his feet. "So, I'm due back. I must return to my quarters tonight. But tomorrow we'll make our vows and tomorrow night we'll all stay here."

"One thing, Remy. How did you find me tonight?"

He touched the side of his head. "The same way I found your telephone number a week or two ago. Gestapo, remember?"

"They have all that?"

"Oh, they have that and so much more. Hitler spent from 1934 to 1938 refining government records. They know everything, Claire. Everything except Lima. The little one they don't know about. I'll put myself as her father on the marriage license."

"Wonderful. What time should we be ready?"

"I'll leave work at noon, jump over here, and we'll take a cab to the town hall. We'll get married, and then I'll call in and tell them I'm taking the rest of the day for personal business. It won't be a problem."

"We'll see you then."

Standing, there was an awkward moment as he was turning to the door. But then she stopped him, touching his shoulder, and she leaned in and brushed his lips with hers. It wasn't their first kiss, but it was the first that meant something to her. She liked the feeling.

"My Claire," he said in wonderment. "Who would have guessed?"

"Not I," she admitted. "But I'm glad it happened. I've missed you."

The next day, Remy's predictions of the ease of getting a marriage license and a ceremony turned out to be correct.

The deputy mayor married them the next day at three. They celebrated with their new daughter at a restaurant serving expensive French food. Lima was silent through dinner, but her eyes lit up at her glistening chocolate cake at dessert time.

When they had paid their bill and were leaving, Lima at last spoke, "Where's my Maman?"

16

Claire's mother agreed to watch the little girl Saturday morning while Claire visited the train station. It occurred to Claire—yet again—that her activities were putting her family at great risk. And that what she was about to attempt could do even more harm to them if she was captured or shot. She decided she had no right. It was time to begin looking for a nanny of Lima's own.

"I'm torn," she confided in her mother that morning. "Our country needs the train station pictures. Maybe they can even influence the Americans to join the war. But on the other hand, there is my family and Lima. If I'm caught, it goes badly for you."

Her mother scoffed, "If you're caught, we likely go to the camps. Especially when they come to our home and discover Lima in hiding."

"What do I do?"

"Who else might take the pictures?"

"Jacques has told me he trusts me with the assignment. There probably won't be a second chance."

"Then he should go himself."

"That's not his job. Suppose I leave Lima at my flat with a nanny. That way, I don't involve any of you if I'm caught."

"Nonsense. You are married with a husband and child. She's one of us, now, even brand new. If we're going to raise her as ours, that begins now."

"That's brave and makes me feel so good, but it's still not fair. No, I think she goes back to my flat with a nanny."

"That's not going to happen. I won't allow it."

"Allow what?" asked her papa, coming into the room.

"She wants to leave Lima with a nanny while she goes to the train station. I told her no, the child stays with us."

"Come and let me show you something," her papa said.

Claire followed the man out into his garage. They stopped next to a tall cabinet filled with tools. Her papa reached up and far back on the top of the cabinet. He sprung a latch there, and the entire front shelf area of the cabinet swung forward. It was a false front. "See? Lima waits here if they come. She's our cabinet baby. That's what I call her now."

"You made this for her?"

"We're surrounded by Jews in our neighborhood. Wonderful people, just like our family. I thought one of them might need it. Just finished. There's food and water in that small cabinet. I've already shown Lima how it works. She knows. Plus, I've made it soundproof with these liners. No one can hear her cry."

"*Mon Dieu*! You really are going to be grandparents."

"Our first—and hopefully not our last—grandchild. She's part of the family now, Claire. Let's all act like that. No need for a nanny and all that. She's much safer with us."

"Now, I see."

They went back inside the house. Her mother was beaming. "Well?"

"I'm speechless. I had no idea you were doing that."

"Thank your father. Never forget he's a design engineer. These things come easy to the man who designs the cabriolet."

"I'm so grateful. I don't know how to thank you enough."

"No need. Now, let's see about getting you there. The taxi just pulled up."

The physician and surgeon mother helped Claire's driver load a wheelchair into the boot of his cab. Claire was assisted out of the house by her younger brothers in the manner of one who couldn't walk.

Off they navigated to the Paris north train station.

The taxi pulled up at the building that said NORD across the top and housed six train tracks within. Paris's Gare du Nord was the busiest train station in Europe and, with the coming of the Poland-bound freight trains, getting in and out was all but impossible, thanks to the constant crush of people and the constant body and luggage search by the Paris police and Gestapo. They used the second and fourth entrances for Paris Jews and Gypsies on their way to camps. The third entrance they used for continental shipping of goods and products. It was all choreographed and the normal uses of the station had been turned on their head to have the Germans processing and shipping Jews and other so-called "undesirables" out of Paris.

As the taxi rocked to a stop, the driver hustled out, came around to the boot behind Claire, opened the lid, and worked her wheelchair out of a tight spot. He unfolded the chair and wheeled it around to the right rear door of his cab. Claire, clutching her handbag and her shawl, allowed herself to be lifted into the wheelchair. The cabbie then stood back. "You can wheel it?"

"Yes, I can make it go." She paid him with francs. "You've been wonderful, and I thank you, Renz."

"Thank you, Mademoiselle Schildmann. Have a pleasant journey."

"I will, I'm sure."

The man got behind the wheelchair, seized the two handle grips, and tilted her back then rolled her up and over the curb. She then nodded her thanks, pulled on her black gloves, and rolled the wheelchair in the direction of the train station's main entrance.

One of the unique features of the railway station was the 23 female statues that adorned the façade. Each statue represented a particular destination served by the Chemin de Fer du Nord rail company. The destinations sculpted on the façade included Paris, London, Berlin, Warsaw, Amsterdam, Vienna, Brussels, and Frankfurt. It was the Warsaw connection that was the busiest by a thousand percent.

Looking upward, she viewed the nine statutes situated along the cornice line of the façade. Realizing she had reached her destination, her heart skipped a beat and sweat beaded across her forehead. She didn't hesitate; the sweat would look like the normal exertion of one operating one's wheelchair around the station as would be expected.

She passed through the main entrance, got her bearings from past trips there, and rolled off toward the door leading out to the tracks. She was fairly confident she would find almost anytime day or night a train being loaded with Jews and all the horror associated with it. She edged over to the second entrance passageway to the tracks and rolled right on through. Sure enough, a train was loading.

It was a freight train loading up with civilians young and old, male and female, all with shocked and dismayed looks on their faces, many weeping and extending their arms to loved ones being taken to different parts of the train.

Claire knew she would only have minutes to get her pictures before being ejected by the Gestapo. From beneath her lap shawl she opened her handbag and withdrew her Exakta camera.

She began snapping and winding, winding and snapping again. Here was an elderly couple in the process of separation as he was dragged forward several boxcars and pushed into the car while she was held back and pushed inside the second car. Here was a mother screaming and reaching out for her twin girls who were being dragged along the walkway that would take them to the first car which, Claire saw, was loaded with children. On and on it went —husbands and wives, lovers, brothers and sisters, parents and children, grandparents—a scene of chaos and horror and tears and screams. Intermingled were cries from the Paris police, working in league with the Gestapo to load all passengers according to prescribed methods and rules.

Suddenly, Claire saw in her mind's eye the old hospital patients of her youth and the looks on the faces of family as the ill were separated from the well, the dying from the living. She shuddered at the horror and applied every ounce of willpower to keep her eyes clear and her hands steady so the pictures could be framed. It was everything she could do to keep from standing and running, screaming from the hell she had wheeled into.

A dozen pictures in, she quickly returned her camera to her handbag, tucked it beneath her shawl, and abruptly spun her wheelchair about, shouting at the approaching Gestapo that she had blundered into the area by accident and was looking for the Metro tracks. The nearest soldier held up a stiff arm and uttered a directive that she leave the area immediately. She could, he said, get her directions on the other side of the wall separating the tracks from the station. She thanked the man and rolled back inside the station.

But she had her pictures. She had been successful, and she was headed to the darkroom of the *Paris-Soir* newspaper.

From the *Paris-Soir*, the photographs were distributed by the Associated Press. One, in particular, of a child being ripped from its mother's arms while the child fought to lean toward the mother for a final touch of the hands got published in editions worldwide.

Photograph:

camera - Kine Exakta

Plano-convex magnification

Xenar 1:2 f = 5cm fast lens

film - monochrome

background - black train car full-frame

open door

100+ children inside

foreground - young Jewish mother, light tight-waisted dress and white apron

5-year-old daughter, torn white dress with puffed sleeves; pigtails

SS Officer, black tunic with black peaked hat; Nazi insignia left arm

Descriptor: "100 wailing children's faces - backdrop SS officer tearing one of the girl's arms from her mother - Mother and child screaming."

Title: "Anguish"

It just so happened American President Franklin Delano Roosevelt found his resolve to keep America from another world war softened upon viewing the tear-stained faces of the victims. For history, it would be recorded that staff found the president with the *Post* spread on his desk, Claire's picture facing him, using his handkerchief to wipe away his tears.

Claire's photographs were all at once in high demand.

17

All was well for another six months until Remy's training in explosives served to see him deployed to antitank warfare. He would leave the next day.

Remy departed Paris on a northbound train out of Gare du Nord station, heading toward Bruges, but then veering northwest in the direction of Normandy. Several hundred other SS and Wehrmacht soldiers filled the dozen train cars, officers separated from the soldiers, and both groups treated quite differently. Where the officers were fed steak and potatoes, the enlisted men were fed sausages and sauerkraut. Where the officers received Cuban cigars and stank up their cars, the enlisted received German cigarettes of such inferior quality that only the diehard nicotine addicts would partake.

The train ride lasted sixteen hours, stops included, time that Remy passed sleeping and reading a certain military manual on tank warfare, *Militärhandbuch zum Panzerkrieg*. It was a manual which he read and then immediately turned to the front and started over again. He wanted to be ready for his first engagement with an enemy tank. Foot soldiers such as Remy would be no match for enemy tanks unless the ambush was executed perfectly and the tanks disabled by the first round of explosives and antitank gunfire. Anything less, and the tank's machine guns and cannon would win the day, and Remy would be dead.

And he wouldn't die. He had Claire and Lima to go home to. Their last day together for an unforeseen amount of time was yesterday.

They were still living in the flat on rue des Amis. They didn't know Lima's birthday, so they created a birthday for her of June 1. On that date, they celebrated her fourth birthday—also a guess as to her exact age, but supplemented with comments made by the family dentist as to her age based on dental development.

She had watched him around the house that last day. He spent most of it working on his gear and getting his uniforms ready for deployment. As he worked in a T-shirt and khaki pants, she saw how the officers' training course had caused his upper back muscles to develop. He was no longer the young boy whose physique resembled the old men around the city parks. Now he looked taut across the back, and his shoulders and upper arm muscles bulged. Watching him, she felt a twinge of desire uncoil deep inside, and she stopped him at one point and turned him to face her. "I'm going to miss you," she whispered.

"Me, too."

"I want you terribly right now. Can you set that task aside and make love to me while Lima naps?"

"I would like that."

They went into the bedroom, and she lifted Lima from the bed where she was napping, carrying her into the living room couch. She covered the sleeping child with a comforter. Then she went back inside the bedroom and joined Remy on the bed. He was lying on his back as she put her head on his chest. "I miss you already," she whispered.

"I know. I'm trying to be strong right now. You and Lima are all but impossible for me to leave alone in this terrible war. I need to be with you where I can take care of you."

She slipped her left hand onto his belly and began softly circling the spot with her fingertips.

"That's so nice," he said.

"Tell me you love me, Remy."

He smiled. "I've loved you since first grade. You know that."

"I want to hear how the man loves the woman. Childish love is far, far away just now."

"I want inside your soul. I want to let my soul join your soul and look deep into your eyes while I enter you."

"Do that, please."

He turned over to face her and began removing her blouse. Ever so softly his free hand brushed her upper arm. She closed her eyes and inhaled him, inhaled his scent, his breath, his soap smell. Then she lifted her leg and placed her foot flat on the bed. Now he touched her and she cried out.

When it was over, she turned onto her back and found he was holding her hand. She left it there, feeling his gentle finger pressure while they were joined at the hands.

Now she knew: the young had been replaced by the new lovers. And what was old had become young.

Then Lima could be heard stirring on the couch. The lovers looked at each and abruptly began laughing.

"Maman!" came the call. "Maman!"

It was family time, the best time of all, if only for twelve hours more, and they meant to be present for every last precious second.

"Coming, precious one," called Claire.

"Papa is coming, too," called Remy in a voice that sounded more confessional than confirming. For he knew it wasn't true: Lima's father would never be coming back, nor would her mother. And it all came down to Remy and his actions in this horrible war. He wouldn't have done this to a child for anything the world had to offer. Yet he had done it, in a way to save his own life from the Nazi machine. He climbed from the bed, suddenly weary, suddenly fighting back tears as he went to the child he now called daughter.

"Papa is coming, too."

18

Claire was horrified that Remy had deployed to the battlefield. Each night, after Lima was asleep, she crept into her small living room and switched on the wireless. One station in particular, beamed out of Cologne, provided a nightly listing of the Germany army casualties from the day. Each night she sat on the near end of her couch and strained to hear the names read one-by-one, praying with each syllable she wouldn't ever hear "Schildmann" read off or "Remington"—Remy's full name. And each night, thank God, it was the same. No Remington Schildmann. After the radio airtime, she would creep into the kitchen and retrieve a bottle of wine. A half-glass did the job nicely, making her relaxed enough to sleep without the terrible dreams she sometimes had of Remy. They were rare, but they were horrid enough for all the other nights. Just as she nodded off, she asked God to keep her family safe—all of them.

One day walking up rue de Picardie, looking for photographs the papers and newswires might use, Claire found herself seized at the right elbow by a woman in a red coat. The woman began pulling her to the side and said, clear as a bell, "Remy sent me."

Claire stopped struggling. She was pulled sideways into the next alley where two men waited. One of them was a man she thought she'd seen before but couldn't remember where—tall, thick-boned, with a face that looked like it was locked in mortal combat with itself—which Claire realized was probably the result of having been tortured. The second man was very dark and hid beneath a bucket hat. She saw his eyes study her up and down then look away to both ends of the alley as if on guard.

"Claire," said the first man, "Remy asked us to give you his hello. He is well, and he is surviving. He wants you to stop worrying about him so much."

Tears flowed into her eyes as the inner dam she held back suddenly exploded with happiness. "*Mon Dieu*, an answered prayer!"

"He also says you wanted to be with us."

"I do," Claire answered without hesitation, for she knew with whom she was speaking.

"We'll be in touch. First, there will be training."

Claire was determined to accompany the Resistance fighters whenever possible, on any mission, no matter the maelstrom, no matter the shots fired or the bombs dropped, because her role was in the middle of it all. After all, where else would the story be found that she was sworn to provide to her readers? If not in her photographs and reportage of fighting, then where was the truth? Certainly not in the mouths of the politicians and government leaders. Only in the eyes of the soldiers and the citizens caught in this endless Hell—there, she would be among them, reporting the real truth.

After months of witnessing Resistance attacks, Claire had photographed dead Germans and burning tanks and battle lorries. She knew what it was like to photograph real people shooting at real people instead of targets. She would do whatever was necessary to protect her home, her friends, and her family, and Lima, most of all Lima, with the photojournalism that would encourage resistance and redouble national determination to survive. Photographing an enemy killing, raping, and plundering was a horrible, heart-breaking task, but she put her head down and waded on. Who could say? Maybe her photographs even provided a form of intelligence to the Allies that resulted in more enemy dead. She'd never been to war before and had amazed herself with her bloodlust. But she had not been a mother before either.

There was another aspect for Claire, as there was for all parents: she wanted a safe place for her daughter to live and grow up. She had become Lima's mother for all purposes. She wanted a France that nurtured Lima, that offered opportunity without regard to the same things that motivated the Germans to kill her kind. And a fierceness had taken over Claire. She was the she-lion, the mother bear who would attack anything, soldier or not, that threatened her daughter. In this frame of reference, then, she became willing to do anything, no matter how degrading, no matter how dangerous it might prove to be.

Her life in wartime Paris, and without Remy fell, into a certain cadence. Even during times of conflict, humans will find a way to structure their lives, for it's in this structure that they are able to survive. It was the same with Claire. She went to school and work, she took care of Lima, and on the weekends, she was all about the Resistance.

19

Remy's expertise in high explosives had led to his commanding a troop of tank killers. These were soldiers who set ambushes for enemy tanks to take them down with satchel charges and antitank guns. Before he left, he'd had a talk with Claire. The gist of it was that, while he was forced to perform for the German army, he would be taking every opportunity to sabotage the army's efforts, even going as far as allowing enemy forces to breach the ambushes he had set. He told Claire that she was free to do the same: whatever fights she would undertake against the invaders he, Remy, would support her in totally. There was one aspect of this that had been plaguing her, a delicate matter that she wondered if she even should chance to discuss with Remy. She decided she had to; they'd known each other all their lives and had no secrets.

"You know," she said, "there are women who are collaborating with the enemy."

He'd frowned. "I know."

"Given the right circumstances, I might be willing to engage an enemy officer and steal secrets. I'm not saying I'm going to. I just want to talk to you about how far I'm committed to winning this war for Lima. If we don't win it, and win it soon, I fear for her safety."

"Let me be sure I understand. You're saying you would sleep with the enemy for information?"

"For maps, for secrets, for ways to save Allied lives. Tell me how you would feel about that."

"How do you think I'd feel? It would kill me!"

"All right, it would be the same for me if it were you. Now, what about this? What if it took me collaborating with the enemy to steal information about an attack the Germans were planning against our friends. Sleeping with the enemy could save lives. Now, what do you say?"

"That's not fair. I'd still feel terrible, but I'd say go ahead."

"You see where I'm going with this? I would hate doing it. I would hate, even more, seeing French people die because I didn't. Now what do you say?"

"I feel like you're in a unique position, Claire. You're young, you're beautiful, and you have a daughter you're in love with and want to protect. So tell me this. What if I weren't even in the picture? Then what would you do?"

"I'd do it in a second. If I thought it would help kill Germans, I wouldn't think twice about it. Oh, I'd despair afterward and hate myself for what I'd done with my body. But by then it would be too late, and the good would already be done."

"I'm going on deployment. You must do what you feel would help as if you don't even know me. Who knows, we may never see each other again. But both of us owe everything to Lima. We brought her into our lives, and so we owe her our lives. I can't even think about her and Auschwitz without breaking down in tears. Yes, my love, do whatever you can to help save that baby. Nothing is off-limits."

"My feelings, exactly."

Then he was gone. They'd had their talk; she had her freedom to act. She'd expected no less from Remy. But she'd wanted him to know so there'd never be a need for coverups.

20

The Germans had marched into Paris without a single shot being fired. On 14 June 1940 at precisely 0800 hours, the German Army had set up its first Paris HQ at the Hotel Crillon overlooking Place de la Concorde. Simultaneously, a German flag was soon placed over the Arc de Triomphe. General Nether von Stülpnagel was the Wehrmacht's new military commandant of Paris. Claire watched all this from close-up, recording the changes with her camera and posting her pictures to *Paris-Soir* where most were published without interference from the Germans.

The worst of a certain class of Frenchmen had begun to emerge as a group in Paris immediately began collaborating with the Germans. The intermingling began at the Ritz hotel, a popular spot for the Nazi command and SS to eat, board, and party. It was also frequented by the French elite collaborators. Madame Ritz herself lived in 266-268. French Actress Arletty, born Leonie Bathiat, resided at the Ritz with her Luftwaffe officer lover Hans-

Jürgen Soehring. Arletty was also a very close friend of Josée Laval, daughter of the Prime Minister and notorious collaborator, Pierre Laval. Arletty died at the robust age of 94 years old in 1992. Arletty's famous line in the war was: "My heart is French but my ass is international."

The collaboration was not lost on Claire, who had realized early on that this was a possibility. Who better to get the Resistance behind German walls than a woman who was sleeping with the enemy? She was driven by terrible nightmares of the lost and dispossessed Jews of Paris, departing on nameless trains in the middle of the night, bound for Auschwitz. Lima's parents haunted her dreams. Worse, the little girl still asked for them, as if their return was imminent. Claire had no idea where they were or even if they were still alive, but it was always in her mind, lurking there, that one day they would have to be dealt with, living or dead, insofar as Lima's ethnicity.

As part of the Resistance she knew that if she were caught, she would find herself on the next outbound train loaded with Jews bound for Auschwitz as well. To sleep with the enemy was all but unthinkable to the nineteen year old, yet doing nothing while all around her Jews were disappearing was even worse. She'd already had the talk with Remy before he was deployed to antitank warfare. They'd decided, together, they both would do everything in their power to help win the war for Lima. Her safety—her very life—demanded they stop at nothing. Claire decided she would do it, that she would appear at the Ritz and worm her way inside the Nazi hierarchy, repulsive as the whole idea was to her. Finally, if caught, she would likely end up in a camp such as her editor would've wanted. Upon mentioning her plan to Jacques Marseille, he approved but left no doubt how dangerous he thought collaboration could be. While there was no Remy to discuss it with this time, she already had the answer she needed from him. It was wartime; anything went.

The doing turned out to be easier than the thinking about it. First, she imposed on her mother to watch Lima for an indeterminate time, telling her parents only that an operation was upcoming that would take her away for an extended period of time. Her mother stood in the gap for her, promising the little girl's needs would be met just like her younger brothers. Claire gently approached the subject with Lima.

"Lima, I need to go on a long trip. I'm going to leave you with Grand-mère for a little while."

All color drained from the little girl's face.

"No, Maman stays with me now."

"I know, but this is important."

"Are you bringing my other Maman?"

"No, I don't think so. I must go and help Papa win the war."

"But you will be back."

"I will, I promise."

"And bring Maman back, too?"

"I don't think I can do that. I think it will just be me coming back."

"Come back soon."

So, Claire, one Saturday night, dressed in her most alluring black dress and wearing graduation pearls around her neck, presented herself at one of the three lounges inside the Ritz. It was a mild night in September when she sauntered into the lounge, saw that it was totally packed with German officers and young girls, and made a beeline for the bar. She found no empty barstool. But she was noticed almost immediately by a young, blond German officer wearing the uniform and collar pins of the SS. He stood, snapped himself to attention with a wide smile, and motioned that she should take his stool. She smiled vivaciously but not cheaply, not as a woman of the night might smile, or leer, and settled onto the proffered stool. The young officer immediately placed himself between Claire and the next stool, leaning sideways between them and planting his elbow on the bar. Then he smiled again, and Claire realized that he was a very attractive man and it was going to be a real effort to always remember why she was there and that her true purpose had nothing to do with romance.

But her acting days from playing Joan of Arc provided her with a reservoir of facial expressions and body language suited for the task of presenting just the right look, smile, and vocal range to charm her young soldier into a state of mild frenzy. Mild at first. Two drinks later, it was clear he was in love. Two drinks later, Claire was telling herself over and over that she would kill the beautiful young man if necessary, even though her feelings were screaming otherwise. His name was Friedrich Ehrlanger, and he was a lieutenant in the Schutzstaffel. On their fifth drink, she agreed to go upstairs to his room with him for a late room-service dinner. The ostensible reason for retreating to his room was dinner, but she knew the real reason she was going there and, even intoxicated and with her inhibitions aired out, she nevertheless had to steel herself for what was about to happen that night.

Claire's flawless mastery of German provided access to a make-believe history that had her growing up in Berlin until the age of eleven when her father's business moved the family to Paris. Relying on half-truths—her father was employed by Mercedes-Benz, her mother was a German patriot working as a physician— she spun a web of deceit that, she worried she might be unable to remember when tomorrow and sobriety dawned in the expensively furnished room. But she plunged ahead. Lieutenant Ehrlanger liked what he heard, chewing slowly as they dined on *foie gras* and sipped a modest, celebratory, chardonnay. Later on she would learn that the expensive meal cost Ehrlanger nothing—Germans ate and drank free at the Ritz. Even the rooms were free, and the right among the officer cadre to preempt a room for lodging depended wholly on the importance of his work for the Reich. In Ehrlanger's case, Claire learned after several nights with her new soldier, importance was a given, for his role was the location of and mapping of the French elite, the data to be used as a key resource for the conquerors when the military required a resource that only the French could supply.

One evening at six p.m. As the couple prepared to go downstairs for drinks and song, Claire, in her most off-handed, disarming manner, asked her young officer exactly what he did during his days.

"My job? It's nothing, really."

"Oh," she said with a smile of polite disagreement, "it's something, I'm sure, judging by how you live."

"I make maps. I make maps of where French people live."

"Really?" she asked, "am I in your maps?"

He laughed. "Not unless you own an automobile plant we might convert to making German tanks. Not unless you're a military manufacturer of uniforms or, better still, munitions. Then you'll have a starring role in my maps."

"Can I see your map?"

He stopped brushing his straight, blond hair. "Why would you want to see my maps?"

"I'd like to know who has what. Relax, love, I'm not a spy. I'm a young girl who is easily impressed with name-dropping. That's all. Forgive me if I've overstepped." This last sentence was said with a sniff and a toss of her head not unlike Saint Joan might have done when facing the stake in her most cavalier moment. She could take it or leave it said her tone and her look. Which meant, she was quite sure, she owned him now.

"I'm not worried about spies. It's just that most people would find my maps very boring."

"And I, my young lieutenant, am not most people. I'm totally enthralled with how my soldier spends his days. I belong to you; my daily thoughts are of you. Forgive me for being so forward. It won't happen again."

He went behind the wall divider that stood between a small sitting area and the bedroom and returned with two folded documents. He placed these on the table where Claire sat and began unfolding the top sheet.

"Look, here is avenue Foch. This is where it's all happening in Paris."

"Meaning what? All I see are streets and numbered buildings. What does it all mean?"

"These are wealthy houses and mansions belonging to your city's elite upper class. It begins here at the Arc de Triomphe and ends way down here on the southwest end at Bois de Boulogne."

She followed his finger used to trace avenue Foch, the same finger used to trace her mons when he toyed with her body before entering her.

"But I thought the avenue was named for General Foch."

"Indeed, your French general who accepted Germany's surrender in 1918. Rather appropriate that much of it now houses Nazi officers and French collaborators. The Führer does have a sense of humor."

"Give me some names. It would make me feel important to know."

He was inspired by her request. "19 avenue Foch, once belonging to Baron Edmond De Rothschild, is now occupied by Helmut Knochen, senior commander of the Sicherheitspolizei, the Security Police. This is just one of our prized residents. Please, look over the map while I go in and shave. You're about to get your baby's ass." The odd reference being to her comment one drunken night that his face that morning had reminded her of a baby's ass. It was said because she was playing a role, not because there was truth in such a reminder.

She read down the map and its notes:

31 avenue Foch, former home of Madame Alexandrine de Rothschild, a family of bankers, now occupied by Theodore Dannecker, Head of the Gestapo's Jewish Affairs, colleague to Knochen. Later, Claire would learn Dannecker had a vicious hate for the Jews. From this address, Dannecker would heartlessly send thousands of French men and women to the death camp at Auschwitz Concentration Camp.

The Resistance soon had mapped out the residences on avenue Foch and, most importantly, the names of the residents in each dwelling:

31 avenue Foch, Adolf Eichmann, SS-Obersturmbannführer, author of *The Final Solution*, the Nazi plan for the extermination of the Jewish nation, arrived in Paris and set up an office at this same location.

41 avenue Foch, Comtesse Hildegard von Seckendorff, code name Mercedes, Knochen's informer.

70 avenue Foch, Knochen's offices had expanded to this address.

72 avenue Foch, Gestapo HQ, a five-story Villa, taken by Helmut Knochen.

74 avenue Foch, occupied by the KRIPO German Police.

76 avenue Foch, occupied by Hermann Bickler, "Brutal Alsatian," in charge of the French unit (police) responsible for tracking down Resistance fighters.

84 avenue Foch, occupied by Hans Josef Kieffer, Sturmbannführer, SS Counter Intelligence for the Sicherheitsdienst.

Then, while Ehrlanger shaved in the bathroom and hummed French love songs, Claire produced a small camera and began photographing both maps. It took her all of three minutes to do, a short time, but, had she been discovered, she would have been shot on the spot, no questions asked. By the time she was done, her face was flushed, she was dripping with sweat, and she knew she would have to submerge in a bath before going out that night. She hid the tiny camera inside an air vent on her side of the bed under the window where she kept it now.

At her first opportunity, after Ehrlanger reported for work, Claire dropped her film off with Jean Renoz, her co-writer on the "French" edition of Shaw's *Saint Joan*. Jean, who had earned her position in the Resistance with her Thompson submachine gun, was now second-in-command of the 2nd Battalion of the Secret Army. The film was dropped in a cash register drawer at Lusanne Cafe on the West Bank by Claire. Hours later, it was picked up and developed by Jean herself. Then it was turned over to the Resistance. The leaders were ecstatic. Here, at last, was strong evidence of the location of key Nazis, German army officials, German police officials, and French collaborators, any of whom—or all of whom —were valuable targets. The esteem with which the Resistance High Command held Claire went up several notches. Here was someone who had, as her parents had insisted, made her life stand for something. Had those parents known what their eldest was up to—which they did not—they would have been immensely proud. They would have also been horrified and so, when Claire would disappear for weeks, sometimes months at a time, they were wise enough not to ask, and Claire definitely wasn't telling.

The 2nd Battalion High Command of the Resistance focused on Claire's intelligence. The avenue was target-rich. They could almost drop a bomb from inside a cloud and hit a key strategic target.

With back-and-forth questions and answers, High-Command-to-Claire, a plan began to develop. Claire would soon be asked to risk everything for a shot at a key German asset. When asked, she volunteered for the assignment on the spot. She had come to loathe the Nazis and their death-dealing to such a great extent that she was ready to die for whatever attack the 2nd Battalion might ask of her.

Lieutenant Ehrlanger knew none of this, of course, as he continued to wine and dine his beautiful friend, oblivious to what she was easily learning from him with her questions, partly because he trusted Claire by now but mostly because he forever wanted to impress her. He was in a contest with himself in that regard, and now he couldn't tell her enough fast enough.

"What did I do today?" he asked. "I located all German munitions and weapons dumps in Paris. Another map, my beautiful Claire. Very boring."

"It doesn't sound boring. It sounds like very important work."

He smiled and hung his uniform jacket on a wooden hanger. Then he brushed it with a stolen clothes brush. "There."

"I said it sounds important, love."

"Well, it is important, but I don't want you to think of me as a braggart."

"Never. You're a humble man through and through. Maybe later tonight you can show me what you learned, and I can feel closer to you for it. I'm very proud."

He hesitated, turning around and pointing the handle of his brush at her. "Show you my map? Is that what you're asking from me?"

"No, no, no. I just want you to sit down beside me—or lie down beside me—and tell me how difficult your job is. You've told me some of it, about your superiors and how they abuse junior officers with their words and their scorn. I just want to help you bear some of that load. I'm right there beside you."

"Ahhh, I see. We are a team, Claire. I love that about you."

"And I, you. Please don't ever be offended or suspicious because I seem to care too much. That's really all it is. I'm way too simple to ever understand a war, anyway. I know that. Heaven forbid I should ever embarrass you with my limited understanding. Part of it is, I just don't care. France, Germany, England—what do I care who rules France? I just want to be with the man I love and be kind to him. That's my whole life, Lieutenant."

"And I love you for that. Let me show you this dumb map I made today. There's not much to it, dear Claire. I think you'll understand what I do once you see it."

"That would be nice."

Nice, indeed, she thought.

She wondered which ammo dump her friends would blow up first.

And she wondered how long it would take the Germans to figure out how they knew.

21

The target was one unearthed by Claire in her study of a Lieutenant Friedrich Ehrlanger map. With his trust of Claire increasing every day, the lieutenant would sometimes depart for work and leave tactical maps on his desk at the Ritz mini-suite he inhabited. Dressed in her nightgown and sipping room-service Colombian coffee, Claire would casually photograph every map she could find. The ammunition dump at 217 rue le Sueur was chosen from among twenty or more matériel dumps Claire's work had revealed. It was chosen because it was the prime storage facility for all automatic weapons ammunition that entered Paris in 1941. The vast majority of those weapons were the MP 40, 9 mm guns used most often in the "spray-slaying" murder of Jewish citizens in the streets of Paris. The Resistance High Command held a particular hatred of those weapons and those munitions for that reason.

217 rue le Sueur was a home located two blocks off avenue Foch. After four days of 24/7 surveillance, Resistance spies Chomill and Luscenne reported to High Command the place was unin-

habited; however, during the day jeep loads of soldiers might come and go once, maybe twice. They would arrive empty-handed and leave with a dozen long cartridge boxes stowed in the footboards of their half-tracks. The boxes were reported to be six feet long and two feet deep. The two Resistance fighters followed the tracks one day, and they were able to confidently report ammunition was being distributed to the troops right off the half-tracks. The intel was turned over to the Allies. The turn-around action-planning was almost immediate. Allied bombing could never pinpoint the target; it fell to the Resistance to strike instead.

"I found it so I want in on the strike," Claire told Jean Renoz at their cell's Tuesday night meetup.

Jean, now heading up the cell, violently disagreed. "Not possible! You're bringing us intel from the Ritz almost every day! I can't afford to lose you in a strike."

"But it's a key strike. That's MP 40 munitions you're talking about destroying."

"Yes, and it will take them all of four days to bring in another load into a different dump. We need you with Ehrlanger and undiscovered. Just keep doing what you've been doing. That is way beyond what most of us ever lay siege to, the spoils of a mapmaking German officer. You'll not be invited along this time out, Claire."

Claire thrust her lower lip forward. She made a noise that sounded like "Phhht!" She repeated it, then, "Ehrlanger's not going to last forever. He's either going to end up shooting me or getting transferred. They move the junior officers around at least every six months so they can't get too close to anyone."

Jean looked up from the latest map Claire had photographed. "We better find you a senior officer, then. Someone with some longevity, though whether that would also apply to his bedroom endowments is debatable."

Her words let the air out of the moment. Claire was salved, somewhat, and decided she'd pushed it as far as possible. She obviously wasn't going to get to lay out bombs and light fuses. Her job was to continue to interdict Friedlich Ehrlanger's supply lines and apply pressure accordingly. There was one problem with that, however, that was slowly forming in her mind. She could foresee that sooner or later Ehrlanger's laxity and his loss of secret munitions locations was going to be discovered by the German army, and he was going to pay dearly. Try as she might, she had some feelings for the young officer and really couldn't stand to countenance what his future held, in large part thanks to her. Shooting a Nazi from a mile away or even ten feet away was something she might reasonably be expected to execute if her own life depended on it, but that would be a stranger on the other end of that calculus. On the near end was Ehrlanger, a friend and lover, a man she knew, whose hopes and dreams were a reality in her own life, a man who she didn't want to see get hurt, maybe tortured, maybe even killed. For once, she had to admit, she knew her work was necessary, but at the same time she actually regretted it.

Her regret was short-lived. Three weeks later, Ehrlanger was transferred back to Berlin, where he would work supply chain logistics from the funnel end. His move was one he'd requested: his wife was seriously ill and his mother was dying. Someone up the line had some heart left, maybe, thought Claire, the only heart in the entire German army, and they took pity on Friedrich Ehrlanger and rotated him back home. His eyes brimming with tears, he shared the news with her one night. She cried with him because the role demanded it. The truth was, she was happy to see him go before her work destroyed him. She was relieved and went immediately about finding her next German to seduce.

Which didn't take all that long. Emil Fleischmann owned a large electronics conglomerate in Frankfurt, Germany. The war effort had denied his request to be taken onboard by the military in the role of an SS officer. Rather, the army explained to him, they needed him in place, running his electronics firm, a key product being the backlights used in almost all German aircraft flight controls. "You make the gauges so our pilots and navigators can read them at night," the SS overlords told Fleischmann. "You are already a national hero."

A hero, maybe; but then he was also needed in France, where a sister company, owned by the French maker of Renault automobiles, manufactured timing devices for aerial bombs. Fleischmann was brought in to Germanize the plant, bring in German supervisors and line bosses, and was given one month to do it. These are the things Claire overheard Emil Fleischmann explaining loudly and somewhat drunkenly downstairs in the l'Auberge lounge one morning at two a.m. Claire was there for a nightcap with Ehrlanger, who'd returned from Marseille late that night, and he'd shushed her so they could listen to the German businessman tell it all, holding back nothing. Ehrlanger thought it horrible and made the man leave the lounge and promise to go up to bed. He returned to their table, shaking his head. "He's one for you to know, Claire. If it's intel you're after, he's your man."

She was stunned. What in the world did he—?

"You've soaked up everything I left lying around. It sounds like the gentleman in the lounge will be a similarly easy target for you and your spying."

"But I'm not—"

The lieutenant raised a cautionary hand. "Don't. No need to say another word. I've known all along but I've loved you too much to care. That's over now; I'm going home."

Tears flooded her eyes. She'd had no idea, wouldn't have guessed in a million years that she'd been found out. He had every right to shoot her or turn her into his superiors who would. But instead, he'd simply requested a transfer so she wouldn't be hurt.

"But here's the warning, Claire. Don't do this again. Next time, you will be shot. Not everyone in the Reich is like me. You have no idea."

"I have some idea. That's why I fight."

He looked at her then and said through clouded eyes, "No, really, you don't. You have no idea who these men are."

One week later, rue le Sueur was the site of a strike by Claire's Resistance cell, 2nd Battalion of the Secret Army. It came on 6 January 1941. The event was reported in the *Paris-Soir* the next morning:

7 January 1941, Canton of Paris:

At approximately 11:25 p.m. in a well-known arrondissement of Paris, a German officer was attacked by three individuals who fired three revolver shots in his direction. Injured in the left arm with a bullet, he was admitted to the General Hospital where his condition is listed as not serious. Just after the officer was taken away by ambulance, the building he'd just exited exploded, throwing flames hundreds of feet into the air and burning down the surrounding houses on all three sides. Fire marshals say they've never seen a house go up like that. The address at 217 rue le Sueur was a terraced house located two blocks off avenue Foch. Today it is dust.

22

A peaceful Paris wartime had plunged precipitously downward in the life of Remy Schildmann. His commanding officer, Captain Daniel Schlossmaier, had been rotated onto the battlefield just south of Bruges where the pockets along the German front were meeting massive resistance from the Allies. The British and French were fighting furiously, and the German army was doing everything it could, with every last man it could spare, to push them into the sea.

Remy had been promoted to Captain based on his service in Paris and based on the rigorous training he had undergone in explosives and tank warfare. Rotated to the battlefield, his primary duty was setting ambushes for oncoming tanks as they rolled from the west toward the south of Bruges. Remy and his platoon had set out a field of high explosives and were awaiting a tank brigade headed east on rue Gille toward the city of Roye in the Somme region. They were hidden on both sides of the road, heavy machine guns in place in an *X* formation, ready to engage. It was raining that morning in January and threatening to snow as the sky fell lower and lower with each hour. Hands were shaking, voices muted, and Remy had issued the no-smoking order. Field rations were being silently traded among the men, meat and potatoes here for sausage and sauerkraut there. They had no coffee, and their only water was a questionable, brackish liquid from a well in Roye.

Two hours after sunrise, the wireless crackled. Three British tanks were seen rumbling toward them. The tanks were evenly spaced, maybe a hundred meters between each one and the next, in order to avoid a total loss in case of the kind of trap Remy and his squad were waiting to spring. Remy's men received the word: the first tank gets through, then fire on the second with antitank weapons and machine guns when the turrets open after the antitank weapons set them afire inside. The first tank would then be engaged as its turret with its big gun was coming around. Same procedure. Only then would the third tank be engaged by the westernmost top and bottom points of the X.

Remy, wearing his field jacket and slicker and helmet with liner, coat collar pulled up beneath, turned to his left and peered through his binoculars at the sound of the first grunting diesel engine. The tanks were coming up an incline—one always sprung ambushes on an incline in order to overload the diesels if possible. Within seconds, Remy could smell the diesel exhaust on the winds sweeping in from the coast. He flicked aside his cigarette—he lit it to flaunt Schlossmaier's order—and patted his machine gunner on the shoulder. "Ready, Wilhelm. But don't fire until the turret opens." Then he turned and cuffed his antitank weapon operator on the back of the neck. "Any moment now, Andrus, at the ready. Remember, if you can take one off a track, we own him."

Andrus nodded ever so slightly. When the first tank came up the hill and began climbing past, Remy whispered to his squad, "Easy,

easy now, we want number two. Here he comes, coming, all right now!"

At that moment, the air was split a thousand different ways by the roar of antitank shells screaming and connecting with the tanks, first number two, then shortly after, tank number one, and now the machines were opening up, and as they turned back down the road, the antitank gunners unloaded on tank number three. Turrets were cranking open and men were attempting to climb out, but the machine gunners were ready. Bursts of fire, cries, some return fire, then all was still. Within minutes, nothing was moving. The tanks were in place, diesels stilled, when, suddenly, fires began breaking out from magazine stores and diesel fuel tanks. A man in the first tank, on fire, jumped from the tank's midsection onto the ground and ran twenty paces before he fell, enveloped in flame.

While all this was going on, neither Remy nor his men realized they had been flanked on both sides of the road by French soldiers who had been tracking the tanks' progress, waiting for just such an ambush so they could launch a counterattack. Which they did now, firing mortar round after mortar round at Remy's position, raking both sides of the road where the Germans were hiding with fifty-caliber machine gun fire. Remy's squad turned and faced outward on either side of the road and engaged with machine guns and small arms fire. The machine guns and mortars were soon replaced with the *pop, pop, pop* of hand grenades as the outer band of soldiers closed on the inner band. Then the French were overrunning the other side of the road and the French commander was calling across the road to Remy, demanding his surrender. Which Remy ignored.

His wireless man keyed his mic, trying to alert other German patrols to their predicament. A muffled response could be heard but Remy's wireless man didn't dare speak out loud. He only keyed his mic again, and again the remote voice asked who it was. There was no way to get a message out.

"Sir," a voice called out in French, "I can see your head, and I am going to shoot you there unless you drop your weapon and stand."

Remy heard the voice, recognized the thin line he occupied between life and death just moments away. He stood as he pushed his MP 40 machine gun forward, letting it drop harmlessly into the mud along the trench. "I am unarmed," he said steadily. His machine gunner did likewise.

Within minutes, they were surrounded by the French army and Remy was explaining in French that he was Parisian but that he'd been conscripted and wanted to return to Paris and home. His machine gunner, a wide-eyed German brought up through the brown shirts, stood speechless beside him. Remy could only shake his head at the man and shrug. "Nobody ever asked me," he finally said to his comrade. "I didn't want any of this."

Remy's final day in a German uniform had arrived. His machine gunner was bayoneted ten minutes later when he made a play for a Frenchman's sidearm. He died with his hands at his chest trying to dam the blood gush, his eyes rolled back in his head, his throat gurgling.

"Just as well," said Remy without emotion. "It's going to be a long war."

23

Young Lieutenant Friedrich Ehrlanger introduced Claire to Emil Fleischmann on the lieutenant's way out of town. It happened quite by accident one night as Claire and her lieutenant were finishing their nightcaps in the Ritz Hotel main lounge. It was the night before Ehrlanger would leave Paris for Berlin, and the duo was quite subdued. Until who should walk into the lounge but Emil Fleischmann.

Obviously laboring under a full complement of Schnapps and champagne, the maker of the Luftwaffe aircraft night lights, Emil was beginning to lose control. This time he was in the company of a woman about his age—mid-forties, maybe—who was much more sober than he and who was not amused with the running mouth of her husband, for he stopped at every table to introduce himself, buy a round, and make the clientele laugh like they were glad to have just met him.

"Oh, don't tell me, he's coming this way," Claire whispered to Ehrlanger and kicked his ankle as if to prod him to stop the man's progress toward them.

Ehrlanger stood and came around the table. He threw his arm around Fleischmann's broad shoulders and whispered to him, "Not right now, dear man, my lady is feeling poorly."

Fleischmann, even stuporous, managed to sidestep Ehrlanger and his grip and stagger up to where Claire sat nursing an aperitif. "Not well?" he asked. "I have just the thing for you. What did the Nazi say to the farmer with the cow?"

"I don't know. What did he say?"

"She's cute, but I was thinking fewer legs."

With that, Fleischmann bent double and slapped his knee. The crudity of the joke was lost on no one, yet he never did fully appreciate he was the only one laughing.

"Come on to the bar, then, son," said Lieutenant Ehrlanger, "and let me buy you a drink."

"Not for a minute!" cried Fleischmann. "I need to meet this beauty."

He meant Claire. When he said the words, his wife turned on her heel and hurried from the lounge. Her huffy departure was lost on Fleischmann, obviously taken with Claire's retiring manner and cool look. She was, he saw, a major challenge, but he was certain he was up to it. So he took the seat beside her at the table and indicated Ehrlanger should scrounge up another chair if he wanted to join them.

An odd thing happened; Ehrlanger decided the time had come for him to bow out. Claire was on the prowl for her next target, and this whale had presented himself to her, ready to be harpooned and cut open. So he, too, left the lounge, heading for their room and a round of suitcase patrol. It was time for him to pack.

Claire immediately understood what had just happened. She had been passed along, for better or worse, German to German, Ritz resident to Ritz resident. Ehrlanger had left her still in the running and unrevealed for what she really was. It was difficult but, taking all this in in a fragment of a second, she decided it was time to let go and make the leap. "Why not Fleischmann?" she asked herself. His companies employed the technology and workers that kept German aircraft aloft in the night skies and German bombs accurately fused. He was every bit as much the target as Lieutenant Ehrlanger—maybe even more.

She learned that night just how fluid was her situation. Down with this man now, down with this one two minutes from now. And on it would go, she supposed, for however long the war lasted. Her youth and her German opened all kinds of doors; her intelligence and accomplishment with cameras of all sizes, in all light conditions, was just frosting. She was, had become, the perfect spy. She had stolen German war plans from Ehrlanger, and she would steal Fleischmann Aero Industries manufacturing plans in the next little while. She was every bit as effective as the Resistance fighter with her Thompson submachine gun, the Allied soldier with his carbine, the British RAF bombardier with his bomb bay release pickle. She had become death as much as any of them.

It was her time. Again.

Fleischmann took her to his room the same night she met him. His wife had, conveniently, stormed downstairs with her bags, intent on returning to Berlin, away from her husband's alcoholic crazies. Claire never had a problem because a man was married. It meant nothing to her, not in the face of the thousands of Jews being loaded on freight trains and spirited out of Paris with each passing day. Knowing those Jews were off to their deaths, the marriages of her targets became meaningless. So it was with Emil Fleischmann, recently relieved of his own marriage by his wife's anger. Good riddance, thought Claire. Now he belongs to me.

"How shall we do this?" asked Fleischmann in the privacy of his bedroom. "You are going to collaborate with the enemy? Collaborate with me?"

"I am. My dalliances with German officers and business people keep me in the best French restaurants eating the finest French food, drinking the finest French wine, and sleeping between warm, silk sheets during the night. Consider that I am collaborating as of tonight."

He poured two brandies out of a decanter on the wet bar. "And what do I get from you in return?"

She was always ready for this. "Nineteen-year-old flesh. It's what all men secretly want."

She had him there. He didn't ever bother to ask again. Claire listened in on telephone conversations and accompanied her mark on certain visits to manufacturing plants in Germany and France. It wasn't long before she knew locations and business facts that were golden to the High Command. Moreover, British bombers now knew where to target those buildings twenty-five-thousand feet beneath their wings. Those were the priority targets because their destruction all but guaranteed to slow or even stop the production of German aircraft. Without Fleischmann's navigation lights, the German planes could bomb only during daytime, the riskiest proposition of all, for they were easily seen and easily attacked by British antiaircraft emplacements and British Spitfires.

One night, sleeping beside Emil Fleischmann, Claire and her lover both jolted awake by pounding on their hotel room door. Fleischmann, cursing, leaped from the bed and pulled on a robe and eyeglasses. He angrily swept to the door and threw it open. There stood four SS soldiers and one officer, heavily armed, demanding to see Claire Vallant. Fleischmann stood aside, and the men burst into the room. They rousted the frightened Claire from bed and roughly pushed her toward the door.

"Where—where are you taking her?" bleated Fleischmann obsequiously.

"Never mind that. Don't let this one back inside, or you will suffer the consequences," the officer sharply replied. "She is finished here. You would be, too, but my orders say you're to be unbothered by us. Traitor that you are, I would just as soon take you out into the street this minute and shoot you. But I have my orders, fortunately for you, Herr Fleischmann."

Fleischmann recoiled as if from a hot flame and made his way to the brandy decanter. He had poured himself three fingers before Claire was bundled up in her winter coat and trundled away. "My sweet Lord," mumbled Fleischmann. "What have I done?"

They threw her roughly into the back seat of their long black car. She shuddered from the cold and from her fright, and by the time they reached Wehrmacht headquarters, she was violently ill, throwing open her door to vomit into the freezing night air.

Inside the building, they took her down two flights of stairs, down into the bowels of what once had been part of the city's jail system. There, she was tossed into a cell with perhaps a dozen other men and women in various stages of dress, like her, from nightgowns and pajamas to glamorous evening wear. She would learn from her cellmates, that night, that collaborators had a shelf life of maybe six months, rarely nine months, until they would wind up here, in jail, waiting to be deposed by SS intelligence services.

AT NOON THE FOLLOWING DAY, THEY TOOK HER BEFORE AN SS intelligence officer by the name of Hans Willsan. He was a rough-hewn Austrian-by-birth Nazi SS officer whose cold eyes immediately terrified Claire, though she did everything she could not to show her fear because, if she did, she would already have lost.

She was placed at his desk.

"So," he said, whipping a pair of rimless spectacles from his smooth face, "you have been feeding the Allies information on Herr Fleischmann's factories. Good for you, if you're a French Resistance member, which we know you are. My first inclination is to have you shot without further ado. But there's a side of me that likes to even things up, so here it is. You will now feed false intelligence to your High Command. You will feed them false intelligence that will cause the loss of Resistance lives. Or you will die, right here, right now, if you refuse to cooperate. So which is it, Mademoiselle Vallant?"

She hadn't been prepared for this man and this demand. The Resistance had never discussed what should be the proper response to such a demand if they were captured. Usually capture meant death—they all recognized that. But this time, capture meant acting as a double agent. She'd heard of it before, and she'd wondered how someone could ever stoop so low as to mislead one's own friends, but here she was being given the opportunity to remain alive by doing that very thing. What to do?

"And if I cooperate with you, my captain, what is my reward?"

"That's easy. You get to live. Your family gets to live. Dare to cross me, Mademoiselle Vallant, and you with your father and mother and your siblings all die. Without further inquiry and without exception, your family will be erased from the earth, along with you. Where does that leave us?"

She sucked in a hard, deep volume of air. It was over and she knew it. She now belonged to the Germans. She could not forsake her family and especially her beautiful Lima, who had her whole life in front of her if Claire acquiesced. The SS might not know about Lima yet, but they would do.

"Moreover, you will feed disinformation that results in the death of members of your Resistance. Failure to do so will likewise result in your death and your family's death. Are we clear on your new assignment?"

"We are clear."

"And how do you vote, my dear? Life or death for all?"

"Life. When will I start?"

"You started five seconds ago. I own you now, my lovely girl. You now belong to Captain Hans Willsan, your very own SS officer. Memorize my name and, remember, to utter it anyplace outside this room is to die. I might not learn of your next deceit right away, but I'm watching you now. I own you, remember. Do not let me down."

"I won't let you down."

"Good, then here's our first plan. We are going to entrap Resistance fighters by directing them to plant a bomb inside one of our munitions stores. They will be captured and taken into the street and executed on the spot. You, who are working for *Paris-Soir*, will record the event with your camera and make sure it appears in the newspaper's pages the next day. Other so-called freedom fighters will take heed. Many will quit the Resistance when they see the dead bodies of their friends paving French streets. Oh, we are so ready for you, mademoiselle. How pleased we are to have you onboard with us, and welcome!"

What to do? she wondered as she curled up in a corner of her cell and tried to sleep in her overcoat and nightdress. She drew her knees to her chest. Horror of horrors, and she couldn't even think straight. Her heart beat like a snare drum in her chest, rat-a-tat-tat, rat-a-tat-tat, as she struggled to calm her thoughts and imagine a solution.

But no solution came. It was a basic, horrifying choice: family or friends? Which would she protect? Would she sacrifice her family for the cause? Would they really murder her loved ones if she refused to cooperate? She thought of Captain Willsan's lifeless eyes as she considered these things. Clearly, he was SS beginning to end. She had no doubt he would personally execute her mother and father, brothers and Lima, if she attempted to deceive the SS, attempted to injure the German army in any way. Which left her with one solution: she would have to remove herself from the picture. She would have to disappear from view, maybe even commit suicide. But would even that final act protect her family? Would the Germans go for them even if she did kill herself? She had to admit, she knew they would. That was part and parcel of her new deal: she had no way out, not even by death.

Except if the SS couldn't find her family. What if they were to disappear instead of her? What if the High Command provided them with new identities and a new life? Was that even possible? Did the Resistance of 1941 have the capability to even pull off such a disappearing act, the ability to invent new lives, new papers, new jobs, new everything? It seemed, to Claire, to be far beyond the reach of the Resistance still in its infancy. It seemed impossible, based on what she knew of her group.

So it was with pounding pulse and a heart full of self-hate that she fed Jean Renoz with false information about a munitions dump in the twenty-first arrondissement. It was all that, but it was also going to be a trap. The Germans were ready to make a spectacle out of any attempt to bomb or attack their emplacement. Claire knew that; Jean Renoz did not. But Jean read her friend's demeanor immediately.

"You've been turned-out?"

Claire could only nod furiously.

"You've been discovered?"

"Uhhhh."

"And your family is threatened."

"Uhhhh."

"All right. It happens. We're ready for it. Return to your master and tell him we fell for it. That's all you need to know."

Which Claire did. She returned to Willsan and told him it was on, that the Resistance had taken the bait. Willsan seemed pleased and sat down with Claire to get the details from her. Claire told him what she knew, that four freedom fighters would converge on the location along Rue de la Roquette, a block from the cemetery, just at midnight, Friday. Willsan then reiterated to Claire what her role would be—she was to take pictures and make sure they were in the *Paris-Soir* the next day.

On Friday night, Claire was driven to the scene in the backseat of a navy blue Citroen sedan. The vehicle was parked a block away, and Claire was left there with an SS officer. She had been told to bring along her camera, which she had with her, and she had been told that her vehicle would converge on the scene once the shooting ended. Claire was in agony as she waited with her guard, amid thoughts of what her friends would be facing when they breached the small compound. Her hands were clammy and her heart raced as she worked to arm the flash attachment on her camera. The time was 11:40 p.m.

Two minutes past midnight, the sound of automatic gunfire could be heard hammering down the street as the German MP 40 machine guns opened fire. The shooting lasted less than twenty seconds. Immediately the Citroen roared to life and hurtled down the street, squealing through a right turn and then abruptly screeching to a stop as bodies were encountered lying in the road. Claire was told to start shooting pictures. She quickly shot one roll of film and was loading a second when Willsan himself approached her.

"Do you know these people?"

Claire looked beyond Willsan at the bodies lying broken in the street. "I do. I know them all." She opened up then, and the tears began. Her shoulders were shaking so badly she fumbled her camera to the ground.

Willsan bent to scoop it up. "Well enough," said Willsan as he returned her camera. "I want a complete writeup from you on my desk first thing in the morning. I want the names of all persons who were shot dead tonight. Plus I want addresses. You will see what happens to the families and friends of scum like these," he said, waving his hands at the dead and dying fighters. Even as he spoke, soldiers wandered among the shooting victims, dispatching those still living with a single gunshot to the head. Minutes later, the scene was perfectly still, perfectly quiet, as the soldiers loaded onto their trucks and sped away.

"What about—what about their bodies?" Claire asked.

"Notify your High Command. Tell them to come and take them

away—if they dare. If they don't, our Jewish workers will load the bodies onto wagons and take them away to be burned. That's what happens to these fools."

"Oh."

"I also want all pictures developed by eight a.m. and on my desk. I will decide which photographs you will turn into your newspaper for publication later today."

"I see."

"You mean, 'yes, sir.'"

"Yes, sir."

"And while we're at it, I've been notified you might have a sister by the name of Esmée, same last name. Would that ring a bell?"

Claire's heart fell. More than anything else she'd wanted news of Esmée, that she was even alive, but not like this. The last thing she wanted, in fact, was to have Esmée linked to her, a failed Freedom Fighter. It could only mean a dark future for poor Esmée.

"That would be my sister," she admitted in a small voice. She kept her eyes averted from the captain's burning eyes.

"Indeed. Well, I will certainly do what I can to ease her passage through the war now that you're cooperating. That would help you feel good, am I right?"

"You're right. I need to know Esmée is all right."

"She's with Colonel Sigmund Schlösser. He's one of the rare SS army field commanders. A perfect soldier and a man to be looked up to. Do you know why your sister works for him?"

"I didn't know she did. I thought she'd been taken captive."

"Dear girl, we don't take captives. We arrest troublemakers like yourself, and we either convince them to work for us or we send them away to a place like Auschwitz or Treblinka. We don't countenance troublemakers at all."

"I'm glad she's working for you, then."

"Just like you are. The two Vallant daughters."

Claire cringed then. She had felt it coming, felt him driving to the point where he would raise his arms to pull her close.

But it didn't come. Not just then, anyway. Claire backed out of his office, humbling herself with bowed head and shuffling feet as she went.

"Son of a bitch!" she cursed once she was outside his office and headed for the end of the hall. She had a dozen pictures to develop and print before morning and needed to access the company's dark room before then. It was going to be a long night and an even longer day tomorrow.

And what of Esmée? How would Claire's involuntary service impact her sister?

She shuddered as she walked outside the building and headed for the press Quonset hut and darkroom. It was time to concentrate. Time to concentrate on faces and try to give addresses that seemed accurate but were wildly ineffective. That was her last remaining ploy. Unless...

Unless she could locate other death pictures and use those in place of the real ones. Why would she do that? To protect the living, the families left behind, the wives and loved ones. Especially the children.

Her step quickened. Where would she locate other death pictures?

The Quonset hut housing the press bureau was the place to start. She was certain the public relations arm of the Third Reich would be keeping pictures of the dead.

After all, death was the currency of the realm.

She would start there.

24

Esmée persevered, keeping Sven's memory alive with the nightly POW broadcasts. She had taken to broadcasting news not only of French and British captives but of German wounded as well. There had been shortwave calls to her call sign that German families had no other way of getting news of their loved ones than the shortwave wireless broadcasting from France —there were hundreds by now—and would she please keep it up? So she did, broadcasting in three languages every night.

Sigmund Schlösser knew none of this. If he had, she would have been shot. But her love for Sven and his commitment to the wireless outweighed her fear of death. By now, she could think of much worse things than death.

One night, as she was broadcasting from the dark of her room, she looked up to find her door ajar and two eyes peering into her room. Her stomach contents immediately washed into her mouth, so frightened was she. Esmée swallowed hard and paused her broadcast. Then the door opened. The figure entered her room and closed the door behind. It was a young German officer, a new lieutenant, wearing the collar pin and uniform of the SS. She imagined she would be dead in minutes. He sat beside her on her bed.

"What do you think you are doing, miss?"

"I'm giving out the news of our wounded."

"But you were speaking French."

"I give news in English, French, and German. It harms no one."

"What about the Führer. It harms him because he has said no information can be passed out of our hospitals and camps. Would you like me to take you out and shoot you for this?"

"No. I don't want to die. I'm only eighteen."

He slipped an arm around her shoulders. "What are you willing to do to stay alive?"

Esmée shivered under his arm. "What do you want me to do?"

"I want you to lie back and let me make love to you. Then you may resume with your broadcast. It is the only way you can stay alive tonight."

"And if I do, will you demand it again?"

"Yes, every night. I'm a very lonely German officer, and you're a beautiful French girl. I'm told I'm easy to look at. We have enough to have a love affair, I would imagine."

He slipped his free hand across her breast. When she recoiled, he placated, "There, there. Let me touch it now."

Esmée didn't resist again. He did what he'd come to do, and she kept her eyes shut the entire time, imagining that Sven had returned and was making love to her. Actually, the German was gentle and, while she was disgusted and hated him for his rape, it wasn't enough to make her give up her wireless broadcasts. If this was to be the trade-off to continue her late-night work, so be it.

The rapes continued in this way, and Esmée continued with her broadcasts. Her audience continued to grow as the field hospital grew and increased the volume of prisoners and German wounded almost every day. So it was taking two hours each night to get her message out. Plus Harold—her rapist—took another half hour with her. So her nights were busy, making her days miserable from lack of sleep and lack of healing in between shifts.

Schlösser began to notice she was late getting to work in the mornings since she was oversleeping. In his thick German accent, he confronted her with, "What's got you in bed so late, my lovely? Have you met a boy you like?"

Esmée almost lost it, almost broke down in tears, but fought it off. One thing would lead to another if she told the truth. She couldn't afford that, so she prevaricated, "I've just had trouble sleeping, sir. Too much blood and bad things are making it hard for me to sleep. I think some time away would be nice."

"We can make that happen, mademoiselle."

Later that day, she found herself in the backseat of a jeep, with Schlösser up front riding in the passenger seat. She knew they were going north, but didn't have any idea where. Hours later, they entered Bruges, now a German-occupied city. Schlösser directed the driver. Soon, they pulled up in front of a hotel marked *Wilhelm* and pulled beneath the portico. Schlösser took his young charge inside and demanded "the best room." They were taken upstairs by a bellboy, who led them to a corner room with windows on both outer walls. Esmée parted the curtains and looked out. Bruges was beautiful. It was dusk by now, and lights glittered like a thousand points upon a dark sea. She was mesmerized.

"Will this do?" he asked gently.

"I'm staying here?"

"You're here for a week. I'll be leaving you now."

"But I have nothing with me. No clothes, no bath essentials, toothbrush—"

"Esmée, this is a very nice hotel. They will have everything you need. And you can shop to your heart's content with this."

He handed her a letter in an envelope. She opened and read. It was a *To Whom It May Concern letter* and advised the holder that they were to provide to Esmée any goods or services she might request. Payment was guaranteed by Sigmund Schlösser, Colonel, Third Reich. It was impressive, even embossed.

Her eyes clouded over. "Thank you, sir. I don't have words."

"No words necessary. You are like my daughter, the one I lost to smallpox, now grown up. Be well."

With that, he turned and left. Then he returned moments later. It was clear he wanted a hug, so Esmée, trembling, hugged her captor. It only lasted a moment, but it brought tears to her eyes and, for the first time in months, she felt safe.

Then he was gone, and she was alone with his letter and without Harold the rapist lurking around the corner. She wondered if she should tell Schlösser about Harold. Might he overlook the wireless? Definitely not, she decided. He was German before he was love. She must always keep that in mind and not weaken just because he had. Honesty with her captor had to be avoided at all costs.

France had surrendered to the Germans, Belgium was occupied, and her world was looking more and more hopeless every day. She determined that she would enjoy her time in Bruges. She'd never been away on a lark before by herself. She'd just have to see what happened.

Who could tell? She might fall in love.

Or maybe even flee to Paris.

25

In the end, Claire had taken the pictures of her dead comrades lying in the street outside the munitions dump, and she had exchanged those pictures for photographs of other civilian murders, pictures of dead young people who might just as well have been members of Esmée's cell. She withheld all real names as well—of course. In this manner, she successfully threw off the investigations Willsan had begun in order to punish the families of the murdered freedom fighters.

Claire made a decision Friday night as she sat alone at Café de Flore, a café on boulevard Saint-Germain, that she wasn't going to be used by Willsan again. True, he had caught her spying and, true, he might yet have her shot on a whim. But after the disastrous ambush at the munitions dump, she'd vowed that would never happen again, or anything like it, just because she'd been forced to collaborate with the Germans.

As she stirred her scotch and soda, she calculated what it would take to disentangle herself from Captain Willsan once and for all. For one, she knew that whatever else she might do, it would leave her family at risk as long as there was a war. She decided to warn them, to tell them that she'd been caught and forced to betray France in order to safeguard her family, and to ask them to take steps to protect themselves. Her parents were smart people. Surely, they would have a plan to deal with the situation Claire had created. Additionally, she herself would disappear. She'd take her bag of tricks and the bag of beautiful clothes gifted her by Ehrlanger and Fleischmann, scoop up Lima, and flee the city. Or at least go underground, never to collaborate again. Armed with her camera, as was her original plan, she would record Resistance successes and publish photographs guaranteed to motivate even the weakest of Parisians to action. Only good could come of pictures like that. Besides, she was disgusted with herself and her so-called collaboration. She was finished living her lies, no matter the need, no matter the part of France she'd strived to protect.

Her deceits with the substituted photographs and phony names would surface soon enough and Willsan would come for her. It was time to move on, time to disappear. But motivating her more than any of her successes—or failures—was the evolving Jewish problem. Jews were disappearing from Paris by the thousands. Claire knew where they were going; her comrades knew where they were going. A renewed call to arms went out from the High Command. All fighters were needed now more than ever. Claire vowed that she would do whatever it took to help the Jews—for they were everyone's neighbors, often, people just like her who were being taken to the camps as part and parcel of the undesirables the Nazis meant to eradicate.

In 1941, the Germans, with the help of the Vichy French Government, had established four primary internment camps just outside of Paris where they interned Americans, political dissidents, resisters, and Jews. They were typically housed according to their categorical label. The Jews, unless freed for some obscure reason from the internment camp, were always transferred from the Paris camp to Polish concentration camps where survival chances were nonexistent. Those four internment camps were Compiègne, 50 miles northeast of Paris, Drancy La Cité de la Muette (operated by the Vichy) near St. Denis just north, of Paris center, Pithiviers Beaune-la-Rolande, and Fresnes. The Resistance knew everything about every camp and knew they were impenetrable and any attempts directly against the camps would most likely result in prisoner deaths. So it was decided nothing could be done from the outside. A call went out: who would volunteer to go inside the camps and take the Resistance there? Claire would answer the call. But first came her family.

After meeting with her parents, they decided they would sell everything and move to America. That Claire's mother was a physician and surgeon made her chances at immigration very good. She would also take Lima with her for the duration of the war. So the process was begun and, with the exchange of a large number of francs for German marks, the move occurred in the dead of night in April of 1941. With her family in a safe place, Claire was freed up. She could now resist the Germans in whatever way she chose, without worry of possible implications for her family. Her first move was intended to return her to journalism.

She participated in the Resistance and helped produce clandestine publications, including leaflets such as *L'Université Libre* and Georges Politzer's pamphlet *Sang et Or* (Blood and Gold), which presented the theses of the Nazi theorist Alfred Rosenberg. She also worked on a clandestine edition of *L'Humanité*. She strengthened the relationship between the civil resistance (Conseil National de la Resistance or CNR) and the military resistance (L'*Organisation spéciale* or OS), which later became the *Franc-tireurs et Partisans Français* (FTPF), French Snipers and Partisans. But she soon was back to old ways, venturing into the field again, where she even transported explosives.

But the photojournalism was where her true strength lay. She proved to have a knack, like all outstanding photojournalists have, for being in the right place at precisely the right moment with her camera primed and aimed in exactly the right direction. Her first internationally acclaimed photo was of a group of pre-teen boys, young Jews, clinging to a barbed wire fence in the dead of night while a crew of German camp guards and police dogs attacked them from behind just as they were being herded into the gas chambers. The looks of terror, of abject horror, found their way onto the front pages of newspapers from Paris to London to New York to Chicago to San Francisco and around the world. Where before in America, there had been a lurking sense of trouble in France and Poland, now there were actual undeniable photographs exploding again and again from the Exakta camera of Claire Vallant. Suddenly, the world was on fire, Pearl Harbor was attacked, and America came into the war in December 1941.

26

E smée had told the hotel desk absolutely no telephone calls. They were to allow the calls to ring without answer. The desk complied. On Wednesday afternoon, Esmée rode the lift down to the lobby and stepped out into the early August sunshine. Two blocks down, she found herself at a sidewalk cafe with a newly-posted menu written in chalk on a board in German. This sign—at last—she could read, and so she took an empty two-chair table facing toward the street. At her left was a couple obviously in love, he wearing the uniform of the Wehrmacht, she wearing a horizontal striped boatneck shirt and a black beret. Esmée immediately understood: the soldier and the collaborator. In a way, she didn't blame the woman at all. The Germans were unavoidable now and irrepressible. They were loud and rude and got their way in all things civilian. She turned her back slightly to the couple and found herself not more than a meter from an elderly gentleman on her right. He was dressed in a summer suit with vest and had thin white hair, a white mustache, and rimless eyeglasses. A local paper—she couldn't decipher the headline—was propped open before him on the table as he ate a dinner roll and sipped what she guessed was coffee. Within moments, he felt her eyes playing over him.

"Excuse me," he said in French. "Do I know you?"

"How do you know I'm French?"

"Your clothes. All French designers. Which tells me, as well, that you're quite well-off. Are you a collaborator?" This last part was said with a smirk and sour expression. Obviously, he had no use for collaborators.

"No, actually I'm a prisoner of sort."

"Really? You seem to be on a very long leash."

A waiter came and took Esmée's order for a fruit drink and a shaved roast beef roll. Rationing was strict, and it was the closest she knew she'd come to protein on a Belgian street that day.

"I am on a long leash. My master is a colonel in the army. He's off fighting, maintaining German control of Dunkirk."

"Ahh, the miracle of Dunkirk. Was he there?"

"At the retreat? I'm not sure. He doesn't tell me much about the war. I think he wants me to forget it sometimes. What do you do?"

"I'm retired. So now I pester the newspapers with my letters to the editor. I'm reading one of my missives right now."

"What sort of letters do you write?"

"I write under a pseudonym. I complain about the occupation. I hate your Germans in my city, and I don't try to cover it up."

"Not my Germans, please. I'm Parisian."

"Understand. My apologies."

"So, bring me up to date. What is the latest in your city?"

"Well, shortly after the invasion, the Military Government passed a series of anti-Jewish laws. Don't tell anyone, but I'm a Jew. They are laws similar to your Vichy laws on the status of Jews. The Belgian government, however, has refused to pass any anti-Jewish laws. They are at an impasse with the German Military Government. That will change, however, unless I don't know my Adolf Hitler."

"Goodness. It must be awful. I'm so sorry this is happening."

"Two days ago, without orders from the homeland, members of the Algemeene SS Vlaanderen pillaged two synagogues in Antwerp and burned the house of the chief Rabbi of the town in the so-called Antwerp Pogrom."

"Persecution has begun then."

"A Judenrat has been passed. We are now forced to wear the yellow Star of David."

"Which, I see, you have chosen not to do."

"I have chosen not to do, exactly. Don't tell anyone."

"I'm French. There's no one to tell."

"Now they are deporting us to Poland. I am using a fake name, and I have refused to inscribe. They don't know about me. Why am I telling you this?"

"Because you know I'm French and you know I hate the Germans as much as you. If I could help you, I would."

"Save me from the Mechelen camp. The place horrifies me. My brother has gone there, as well as my sister and her children. I'm too much of a coward to follow orders and show up there. If they catch me, I'll be shot on the spot. This roll and coffee are a rarity. I never leave my apartment anymore. The less seen of me, the better. What's your name?"

"Esmée."

"Reynauld. That's my real name. No last names, though."

"Okay."

Her roll appeared with her fruit drink, and she began nibbling. Reynauld returned to his letter to the editor and allowed her to eat in peace.

In the next moment, she raised her eyes and found, standing in front of her, Colonel Sigmund Schlösser and three SS men. He was wearing his summer grays and officer's cap and was all polish and knife edges on the seams of his trousers and jacket, a very malevolent look to any civilian in any German-occupied city or town.

"So. You refuse to answer my calls?"

"Calls? I've been in my room."

"The desk tells me you have left instructions for the phone to ring through."

"That's because a certain German soldier has been pursuing me. He raped me at the hospital."

Schlösser took a step forward, his face turning white. He bit out, "Give me a name. He is a dead man."

"His name is Harold. I don't know his last name, but he is on sentry duty at the barracks."

Schlösser snapped his fingers. A senior enlisted man stepped forward. "Bring me this man. Harold, sentry, barracks. Don't hurt him."

"Yes, sir. Don't hurt him."

"Leave that to me."

He turned his attention back to Esmée. "Why didn't you come to me?"

She began crying. "I was so scared. He said he would turn me in if I cried out or reported him."

"How long did this go on?"

"A month or more. He came to me every night and had his way."

"We are going to bring him here. I want you to point him out so I can be sure it's the right man."

Schlösser turned to Reynauld. "And who is this old Jew?"

Esmée turned away. Suddenly, she couldn't watch.

"Is this old fool bothering you, daughter? I saw you talking from a distance."

"He only wanted to borrow a napkin. Nothing more. Please leave him alone."

"Take this old Jew out in the street and shoot him!" Schlösser ordered the youngest soldier. Without a word, the youngest and the third soldier reached and took Reynauld by the arms and pulled him into the street. The old man fell to his knees, his hands clasped in prayer. "No, no, no," he cried. "I've done nothing against the Reich!"

"Nonsense," Schlösser called to him. At this moment, all diners were frozen, some were turning away for they knew what was coming.

Suddenly, Schlösser turned on the heel of his jackboot and strode up to the old man, unholstering his Luger 9 mm pistol as he went. He boldly walked up and pointed the muzzle right between the man's eyes. Without a second letup, he pulled the trigger and kicked the old man over, dead. "Call the OD," Schlösser ordered. "Have them come take him away."

Colonel Schlösser returned off the street and seated himself in the old man's chair next to Esmée. "Now. Where were we?"

THREE HOURS LATER, HAROLD WAS BROUGHT TO HER ROOM. Schlösser and his soldiers were waiting there with Esmée. The men were drinking coffee and laughing at the fools on the side-walks below, leading away from the corner room. The young sentry was manacled and waist-chained and white from the collar up. Obviously terrified, what blood was left in his face drained away when he was dragged into Esmée's hotel room. Their eyes met, and Esmée looked away.

Schlösser gave her a testy look. "Well?"

She nodded.

"So, this is the rapist?"

She couldn't speak. She could only nod her head. Again Schlösser drew his pistol. He dispatched the young man with a single shot to his temple. A towel was brought from the bathroom to staunch the flow of blood, which was but a trickle, after all. Then the two arresting soldiers dragged the body out of the room.

The colonel turned back to his captive, his putative daughter.

"So," said Schlösser. "What else is bothering you that you cannot take my calls?"

27

Following his capture as a German POW and the discovery that he was a conscripted Frenchman, the French army transported Remy south toward Paris. Halfway there, a Resistance fighter and his wife intercepted the procession and said they would drive Remy into the city. It was the only chance he would have at remaining underground. Just outside of Paris, on the autoroute du Nord, a German roadblock suddenly loomed up in the nighttime windshield of their borrowed Volvo sedan. A red and white checkered arm had been lowered across the road, blocking anyone from coming into or leaving Paris without first having their papers checked by the German authorities. The Military Government was now regulating all traffic at all points leading in and out of the city.

Denis LaRue was driving, his wife Monique in the passenger seat, and Remy occupied the backseat with the family dog as they approached the checkpoint. Wolfhound—the dog's name—became disgruntled with being awakened from his long sleep overnight and began barking, shrilly and without letup despite the threats or cajoling from his owners. The vehicle inched forward in the long, slow-moving line that crept forward a car at a time as papers were turned over and questions posed and answered.

"I have no papers," Remy whispered to his hosts.

The driver, Denis, looked around. "We have papers for you. You're my brother."

"My name?"

"Henri LaRue. You're a baker."

"But I don't know anything about baking!" Remy harshly whispered.

"Neither do they," whispered Denis at his rearview mirror. "These are farm boys and city kids who don't know anything about anything. Just remember, Jewish bread is unleavened and we never bake unleavened bread. That they might know."

"Jewish bread is unleavened, of course."

The German road guards reviewed papers and waved the Volvo on through.

A mile down the road, Monique passed a sheaf of papers into the backseat with a flashlight. "Read this," she instructed Remy.

"What is it?"

"We have prepared this brochure. It's entitled *Manuel du Légionnaire* and contains detailed notes on how to fire guns, manufacture bombs, sabotage factories, carry out assassinations, and perform other skills useful to the Resistance."

"My God, if they had searched this car, we'd all be dead. Including the dog."

"The brochure is disguised as informational material for fascistic Frenchmen who volunteered for the Legion of French Volunteers Against Bolshevism on the Eastern Front. It has taken occupation authorities some time to realize that the manual is a Communist publication."

"You're communists?"

"Yes. You must be, too. It's the only way."

"Much has changed since I went away," Remy sighed. "I feel lost and frightened by it all."

Monique slipped her hand between the front seats and gave Remy's knee a squeeze. "We all feel that way. Life is short, here in France. Tonight we will drink wine and eat leavened bread and cheese and see if we can find you a girlfriend, Remy. Do you like that?"

"I have a wife. She's also with the Resistance."

"What name does she go by?"

"Claire."

"The photographer?"

"Yes. You know her?"

"Claire Vallant is very famous now. We beg her to come take photographs of our resistance activities. She can't be everywhere, though. Only at important events. Soon, we have an event so big she won't be able to resist."

Remy's heart skipped. A chance to see Claire? So soon?

"What are you going to do?"

"We're bombing the German headquarters."

"That's impossible. There are guards four deep around the Wehrmacht HQ."

"We know a way in. A very secret way, Remy. You must come with us. Do you know bombs?"

"I specialized in high explosives in the army. I know everything there is to know about bombs."

"Good. Then you've officially joined our group."

He didn't know about that. Denis and Monique seemed so *loose* with their secrets, the way they'd opened up to him, that it was worrying. Who else knew about them, about their activities? Or even about their plans? He was uncomfortable. It felt like he was being drawn in. Then the thought came to him, what if these people were really Nazis who were undercover tracking down the Resistance? What if he was being set up and he was one exercise away from being executed by the SS for subversion? His hands were suddenly damp, and he felt sweat beads break out along his spine. It was unnerving, never knowing for sure who was who. Then he reminded himself that it was the French army that had turned him over to these two. Surely they knew who Denis and Monique really were. Wouldn't the French army have to be convinced of their identity, their allegiances? He felt himself relax just a mite then. Maybe he would go with them Friday night. Maybe he would see about their bomb.

Monique was speaking, and it broke his reverie. "We want you to come stay with us in Paris. We live above a noisy shoe repair shop with the yammering of machines and supplies and people coming and going all day, so we've got an anonymous silhouette. You can join us there, and no one needs to know you're even in Paris."

"I'm going to need papers and ID. The German army isn't my friend."

"We can do that. Our group has the best forgers in all of France. We'll have your passport and driver's license made up, and we'll prepare membership cards with local groups and libraries. You'll fit right in."

"I can't thank you enough for this. I want to help in any way I can."

"Are you familiar at all with the German High Command in Paris?"

"Somewhat. My father is stationed in Paris. He reports there."

"Goodness, who is that?"

"Major Wilhoite Schildmann. He was in Africa with Rommel. Then with the tanks in the Ardennes. Now he's here in Paris."

"SS?"

"Yes, SS. He's a bitter old man who suffered lung damage in the First World War. Now he's slow to get around, but the Führer made him a hero. He's been kept around as a lesson in loyalty."

"So he's not someone you want to run into?"

"What do you think? He's there at General HQ. Here I am, thinking of blowing him up."

"The explosion is middle of the night, Remy. Not much chance of killing your own father."

"Even so..."

"Don't dwell on it. That's why they call it war. People get killed."

"I hate it."

"War?"

"War." He sighed a long sigh.

"Have you been in touch with Claire?" Monique asked.

"It's been a year since we talked."

"Come to think of it, she might have gone double with the Germans."

"A double agent?"

"She was seen around with at least one of them. I think she was secretly turning over target information to the Resistance, though."

That gave him pause. If these two were Nazis, they'd have had her killed by now if they knew these things. He felt himself relax another step.

"That sounds like her. Nerves of steel, that one."

Monique turned and looked out the windshield. It had begun to rain, and Denis was feeling around on the dashboard for the windshield wipers knob. Monique found it by lighting her cigarette lighter and putting her face close to the knobs and dials. "Ahh, here we go." The wipers leapt to life and Denis leaned back, satisfied with the improved vision up ahead.

Remy peered beyond him from the backseat. The lights of occupied Paris lay ahead through a sweeping sheet of rain. He was glad to be going home. He was glad to be setting high explosives— whatever it took to drive the mad Germans out of his home.

His mind advanced beyond the rain, beyond the remaining distance, advanced beyond Friday sundown. His fingers twitched as they lit off the fuse he would lay.

This time he would watch.

Then he would find his wife and daughter and steal them away.

They would go someplace where there was no war. Where there would be warm, white beaches and orchid air at night. He would draw his little family close and do nothing but share love thereafter.

After the bomb.

28

America had been in the war two months when Claire, one gloomy February afternoon, was summoned to rue d'Orly to observe an attack in progress. First, however, the High Command wanted her to photograph the making of the bombs for the attack. The photographs were to serve as a warning to the Germans that the French Resistance was going to fight them every step of the way in the battle for the Jews of Paris.

A committee consisting of SS *Hauptsturmführer,* Theodor Dannecker, the Commissioner for Jewish Affairs, Louis Darquier de Pellepoix, and General Secretary of the Police, René Bousquet, had begun planning a *grand rafle* (great round-up) of Jews to deport to the death camps. Word of the plan had been passed along to the Resistance, and the bombs were being prepared for Dannecker's home. The plan was to make the great round-up so painful that the SS would turn away.

But the attack never went off due to a shortage in bomb ingredients, and on the morning of 16 February 1942, the *grand rafle* began with 9,000 French policemen rounding up the Jews of Paris, leading to some 12,762 Jewish men, women, and children being arrested and brought to the Val d'Hiv sports stadium, from where they were sent to the Drancy camp and finally Auschwitz. That morning, as Claire observed from the shadows of the sports stadium, she learned the *grand rafle* was a Franco-German operation. The overwhelming majority of those who arrested the Jews were French policemen. Twenty-four Jews were killed resisting arrest.

Claire noted about the watching bystanders that their expressions were empty, almost indifferent. She heard one woman shout at the policemen, "Well done! Well done!" while the man standing next to her warned, "After them, it'll be us. Poor people!" Claire, with her Exakta camera, recorded the entire roundup, beginning to end, her final photograph being the end of a freight train leaving Paris on its trip to Auschwitz concentration camp in Poland.

Her pictures were bought up by *Life* magazine, and one week later were seen around the world. Pictures of old and young people, men and women, children and infants, wearing threadbare garments as they'd been ordered to leave all good clothes at home, standing in ankle-deep snow in the sports stadium while orders were shouted at them by the SS guards. She shot pictures of SS men beating down stragglers with their quirts and others being dragged away and shot inside the goals of the soccer field where the dead bodies were being stacked like firewood in a fireplace.

Then began a forced march to the train station. Claire followed from a discreet distance, again running through rolls of film while she recorded the inhumanity of the march and especially what happened with the children when their parents began to stagger and could no longer carry them. At first, the kids were passed between adults who shared the weight of the very small ones who couldn't walk. But the Nazi guards put an end to it, beating and shooting any helper so they soon became cowed and turned their heads away, leaving the horrified parents lying in the street with their children, holding and cuddling them as they waited for the following trucks with men who would leap out, shoot them, and load their bodies onto flatbed trucks like cords of firewood.

Tears streaming down her face, Claire grew bolder and began taking close-up shots of the Jews when the SS guards increased the marching speed to a double-time, leaving behind many old and infirm who were now being shot on the spot and loaded onto the trucks. Claire heard the guards tell the moving mass that they were going to be a work camp with hot meals and feather beds where they would be left to work in peace under the eyes of friendly German managers. But the Jews knew better, and many were angry and would lash out at the Germans in French and, occasionally, swing a fist or a suitcase at them. Which always resulted in summary executions and greater stacks of bodies on the flatbeds.

At long last, they reached the train station where, to their horror, they found that the promised comfortable lounge cars were actually freight and cattle cars without heat, without toilets, and without even a place to sit. They were forced inside, body against body, until, literally, the last loaded in would have to hold their breath while the giant doors were shut and locked from the outside. Claire captured this on camera but backed away when two guards began motioning for her to join the load-in. "I'm German. I'm not a Jew," she told them in her perfect German, and they nodded and waved her away. One tried to confiscate her camera, but she immediately backpedaled then broke into a run back down the platform toward the station house.

More pictures sold to *Life* and *Look* magazines later that week; more exposure, more acclaim for the French Camera Lady, as she was called in order to protect her identity in the magazines. *Paris-Soir* still paid her salary, but now there was money coming from the giant American news conglomerates, including the magazines and newspapers like *Time magazine*, *The Times* in New York, and the *Associated Press* wire service.

But it wasn't all acclaim without some downside. Now the SS and Wehrmacht were looking for her. Her real identity was known to the Germans, but her habits and her address were unknown. At this time, Claire was spending her nights at the homes and apartments of different Resistance fighters on a rotating basis, laying low, hiding among friends and fellows who would give up their own lives before they would allow her to be taken. Lima was still living with Claire's mother and was heard to be thriving, for which Claire was grateful. Still, she missed her little girl and wept for her many nights. The war was taking its toll in more ways than one. At times, she thought she would leave the war effort to others and just return home to her mother's house. But each time, she remembered there was no one to do her job as well as she. So she continued putting one foot in front of the other and doing what she could to help win the war and send the Germans packing.

It was on one of these nights, in a flat located in the twelfth arrondissement, that she found herself walking into a living room only to find a man she hadn't seen in over a year: Remy Schildmann.

29

"This man is going to hide you from the Germans," said her hostess that night, a woman with a small secretarial service. "His name is Remy."

Claire and Remy fell into each other's arms. He encircled her with an arm and with his free hand tilted her face up to his. He kissed her fully on the lips. Startled at finding her husband so suddenly, without warning, Claire pushed away to take stock.

"You were sent to the battlefields!" she cried. "But here you are!"

"I was captured by the French and made my way back to Paris."

"Did you fight for the Führer?"

"I did. But I was a captive myself."

"I didn't know! We've received no mail, no word since you deployed."

"And where is everyone from the 2nd Battalion of the Secret Army? Are they still around?"

"Jean Renoz was captured. They hanged her New Year's Eve. Jacques Marseilles was either shot earlier or rounded up with other pro-French newsmen from the *Soir* and taken away. We're looking for him, but nobody knows anything."

"And what about our Esmée? Has she been located?"

Claire's face fell. "No. We've asked everyone, looked everywhere we dare to go. But so far, nothing. It is my opinion that she's being held in a camp. Otherwise, how has she disappeared off the face of the earth? Only the camps can do that. God forbid, she might even be dead by now, Remy. Nothing would surprise me."

"God forbid. We must find her. And now the most important of all. How is our Lima?"

"She's with my mother. It's been a long time while I've been doing what I can."

"I've been ordered to take you into hiding, Claire. The Germans want to find you and put your picture in the papers—after they hang you first. We'll be leaving Paris in the morning."

"I can't do that. My photographs are too important to the Allies. I won't leave Paris."

"Maybe we won't have to go far. Maybe you will agree with my plan to take you underground on the outskirts of town. I've been authorized for a farmhouse there, a deserted one in the hills where the Germans don't go. It's got fruit trees and good well water and even has its own electricity. You'll be safe there."

"And you'll be with me?"

He half-smiled. "Yes and no. My orders are to protect you. I will spend my days scouting and my nights standing guard. You won't be seeing that much of me, dear Claire."

She relaxed and accepted a glass of wine from the host. "Merci. Just to be with you at all. It feels like a dream."

He walked across the room and sat beside her on the couch. "I haven't changed. I've loved you more each day."

"Now you've learned how to say what a woman wants to hear," she said with a laugh. "Hopefully, I'll see more of you at the farm than your plan anticipates."

"There will be moments," he said and accepted his own glass of wine. "We will have our times."

"Good, then. Let's make our pallet and settle in for the night. I'm exhausted."

"You go ahead. I'll be outside in the hall watching over you. Those are my orders."

"When they relieve you, come to me. Promise?"

"Maybe in the middle of the night. Maybe for ten minutes."

"As I remember, ten minutes is long enough."

"More than enough, dear Claire. I'll be here."

NOW LIVING OUTSIDE THE CITY IN A REMOTE AREA WHERE A FARMER had once raised sheep and barley, Remy and Claire had tried to settle in and live a life of normalcy for however long they might until duty—the Resistance—called. The next several days passed peacefully. Now it was mid-March, approximately one month after the roundup of the Jews. The Resistance was grief-stricken. Its members felt as if they'd failed, and they had, to some extent, because tens of thousands of Paris Jews had been lost to the Nazis.

Remy and Claire would wake up in the morning, have long, slow breakfasts, make each other cups of coffee, and languidly read the paper. Then they ran out of coffee and began making barley coffee. It tasted terrible, but neither one complained. Claire would then put on a dark hat and dark glasses and go for walks with Remy. They would stroll about, talking about such diverse subjects as their childhoods, the people they knew, where they had been, and what they had accomplished over the last year. While their paths had diverged, their activities had been similar. Mostly, they had been engaged in the war in their own way, she with her photographs and pamphlets, he with his bombs and bullets. They discovered they had missed each other greatly and were thankful they were getting to spend some time together.

One night, Remy returned from a meeting with the High Command. He had news of their next engagement.

"They want us to get the group here and plan an attack on the Commissioner for Jewish Affairs. Denis and Monique LaRue, who drove me to Paris last month, are in charge of the bombing. There will be others coming, too."

"I'm ready," said Claire. "I was wondering when we would strike again."

"This time, I'll be making the bomb, you'll be photographing the incident, and Denis and Anders will plant it. Monique and Liane will locate the records system and make sure it is targeted with the bomb Denis and Anders will plant. It will actually be more than one bomb, I'm thinking. We'll see what Monique and Liane learn."

"Why Monique and Liane?"

"Liane actually works in the commission. She's a file clerk there, which is why she was recruited. It's her first action."

"Where will you obtain explosives, Remy?"

"I have a contact bringing me enough British RDX to take out the entire building. I'll only use maybe half so we'll have enough left over to strike again somewhere else."

"We'll be meeting when?"

"Tonight, actually. Right here in our living room."

She knew enough about how the 2nd Battalion operated to know the clandestine meeting would go undetected. The agents were highly trained in evasion techniques and wouldn't be followed. Claire went into the kitchen and stood at the window, looking out on a meadow dotted here and there with grazing sheep. Her gaze shifted to the sweet potato she was growing on the windowsill in a small water glass. It was filled halfway with water. The potato was supported half in the water by three toothpicks holding it in place. The plant had sprouted, and runners were eight and ten inches long at that point. It was her baby, a joy to her, recipient of her great care and attention every day. Why did it mean so much to her?

"Because it's real," she told Remy. "It's real, and it's not about the war. I hate the war. I hate the Germans, hate what they're doing to our Jews."

"Our Jews?"

"Yes, they're our Jews. France, Paris. Wherever, it's wrong and it's horrible and I hate them for it."

"I know you do. I do, too."

"Did you have to persecute the Jews when you were in the Army?"

Remy's face clouded over. His intelligent, blue eyes narrowed, and his look turned far away. "I did. We ripped them out of their homes. I was responsible for loading many families onto the trucks. You know all about Lima's family. I did that every night. They went to the Paris camps and then to Auschwitz and Treblinka. It broke my heart, and I drank heavily every night until I passed out."

She looked at him with sympathy. "You were forced into it."

"They would've killed me had I disobeyed."

"So you killed Jews instead."

"Not personally."

"There's a difference between sending them to Treblinka and killing them personally? How's that work?"

"I don't know. It doesn't work. I was guilty, and so I drank. I'll never forgive myself, and it's fair if you don't ever forgive me either."

"It's not my job to forgive you. But I have, for the record. I'm your wife and love you regardless."

He looked at the floor. Then he went outside with his gun and was gone for several hours. When he returned, he was red-faced from the wind, and his collar was turned up and had chafed his neck.

"I don't blame the Jews who hate me," he said after he hung up his coat. "I don't forgive myself either. It's impossible. So I'll do what I can to make it right. I'll make my bombs, I'll shoot Nazis wherever I can, I'll do whatever I can to help the Resistance. But I won't expect them to forgive me. I won't forgive myself either."

They embraced and held on against the night, against the coming bombing, against the people who hated them, Germans, Jews, whoever. It wasn't a romantic embrace at all; it was a long farewell, for they knew they might not see each other after the bombing. She was a notorious photographer, the one whose identity was never far below the surface. They would hang her publicly. But Remy and the others would be killed on the spot if they were discovered. An hour later, she went to her sweet potato again. She looked long and hard at it. With a shallow sigh, she plucked the growing plant from out of its water glass, tore the shoots away, and threw it part and parcel into the trash. Then she washed the glass and replaced it in the cupboard.

Their time together was done.

30

The 2nd Battalion cell met at their house that night. Denis and Monique arrived first, out of breath and panting from a dash around the back meadow, through the oak and hickory trees, up the hill into the low-swept pine trees and in through the rear door of the cottage. Next came Anders and Liane, arriving by motorcycle and sidecar. The machine ran very quietly, Anders explained, thanks to a one-off muffler system he, a lathe operator by day, had built and installed. The machine was made to run perfectly quietly and, at night, it was very difficult to see and follow, especially after he shut off its running lights. The motorcycle would be used in the bombing of the Commissioner for Jewish Affairs' office as a getaway vehicle. "It shouldn't be all that necessary to make a fast getaway," Remy explained to the group that night. "The fuse will give us ten minutes lead time so we could, in theory, be all but out of the city by the time the blast goes off."

"Nevertheless, we'll use the motorcycle to come and go," said Denis, who was in charge of the operation. Anders will pick you up here at home—with the bomb—and take you to the office. There's an alleyway down the side of the building where Anders will park and hide with his engine running while you string the fuse cord and locate the bombs where you wish them."

"What am I looking to target? And how do I get inside?"

"Liane has a key. Explain the system to us, please," Denis said to Liane. Liane—who, it turned out, was the sister of Anders—explained the record-keeping system that tracked all Jews in Paris and its environs. The records were being systematically marked up to track Jews who'd been dealt with versus Jews who remained. It was no secret they were being addressed arrondissement by arrondissement—political districts—which had led to the more well-off of the Jews being able to move from area to area and stay ahead of the SS devils, as Liane called them.

Denis said, "Let's figure where Remy needs to place his bomb. What kind of bombs, Remy?"

"I have a supply of RDX. It will create an explosion with a flash fire. If the records are microfilm, they will be gone in less than a second."

"There are both," Liane continued. "There are thick registry books containing names, addresses, spouses, and children. These books are what's used on a daily basis inside the office. Then there is microfilm which contains all of the books and more. The microfilm is kept in a safe which, I'm going to hazard, is probably fireproof."

"A perfect place to attach a shaped charge then," Remy said. "With my RDX, I will blow the walls out of any safe. Everything inside will vanish."

ON FRIDAY NIGHT AFTER DARK, CLAIRE AND REMY DOUSED THE lights in the farmhouse. They crept outside and hiked down to the end of lane, staying in the center of their walking path for orientation in the dark. Off to the west, they could see the skybursts and flareups from exploding bomb and artillery shells as the fighting raged on miles and miles away. It seemed the sky was filled with hundreds of airplanes. The buzzing and accelerating noises that planes made when they banked all but drowned out the gathering wind.

The motorcycle was upon them before they were aware it was even in the area. One minute the wife and husband were standing at the roadside pointing out war zones beneath the erupting sky, and the next minute the motorcycle was there, passing by. It turned at the next crossroads, then returned and slowed, finally stopping to take on its passenger. Remy, wearing a large knapsack containing his bombs and fuse, climbed on the motorcycle behind Anders. Claire climbed down into the sidecar, her camera held in place against her chest by a series of straps. The Exakta was made with a waist viewfinder and she planned on taking advantage of its versatility that night.

They bounced along the lane until they came to rue Henry Barbusse where they turned left or south. The wind hammered their faces and making their eyes weepy. Remy wondered what might happen if they crashed the bike—would the RDX explode in his knapsack? The truth about the high explosive was that it took another explosion to set it off, mere concussions or flame wouldn't do the job. The fuses he had coiled in his knapsack ended on all three ends with blasting caps, enough force to make the RDX explode and bring down walls and roofs.

When the road turned to avenue de Flandre just inside the city limits, they took back roads around the city until they reached rue

Royale, which they took to place de la Concorde, and then went west on avenue des Champs-Élysées until they were two blocks away from the office of the Commissioner. There, they parked in an alley and stole along the shadows until coming to the street where two other Resistance fighters were waiting with a tool to dislodge the sewer cover. They uncapped the hole in the ground and Anders, Remy, and Claire climbed inside and scurried down the ladder to the waiting walkway ten feet below. One of the Freedom fighters—a man named Herzog, went ahead of them. He switched on a powerful flashlight as they made their way beneath the Paris streets.

The whole thing was a labyrinth, a maze, turning them this way and that as they stole along the walkway. The smell was noxious; twice they had to pause momentarily while Remy and then Claire emptied their stomach contents into the slow-moving river of filth beside them. But vomiting aside, the quartet continued bravely in the dark, at times getting their feet wet up to the mid-calf line from those parts of the sewer where the walkway dipped down— at road intersections overhead—before emerging up out of the sewer contents again.

"Wait here," Herzog said at last, turning to them and raising a cautioning hand. "We've arrived."

"Where does this put us?" Anders asked.

"We're two car lengths from the Commissioner's building. Just inside the area covered by German foot patrols every five minutes. It's a small window of time, but Liane has gone ahead and is waiting inside one unlocked door. She'll take you to the registrar's office."

"Got it," Remy said. "Just let me set my bombs and goodbye to their records. Bastards!"

"Claire, ready with the camera? You're going to wait outside in a small park directly across the street. Once the bombs explode, you'll run back across the park, and a car will pick you up, a yellow Citroën. Got it?"

"We've been over this, so yes. Shoot my film then flee across the park. Yellow Citroën waiting there."

"You'll then direct the automobile to the location of your current film drop. Drop off the film and meet Anders north of the city for egress. He will return you to the cottage with Remy. We all good with this?"

"I'm good," said Claire.

"Same with me," Remy said. "But I'm getting away in the sewer system back to the way we came, correct?"

"Correct," said Herzog. "You and Anders will connect back up with your motorcycle and leave town by way you came."

"Good enough. I'm ready," replied Remy.

"Everyone?"

"Ready," confirmed Anders.

"Ready," said Claire.

Using his powerful upper body, Herzog lurched up against the overhead sewer cover and, seconds later, Claire was smelling fresh air again. She inhaled mightily as she climbed the ladder hand-over-hand, taking care not to bump her camera lens against the ladder's metal rungs as she climbed. She took just seconds to get her bearings, waiting until Herzog patted her on the back to signal it was safe to dash across the street to the park. Then she was gone.

Herzog turned and disappeared back inside the sewer and loosely replaced the cover overhead. He would be called by the others after the bomb was set.

Remy, meanwhile, was inching along the shadows cast by the target building and then scurrying up a flight of a dozen steps to the door that Liane was now holding open as she motioned them to hurry up and join her. She gently closed the door behind them and gave hugs. The group was filled with relief that they had made it inside while the German foot patrols were on the opposite side of the building. It was matter of timing, and it had gone off perfectly.

Liane would lead Remy, but Anders would remain at the door with his machine gun to prevent any patrol or watchman from coming inside until the bombs were set. If it came down to it, all of them were prepared to go up with the explosion if necessary while Anders blocked the entrance.

The main registry, books, and microfilm safe were on the first floor of the building. There were no lights, and flashlights weren't possible, so it was up to Liane to take them straightaway to the target. She led the way, hurrying and staying low so as to not cast silhouettes as they passed by exterior windows. Then they turned into a large room fronted with a long counter. She touched Remy on the shoulder and indicated he should follow her and stay close as some of the aisles back to the safe were a very tight fit to pass through. Plus there was the fear they might inadvertently trigger the alarm system and bring the Hounds of Hell down on them.

She then stood aside and pointed in the dim light. The safe was situated inside a small closet. Remy went inside and inserted his penlight into his mouth as he dropped to his knees. The small light was just enough for him to shrug out of his knapsack and begin molding the RDX to fit in the center of the two sides—the weakest points on the Merced safe, an older model of safe probably left over from World War I years. It took Remy only minutes to set his charges and run his blasting caps into the Composition C material, a gray, claylike substance that would one day be known as C4.

He then walked backward out of the closet and set another charge at a pillar directly across the aisle from the counter where the Jewish registry books were kept on a lower shelf. It was enough RDX to bring down the building. He wanted to be sure he'd take out the first floor and, at the same time, cause a flash explosion that would vaporize the Nazi records. All of this work had been preplanned from drawings with measurements provided by Liane over the past week in preparation for tonight.

"Ready?" he asked her at last. They hadn't been inside the registry for more than five minutes but his work was done. "I'm going to light off the fuses." Remy then hurried from fuse to fuse, lighting them with his silver cigarette lighter and waiting seconds until he was sure the fuse was ignited. "We've got ten minutes and counting. Get us out of here, Liane!"

Retracing their steps, Liane led them around and through various hallways until, suddenly, they had reached Anders. He was positioned just off to the side of the double entrance doors, machine gun at the ready.

"Where are they?" asked Remy.

"They are two minutes away from here, around to the first side."

"Safe?" asked Liane.

"Safe," said Anders as he cracked open the door and led them back outside. His machine gun was still at the ready. They had agreed they would shoot it out with the Germans if they were spotted, rather than allowing themselves to be captured. It was better that way.

Twenty-five meters to the left they located the manhole cover in the street and tapped it three times with a screwdriver—the signal to Herzog to open up. The cover slid up and off to the side, and the three adventurers were quickly back down inside. Herzog scaled the ladder for a last time, replacing the manhole cover overhead. Then he turned to Remy. "Time?"

"Eight minutes thirty-five-four-three-two-one seconds and counting."

"Perfect," Herzog said. He turned on his flashlight, and off they trekked the same way they had come.

"What happens if it goes off prematurely and we're still down here?" Liane wondered aloud.

Herzog, in the lead, shook his head. "The sewer will fill with water and filth, and we'll drown. Let us not tarry now."

It was enough to promote a jog, thoughts of what might happen, and then the quartet was running through the sewer, feet flying, kicking up sewer water here and there, scrambling away from the horrible possibility of death by drowning.

"Time?" Herzog called back as they neared the end of their run.

Remy shouted to him, "Three-fifty-five and counting. Get us out of here!"

At last, they arrived. The original manhole was open. Anders went up the ladder first then pulled Liane out behind him. Then came Remy, followed by Herzog, who replaced the cover then, without a word, vanished down the alley without even a farewell. The motorcycle was waiting where Anders had parked them. The trio climbed on, and off they roared down to the other end of the alley and then back onto Trochee road where they went left and blasted down three blocks, running with green traffic lights all the way. Then they were on the main road and heading north.

Claire had moved across the park and was waiting just south of the Citroën in order to maintain a clear view of the building. She had seen her comrades exit the building and knew the explosion was imminent.

Suddenly, "KA-BOOM! KA-BOOM! KA-BOOM!" went the three RDX charges, and the building was on fire, windows blowing out, alarms suddenly erupting. Claire was shooting her pictures almost from the first second and ran through a roll of film before turning and sprinting for the waiting Citroën. Someone was holding open the door as she leapt inside, and the car sped away.

A familiar voice spoke up in the backseat. "It's Jacques Marseille, Claire. We've been watching you."

"Jacques!" she cried out and gave her boss from the *Paris-Soir* a long, happy hug. "Where did you go?"

"I've been underground. When they came for my colleagues, I decided it was time to disappear. I've been running the photojournalism effort from safe houses. And you? I've been following your exploits by the pictures you've been turning in to us."

"Yes, nothing has changed. They're looking for me. I don't kid myself, Jacques. I'm dead if they find me."

"Aren't we all," said a voice from the front seat.

"Raoul?" asked Claire. "Raoul from the Second Battalion?"

"At your service, miss. I wouldn't have missed tonight for anything."

"Thank God you came for me!"

"We all have our work."

"Thank you, both of you."

By now the streets had erupted with German vehicles going the opposite direction as the Citroën, heading for the area of the explosion.

There would be a massive manhunt. What had been lost in the explosion represented days and even weeks of inscriptive listings as the Jews had appeared and announced themselves—by law—and seen their names entered into the records. Now, it was all gone, and those same Jews were again going to be able to fade back into the general population. Much had changed since they had signed up as ordered. Much had changed in that now it was known all names were being rounded up and sent by train to Auschwitz and Treblinka.

But now those records were vaporized, and the German Final Solution would be stymied, if not completely, at least long enough for the Jews of Paris to seek other lodging, other hiding places, other identities and lives.

It was done.

Except for two things. First, it would turn out that the SS was much more careful. A second cache of microfilmed records was kept offsite. The Jewish enrollment was still intact. And second, Raoul was a double agent.

Stopped for no reason at a green traffic light at the intersection of rue de Rivoli and rue du Renard, the back doors of the Citroën suddenly were thrown open and Claire and Jacques were dragged from either side of the car. They were hurried over to an SS night truck and forced inside. Two leering SS officers waited inside, carbines pointed directly at them.

"Welcome to the rest of your lives," said the larger of the two. "Short as that may be."

"You are dead, you know," said the smaller man, the lieutenant. "But first, a debrief. How are you with pain?" he asked Claire before he reversed his weapon and slammed the butt of the gun into her head.

She was knocked unconscious, slumped forward, plunging head-first onto the truck bed.

The larger man unholstered his sidearm, worked the slide, and shoved the muzzle against the side of Jacques' head. "Any last words?"

Jacques, staring straight ahead, only said, "I don't do words. I do photographs."

The man pulled the trigger, and the 9mm bullet entered Jacques head. He was dead before he hit the floor beside Claire.

"Now you don't do words or pictures," said the SS foot soldier.

"Good riddance," the lieutenant said. He spat onto the back of Jacques' head. "Pig."

"Where are we going?"

"To the camps. She goes to the camps."

"Then Auschwitz with her."

"Yes, then Auschwitz. First, they will get the names they want. Then she will be transported to Poland."

"She'll never last that long."

"Never."

Claire stirred on the floor. Hearing voices, she kept her eyes closed and didn't move again. She had heard—had she heard a gunshot?

She decided there had been a gunshot. Was it her?

No, it wasn't her. It was Jacques. Tears filled her eyes.

But still she didn't move.

31

C laire was arrested in a trap by Marshal Philippe Pétain's police, with other Resistance activists who had been active in the attack on the Commissioner for Jewish Affair's building. Among them were Jacques Marseille, Georges Politzer, Georges Solomon, and Arthur Dallidet, all of whom were shot by the Nazis, most of them at Fort Mont-Valérien.

Claire was interned at the Dépôt de la Préfecture, then was secretly moved to La Santé Prison. Here she stayed until August when she was transferred to Romainville, an internment camp under German authority. Like her companions, she was deported to Auschwitz-Birkenau via the internment camp of Compiègne in the convoy of January 24, 1943. This convoy of 230 women, Resistance members, communists, and Gaullist wives of Resistance members, was illustrated in *La Marseillaise*; only 49 of these 230 women arrived alive at the camps.

Arguably, she was among the lucky ones who survived long enough to make it to Auschwitz. Equally arguable, she was not one of the lucky ones for she did survive and made it to Auschwitz.

Maybe survival was the less acceptable fate, she thought as she rode inside the cold and drafty cattle car on her way through Poland.

She was surrounded by a crushing mass of bodies, many of whom were still standing after hundreds of miles of freezing days and nights, gray skies mixed with rain, sleet, and snow, and a hollowed-out feeling in the soul that said all is lost, survival is futile. Some took their lives inside the train car by wrapping one sleeve of their shirt around their neck, the other through the slats of the cattle car and then slumping forward. No one made any effort to prevent the suicides. Everyone understood, especially the elderly, who would die upon arrival at the concentration camp.

There were no toilets, no water, and not even a board to lie down on at night. Excrement piled up in all four corners. Some among them passed out from the smell and filth which began flowing across the cattle car's floorboards. But the cattle car had seen all this before, both with animals and with humans and it was not deterred from reaching its destination in the heart of Poland.

On the sixth day, after layovers and unexpected stops and starts and loading and unloading, the train pulled in through the gates of Auschwitz concentration camp. The weather had flipped back to below-freezing temperatures and freezing rain, yet everywhere she looked people were dressed in paper-thin cotton shirts and pants.

Claire smelled the place before she saw it as they arrived at 3:20 a.m. in the midst of blowing snow and icy winds. Of course the slats on the cattle car in which she was riding were open to the elements and, as usual, there were deaths around the outside of the rectangle of people, usually the old and infirm freezing to death. Those cadavers remained on the train while the living disembarked among lunging, furious dogs and lowly Wehrmacht guards with whips and canes driving the refugees down a long, sandy path toward what appeared to be a barracks. Hours passed while she waited in line. More Jews fell and died where they had been standing minutes before. Soon, the sun was rising behind a thin layer of gray clouds, its rays struggling to pierce the gloom below.

———

CLAIRE ARRIVED AT AUSCHWITZ WITH THE 230 FRENCH WOMEN from two freight cars. She had learned some of their names. Among them were Danielle Casanova, Mal Politzer, and Helene Solomon. There were some elderly and some very young. But for the most part they were housewives and students of a young age.

Upon arrival, they were taken to the Birkenau Camp, a section of the Auschwitz Camp. It was situated in the middle of a great plain which was frozen. During that part of the journey they had to drag their luggage. As they passed through the gate, they knew only too well how slender their chances were that they would come out again, for they had already met columns of living skeletons going to work; and as they entered, they sang "Le Marseillaise" to keep up their courage.

They were led to a large shed, then to the disinfecting station. Their heads were shaved and their registration numbers were tattooed on the left forearm. Then they were taken into a large room for a steam bath and a cold shower. In spite of the fact that they were naked, all this took place in the presence of SS men and women. They were then given clothing which was soiled and torn, a cotton dress and jacket of the same material.

After that they were taken to the block where they were to live. There were no beds but only wooden bunks, measuring two-by-two meters, and there nine of them had to sleep the first night without any mattress or blanket. They remained in blocks of this kind for several months. They could not sleep all night because every time one of the nine moved she disturbed the whole row. This happened unceasingly because they were all sick or injured or both.

At 5:30 in the morning the shouting of the guards woke them up, and with cudgel blows they were driven from their bunks to go to roll call. Nothing in the world could release them from going to the roll call; even those who were dying had to be dragged there. They had to stand there in rows of five until dawn, that is, seven or eight o'clock in the morning in winter; and when there was a fog, sometimes until noon. Then the prisoners would start on their way to work.

For roll call they were lined up in rows of five; and they waited until daybreak until the Aufseherinnen—the German women guards in uniform—came to count them. They had cudgels and they beat them at random, no provocation required.

32

W hen, six hours after the attack at the Commissioner for
Jewish Activities building, Claire still wasn't back at the
cottage, Remy knew it was time to grab what few things he could
out of the cottage and disappear. He called the 2nd Battalion for
help, and a car was sent to pick him up. The driver and his
passenger took Remy to a safe house just north of Paris and
dropped him there. It was a very old, thick-walled villa that looked
out over a pool on which swans paddled, a place where Remy had
his own room with bathroom and privacy. He then launched into a
hunt for Claire with the rest of the 2nd Battalion's help.

The word was put on the street and, within hours, they had their
answer from sources inside the SS: Claire had been captured in an
undercover operation and taken away. No one knew where she
was. Remy was told by High Command that continuing to pursue
her was hopeless at that point because the SS would have her
under lock and key, given how well-known she and her photographic work had become around the free world. So he broke off
his search and turned to helping the Resistance in the best way he

could. His bomb-making abilities were now well-known and he was in high demand, which he obliged in every request for help.

And Remy began having deep conversations with R.P. Langierre, one of the general officers of the Resistance, a man left with one arm and one leg after suffering at the hands of Nazi medical experiment doctor, Joseph Mengele. He'd escaped, narrowly, with his life and was dedicated to fighting the Nazis with every last cell in his body. He met several times with Remy in the weeks and months following Claire's capture.

"Think of this, Remy," Langierre challenged him. "What can you do now to prepare for the world of the post-war?"

"How do you mean?"

"Will the Allies punish those Germans who committed these war crimes? God knows they will. And how will that happen? Will it be summary judgment and execution at gunpoint? Or will there be trials in courtrooms to show the world the Allies are fair and intent on giving due process, even to the murderers?"

"I would have to say there will be trials," Remy answered. "But how does that involve me?"

"Well, how many war criminals do you know?"

"Counting myself and what I did to the Jews before? Dozens."

"Do you know their names?"

"Some, I do."

"Then write them down. There's your start. The Allies are going to be searching for the likes of you, German soldiers willing to help bring the perpetrators to justice."

"I know so many. Some of them are friends."

"They can be friends but also be murderers. Do not muddy the lines."

"I'll start writing them down. Can I bring you the list and talk some more?"

"Certainly. In fact, I'm going to appoint you Commissioner of War Crimes. Your job will be to collect from all sources such names and ranks. We have members to be interviewed, and we have confidential sources who will help. Your commission is to stop at nothing. Be ready for the Allies when the time comes to strike! Don't let us down, Lieutenant Schildmann!"

"I'll do it thoroughly, and I won't miss any names given to me. What if I investigate the more famous criminals? The most wretched leaders? So that they can be tracked as the Nazis lose the war?"

"That would be a top idea. Enlist others from our group and make assignments. Track the Goerings, the Hesses, Himmlers, the Hitlers. Let no one get away."

"I accept this commission, General Langierre. Now I know my true purpose."

"Just be ready. There will be trials, and we want front row seats."

"I will start the book of crimes with my own participation. If I make my own crimes known, and become willing to suffer my own consequences, then I have nothing to fear after that. Yes, today I'll start with my story."

"Remember, all the names you can enter in your book. We need to be ready for the Allies' prosecutors."

"I'm on my way, General. Thank you."

"Godspeed, Lieutenant Schildmann. Your courage is remarkable."

"My trespasses are many. I have only my shame and fear to blame. Now I open the book."

"Godspeed."

With that, Remy returned to his room back at the villa, taking with him a thick book of accounts that he had labeled, *War Crimes: Volume 1.*

Two days after, he had written out his own war zone actions and shortcomings. He had robbed and dispossessed Jews of their homes, their property, and their lives. He had transgressed. Even though he was frightened and at times hated himself beyond words, he put it down on paper nonetheless.

He even considered taking his confessions to a minister but decided against it as too risky. No one could be trusted at this point in France, not even the cloth; collaborators lurked around every corner. So he could turn only inward for forgiveness. He did that, in thought and prayer, shedding tears late into the nights and early in the mornings of three straight days. At last, he was cried out. At last, his self-hate lessened its hold.

Four days into his new assignment, Remy began listing the names in his rouster squad, the squad that had spent almost a year driving Jews from their homes, forcing them to load into trucks for transport to the camps around Paris. Selling their furniture and stealing their jewelry and precious items in order to line their own pockets. The first man, Sergeant Kirk Heinrich, a high-energy non-commissioned officer from Heidelberg. Where was Heinrich now? Most likely he, with the rest of his squad, would still be under arms, under the flag.

But of all the men Remy served with, he had been closest to Heinrich. They had shared food and water on the fields of war and food and drink in the clubs and cafes of Paris. They had become friends—no, more than mere friends. They had become like family. They might one day hate each other, but they would never forsake each other. So Heinrich came to mind, and Remy decided it wouldn't hurt to make discreet inquiries. Maybe Heinrich would be ready to tell what he had seen and done. There might be others from his squad, too. But where to start looking? He couldn't go to any war offices or army bases—he would be arrested and shot without any due process. He couldn't go to their homes; they all lived everywhere and nowhere. This wasn't home for them. This was a foreign land where none of them had roots. So how did he contact Kirk Heinrich? Was there another way?

Remy remembered the sisters he and Heinrich had taken dancing, dining, and drinking. But that had been over two years ago. Would there still be any contact between the women and the sergeant? After rolling it around in his head, Remy decided he would pay the girls a visit. They might be collaborators and they might not, but they would let him know either way. They owed him that. They were Schmidts, Sina and Lyn, and they had shared everything with the dashing young soldiers, Heinrich and Schildmann.

He remembered the nightclub where they sometimes danced. On Friday night next, he dressed in his most inauspicious suit of clothes and prepared to attend there. It was a long shot and a risky one, but nothing good had ever come from being fear-based. In fact, fear is what had kept him under his father's thumb and what had gotten him conscripted into the German army in the first place. He terribly regretted that he had ever just come right out and told his father no. Well, those days were past.

He was going to *Les Deux Magots* on Friday night and that was that. He would find Sina and Lyn, and they would point him to Heinrich. Then he would net his first cooperating witness.

His witness panel would increase by one.

33

The work at Auschwitz consisted of clearing demolished houses, road building, and especially the draining of marsh land. That was by far the hardest work, for all day long they had their feet in the water and there was the danger of being sucked down. It frequently happened that they had to pull out a comrade who had sunk in up to the waist.

One morning at 3:30 the whole camp was awakened and sent out onto the plain whereas normally the roll call was at 3:30 but inside the camp. They remained out in front of the camp until five in the afternoon, in the snow, without any food. Then when the signal was given they had to go through the door one by one, and they were struck in the back with a cudgel, each one of them, in order to make them run. Those who could not run, either because they were too old or too ill were caught by a hook and taken to Block 25, the "waiting block" for the gas chamber. On that day ten of the French women of their convoy were thus caught and taken to Block 25.

Block 25, which was the anteroom of the gas chamber, was well known to all because at that time they had been transferred to Block 26 and their windows opened on the yard of Number 25. The rate of mortality in that block was even more terrible than elsewhere because, having been condemned to death, they received food or drink only if there was something left in the cans in the kitchen; which means that very often they went for several days without a drop of water.

One of their companions, Annette Epaux, a young woman of thirty, passing the block one day, was overcome with pity for those women who moaned from morning till night in all languages, "Drink. Drink. Water!" She came back to their block to get a little herbal tea, but as she was passing it through the bars of the window she was seen by the Aufseherin, who took her by the neck and threw her into Block 25. Two days later they saw her on the truck which was taking the internees to the gas chamber. She had her arms around another French woman, old Line Porcher, and when the truck started moving she cried, "Think of my little boy, if you ever get back to France." Then they started singing "Le Marseillaise."

Another cause of death was the problem of shoes. In the snow and mud of Poland leather shoes were completely destroyed at the end of a week or two. Therefore their feet were frozen and covered with sores. Claire quickly learned she had to sleep with her muddy shoes on, lest they be stolen. When the time came to get up for roll call cries of anguish could be heard: "My shoes have been stolen." Then she had to wait until the whole block had been emptied to look under the bunks for odd shoes. Sometimes one found two shoes for the same foot, or one shoe and one sabot. After having her shoes removed from her feet while she slept, she went to roll call wearing sabots but it was an additional torture for work because sores formed on her feet which quickly became infected for lack of care. Many of her companions who went to the

Revier or infirmary for sores on their feet and legs and never came back.

Those assembled at roll call without shoes were immediately taken to Block 25. They were gassed for any reason whatsoever. Their conditions were moreover absolutely appalling. Although they were crowded 800 in a block and could scarcely move, the Jewish internees were 1,500 to a block of similar dimensions, so that many of them could not sleep or even lie down during the whole night.

Generally, the SS economized on many of their own personnel by using internees for watching the camp; SS only supervised. This happened to Claire many times, as she retained her health—for the most part. By accusation and terror the SS succeeded in making human beasts of them. During this time, the continued assaults resulted in Claire losing all sense of identity until she was going through her days as if sleepwalking. The SS beat beat just like everyone else, no matter her role. There was no difference.

The system employed by the SS of degrading human beings to the utmost by terrorizing them and causing them through fear to commit acts which made them ashamed of themselves, resulted in Claire being no longer human. This was what they wanted. It took a great deal of courage to resist this atmosphere of terror and corruption and, as for Claire, she became unable to resist anything.

Punishments were meted out by the SS leaders, men and women. The nature of the punishments were physical. One of the most usual punishments was fifty blows with a stick on the loins. They were administered with a machine which Claire saw, a swinging apparatus manipulated by an SS. There were also endless roll calls day and night, or gymnastics; flat on the belly, get up, lie down, up, down, for hours, and anyone who fell was beaten unmercifully and taken to Block 25.

At Auschwitz there was a brothel for the SS and also one for the male internees of the staff who were called "Kapo." Moreover, when the SS needed servants, they came accompanied by the Oberaufseherin, that is, the woman commandant of the camp, to make a choice during the process of disinfection. They would point to a young girl, whom the Oberaufseherin would take out of the ranks. They would look her over and make jokes about her physique; and if she was pretty, and they liked her, they would hire her as a maid with the consent of the Oberaufseherin. Claire was put into the brothel at one time for a period of nine months. During her time there she became pregnant several times and suffered miscarriages and underwent crude abortions.

Whenever a convoy of Jews came, a selection was made; first the old men and women, then the mothers and the children were put into trucks together with the sick or those whose constitution appeared to be delicate. These people all went immediately to the gas chambers. The guards took in only the young women and girls as well as the young men who were sent to the men's camp.

At this selection also, they picked out women in good health between the ages of twenty and thirty, who were sent to the experimental block. Medical experiments were performed to discover the most effective way of sterilizing an entire population and wiping it from the face of the earth in one generation.

There was also, in the spring of 1944, a special block for twins. It was during the time when large convoys of Hungarian Jews— about 700,000—arrived. Dr. Joseph Mengele, who was carrying out the experiments, kept back from each convoy twin children and twins in general, regardless of their age, so long as both were present.

Claire was an eyewitness to the arrival of the trains. A side line took the train practically right up to the gas chamber; and the stopping place, about 100 meters from the gas chamber, was right opposite Claire's block though, of course, separated by two rows of barbed wire. Consequently, she saw the unsealing of the cars and the soldiers letting men, women, and children out of them. All these people were unaware of the fate awaiting them. They were merely upset at being separated, but they did not know that they were going to their death. To render their welcome more pleasant at this time, an orchestra composed of internees, all young and pretty girls dressed in little white blouses and navy blue skirts, played during the selection, at the arrival of the trains, gay tunes such as "The Merry Widow," and the "Barcarolle" from "The Tales of Hoffman." They were then informed that this was a labor camp and since they were not brought into the camp, they saw only the small platform surrounded by flowering plants. Naturally, they could not realize what was in store for them.

Those selected for the gas chamber, were escorted to a red-brick building. The red brick building bore the letters "Baden," or "Baths." There, they were made to undress and given a towel before they went into the so-called shower room.

Claire watched this process repeat day and night. The trains never stopped arriving, the band never stopped playing, the march to the showers never slowed, never varied.

There came a time when she could no longer watch. When the trains arrived she merely looked away.

What else was she to do?

34

One year later, Claire was ready to die. She had lived in hell —they were all sure of it—for a full year.

She had recently been in quarantine, where conditions were vastly better than in Auschwitz general prisoner population, the street address of hell. Any remnants of the child she had once clung to inside her soul were tattered and shed. She had been beaten, starved, kicked, savaged, frozen, raped, forced to work on broken feet, suffered typhus, blood poisoning and forced abortions. Only a shell and a tiny ember of the old spirit survived. She was about to return to Auschwitz inside the wire when, during processing, as she was about to enter the camp, she was stopped by a guard.

She was asked, in German, whether she had any gold teeth or gold jewelry. She answered back in perfect German that she had neither. Whereupon the guard, a young SS soldier in his winter gray uniform, gray overcoat, jackboots, and pitched hat, stood and called to an officer. Claire could hear most of their conversation, which basically centered on the fact she had excellent German and they could use her for work. Finally, the SS officer nodded and turned away; she was pulled out of the line of new arrivals and ordered, in German, to follow close upon the heels of the officer.

She followed the man down a long inner path, leading beyond a dozen barracks, past various structures with chimneys and hooded masts, then down through a gated garden where blackbirds scratched and pecked at the ground, into an islet of nice houses with staff cars parked in the driveways and a grocery or commissary, she wasn't sure, at the far end. The sign said *Supermarkt*; women with bags, evidently of groceries, were leaving singly and in pairs, smiling and laughing out on their lark. Claire guessed that if there were children in the compound, they must have been in a classroom some place nearby, for she saw no children anyplace she looked. Midway down the main street, along the right-hand side, were a set of long, low buildings with blackout curtains and white smoke streaming chimneys. She recognized this as the administration building, the heart of the entire camp, based partly on what she'd seen coming in as it was lighted at night. She saw many officers coming and going in their perfect uniforms, sparkling boots, black patent holsters, and chauffeured cars. It was a high activity zone; not a rock or a stone was out of place, everything trim and recently painted. She wondered how such a place could exist as this compound inside the concentration camp in view of what was actually going on here. *Women shopping in the food store while three-hundred yards away other women and children are being put to death in the well-publicized German gas chambers? How could that possibly be allowed to happen any place on earth? How could these sane, normal-seeming women abide such a thing? Aren't any of them asking questions? Aren't any of them complaining that the place is detrimental to the children, given what they all know is going on here?*

These thoughts flashed through her mind as she followed the officer. Then he abruptly turned left and led them up a snow-covered path to an imposing, but not grand, two-story house. There was a hedge across the front yard, there was a low stone fence, there were two dogs in the yard, one white and one black, sniffing and barking as people went by. The place looked totally normal and sensible to Claire. Up the path they walked, up to the porch where, coming to an abrupt halt and pulling himself perfectly upright, the officer spun around and said to her, "My name is Sigmund Schlösser. I am the second-in-command of this entire camp. You have been selected to help in my house. My daughters need help with their German verbs and you have perfect German. You are their new teacher."

She wanted to blurt out, "Colonel Schlösser, I'm not a teacher!" but she didn't, instead realizing that if she interfered with this last-second chance of survival, she would likely be sent to the head of the line outside the shower room of Block 25 and forced to enter with the next ones. She kept her mouth and said nothing for several moments, then, "I am a student of German. How lucky for them all! I will be a wonderful teacher for your children, Colonel."

"What is your name?"

"Claire Schildmann."

"Is your father in the German army?"

"My father was, but he died in the Battle of Bruges at the start of the war. He was decorated a hero." She was lying and praying the Colonel would never check her story.

"And your mother?"

"My mother is a German physician."

"Why are you here?"

"I wrote articles in support of the Jews."

"Do you still support the Jews?"

"I support the people of France and Germany."

"But you didn't answer my question. Would you support Jews knowing they were bad for Germany?"

She paused. Warning signs were flashing. She did not—could not —go back to the camp. Yet she could not give up the final shred of Claire she had left. She could not denounce Jews or she would be gone in a puff of existential smoke. She read Camus and Nietzsche before the war. Along with Remy, she had dissected their approach. The French and the Germans had them in common.

She plunged ahead. "Here is how the *Übermensch* would answer your question. It requires one to say, 'Jews are bad for Germany. But Germany is good. Therefore, Jews are not German.' You can see the weakness, Colonel. So I see my Jews. They are not bad for Germany and neither are they good for Germany. They just are: some good, some bad, no different from anyone else."

"You know your Nietzsche," he said. He might just as easily have sent her off to be gassed just then. It was a chance she had taken, yet she had no choice if she were to keep one atom alive that was Claire.

"I have only myself today, Colonel. Nietzsche failed me long ago."

"But you have a German mind. We are at war in a foreign land so accommodations must be made. My girls will benefit from your teaching."

"It would be my honor to teach them."

He allowed a small smile. "Then, you will like it here, Fräu. Now you must come inside and meet everyone. After that, you will be shown to your room. You will be expected to de-louse three days in a row, and you will visit the Reich camp doctor and dentist so they can be sure you have no communicable diseases and no gold teeth."

"What would happen if I had gold teeth?"

"You're a German girl?"

"I am," she lied.

"Nothing would happen to your gold teeth." He laughed. "Maybe a good cleaning. There's a rarity in wartime."

"Indeed. That would be good. I will go and do as your say, Herr Kommandant."

"Not yet the kommandant. Not quite yet. But who knows?" He laughed and pieces of white spittle flew into her face. She kept her lips tightly shut against the storm and reminded herself she would need another two feet of separation when conversing with the colonel. He also seemed to appreciate that she joined in with his simple attempts at humor. His humor was the kind of inanity that powerful men express then look at lesser men and laugh so they would laugh too. That was this man, she knew already.

He turned and started climbing the steps, his daughters' new German teacher close on his heels.

35

Nonna and Necci were the Colonel's twins, aged nine, nice enough kids but lacking even rudimentary skills in reading and writing their native tongue. Their German was pre-school in vocabulary and spelling; Claire saw huge room for improvement, which, if anything, guaranteed a long term of employment for her. She met them the next morning after she had arrived, at breakfast, where, she learned, she would be eating with the family.

"Usually, the help eats in the kitchen," the colonel announced at the table. "But Claire Schildmann will be treated as one of the family. After all, her father died a hero's death, a German officer, giving his life for blood and soil. She eats right here!"

Which suited Claire just fine. That way she could monitor the family's emotional health, know the father's concerns, and learn to talk with the mother in the way grown women talked. Sometimes they would find themselves alone and it was everything Claire could do not to ask if the woman how she lived in that hell of Auschwitz. She didn't dare ask such a thing, however; if it got back to the colonel, she would be taken back and thrown into the gas chambers. So she learned to hold her tongue, to be circumspect in dress, attitude, and conversation.

One night, after the house had gone to bed and Claire was in her basement bedroom preparing to sleep, a knock came on her door. She slipped into her robe and opened the door. There he stood, yet in full uniform, a newly lighted cigarette dangling from two fingers, the remaining fingers tapping her door frame. He was impatient and upset. She drew the door fully open and stood to the side. He entered without asking and took the seat at her desk. That left the bed for her to sit on, which she did. He crossed one booted lower leg across the other knee.

"Now, where were we?" he asked in a tangential thought that left her far behind.

"Uh, where were we when?"

"When we came here the first day. When we spoke before coming inside the house."

"Where were we? You told me I would be teaching German to Nonna and Necci."

"No, no, farther back. Why were you brought here with the Jews? You're surely not a secret Jew?"

"No, I told you, my father fought and died in the German army."

"I've done some looking through our records. Headquarters cannot find any Schildmanns who were officers who died at Bruges. Are you sure it was Bruges? Not the Ardennes? Not Roye?"

"No, it was Bruges. I can't vouch for the accuracy of the Wehrmacht's records. It's wartime, Colonel."

"Most important question, Claire: why were you sent here? Your file says you were taking pictures the night the Commissioner of Jewish Affairs' office was bombed. Why were you there?"

"I was on assignment from the newspaper."

"Assignment, why?"

"My editor had word there was going to be trouble in the Commissioner's office at some point. I was on duty that night."

"It was below freezing and you were waiting in a park?"

"I am very dedicated, Colonel. Look at the progress I'm making with the children."

"Who sent you here? Your file jacket says the SS arrested you for being a Resistance fighter who plotted with the others to bomb the office. But you never had a hearing, so there is that question mark about it. I'm giving you the benefit of the doubt because there is that question mark."

"It turned out my editor was in the Resistance, I have been told. But I was unaware of all that. I was just a staff photographer with no special skills."

"Not so, Fräu. I have learned your photographs have appeared in magazines, newspapers, and journals around the world when your last name was Vallant. You have even been known as Lumiere. You're quite well thought of. Even famous. And yet you're here, teaching German to my children? Why did your pictures appear in the pages of the Allies' publications? Why not in the German press, in German publications?"

"My father was stationed in Paris. It's where I went to school before the war. It was only natural that I would get a job in Paris while my family was living there. We were very close. We didn't live apart."

"I see. That could explain that, I suppose. Yes, that explains that."

"We were never political. We were military, yes, but we also had to work, so I was employed by the French newspaper. It meant nothing except it was my work. I knew that someday we would return to Germany and my skills and experience would transfer. It was how my father intended. He demanded his children work and help the family so I was working. Nothing more was intended. We were German and German army."

"Very good. Like I said, I'm giving you the benefit of the doubt because you had no hearing. Without a hearing there is no guilt unless I view it with my own eyes. I have not done that. You are on probation, Fräu Schildmann. Do not let me down. My girls love you, their language is improving enormously, their mother and I are very pleased. Now off to bed and think no more of this. I'm satisfied."

"Thank you."

"That doesn't mean I won't be watching."

"No, of course not."

"So sleep well. Don't let me down."

"Of course not. Good night, Herr Kommandant."

This time he didn't argue. SS Kommandant Rudolph Höss was the only thing between Schlösser and the real title. The war made massive changes every day. Maybe tomorrow Höss would be a memory and Auschwitz would be his, Colonel Sigmund Schlösser's. That would be difficult though because Rudolph Höss had already supervised the extermination of one million Jews. Hitler would never replace one who had served with such honor.

There was the real reason for his suspicions about Claire. He made a mental note to himself. When she had his girls up to reading and writing at their grade level, he would make a change and find a different teacher.

This one? She would be fed to the gas chamber with the rest of the Resistance. Allied publications featuring her pictures and words?

Damn her to hell, anyway.

36

She remembered Remy, six feet tall, blond hair with a wave, light blue eyes, straight white teeth, a strong jaw, a slightly enlarged chest from weightlifting and running long distances. She remembered him but realized the images of him were fading.

Claire tried to force her daydreams. She struggled to see Remy, going inside her heart to find him in those times during the day when the twins were reading or writing quietly by themselves. During such times, her mind could wander, could plan future lessons, and could pretend to meet with her Remy. In truth, she had no idea whether he was even alive. She had no idea about Lima in America. Was she safe there? Were there Nazis in America? She fully expected to see none of them ever again.

In the middle of all this, Pietor Berglund walked right into her life, the perfect German soldier—her Remy—walking, and talking. Which just proved how desperately she missed her husband: she was inventing him now.

They met at half-past five one Wednesday evening when Colonel

Schlösser was entertaining junior officers over Wednesday cocktails and dinner. It just so happened that on this particular Wednesday, Ilyana, one of the usual waitstaff, had taken ill and the kitchen was short-handed. When asked, Claire happily jumped right in. She'd never attended a German dinner party of SS officers and wouldn't miss the opportunity to do so now for anything. So she donned the black serving dress and starched white collar of the Schlösser household waitstaff, listened to her orders from the head waiter, and promised an exceptional performance.

First up was the taking of drink orders. She circulated among the guests and took the orders five at a time before returning to the sidebar where another of the staff was furiously mixing drinks and pushing them onto the bar for serving. This process went on for thirty minutes. Toward the end, just before dinner was announced, she approached Pietor Berglund, who was sandwiched between Schlösser himself and a major by the name of Hanzel. The young lieutenant was immediately interested in speaking to her about more than just his drink refill. He stepped away from the two superior officers and touched her on the shoulder as she was making her way back to the bar. "A word?" he said simply. She turned around.

"Yes? Did you change your mind about your drink?"

"No, I changed my mind about talking to you. Do I know you, Fräulein?"

"I'm still new here and don't know many people. But I remember faces and yours isn't familiar. How can I help?"

"By going to the movies with me this Friday. How would you feel about that?"

"They would never let me go."

"Why not? You're not Jewish."

"But I'm a prisoner."

He smiled. "The Colonel already said you could accompany me. He likes me."

"I don't know you," she said, feeling her skin tingle as she realized he was actually interested in her. Her initial thought was that maybe she could use him to get information for the Resistance but she was out of touch with the Resistance. If she were to accompany him to the movies, it would have to be because she might learn useful information about the camp, about conditions, maybe even ideas for escape. So, she took him in and was instantly swept off her feet—she led him to believe, never forgetting for an instant that he was, on the bottom line, the enemy. And she wasn't about to do anything but use the enemy anyway she could. Still, there were the eyes, the perfect skin and handsome smile. She felt her resolve weakening because she was overall exhausted anyway. The camp, the deceit, the terrible fear of death lurking and waiting to grab her at any moment—all of it had taken its toll. What could it hurt to go see one movie if she might learn something useful? After all, wasn't that her true motive, to learn useful information? Even Colonel Schlösser approved.

"You don't know me," he agreed, "but nobody knows anybody at first. That's how people meet and begin going out, Fräulein. The first risk, I call it."

"I can ask Colonel Schlösser."

"The Colonel said it would be okay to ask you out. I approached him about it thirty minutes ago when I first saw you."

She felt herself losing whatever antipathy she had promised to maintain against the enemy. Then, it was gone, and she heard herself saying, "I think it would be good for me to go to the movie with you. I haven't been out since coming here."

"Are you a prisoner? You're not Jewish."

"I'm a teacher. I teach German to the Colonel's daughters."

"So you're not a prisoner."

"You'd have to ask the Colonel about that. Much has changed since I was first brought to Auschwitz."

"Brought here against your will? You were arrested?"

"I was. But it was a mistake," she hurried to add, feeling uncomfortably defensive. "There was no hearing for me."

"Ahhh, now I see. It's a gray area you occupy, then. I'll be here to pick you up at six on Friday night. We'll go early and get dinner."

"Wait. What do you do?" If he were involved in death dealing, there was no possible way she would see him. She needed to know.

"I'm a doctor. I run the infirmary."

"Do you treat Jews?"

"Does it make a difference?"

"Yes, it makes a difference."

"I treat the Jews who are brought to me. These will be people doing administrative tasks."

"All right, then."

"The restaurant is good for you?"

"Yes, it's fine."

There was only one restaurant on the entire compound. Realizing that, and considering where she was for a moment, she almost changed her mind about going. How could she enjoy herself when five-hundred meters away people were dying day and night? But she remembered that she was of no use to them just teaching. Perhaps this would open into some kind of opportunity to do some real good for the real prisoners. She kept her resolve and said dinner sounded wonderful. Then she continued on to place and distribute the next drink order she'd taken.

She helped serve the meal that night and was exhausted when, two hours later, the twenty diners had all been fed, the cognac and cigars passed around, and the dishes and dinnerware all cleared away. Now the men had broken up into five small groups and were dealing cards and making bets on poker hands. At that point, Claire was relieved of her duties, the rest of it being anticlimactic in a way. She returned to her room and took a long, hot bath.

Thirty minutes later, she stepped from the bathtub and walked in front of her full-length mirror. She was a skeleton. Even while she'd been at the Colonel's house there were few snacks as the help didn't have free access to the kitchen so the occasional treats never made it her way. Plus, her appetite hadn't returned. That was part of it. Also, she was full of worry. She plotted and worried herself sick day and night, trying to come up with a plan to help the Jews—*to do something for them*. But she could come up with nothing.

She left the mirror and slipped into her nightgown and climbed upon her bed. Time to read. She thought she would continue with the American, Hemingway, as she was loving his books. The colonel had allowed her to borrow from the camp's small library and, while Hemingway wasn't on the approved list, the librarian, herself a French woman, kept a few books in her private room. One of them was Hemingway.

That night, for the first time since her capture, Claire began thinking about escape. She was doing no one any good in captivity as there was no opportunity to use her photography and no opportunity to join with Resistance activities. Or was there? She began wondering whether there was any kind of Resistance among the prisoners. She had been so wrapped up in her own situation that she really hadn't looked up to that point. But now it was time.

37

F riday night, December 1942, Auschwitz, Poland, the Colonel was hosting a Christmas dinner party. Again, Claire had offered to help with serving the meal and drinks, more out of a sense of possibility than a requirement put to her by Colonel Schlösser. She wore the little black dress, flat, comfortable shoes, and the starched white collar of the serving staff. Though the concentration camp was remote, about forty miles west of Krakow, the facilities, clothes, furnishings, and dinnerware were all the highest quality Poland had to offer. The theory was that the mass murderers, in executing such a key part of Hitler's Final Solution, should have the finest of everything. Hence, the movie theater, the restaurant, the library, the commissary, the bowling alley, and the community hall were dances were held for the working soldiers and overseen by the officers and their wives. There were also two beer halls for after-hours tippling and darts and brotherhood among the soldiers who were making the mass murders happen.

Claire had just served the second round of pre-dinner cocktails and was heading back to the bar when she heard a voice, a familiar voice, say over her left shoulder, in perfect German, "Fräulein, would you please pick out another cognac for me?" She turned around and was stunned to see seated on the sofa, between two aging SS officers, none other than her sister, long-lost Esmée. Claire was stunned. Esmée was smiling solicitously at her, fighting to stay in role so that her connection to her sister wasn't betrayed. Claire immediately understood: no one could ever know of their relationship as it would only give the Germans leverage against both of them when that time came, as it always did with the Nazis. Nevertheless, tears flowed into her eyes, and it was all Claire could do not to cry out and run to her sister.

"I will pick up a fresh cognac, yes Fräulein," Claire managed to say.

"And could you direct me to the ladies' room?"

"Certainly, just follow me, please, Fräulein."

Esmée followed Claire down a long hallway. The restroom for the main floor of the house was on the left, across from the master bedroom. Esmée went inside. Claire looked both ways, saw no one coming, and slipped in behind her.

They instantly collapsed into one another and began weeping and crying with joy.

Then, "What—what—how—we were so afraid you were dead!"

"And I was so afraid for you, dear Claire. What has become of mother and father and the boys?"

"They have gone to America. With Lima, my daughter." Claire waited for that to sink in, and then Esmée burst into tears.

Esmée leaned into Claire, holding her tight. "I was taken captive by that horrible Schlösser. And now you work for him."

"And what about you? Why are you here tonight?" asked Claire of Esmée.

Esmée said, "He's dreadfully confused, that one. He has me confused with a daughter who died. He's taken me to replace her in his life."

"Does he—bother you?"

"No, never. He's never laid a hand on me. In fact, he's killed other men he perceived as bothering me. Everyone's terrified of him; no one dares look at me."

"I'm teaching German to his twins."

"So you're living here in his house?"

"I am."

"Sweet Jesus," said Esmée. "I live across the road in a block-house set aside for women working as clerks in the adminis-tration."

"What do you do there?"

"Mainly order supplies from Berlin. It takes huge amounts of food and coats and guns and bullets to keep this place going."

"What a horrible job, feeding and clothing these snakes. I'm sorry you have to do that."

"They're not so bad to me," Esmée said. "I'm well-fed and fairly happy."

Claire was taken aback. "Happy? How can my sister be happy, knowing what they're doing here?"

"I just leave that up to the French army. Or maybe the Americans and Soviets. That's way more than I can think about."

"But you should be feeling miserable about it," said the older sister to the younger.

"There you go, dear sister, telling me what to feel. Nothing much has changed in all this time."

"You're my sister. I would die for you, Esmée. Someone has to look out for you. On the day they took you away, did they hurt you then?"

"At first I was tethered to a chain with two others prisoners. But then the colonel interviewed me and commented on my perfect German—thank God for mother making us learn the language. He then found out I was only sixteen, and that's when he realized his daughter would've been my age. From that moment on, I could do no wrong. I worked in a triage station that became a field hospital and now is a huge complex the Germans have built to treat their injured. They have long-term care facilities there."

"I was captured the night we blew up the office of the Commissioner for Jewish Affairs in Paris. They made a trap for me, and I walked right into it. They put me in the Paris camps, moved me around, and then sent me here to Auschwitz. I was about to go into the gas chamber when mother's German saved me, and I was brought here. Ever since, I've been teaching the girls their own language. Have you heard about any of the others of the Resistance?"

Just then, a knock came on the door. "Fräulein," called a gentle woman's voice, "are you about finished in there?"

Claire answered, "I'm in here helping a guest who became ill. We'll be coming out momentarily as soon as I clean up the facilities."

"Take your time, please," came the reply.

Claire turned and ran water into the wash basin then flushed the toilet twice.

"Are you feeling better now?" she asked Esmée in a sing-song voice for the benefit of the woman outside the door.

"I'm doing much better. Thank you for cleaning up after me, Fräulein," Esmée sang out.

"I will see you again soon," whispered Claire. She then spoke loudly, "Happy to help."

The two sisters then opened the door, and Esmée greeted the female guest by name. Then they slipped beyond, and Esmée went wordlessly back into the family room while Claire headed for the bar. After Claire's drink order was filled, she returned to the party to distribute the drinks. She looked down and saw that her hands were shaking and causing ice cubes to chatter against their glass containers. It had almost been too much for her. Her thoughts were racing as she thought of Esmée, her own sister, working contentedly inside a German extermination camp, going about her job, and not sick at heart with what was going on all around her. Had they injured her? Frightened her into submission? She didn't know.

THAT NIGHT, SCHLÖSSER CAME TO HER ROOM. THERE WASN'T A polite knock followed by a request to enter this time. He threw open the door without a word and without warning and sailed right in. Fortunately, Claire was wearing her robe, seated on her bed and brushing her hair.

He set right in. "It was reported to me that you and my helper,

Esmée Vallant, disappeared into the bathroom today at the party. What was going on there?"

Without being cowed and missing a beat, Claire purred, "She was taken ill, Herr Kommandant. I merely went inside to clean up after her."

"How did you know she was ill?"

"I went to the bathroom to relieve myself and found the door locked. I could hear her being ill inside and offered to help."

"What did you do?"

"Do? I helped clean off the front of her dress, washed up the basin, and cleaned all around the toilet. She had been quite ill."

"Had she had too much to drink?"

"She appeared completely sober. She didn't slur her words or wobble on her feet, if that's what you mean."

Schlösser eyed her closely. He came nearer her bed until he was hovering dangerously above her. "Did you know her from before?"

"Before the war? I think not. She was merely a guest in my employer's house, and I went to help."

"She resembles you. Are you sure you're not related, the two of you?"

"I think not. I was an only child, Herr Kommandant."

"Yes, you've told me as much. But be warned, I'm headed across the street right now to ask her the same questions. Her answers better damn well be the same as yours, Fräu, or there will be hell to pay."

"I understand. I cannot vouch for what she'll say. My guess is you'll hear the same from her, however."

"That remains to be seen. Goodnight, Mademoiselle Schildmann."

"Good night, monsieur."

With that, he turned and exited her room. Claire pulled a pillow to her face and began gasping into its cover. Her breath came hard and fast, frightened as she was. It was all she could do to keep from running and calling out to Esmée what to say. But she couldn't do that; she knew Schlösser was halfway across the street already. All she could do was pray and hope, hope and pray. She closed her eyes and said the best prayer she could remember from her childhood and church school. Was it enough? She didn't know. Only time would tell now.

SCHLÖSSER IN FACT KNOCKED AND ASKED TO COME INSIDE OF Esmée's room. Esmée, who was reading a German magazine, called to him to come right in.

"Fräulein," he began gently, "I learned you were ill today. How are you feeling by now?"

"Much better. Who told you I was ill?"

"Someone heard you in the bathroom being sick."

Esmée looked at him and immediately understood the lie. No one had heard her being sick because she hadn't been sick. It was a trap. Another one of his million-and-one traps he'd laid for her over time. He would never trust her, she thought. And he shouldn't. Suddenly, it came to her. He'd been talking to Claire, and she'd told him she heard someone being sick.

She answered, "I hope I didn't interrupt the party."

"Only someone waiting outside. You were seen coming out of the bathroom with my daughters' teacher, Claire. Did you meet Claire?"

"I did. She came in to help me clean up."

"She's a nice person, yes?"

"Indeed. She's charming. I can see why you selected her to help your daughters."

"Did you talk to her about anything in particular?"

"Not at all. She asked if I was going to be okay, and I told her yes."

"Did you know her from before the war?"

"I did not. She's from a different area of Paris than I."

"So you did talk about Paris?"

"Of course. She immediately knew I was French from my German accent."

"You have no German accent. What are you telling me?"

"Maybe that's why she's the language teacher and you are the Colonel, Herr Schlösser. She hears things you do not."

He felt only slightly chastened. Not quite enough to back off. "Is she your sister?"

"I don't have a sister, Colonel. I thought you knew that. I'm your only child."

"I think you are my only child. All right, then. Good night. I'm glad we can talk like this and be honest."

"Yes, Colonel."

"But be warned. Should you ever lie to me about things like this, it would be very hard on you, Esmée. You would be hurt very badly."

"Yes, Herr Kommandant."

"Goodnight, then."

"Goodnight."

He stormed back across the street to his house. The front door slammed when he passed through, continuing into the study where he flopped back in his easy chair and waited for a maid to remove his boots. "Damn her! She knows the other. It's her sister. I know it!" he cried about Esmée.

It was then that he made a plan for Esmée. He was going to make an example of her, an example for the entire camp. Then he would see if the other one sprang in to help her sister. If she did, someone was lying. If she didn't, death to Esmée. What message would that send?

That they should abandon hope, all who entered there.

38

Friday night in June 1943, Remy choose the 11 Bus to ride downtown from the villa. His destination was *Les Deux Magots*, where he hoped to find the Schmidt sisters and ask after Kirk Heinrich. He sat midway back, in a seat by himself, and watched Paris slide by outside his window, a museum tableau frozen in time and place. The German flags and red and black bunting thickened the closer he got to downtown until finally the windy roadside was fluttering in a sea of swastikas and iconic eagles in rich, heavy colors of the Third Reich as if Paris had been reborn, as if the original Paris itself had surrendered to the Germans. Which, in fact, it had.

Les Deux Magots was a French institution, located in Saint Germain des Prés and just across from Café de Flore, it was one of the city's most famous cafés. One saw the likes of Sartre, Simone de Beauvoir, and Camus sipping coffees on its banquettes. The Surrealists, such as André Breton, Picasso, and Léger had also congregated there. Remy had great affection for the place and, sadly, so did many German higher-ups who appeared in uniform and, with much pomp and flair, hoped some of the culture might rub off on them.

He arrived at half-past nine and headed for the bar. All stools were taken, so he slipped in sideways at the end and tried to get one of the bartenders' attention. No one looked at him, alas, and so he waited and waited. At long last, the female on his end took pity on such a plain-looking man and served him a *Soixante Quinze, a cocktail made from gin, Champagne, lemon juice and sugar.* When she returned with his change, he told her to keep it and quickly asked, "The Schmidt sisters, Sina and Lyn, do they still come here?"

"I don't know, monsieur. Ask the other bartender."

He did look to be a much older and maybe a more permanent employee, the bartender at the other end. Remy handed her his remaining francs and asked her to bring the man to him. She did, the troubled-looking bartender coming up with a flounce and a hurried look. "Well? Make it fast, monsieur!"

He asked again about the Schmidt sisters.

"Of course," the bartender said without hesitation. "Have you even bothered to look around? I think I saw Sina here earlier. Good evening, monsieur." Then the man was gone, returning to his station at the far end of the bar.

Taking his drink in hand, holding it near his chest to protect it from the dancers, Remy began snaking through the crowd, eyes wide, looking for a familiar face and hoping it would be a Schmidt and not a soldier from his old squad. That would be a catastrophe, to be recognized by a member of the German army. Just as he made the far wall, he was shocked to suddenly find himself looking into the face of none other than Kirk Heinrich himself, his old drinking buddy. Would the man hug him or have him arrested? That was the thought uppermost in Remy's mind.

"Remy!" cried Heinrich. "My God, man, it's been forever!"

Remy extended his hand, and they shook. Almost breathlessly, he said, "You don't know, I've been looking for you. I need your help."

Heinrich looked around at the tables. "Come in the back. There's a card game, but there's also a side room. We can talk there."

Remy followed Heinrich as he led them out of the main club area and into a very dark, candlelit area with several rooms off to the sides. Heinrich chose the last room on the right and motioned Remy inside. The German soldier shut the door.

"Now, what's so important you would leave the safety of your flat to come here? Don't think I don't know you were captured and eventually escaped. There's a warrant for your arrest from the Wehrmacht. It says you're a deserter now."

"So you've been keeping track of your old friend, Heinrich?"

"The warrant was given to me to execute, but I had no idea where to find you. For which I was grateful. They would probably take you out and shoot you if they knew you were free and walking around Paris with such abandon as to come here. It must be important."

"That's just the thing. I've dropped out of the war, Heinrich. I was never meant to be a soldier."

"You were wishy-washy about it. We all knew that."

"Now I'm on neither side. I'm compiling a list of war criminals and need your help."

"Jesus, man, listen to you! I'm an officer in the SS, and you come to me with that? Hell, man, my name would likely be at the top of your list."

"It is."

"Schildmann, listen to yourself! You're calling an SS officer a war criminal?"

"Damn it all, Heinrich, we're all war criminals. Some of us are going to have to answer for the things we did once the Americans arrive in Paris."

"That won't happen. Our army is destroying them every day."

"Nonsense! The Americans are going to come here and arrest us all, Heinrich. The smart ones among us will be ready to cooperate with them, to give up the worst of the worst in return for immunity."

"What do you know of immunity, Schildmann? Does your God grant immunity?"

"That isn't why I'm here. That's between you and your priest. I'm here because we must do the right thing, you and I. We hated those things we did. We drank ourselves silly for them. I was there, Heinrich. I know your heart. Help me, now."

Heinrich backed up to the table and let himself down into a chair. He rubbed the side of his face with the palm of his hand. "You're insane, Schildmann. You've gone off and lost it, man."

"Please, at least talk to me. You're a good man, Kirk. I know you as well as I know myself. You carry the same shame I carry. Turn away, man, and help me make this right."

Heinrich looked up, the color gone out of his cheeks. "We can never make it right. We're too far gone for that."

"Never! There is always room for confession and redemption! It's never too late to redo our own history."

"How do you know these things?"

"I don't, but I've found redemption. You should too, Heinrich. You'll feel better immediately. How many Jews have you personally killed by now?"

"I couldn't say. Maybe a hundred. Maybe twice that."

"You've shot them yourself?"

"Or beat them to death. I don't like talking about it."

"Of course, you don't. Come with me, Heinrich. Abandon your post and come with me. I can hide you out. I can help you disappear. I can help you regain your decency. I can help you make amends."

Heinrich slowly unbuttoned the top button on his gray tunic. The SS lightning bolts loosened their grip on his throat, and Remy was encouraged for the first time.

"I'd have to think about that. Initially, I must say no. Initially, my reaction is to arrest you and take you in, Remy. But we were once friends, so I won't. But the rest of it... Lord, man, do yourself a favor and don't go around saying these things to people. I don't care how much redemption you get for it. Someone will shoot you if you carry on like this with the Wehrmacht."

"I hear what you're saying. But let's keep this between you and me, Kirk. I'm offering you a way out of your nightmare."

"That's where you're wrong, Schildmann. I'm proud of my service. I'm glad I'm not weak like you. My advice to you is that you leave this place now and don't come back here. Next time I won't sit and listen. I'll arrest you. Be off, now!"

Remy hadn't expected that at all. He'd thought he was making progress. He'd thought he saw a chink in the man's armor, but evidently he was wrong. With a sudden start, he realized the terrible risk he'd taken by coming to the club and suddenly felt compelled to leave immediately.

"I'm going to go now, Heinrich. I hope you will think about these things."

"I won't. You should leave now, Remy. Leave and Godspeed in your insanity. I hope you come to your senses, however. But it's probably too late for that anyway."

With that, Heinrich stood, rebuttoned his tunic collar, and strode past Remy and out of the room. Remy knew he should leave at once. He had no idea whether Heinrich was going to turn him in right then or turn his back for ten minutes and let him go free. He decided he was finished. He couldn't do this again. There was too much risk. He wouldn't be searching down any other members of his old squad. They probably wouldn't be interested in his redemption, either. Once an SS, always an SS. He would move on, alone.

He'd hated the army. He'd always been alone, anyway.

Claire had forgiven him, but she was gone. Heinrich wouldn't forgive himself—or Remy. So he'd have to forgive himself, just like he'd already begun.

He walked out of the front door and began running for the bus stop. He didn't stop running until he was back on the bus, rear seat, hands in his pockets, shaking with fear.

Was he the only one who saw what was coming?

At that moment, just as the bus pulled off, he had his insight.

The others weren't missing what he was seeing.

They just didn't care.

39

C olonel Schlösser, thinking about his planned speech, had what he thought was a second stroke of genius. He needed pictures of the ceremony. But there was one particular one he didn't want—the moment of Esmée's death.

So he decided that since Claire already was a renowned photographer and capable beyond anyone else here with a camera, and if she is Esmée's sister, she would abandon the camera to come to her sister's aid. And if she abandoned the camera, she would take no picture of the death. It all made perfect sense.

"Claire," he said to her that afternoon after grammar lessons, "I would like you to take a photograph of my family. Will you do that for me?"

Claire immediately agreed. She would like nothing better than to get her hands on a camera. She followed Schlösser into his study. She sat and watched while he took out his keychain and unlocked a drawer on the right pedestal of his long, black desk. She shut her eyes and pretended not to be watching, but she'd already seen all she needed to know: the camera was kept in his desk, the key on the keychain in his pocket. If he ever died, she would have the camera. How else might she get the key? That one, she would work on.

He placed the case on his desk and carefully unsnapped the brown leather cover. When he opened the top, she could she green felt lining. Nicely done, she thought. Removing the camera, he looked across at her. "Recognize this?"

"Yes. Leica 3C, I believe."

"Yes. 3C, the newest Leica. I have the flash connection installed, and here is my flash unit and bulbs."

"And the sync speed?" she asked.

"This camera syncs with flash at one-thirtieth of a second."

"I would've guessed that and been right."

"Yes. Would you like to see it?"

"Of course."

He passed it across his desk.

"Small," she said, "and surprisingly light. This is my first time with a Leica. I should like one, I can see already."

"Germany's finest. Do you find it suitable for taking my family's picture?"

"Oh, certainly. This fine camera would do justice to just about any subject on earth."

"What about a photograph of a rather gruesome death?" he asked without blinking. His voice had turned chilly. She felt a sudden tension in the room.

"This camera could even do that," she said, "though I could not be the operator. I would be unable."

"What if I ordered it? What if I ordered you to take the picture, Claire?"

"Then I would try. I would have no choice so, of course, I would try."

"Well, in one month I will be giving a speech. You are to be the official photographer for the Reich newspaper. There will be death, but if you are to work in the infirmary, you will be familiar with death already in one month."

She skipped ahead. "Wait, I'm to work in the infirmary?"

"I'm transferring you there, effective immediately. The twins have learned their lessons and Dr. Berglund needs you in his infirmary. You have been requested."

"Really? I know nothing about medicine. I—I—"

He sighed. "There we are again. Another prisoner disobeying my order. What am I to do?" He smiled when he said this. "I'm only making light, sort of. You are going to the infirmary immediately. You will move your things to the nurses' floor and you'll be living there. I would suggest you move tonight, now, so you aren't late for work in the morning. That will be all for now. My camera, please."

She passed the camera back across the desk. He reached inside the leather case and plucked out a soft cloth. Ever so carefully, he began rubbing off the fingerprints—hers, she was sure, were his main concern. Then he replaced the Leica inside its case. He snapped the latch and then replaced it in his desk, turned the key counterclockwise and pocketed the keyring. It was all in keeping with his fastidious nature. A place for everything, including her. It was time to move her few things across the street. She knew it would require only one trip. She wouldn't even need a suitcase.

In her upstairs bedroom, Claire gave one last look around and began laying out her clothes. Essentially, she had two dresses she worked in, two bras, four underpants, three sets of stockings, two pairs of flat shoes, black and brown, two towels, and her toiletries. She also owned two T-shirts, one pair of woolen socks, and her winter coat, hanging by the front door. It was easy enough to make one pile out of it all. The pile was easily managed as she made her way downstairs to the front door.

Schlösser stopped her at the front door.

"Take your things over then come back. We'll have good light for the family photograph in about one hour."

"Yes, sir. I'll be back at four."

The sun was shining, but the shadows were beginning to lengthen. She would take the family outside and shoot with the sun at her back. If, and it was a big if, she could find an interesting background. She wanted to see how the camera operated out-of-doors, how well it translated light to film. It was to be the camera she'd be using for the upcoming speech, and it went without saying that she'd better get that right. He'd already told her he wanted to see the pictures in the Reich newsmagazine. She had no option but to deliver a perfect photo story.

Upon entering the infirmary, the first person she bumped into was Dr. Pietor Berglund. He saw her as he was making rounds and immediately broke away from his nurse and came to Claire. He was wearing light blue slacks and a white lab coat, open down the front. Beneath, he wore an SS blouse with a stethoscope around his neck. His blond hair was longer than she remembered and his face was smooth even this late in the day. Her heart skipped when he smiled.

"Claire," he said in a most friendly voice, "are you answering my call for help?"

She stood there holding everything she owned, which wasn't much compared to her French life. Still, she managed to return his smile. "I am answering your call for help. I'll be more helpful, too, once I know where to park my belongings."

"Nurses' quarters are one floor up. You have the entire floor. There should never be a man on that floor so you and the others should feel comfortable and safe there."

"That's good to hear. I feel like I've been studied every minute back across the street. It will be good to be with other women." She said these things and immediately wondered why she felt comfortable telling him how she felt back across the street. But she let it go. He was either trustworthy or he wasn't and, to be honest, she was exhausted from deceits and subterfuges through these many past months anyway. It was time for simplicity, which meant time for honesty.

"Good. Are you still feeling up to dinner and a movie tomorrow night?"

"Oh, I wouldn't miss it for anything." Her heart warmed. She had been planning how she'd fix her hair for days anyway. Even better, now she'd be around other women where she might even be able to borrow a white blouse to wear.

"Excellent. I've been looking forward to it myself."

"Dr. Berglund, I need to ask you something."

"Pietor, please."

"Pietor, why would you ask for my help? The closest I've ever come to medical knowledge is mustard plasters for a chest cold."

"That's a fair question. I requested you because I know you care. The practice of acute nursing is something I can teach you in six months. The caring part is something you're either born with or you're not. You are. That's why I want you, because I need what you have."

"Goodness, I'll have to process that. But thank you. That means so much."

She wanted to say she was on the verge of tears, that she had been on probation, under house arrest, and under suspicion across the street. But she didn't say those things. Besides, Pietor already knew them. He knew about Schlösser and his dark side when away from his home and family. He knew about Schlösser's private floor at the hospital. He knew about Schlösser's hand-picked staff of SS doctors, the Aryans who did his bidding. At Auschwitz, on the Schlösser floor, so-called camp doctors performed vile and lethal medical experiments on concentration camp inmates, tortured Jewish children, Gypsy children, and many others. "Patients" were put into pressure chambers, tested with drugs, castrated, frozen to death, and exposed to various other traumas. Why? For the sole purpose of learning better and faster ways to kill. That was the whole reason for the Schlösser floor. The remainder of the hospital belonged to Pietor Berglund and his staff. It was for patients who retained some value to the administration, usually German staff charged with killing and burning bodies, and Jewish staff who had earned positions of trust and merit with the Nazis. These were far outnumbered by the Germans, but they were admitted, and it was more common than Claire would have thought going in.

"However," said Dr. Berglund, "we must always remember there is a clear and present danger for our Jewish patients when they come to hospital. If even for a moment it looks like they may not return to work, they are bodily dragged from their hospital beds and put into the gas chambers with the very next bunch. SS doctors come downstairs from the Schlösser floor every night and review patient records, tracking down those whose working days may be at an end. If they find one, in the morning when we return to work, the patient will be gone, dragged out in the middle of the night and gassed. What do you make of this, Claire?"

"It's horrible. What do you mean, what do I make of it?"

"What does it mean to you?"

"It means I never make a record entry that might possibly suggest a person won't return to work."

"Exactly. Here's how that works. If they have pneumonia, we write down 'chest discomfort.' For those of us working here, those are keywords that mean pneumonia. If they have cancer, we write down 'viral infection.' Those are keywords that mean to us 'cancer.' If they are dying of heart failure, we write down 'high blood pressure.' And so it goes. If you're not sure what to write down, always ask. The men and women working on this floor are, for the most part, on my team and helping me save lives. Even lives we will eventually lose from natural causes. But you cannot trust everyone here. For that reason, I liken working here to treading carefully through a minefield. Now do you see why I needed someone with your brains?"

"What do you mean?"

"If you know how to take exquisite photographs, then you are a student. Your job is to find hidden points of light and display them. Our job here is the same. We always look for reasons patients are going to recover and return to work and those are the things we place in their medical charts. Those are points of light, we might call them, to a photographer. Not so unlike developing your film, am I right? What comes out depends on what goes in. We are the same here. Take care all around, in this place. But take the greatest care in what you commit to writing."

"I promise I will."

"One more thing. What do you think is the other side of this coin?"

"I think I know. If we write a patient is hardly sick, we risk seeing them put right back to work without treatment."

"Exactly. I'm impressed with you, Claire. You already see the fine line we must tread here. Just enough but not too much. Just enough but not too little. Just enough. Again, if you're not sure, come get me. We'll figure it out together."

"Do you lose many patients to the gas chamber?"

"I do. Even one is too many. Our records show we're losing thirty percent. I know that sounds high, but one-hundred percent would have died if we hadn't been here. So I try not to look at it like losing three. I try to look at it like saving seven. In this way, I can live with myself. Can you take the same view as me, so when the time comes to lose someone you've grown fond of in here, it doesn't drive you mad? Can you stand with me in this? I lose some nurses who cannot. But here's one thing. I've never had one nurse accuse me of manipulating patient records. Even the Nazi nurses haven't crossed me. Among the great majority of German doctors and nurses, the Hippocratic Oath is a reality. Then there is Schlösser's ward. How they live with themselves, I absolutely cannot say."

She heard all these things and was astounded. She'd never been

around such a principled man in her life. She found herself
drawing ever closer to him by the magnet of his goodness alone.
She wondered how many of the nurses she would meet that night
were already head-over-heels in love with him. And who wouldn't
be? She decided to avoid that trap, for she knew there was no
permanency in the world surrounding her. He might be here
tomorrow doing his work, but he could also just as quickly vanish.
Wasn't that how it had been with Remy? There with her, then
gone in a blink? That was how it worked. To love in this world was
to lose. And she wanted no more of that, so she determined to
keep her distance. Besides, the patients would be better off for her
detachment from him. She could serve them better.

It was time to return to the Colonel's house and photograph the
family. Which meant it was time to use the camera that, it was
becoming clear to her, might help her—but help her with what?
As she wondered about how she might contribute to those
standing against the insanity, an idea began forming in her mind.
One floor above the nurses' quarters was the Schlösser floor. An
entire collection of photographic evidence against the colonel and
his role in mass murder was waiting up a single flight of stairs. But
would she ever go there? Just the thought of it made her want to
throw up. The thought of it made her pulse pound and her knees
wobble. She sat down in the nurses' break room when the doctor
resumed his rounds. It was going to take several minutes to collect
herself enough to return across the street. She just needed a few
minutes to blank out her thoughts and stop her swimming head.

When she awoke it was two hours later and the sun had set. She
had failed to return and take the photographs. Sweat broke out
across her forehead; he would be furious. What if he took her out
and had her shot before she even began? She looked around the
nurses' breakroom. Surely there was some way, some excuse there
to protect her. But no ideas came.

So she journeyed around the ward and finally located Pietor. When he broke away from his current patient, she told him what had happened.

"Oh, yes," said Dr. Berglund with a smile. "Your colonel came here looking for you."

"You spoke with him?"

"I did. I told him you had serious female cramps and he should come back in two days."

"Oh, my God! What did he say?"

"He actually apologized. He said he hadn't known you were feeling poorly when he spoke with your earlier today. He told me to tell you he apologized for how abrupt he was with you, that he didn't know."

"You saved my life, Dr. Berglund. I cannot thank you enough."

"Go upstairs and sleep now. Be here at six in the morning. Together ,we will save many more lives and I will be repaid. Scoot, now, scoot!"

She turned and left for upstairs, her heart singing.

She had a mentor and a protector. That hadn't happened to her since Jacques Marseille at the *Paris-Soir* when he became her associate editor. But he had died.

She didn't follow those thoughts another step. There was no need and, besides, she was too tired.

It was time to sleep and dream of life before death.

40

Three hours after the start of her first day at the infirmary, Claire was told to take her thirty-minute break. She looked up from a patient she was bathing with warm cloths and realized it was 10:30, that hours had flown by already that day. When she had the patient dried off, she washed her hands in the basin, toweled them dry, and headed for the break room. Then an inspiration hit her, and she turned and walked out the front doors of the infirmary, hurried down the stairs, and ducked next door to the main administration building for the camp.

A young woman wearing a corporal's stripe waited on visitors just inside. "Fräulein?"

"I'm looking for someone. I'm from the infirmary, and we need to order supplies."

"There's a requisition form for that, Fräulein. Are you new here in the camp?"

"I'm afraid I am. I was told by the doctor to come here and speak to Fräulein Vallant. Esmée Vallant. May I see her?"

"Certainly. Let me phone her office."

While she waited, Claire reviewed her tasks for the day. After work, she wanted to have a miraculous recovery from the cramps and go to Colonel Schlösser's. Maybe they'd be ready for the photograph and she could explore the Leica camera. Then, at six that evening, twelve hours after starting her shift, she was to meet with Dr. Berglund and go over some of the day's charts. It was a teaching session where he was to pull typical patient records and begin teaching her how to read between the lines.

"Miss?" said a female voice. Claire looked up. There stood Esmée, wearing a form-fitting gray suit and business heels. Her hair was swept back in a bun, and she was wearing eyeglasses. Claire had never seen her sister wearing eyeglasses before, and she realized her sister looked much older than the day she disappeared. She was still very young but much of the baby fat around the face and throat was gone. She had become a beautiful young woman. "Can I help you, Fräulein?"

"I have an order to make for the infirmary."

"Certainly. Please follow me to my office."

Back through a frosted glass door, past four rows of desks, then a left into a private office. Claire followed her sister inside and closed the door. Esmée immediately came to her and threw her arms around Claire's neck.

"Oh, my God! My God! My God! It really is you. I thought I was dreaming."

Claire's eyes welled up with tears. "I know, I know. I haven't stopped thinking about you for a minute. How lucky we are!"

"What are you doing at the infirmary?"

"Training to be a nurse. Dr. Berglund asked me to join his staff."

"Oh, that man. He is absolutely heavenly. Everyone swoons for him."

"Not me," Claire said staunchly. "My job is to detach and be professional. I don't have time for dalliances, not with death all around."

"Have you been inside the camp yet?" Esmée asked.

"Yes. I lived there for over a year."

Esmée gasped and covered her mouth with her hand.

"But I won't go there again. I'd kill myself before they threw me back into the blocks."

Claire's heart burned when she thought of those she had left behind. "Those poor, precious people just over the fence. Have you thought of how we can help?"

"Forget about that," said Esmée. "There are guards and dogs every ten feet. This is Hitler's secret of all secrets. The place is even rigged with booby traps, I'm told. It will be blown up if the Allies get nearby. The Germans don't want anyone to know what went on here."

"What about mail? Can we send things out?"

"No way. They couldn't regulate Polish mail so no letters get out. In fact, nothing leaves here without the SS personally inspecting it. Why, is there something you want to send out?"

"Maybe. Maybe there will be."

"Such as?"

"I don't know exactly yet. Maybe photographs?"

"The Nazis would never allow photographs to leave the camp. Try something else."

"Letters?"

"Not allowed."

"That's all I can think of."

"No photographs, no letters, no mementos, nothing leaves here. The SS is a very jealous lover of its privacy."

"So I'm learning. Well..."

"Photographs of what, anyway, Claire? What does the photojournalist have in mind?"

"This entire operation must be documented. There will be prosecutions after the war. The Americans will put the German government on trial. The SS will be put on trial, as well as the Gestapo. Many Germans will pay for their lives for what's happened here and other places. I want pictures of it all in order to help. That is how I will do good here."

"You don't even have a camera. It's not possible."

"What about you, Esmée? Can you order a camera for me?"

"What would I say it's for?"

"For the infirmary. We want to do a study on the use of viruses to kill prisoners. We need close-up pictures for our work."

"That I can probably do. Will Dr. Berglund sign for it?"

"You mean I can't?"

"No, you make up the orders but Dr. Berglund signs."

"I don't know about a camera."

"I've heard he is very concerned about his patients. Maybe you can explain it well enough—"

Claire shook her head. "He'll have to be in on it with me, Esmée. I don't have the medical knowledge to sponsor a test without him. It has to come from him."

"He may not want to. It could be very dangerous."

"I have an appointment with him today. I'll ask."

"I can get just about any camera in Germany or Switzerland. Just send me a signed order."

"All right. Well, I better get back. I only have thirty minutes."

"I'll come to the infirmary tomorrow for something or other. Maybe we can get coffee in your break room?"

"Of course. That would be wonderful, little sister."

"All right. One more hug, then."

Claire held Esmée tight and then stepped back. "Before I leave, please give me a blank requisition form. I have an idea."

"Don't tell me."

"I won't, I promise."

AT FOUR P.M. SHE PHONED COLONEL SCHLÖSSER. HE WAS IN HIS office and took her call.

"Herr Colonel, this is Claire Schildmann. I'm doing much better today, and I would like to take the photographs of your family."

"Fräu, so glad to hear you're better. Be at my door in thirty minutes. Goodbye."

He hung up. and she set the phone back down. Abrupt, but it looked like she had her first photography job since France. So be it.

At four-thirty p.m. she knocked on the Colonel's front door and Necci answered. The girl opened the door and gave her teacher a hug. "We heard you weren't well. Are you better now?"

"I am. Much better. Are you ladies dressed for your picture?"

"We are. Everyone's coming down now."

Fifteen minutes later, she had snapped her first photograph on the Leica. The family was standing in ankle-deep grass, the Colonel on one side of the girls and his wife on the other, twins in the middle. All were smiling. The entire setup reminded Claire of late-afternoon family photos she had taken when families were on holiday or on picnics, staring into the camera lens, the sun behind the photographer, that slightest squint on everyone's face from the low angle of the sun.

She then began arranging her subjects. First the twins, back beside an oak tree, each holding a hand to the trunk (as if for support). Then a chair was brought into the yard by the servants, and Mrs. Schlösser took a seat while the Colonel stood behind her, ramrod straight in full uniform, unsmiling. His wife was smiling, however, and Claire knew the photograph would be irreconcilable in the viewer's mind, such a broad disparity in emotion as it was portrayed. Undaunted, she went ahead with her arrangements, and by five o'clock was finished.

"That's about all I can think to do," she told the small family. "I think you're going to be well-pleased."

"Will you develop the film, Fräu?"

"I can. I just need a few chemicals."

"Send over a requisition, and I'll sign it."

Claire's heart jumped. Maybe this was her moment.

"I'd also like to requisition a camera for the infirmary if I may."

"Why's that?"

"We're studying the use of viruses."

He took her aside a few steps.

"Viruses for killing, Fräu?"

"Exactly."

"And what kind of camera?'

"Exakta, German model. I like that it has a reusable flash."

"Definitely that. Exactly what I would recommend. Good, good. Include it on your requisition form, signed by you, then I'll sign it all."

Claire's pulse was racing. She'd done it! The colonel, the second-in-command, was about to give her the tools she needed to collect evidence of his own role in the worse genocide in world history. How had she come to this point? She didn't care. She was going to get her own camera! She thanked the family profusely and promised they'd have a photo viewing session before long, just as soon as the chemicals arrived.

Her step was light as she made her way back across the street.

Then it hit her—he'd said she was to sign the requisition form herself. No need even to involve Dr. Berglund!

She wanted to run, to jump, to cry out in joy. But she didn't. She maintained a measured step as befit one in the medical profession who was embarking on a study of deadly viruses. For all she knew, he was watching her even as she crossed the street. Up the stairs she went, inside the infirmary, where she looked right and left. There was no one around.

So she jumped. Jumped and clapped her hands and then bent double, laughing.

How many Nazi murderers would she trap? She had no idea.

Nor did it matter. Even one was better than none. Using the doctor's math, she looked at it like one caught but nine got away? So be it. She had still caught one who, without her efforts, would have gotten away, too.

The numbers worked.

"How," she asked Dr. Berglund, "can the SS doctors not see in the patient records that we're treating for things far more severe than our diagnosis? We're treating for what we call a viral infection with morphine? They're not stupid."

"That's right. So what we do is we write down penicillin instead of morphine. Or some such as that."

"So our records mean nothing in reality?"

"What, you would have me tell the truth and lose patients over it? I've come up with this system because I didn't know what else to do, Claire. It's the best I know how. It's terrible, it's true, but I don't have anything else to work with."

"I understand."

They were sitting in his office, where he'd just made tea for them on his hot plate and they were enjoying the rarest treat of all, a pastry. One of the officers' cooks had made them and brought them around. They were pfannkuchen, as they were called in Berlin, and Claire thought she'd never eaten anything so good. This from a child of French pastries.

He dabbed his mouth with a napkin.

"So, tomorrow you will meet Mrs. Stanislaus. She is one of my favorite patients."

"Who is she?"

He held up a cautioning finger. "Tomorrow."

"Tomorrow it is, then. Please pass the pfannkuchen."

41

His name was Wilhoite Schildmann, and his wife had been shot to death in a Resistance attack in Paris. He hated everything French. He had raised two daughters and one son. The daughters were in Germany, happily married to Germany army officers, while the son, Remy, had been captured by the French army and then escaped—as near as the father could tell. Which made him what the Americans would call AWOL. He should've reported back to his German army unit when he escaped from the French. So far, he had not.

Wilhoite Schildmann's rank now was *Generalrichter*, approximately the same rank as a brigadier general in the U.S. Army in the judicial service or judiciary. He was, in his posting, a military judge on loan to hear Jewish appeals in Paris, which were appeals from people with Jewish blood, mostly half-bloods or less, who were fighting Nazi round-ups and deportations to Poland. Typically, the litigants would have been people with some means, people who could afford to fight the system, and often, though not always, some money would even be passed under the table for a favorable ruling. Schildmann was not one of those judges who would accept a bribe, however, and woe to the man who offered.

Generalrichter Schildmann lived on rue Marbeau in the 16th Arrondissement, the wealthiest area of Paris, as he had for twenty years. Only a couple blocks from avenue Foch and the Arc de Triomphe, the townhouse was a large two-story one-family home with a nice back garden. Their street was always busy with German staff cars coming and going with prisoners and immigrants in need of Schildmann's court's rulings.

In 1944, Remy Schildmann decided it was time to meet with his father. His goal was to save his father from the coming war crimes trials. Whether his father had been specifically complicit in war crimes, Remy wasn't sure. But he was sure that the Generalrichter had been instrumental in sending Jews to Auschwitz and, he assumed, that in and of itself was enough to see his father stand trial when the Allied war crimes trials began. In short, he wanted to see his father in order to warn him, to encourage him to decry past behaviors, and resolve to join Remy in his search for justice.

The bicycle taxi dropped him in front of the house where he'd grown up. It was after six p.m. so he assumed his father was home. There was no appointment; a son should never need an appointment to see his own father, thought Remy. Nor need he give advance notice. His father would be comfortable with a drop-in— at least so Remy thought. He walked up to the door and rang the bell, expecting to be greeted by his father's long-time maid, Yvonne Gebsmacht. He was surprised when his father answered the door. When the old man saw Remy, his face neither brightened nor fell. He was unmoved.

The father's first words were, "You need to report to your squad. You're AWOL."

"Father, can I come in? I need to say some things to you."

"Come in. I have a dinner date at seven, so you'll need to be quick about it."

Remy followed his father into the formal living room. They sat on two facing sofas in the dim light of the room. There were no flowers, no recent cuttings as his mother would have placed around. The place, thought Remy, definitely missed her touch.

"All right, Lieutenant, get to it."

"Father, I'm no longer a lieutenant or a captain. I'm your son, and I'm no longer serving in the German army. I'm free of all that. But what I am doing is preparing for the war crime trials that are coming as soon as the Allies win this goddam war."

"No need for that language in my house, Remy. That's first. Second, Germany is on the verge of an all-out win. There won't be any Allied war crimes trials. And even if there were, I have done nothing wrong. He has committed no war crimes, no crimes against humanity."

"Father, I know you're sitting in judgment of Jewish families. I know some of them you're sending to concentration camps. That, in and of itself, is enough complicity to send you to the gallows. Please listen to what I'm saying."

"Absurd! I've done nothing other than hear local cases."

"You've ruled on who's a Jew and who isn't. Those who are, you send to the concentration camps knowing they're being murdered there. Don't you see that?"

His father's jaw tightened. "No, I don't know that. I don't know what happens to these people after they leave my courtroom. Nor do I care, because that's outside my purview. That isn't up to me."

"You seriously don't know what's happening to them? That's your defense? When everyone in France and everyone in Germany knows the Jews are being systemically slaughtered by Adolf Hitler, you're telling me you're the one person who doesn't know this? Father, men will die for such ridiculous positions as that."

His father stood and pushed back the sleeve on his uniform tunic, checking his wrist watch. "Time for you to get back to your unit, Remy. Now, excuse me, I have a dinner date."

"You haven't heard anything I've said. I'm not in a unit, for Gods sakes. I'm a free man, Father. You can be too if you'll only renounce and join me."

His father stopped then, taking a step closer to his son. "You seriously expect me to toss aside my career, my life, and renounce my country? What's happened to my boy? You were raised better than this!"

"I've started thinking for myself, Father. So should you."

"Nonsense. Excuse me, Lieutenant, I really must be going now."

Remy turned and led the way to the front door. He knew he was expected to leave without another effort at changing his father's mind.

He turned at the door and extended his hand. "Father, thank you for seeing me."

His father reached beyond him and pushed open the outer door. "I'm sorry to hear you're not owning up to your responsibilities, Remy. You were raised better than that."

"Sorry to disappoint you, Father. Goodnight."

Then he was gone. He had accomplished nothing. But wait, maybe he had. He'd at least given his father the chance to decide his own fate in the presence of the son who would be in attendance at the trials. That in itself was something. Remy stuffed his hands inside his jacket pockets and headed back up to boulevard de l'Amiral Bruix. It was a short walk to the bus stop, enough time to clear his head over what had just happened.

He needed the time alone to mourn his father's recalcitrance, his inability to think for himself.

For that, he was sorrowful.

42

"The patient we'll see next is Elva Stanislaus. She is a woman in her late sixties, a German Jew, who has served as head cook in the officers' mess hall since the camp opened at Auschwitz. Her superior officer has marked her as easily replaceable, but I'm trying to show him there's no need for that thinking and she'll soon be able to return to work good as new. If I'm unsuccessful, she could be taken to the gas chambers at any moment. Please come inside her ward with me."

Dr. Berglund pushed through the double doors of the acute ward, and Claire followed.

"Acute but actually chronic?" asked Claire.

"Now you're getting it," said the doctor. "Tuberculosis, a treatable illness. She would be dead in thirty seconds if her superior officer knew. We have her here for recurring balance problems."

"Good heavens."

"Yes, at least we hope heaven is good. Here we are. Mrs. Stanislaus, please meet a new nurse, Claire Schildmann. She'll be helping you now."

The woman was overweight, but her skin was extremely loose on the parts of her upper body Claire could see. She knew enough to know there had been recent and extreme weight loss, probably from the wasting disease.

"Hello," said Claire and extended her hand to shake. The old woman grasped her hand around her wrist and pulled her near. "Are you a Nazi, miss?"

Dr. Berglund raised a finger to his lips. "Mrs. Stanislaus, none of that matters in here. Let's talk about something else, please."

"You're not, then. That's good," said the woman. "I don't let Nazis touch me."

"No, Mrs. Stanislaus, you're safe with me," said Claire. The old woman released Claire's hand. "Now, maybe you can tell me how you're feeling today."

"I'm doing much better. The sunny afternoons outside are doing wonders for me."

"Good," said Dr. Berglund, "then you're probably ready for a picnic. Some of us are going on a picnic tomorrow. What would you think of that?"

"I think I wouldn't miss it for anything. A chance for fried chicken with my favorite doctor and new friend, here? I'd love to get to go on your picnic."

"Then go you shall," Dr. Berglund said. "We'll come get you in the morning, early. So don't go anyplace in the meantime."

It was a joke. She smiled but it was a tight smile, not a happy one.

"I won't go anywhere unless they come get me and take me to the gas chamber. I know that must be closing in."

"We'll keep you with us, Mrs. Stanislaus, no need to worry about that."

"Good. Then I'm tired. Why don't you talk to someone else now, please?"

The doctor and nurse moved down to the next bed on the ward. The patient was a middle-aged man. He was propped up in bed, his right arm and right leg elevated in traction.

"Meet Mr. Rothstein, Nurse Schildmann. Herman is the camp's locksmith. He is watched every second. But he knows every lock from one end of the camp to the other. Unfortunately, he was attacked by a guard who mistook him for someone else. The beating left him with a comminuted fracture of his tibia and a fracture of his ulnar bone. He's fixable, though, and we'll soon have him fit as a fiddle and back to work."

"Hello, Doctor. Hello, Nurse. I hope your day is going well."

"Very well, Herman," said Dr. Berglund. "How are you feeling?"

"I know I'll never have use of this arm again, doc. And I still can't feel my hand. How do I fix locks with just one hand?"

"Well, let's not broadcast that around, shall we?" said the doctor. "I haven't given up hope for your arm and hand, Mr. Rothstein. I hope you don't either."

"I'm trying. It's just so damn depressing here. I know, I know, it's better than how it could be. I could be dead. But I'd be joining my wife if I died, Nurse Schildmann. They murdered her when we arrived here. I was lucky and they needed a locksmith at the exact moment I walked in. We said goodbye at the gas chamber. There was nothing I could do to save her. You understand that, don't you?"

"I do. No one can withstand the SS," said Claire. "You had no choice about any of it, Mr. Rothstein."

As they were moving on, Dr. Berglund shared with Claire that Mr. Rothstein's "official" diagnosis was strain/sprain of the right arm with a muscle tear in his right leg. His chart said he could return to work in about ten days. "Which is ridiculous. He probably won't ever go back. The beating destroyed his right side, and now he has no use of his hand. He has no feeling from the elbow down. His prognosis for a long life is poor."

"The poor, dear man," Claire said. "I'll make sure he gets extra care."

"He needs a friend, for sure."

"I can be his friend," she said. "I'm quite good at that."

"Yes, you are."

The next patient was a young woman whose tattoo on her forearm was clearly displayed as she slept in her bed, her arms on top of her bedcovers. When Claire first saw her, she thought the woman a bit older than herself, but upon second glance, she realized the young woman might have been younger, maybe in her late teens. The reason she looked older at first was because her face was terribly bruised, as was her neck. Claire looked to Dr. Berglund for explanation.

"She was hung from the gallows and survived. She's from Schlösser's ward upstairs. When I saw them experimenting with new ways to murder people, I pulled rank and had her moved down here."

"You can do that, pull rank?"

"I'm a major in the SS. The other doctors were lieutenants. It was quite easy. Since then, they've tried to take her back two different times, but I threaten them, and they eventually go away. Now I'm wracking my brain trying to figure out how she's essential to the war effort so I can keep her here."

"How about making her a nurse? I can train her."

Dr. Berglund smiled. "I hadn't thought of that, Claire. That just might work. Get her up and moving around and begin training her. I like that. My trainee training her own trainee."

"If it keeps her alive, I'm all for it," said Claire. "It wouldn't hurt to try. We can also train her in some essential skill, maybe phlebotomy, where they can't argue about her usefulness to the war effort. I can start that right away."

"You learned it fast enough. What's it been now, a week?"

"Just. Desperate times require desperate measures, doctor."

"Indeed they do. All right. Get her up and moving around as soon as she wakes up. Let's put her to work."

"Done. What's her name, incidentally?"

"Rhonda Maier. She's from Nice."

"Perfect. I'll check back with her in about an hour. Anything else I should know about her?"

"Just this. She's heartbroken. They took her twin sons and fed them into the gas chamber when she got here. She operates in a haze most of the time. You'll have that to help her overcome."

"Sweet Jesus."

"Yes. But what of it? Everyone here has the same story if they've made it here to our infirmary. They've all lost someone dear."

"Of course. Well, Rhonda Maier and I are about to become very close."

"Excellent. Moving on now."

AT ELEVEN-FIFTEEN THAT MORNING, THEY HAD FINISHED ROUNDS. Claire told Dr. Berglund that she was going to Rhonda Maier. He wished her luck and thanked her for taking on the saving of another life. "No need for thanks," she told him, "that's what we're all here for."

She sent back into the first ward and hurried to Rhonda's bedside. The young woman was curled in the fetal position, eyes wide open, staring.

"Rhonda, my name is Claire. I'm a new nurse. We have so many patients I'm hoping I can ask you for help."

No answer. No indication she'd even heard Claire speak.

She tried again. "Rhonda, I know you're hurting really bad. But those little boys want you to live for them. They don't want their mom to die. I'm here to help you live. Will you let me and the little boys help you?"

Rhonda's head turned. "What? You know my boys?"

"I haven't met them, but I bet you're going to tell me all about them. I need a volunteer to help me with some patients, and you're my best candidate. Will you try getting up to come help me?"

She rolled over. "Seriously? Get out of bed?"

"Yes. Your boys want you up and Dr. Berglund wants you up and I want you up. Your help is really needed."

"Oh. What do you want me to do?"

"Help me draw blood and take samples from patients. Help me give shots. That kind of stuff I'm no good at."

Rhonda sniffed and turned back around. "I don't know how. Get someone else."

Claire leaned and touched her on the arm. "There isn't anyone else. Everyone else is sicker than you."

"Well, then, too bad. I've decided to die."

"Not until you help me over this rough time. Please? I'll pay you back."

"How? Get my boys back?"

Claire's eyes shot around. She couldn't be too careful. "I can't do that. Nobody can. But I can help you hit back at the people who did this to you. I have a plan."

She turned around again. "What kind of plan?"

Claire decided to tell her the truth. "I'm going to make them pay for what they did to you, Rhonda. To your little boys. You can help me."

"That's something I'd like to do."

"But we need to disguise what we're doing so they don't catch us. That's why I need you to help me around the hospital."

"Why didn't you say so? Where are my clothes?"

"I'll chase down your clothes. You go use the bathroom, and I'll meet you back here."

"All right."

Fifteen minutes later, they had rejoined.

"You didn't have any clothes so I brought you some of mine. Here's a dress and underwear. It might not fit perfectly, but it's a start until you get your first paycheck and buy your own."

"We get paid?"

"It's a joke, honey. Our pay is that we don't have to die today. For most of us that's a pretty good trade."

"I don't care."

Claire thought for a moment she was about to lose her back to bed again. So she came on strong. "Let's go. Dr. Berglund wants me to take you over to admin and get you registered as a new nurse. That's what we'll do first."

"All right. What am I doing again?"

"You're going to learn how to draw blood and how to give shots."

"I hate needles, Claire."

"Don't we all. Hurry up with the clothes. We need to get busy this afternoon."

"All right, I'm coming."

After registration with admin—and dodging questions about her experience and training—Claire had walked Rhonda through the process and was returning with her to the infirmary when they were hailed by Esmée. She was walking toward them in the main hallway and called them over.

"I overheard the clerks. They're looking into Rhonda's background."

"I said we'd get her records from school and get back to them," Claire said.

"So, you lied to them, and that makes you a conspirator, too. These people will track down all her records and places you told them she trained, Claire. You need to phony up some records fast."

"We can do that," said Claire. "I'll get Dr. Berglund to help us."

"Don't get him involved, please," said Esmée, "he's the only decent doctor in the entire infirmary. We can't lose him over some useless lie."

Claire found herself agreeing with her younger sister. She was growing up in a good way, and Claire liked what she was hearing.

"What do you suggest?"

"Let me ask around. I know some people in records who might be willing to help."

"That would be wonderful."

"But you'll owe them. Everything we're talking about is very dangerous, Claire."

"I understand. I may be able to pay everyone back before long anyway." She was thinking of the evidence she was going to create with her photographs of Schlösser's ward. Wouldn't that be something everyone would applaud?

"Don't be naive, Claire," Rhonda said. Her interest level in the entire conversation was quite low as she still didn't really care if she lived or died. But just for a fleeting moment, she did care about the people who might be at risk for trying to help her, and she said so. "I don't want anybody making problems for themselves on my account. I'd be happier with my boys. Death doesn't hold any threat for me."

"Yes, but this isn't just about you," Esmée said. "If we can get you in a position of trust, then you'll pay us back ten times over. That's how the camp resistance works."

"We'll make that work just fine," Claire said. "If your people can provide records, I'll make sure she's trained and gets to stay on in the infirmary."

"All right, I'll see what I can do. No promises, but I'm trying. What about you, Rhonda? Will you agree to stop trying to die long enough to help us here?"

Rhonda hadn't expected that. Blunt and direct. She understood what was being asked, however. Other people were going to help, and she owed them for that. They were going to help because it helped them. It was fair. It wouldn't replace her little boys, but nothing ever would. Until she could be reunited with them, she might as well try to get payback for them. She could do that by helping. That could be their legacy. "I agree to stop dying," she said levelly. "I don't want my boys to die for nothing. I'm going to help because they've paid the price for that."

"That's all we can ask," Claire said.

"That's a smart thing to do," said Esmée. "Pay these sons of bitches back for what they did. We're all in, then. I'll do my part and get cover for you."

"All right."

"Claire, you'll also be happy to know Colonel Schlösser signed off on your request for the Exakta camera. I ordered it today."

"With the fixative and the paper and printer?"

"Everything."

Three hours later, Dr. Berglund took both new nurses, Claire and

Rhonda, on a phlebotomy training round with the patients. It was the second of such sessions for Claire, and she was beginning to feel quite confident only halfway through. By nightfall, both were drawing blood from hands, wrists, and arms successfully. It wasn't much, it wasn't medical breakthroughs, but it was enough to keep them out of the gas chambers. At least for now.

Rhonda Maier moved her new dress and underthings into the nurses' quarters that night. She was given her own bed and her own toiletries and several nurses contributed three more work outfits.

Rhonda was back from the dead.

CLAIRE DREAMED ESMÉE INTO HER BED THAT NIGHT. SHE WAS twelve and Esmée was ten again. The child was frightened and had been crying in her sleep. A bad dream. So she had come into Claire's bed to be held. Claire turned back the covers and allowed her sister to snuggle up against her. Soon Esmée was fast asleep, her head lying on Claire's arm, a smile playing across her lips, breathing deeply. Along about midnight, Claire, in her mind's eye, walked Esmée back to her dormitory in the admin building, helped her back into her bed, and tucked her in for the rest of the night. She then returned to her own bed, awaking six hours later with the feeling the dream had been real. It took several hours before the dream wore off.

Her sister hadn't actually come to her.

Not in physical form, Claire decided.

But there was always more than that.

43

Dr. Berglund held a meeting of his trusted nurses and aides. It was on a late Friday afternoon, when much of the Schlösser staff had already left the hospital for the weekend. Berglund called the meeting together in the infirmary's small kitchen and every seat was taken.

He began with a brief summary for the benefit of Claire and Rhonda. "The experiments upstairs have been initiated by Reichsfuhrer Heinrich Himmler, together with SS-Obergruppenführer Ernst Grawitz, the chief physician of the SS and police, and SS-Standartenführer Wolfram Sievers, the secretary general of the Ancestral Heritage Association and director of the Waffen-SS Military-Scientific Research Institute."

"I guess I've never understood exactly what they're trying to prove," Claire said. "Unless they're just looking for better ways to kill Jews and Gypsies."

"Well, experiments were planned to meet the needs of the army, but mainly to reinforce the bases of racial ideology."

"The superiority of the Nordic race. I've heard of that," Claire said.

"Yes, and you will also be enraged to know that many Nazi doctors experiment on prisoners on behalf of German pharmaceutical companies."

"So, what can we do?" asked a charge nurse. "We've been over this before."

"We have," agreed Dr. Berglund. "And I don't think there's anything we can do to stop it. We're medical people, not soldiers. And while we can't stop it, we can make sure they don't get away with it."

"How do we do that?" Rhonda asked. "It looks to me like this whole camp is getting away with everything."

"Pretty much, it is," Dr. Berglund said. "But I'm having ideas about documenting what they're doing upstairs. And I need volunteers. If you want to help, now's your chance. But before we take volunteers, let me add two things. First, this is going to be very risky. Some of us will get caught and probably die for what we're doing. Second, engaging in these spying activities will almost guarantee you a spot as a witness when these bastards go to trial after the war."

"Trial for what?" Rhonda asked.

"War crimes. That's why we need evidence."

"What will we be doing?"

"Most of you will bring us evidence. You will steal into their labs upstairs and bring evidence of chemicals and experiments that aren't a part of normal hospital practices. One of us will actually go in and take photographs of some of the patients there. Claire, by the way, your new camera was delivered to my office today. It's waiting for you in there. Now you all know who will be taking photographs, our very own star photojournalist and sometimes-nurse, Claire."

"I can hardly wait to get my hands on it," Claire said. "I had this same camera before the war. It's a workhorse."

"Do you have the correct lens?"

"If they filled my order, I do. But even the lens it comes with would probably do in a pinch."

"So we're ready, everyone. Now let me see a show of hands, please, from those who want to volunteer."

Claire looked around. All hands were raised. Every nurse and two male orderlies were sitting or standing in the small room with hands raised overhead.

"All right, then, let's begin. Marian Gabryś and Zofia Mydlarz, you will obtain the blue work pants and blouse of the Schlösser wing. They will be kept in our laundry as of tonight. Wear those to work the next two days. Marian, tomorrow you will appear for a shift upstairs and Zofia the next day. You will perform normal medical care on the patients and be alert for proof of the experiments. You might be looking at unusual medications, chemicals, medical equipment, and so forth. Steal what you can and bring it here. We will photograph it and return it. Most of all, do not get caught. If you get caught, they will torture you and you will give them all of our names, too. Do not get caught. If you do, then die as quickly as you can. Try to escape in plain sight of an armed guard so he shoots you dead. That way you avoid torture and do not give up our names. Are we all agreed on this?"

He looked around. There was no disagreement.

He continued. "The rest of you come see me for your assignments.

No one will know more than a day in advance of their assignment. This is also for everyone's protection."

"What can I do?" asked Rhonda. "I know so little."

"For now, nothing. But your time will come, I promise you. You may be asked to work extra shifts to cover for our loaned employees, but we'll see. For now just wait. Claire, let's go have a look at that new camera."

"Ready," she said and got to her feet.

44

That night, Claire crept up to the experiment floor and began wildly snapping photographs.

Photograph:

camera - Kine Exakta

- Plano-convex magnification

-Xenar 1:2 f=cm fast lens

film - monochrome

bed #1 - soiled sheets

patient #1 - 46-year-old Jewish male with experimenter-inflicted malaria, head-to-toe mosquito bites and swellings, shaking, chills

descriptor:

"Patient without visitors. His eyes fluttered as his temperature (41degrees C.) brought on his delirium. He lay on sweat-stained sheets

with arms outstretched in an endless attempt to elicit help that never came. He was observed for signs and symptoms only."

title:

"Torment"

bed #2 - soiled sheets

patient #2 - 22-year-old Jewish female with experimenter-inflicted outdoor freezing session (snow bank, unclothed, -21-degrees C., 12 1/2 hours). Frostbite and her decreased core temperature resulted in black skin with oozing blisters on feet, lower limbs, hands, face and ears; unrecognizable as a person.

descriptor:

"Patient without visitors. Gangrene had set in. She lay perfectly still, her chest imperceptibly raising and lowering, verging on death. She was observed for signs and symptoms only."

title:

"Misery"

bed #3 - soiled sheets

patient #3 - 17-year-old Jewish female with experimenter-inflicted IV of seawater only, no food for weeks.

descriptor:

"Patient without visitors. She was bloated and glassy-eyed with total incontinence—urine and feces. She begged continuously for water. She was observed for signs and symptoms only."

title:

"Anguish"

Claire recoiled in horror but then forced herself to return and continue with her pictures. And there were more. So many more that Claire just wasn't going to have the time to photograph. Tears streamed down her cheeks as she held her breath against the stench emanating from every corner, from every bed. But it reached a moment where she just couldn't go on. The evil overcame her good and won. She fled the floor and vowed she'd never go back. If she did, she feared she would die there, too, which did no one any good because then the flow of pictures to the outside world would cease and her camera warfare would screech to a halt.

45

Berglund called Claire into his off the next day and closed the door behind him. "Let's sit down. We have a problem. I didn't want to say anything at the meeting."

"About the spying on the experiment floor?"

"No, about Mr. Rothstein. Remember they fractured his arm, injured his hand, and fractured his leg?"

"The locksmith. I see him every day. He's not doing well."

"We need to get him out of here to a hospital or we're going to lose him. The SS is complaining that he's not back to work fixing locks. They're getting suspicious because it's taking so long. I'm afraid they're going to come for him."

"How can I help, Pietor?"

"I want to transport him to Oświęcim Hospital."

"Do you want me to drive?"

"No, but I need you to care for him in the backseat of my car. He's on an antibiotics drip again."

"All right. Who's driving?"

"I'm driving. I'm the one who can get him admitted to the hospital without papers. They know me there."

"When do we leave?"

"Now. When it gets dark."

"Goodness. How will we get him out of the camp?"

"I've stolen an SS uniform. The gate guards know me. I'll tell them I'm taking an SS soldier to Krakow."

"But we're really going to Oświęcim."

"Exactly. You should be very frightened just now. We could easily end up dead, Claire."

"But we may save him, too. The risk is worth it to me."

"Exactly how I feel. I'm sworn to save lives and, sweet Jesus, that's what I mean to do."

"Maybe coming home you could stop and buy me that dinner you've been talking about."

"My dear Claire, if we are lucky enough to survive that long, I'd be glad to buy your dinner. Or whatever else you'd like. Believe me, I'll be at your service."

"Well, there is that fur coat...just kidding! Dinner is fine."

"Dinner it is, then."

Two hours later, they were taking Rothstein downstairs on a stretcher with the help of two aides, setting him down inside the doctor's car and leaning his back against the door so his leg could fully extend. Claire got situated in the back so she could help with the antibiotic drip. The doctor had also given him painkiller, so once loaded inside the car, Rothstein was feeling better than any of his helpers.

"Doctor, see you when you get back," one of the aides said. "Until then, we're here for you. We'll be watching out for your patients."

"Thank you, my friends. We won't be gone too long."

"We've got the patients," the second aide reassured the doctor.

"I know you do. Goodbye, now."

After he had pulled the car out of its parking area, the aides asked that everyone say a prayer.

"Great news!" Pietor said from the front seat as he drove away from the hospital. "Admin has provided me with forged papers for Herman Rothstein. We are going to use the identity of an SS guard no longer in this camp."

"Wonderful news," said Claire. "What's his name, just so I know."

"Helmut Manfred. He was a very cruel guard, as I recall."

They were approaching the first gate leading out of Auschwitz concentration camp. The place was double-gated on the theory that escapees might be missed by Gate 1, but they wouldn't be missed again on Gate 2. The whole Nazi mentality about the concentration camps around Western Europe was that information about the camps never leave the camps. Police and soldiers who worked there were sworn to secrecy, as well as the other technical workers who drove in everyday from as far away as Krakow.

The vehicle was a blue over white Nysa mini-van that had once done service as a police car. The first backseat was removed and they had been able to wedge a chair inside for Claire so she was facing the patient and able to care for him.

When they pulled up to Gate 1, Dr. Berglund rolled down his window. He indicated the backseat. "Taking a guard to hospital. He's SS. Show him the papers, nurse."

Claire rolled down her window and handed the forged ID paperwork to the guard. He was middle-aged, beefy, with a very large, round face and a hat a size too big that pressed down on his ears. He studied the ID papers, turning them this way and that, turning them over and reading the backside, and studying the signature for authenticity. The transfer papers were seemingly signed by Colonel Schlösser, and once that was read, he quickly passed them back to Claire. But there seemed to be some confusion around the sick SS guard's ID papers."

"Can he stand up and let us measure his height?" asked the gate guard. "We can compare his height to what the ID papers say."

"He can't stand. He was brutally injured by inmates. They've been punished, but it's left him so he can't stand and can't even walk. We had to carry him to the car."

"His leg. A cast?"

"Yes, his leg is fractured."

"How could a weak prisoner fracture the leg of a strong guard?"

"He pushed him into a grave. The brave guard fell backward into the hole, and it broke his leg and arm. It was terrible. The prisoner was shot right there."

"How long will Sergeant Manfred be in hospital?"

"Whatever it takes to see him fully recovered. Maybe one week, maybe three."

"Is there anyone hiding in the back end of this van?"

"No. Open the back doors if you will. Just don't freeze us out in here, please."

"Pass me the keys to the back end."

Dr. Berglund removed the ignition keys and passed them to the guard. He immediately marched around to the rear doors and unlocked them. It was easy to see there was no other passenger. He returned the keys to the doctor.

"You may go," said the SS guard and thumped the fender of the van. The doctor put it in first gear and passed on through the checkpoint, only to arrive at the second. This time, the lift gate immediately rose, and the vehicle was waved through.

"Evidently, the first gate called the second. So they saved some time and us some aggravation. Good going, Herr Rothstein, to remain silent."

Claire leaned toward Rothstein and lowered her head. "He says he needs water and quiet. He wishes to sleep."

"We can make it very quiet in here. Please get him some water, and we shan't speak again until we reach the hospital."

They sped north on Highway 112 toward the city. The night air pressed against the warm interior windows as the van whizzed through small town after small town, interspersed with fallow fields and fields of winter wheat. "Mr. Rothstein says his pain is increasing," Claire announced. "He wants more morphine. Should I supply another dose?"

"Yes, please," answered Dr. Berglund. "I don't think he can be over-dosed very easily at this point. He's been taking doses of morphine for so long he's probably developed a high tolerance for the stuff.

We'll give whatever he needs to him. Good man, Herr Rothstein," he said into the rearview mirror, calling back to encourage his patient.

"Wow, easy," said Claire in awe of how easily they'd passed through security back Auschwitz.

"I know. Amazing," Rothstein groaned. "Will the hospital be so easy?"

"I don't know. But evidently the papers pass muster, so we'll see."

Two hours later, they arrived at the hospital ER entrance, and Dr. Berglund hurried inside for assistance. Within minutes, orderlies with a stretcher were removing the patient from the van and wheeling him inside the hospital. Claire and Dr. Berglund followed them inside.

"Who is this man?" asked the admitting clerk.

"A patient of mine. An SS guard from the camp."

"His papers?"

"Right here."

"His name is Helmut Manfred?"

"It is. I know him personally," said Dr. Berglund.

"And I know you, Dr. Berglund," the clerk smiled. "So we shall admit your man, and we'll call you after he's registered and assessed. That will probably be later tomorrow morning. Is that fine?"

"That is fine. I'll be at the base hospital."

"Of course, Major. Will that be all?"

"Yes, it is. Thank you all."

Claire watched this with no small degree of astonishment. If only it were that easy for all Jews to leave the camp and get the help they desperately needed. The entire transaction pleased her and made her glad she had come.

Then they reloaded in the van, Dr. Berglund driving. "I know of a great Polish restaurant if you'd care to have some real food?"

"It would be my great honor," she said. "It has been too many years since I've gotten to eat real food. Colonel Schlösser was good enough to us, but the food we were fed wasn't what the rest of the family was getting. We ate mostly potatoes and a small piece of meat every third night."

"I know just the place for you then, Claire."

She was sitting beside him in the front seat now. It was a bench seat, and she was so tired she only wanted to lie down on it and get some sleep. Maybe that would possible later.

Starka Restaurant in downtown Oświęcim was a fancy enough place, leaving Claire feeling underdressed, compared to how the other women were dressed in all their finery for a late dinner. They were coming in from the clubs and movies and social entertainments, most of them a little tipsy, so the crowd was loud and brassy—a perfect place for Claire and Dr. Berglund to slip inside and fade into the background. They requested and received a seat near the rear, across the aisle from the kitchen doors, where it was darker and more remote from the front door where a squad of Germans might just poke their heads in and look around. The waiter came around. "What's a typical Polish dinner?" Claire asked the man.

He pushed his glasses back on his nose and pulled himself to his full height, as it was time to perform. "Well, I would recommend vodka distilled from rye, which is known as the national drink. I would then begin with Bigos, a kind of Polish Hunter's Stew, include a side of Pierogi Dumplings and some Golabki, or stuffed cabbage rolls. You can then try some cheesecake for a little sweet after the main meal."

The vodka was served straight up with a side glass of ice cubes. Dr. Berglund poured and Claire took her first swallow. It burned all the way down, and she asked whether they might get a nice wine. Dr. Berglund followed up the vodka order with a wine order, and soon she was sipping a very smooth Chardonnay from France. Dr. Berglund had switched to coffee after one vodka because he was driving.

"So tell me, Claire, are you unmarried?"

"No, I am married, or at least I think I am. Schildmann is my husband's name. I have no idea if Remy is alive or dead. Or, if he is alive, if he has remarried. I've been gone from him for over two years now. And my sweet Lima, too."

"And who is Lima?" Pietor asked.

Claire paused, but then decided to stick to the truth as closely as possible. "She is my adopted daughter. She would be...almost six years old now."

"Where is she?"

"She is with my mother and father and younger brothers, some-where safe. And I thank God every day for that." She took another sip of her wine. "And how about you? Are you married?"

"I was. She died in childbirth under my hand. I wasn't an obstetri-cian but we had no money while I was in medical college so I tried to deliver her at home. It was a horrible mess, and I almost got arrested for the botched job. I should have been arrested or made to die with her. It was only fair. But my parents stepped in, my father's a surgeon in Hamburg, and they made it go away. So I finished school with a broken heart and have been alone ever since. It just hasn't seemed like the right time to get involved again. Plus the war—how can two people commit in the midst of such uncertainty? It seems dishonest to me now."

"I feel the same. Maybe it is dishonest. Maybe people should just be friends during this time. That would be enough for me." She thought of Remy as she said this. Had he even been real? Or was he another dream, like Esmée at ten?

Pietor smiled and looked deeply into her eyes. "What about while you are away from the prison camp? Would you have time then for a little romance?"

"Like tonight? Is that what you're asking? It seems it would be extremely difficult in light of how things are. There's no safety, and I need to feel safe to have romance. I know it's silly, but that's just how I am right now. Besides, I am married."

"So, I should not make a pass at you?"

She paused, then returned her wine glass to the linen tablecloth. "I've never had a man ask me that. But I am a married woman. Understand?"

They finished their meal while making small talk. At last came the cheesecake and strong, thick Polish coffee. Reichsmarks were the currency of Poland then, and Dr. Berglund paid with several large bills. Change was brought and refused, left behind for the wait-staff and sommelier. Then they loaded back in the van, and the doctor switched on the motor. But that was as far as he went.

"Can I come over beside you?" he asked.

"I don't think so."

"I am going to try."

"I am going to struggle. I love my husband."

"Who may no longer be alive. Do this with me, Claire, while we're still alive. When we return to the camp and they find out, we're both dead anyway."

"Cheat while I'm alive? I can't do that. I won't."

"Then I'm going to force you. Please don't resist."

"I'm going to scream and run away."

"No, you won't. You told me about your sister in Admin. Your sister is their guarantee you will return. They have your sister, and they will hurt her if you run away."

"But they don't know she's my sister."

"They don't need to know. They'll hurt her anyway if our scheme gets revealed by you not returning with me. We don't want them to find out, am I right?"

He moved across the seat and raised his right arm up around her shoulders. With his left hand he reached and gently turned her face to his. His lips passed over the area around her mouth before settling there for a long, gentle kiss. Her lips parted, and she tasted his tongue. He brushed his lips against her ear, and then nibbling and tugging, he finally drew her lobe into his mouth. When he drew her to him, she could feel his arousal, and when he kissed her again, she too, became aroused and didn't resist when his hand passed over her breasts. Then she was gone, her face turned to the roof, letting the pleasure sweep over her. She finally yielded her lower body to his hand, even pulling up her dress herself. They made love, awkward as it was, on the front seat, and it lasted but a short time.

She felt horrible. She wept. "You shouldn't have. I am too weak to resist."

He stayed close, and lovingly whispered in her ear, telling her how nice she was to make love to and how much he enjoyed their time together just then. She took his hands in her own and refused to let go, rubbing his fingers and kissing his fingertips while she wept her regret that she hadn't struggled. It was one more German war crime, she thought.

"It's time," he said simply. "We must go so we don't arrive back at the camp later than would be expected. I've made this run before, and it's about six hours round-trip with the hospital stopover and with the meal at Starka Restaurant."

"Oh," she said sadly. "I suppose I'll nap on the way back if that's okay." She wanted to get far, far away. She imagined she could only do that through the magic of sleep and dreams.

"Please do. We'll have to work tomorrow anyway. So sleep away, dear one."

"Please don't call me that. I am no one's dear one anymore. Maybe Remy's—if he lives."

She closed her eyes and slowly fell asleep with the rumble of the tires on the road, the whisper of the warm air from the heater, and the doctor's slow breathing. It was her time to just let go for a few hours and feel no fear. Only then could sleep come and she be released from Hell.

So she did.

46

Shem Wasilewski was the lab tech on duty the night Herman Rothstein was admitted. He helped with the admission then took Rothstein to his bed and made him comfortable. Part of his lab duties was to draw blood and do a blood study, including type and cross-match. One hour after his break that same night, he was in the lab studying the results. In reviewing the admission notes and the new chart, Wasilewski made a discovery: Helmut Manfred had been admitted to the hospital previously and his blood type was A-positive. He looked at that night's blood test again and blinked twice. Type AB. Had he gotten the results mixed up with another patient? Just to be sure, he went back to Rothstein's bedside and drew blood a second time. This time he personally walked it back into the lab and tested it on the spot. AB once again. Now he was confused because this Helmut Manfred's blood type didn't match the previous Helmut Manfred's blood type. So, Wasilewski did what all careful lab techs would do and called the Auschwitz switchboard and asked to speak to someone about a confusing blood type. He wasn't connected through to the infirmary, however. The sharp-eyed telephone operator connected him to records and ID, a stratum within the SS.

SS records clerk Hiram Goten took the call. He immediately began looking around in Helmut Manfred's records. "It says here," he told Wasilewski, waiting on the other end of the line, "that our SS sergeant Helmut Manfred's blood type is A-positive. What is your patient's type?"

"AB?"

"And who brought him to you?"

"Dr. Pietor Berglund. He's from Auschwitz."

"Oh, yes, we're well-acquainted with our Dr. Berglund. He's treated many of us over the past two years. He said the man's name was Helmut Manfred?"

"Yes, he said he was a guard at Auschwitz."

"Is your Mr. Helmut Manfred wearing steel eyeglasses?"

"No eyeglasses, no false teeth."

"Our Herr Manfred wears steel eyeglasses and has two gold teeth in the back of his mouth, upper."

"This man has no gold teeth."

"Then you don't have our Helmut Manfred, sir."

Said the lab tech, Wasilewski, "Okay, then who do I have?"

"I'm going to admit I don't know. But I will find out. Goodbye."

"Goodbye."

Hiram Goten, upon hanging up the phone, went across the hallway into his sergeant's office.

"Sir? I've had a call from a hospital."

He went on to explain the differentials. The sergeant became incensed, as he'd seen every kind of prisoner smuggling known to man, and he hated to lose even one prisoner.

"Bring Dr. Berglund to me when he returns. Place him under arrest as well."

"Yes, sir."

"And don't report back to the hospital. Just tell their front office we want a hold placed on their version of Helmut Manfred."

"Yes, sir."

"My guess is their Mr. Helmut Manfred is nothing but a Jew wearing an SS sergeant's clothing. Number two, I want you to go to our infirmary. Get a patient list from twenty-four hours ago. Check that list against all male patients presently remaining in the infirmary. When you find one less than those on the list, then we will have the real name of Helmut Manfred at the hospital. My money says he's a Jew."

"I won't bet against you, Sergeant."

"Oh, and one other thing. Once you have the name of the missing patient, go next door to Admin and find out who prepared the ID papers for Sergeant Helmut Manfred's transfer to Oświęcim Hospital. Please bring me the name of the clerk who prepared those papers, Corporal Goten."

"Yes, sir."

"Then we shall report to the Colonel."

Colonel Gabisch Pennske took all of it in very methodically, asking all the right questions but letting his men present the details in order, as well. So far, it appeared that Esmée Vallant of Admin had forged papers for a patient named Herman Rothstein. The papers introduced Rothstein as SS Sergeant Helmut Manfred, a Pole and a non-Jew who joined the SS in Germany before the invasion. He had been injured in the original fighting in Poland, where he served as a special emissary because he spoke Polish fluently. He had lately been serving at Auschwitz but then was rotated to Treblinka where he was serving presently. He hadn't set foot in Auschwitz in over a year. After Esmée Vallant forged the records for Herman Rothstein, he was bundled up by Dr. Pietor Berglund and taken by van to Oświęcim Hospital despite having told the gate guards he was going to a hospital in Krakow. It was all a big lie, which began to unravel when lab tech Wasilewski discovered the differential blood types and the differential dental works.

"So now we are looking for Dr. Berglund?" asked Colonel Pennske.

"Yes, sir," said Colonel Schlösser, who was Pennske's superior officer. "When you find Dr. Berglund, I want him put in the stockade. Jew rations. Now, who else went with him?"

"The only nurse missing at roll call was Claire Schildmann."

"Claire!" exclaimed Colonel Schlösser. "That, I find hard to believe. She worked in my home for over a year. My guess is that she's an unwitting accomplice. The poor girl hardly knows the difference between a Jew and a salamander. She probably has no idea she was aiding the enemy. I'm sure Dr. Berglund lured her in."

"So she's not complicit?" asked Colonel Pennske.

"*Nein.* That would be the last thing I would ever believe about her. She has no idea."

"Corporal Goten, you are to escort Fräu Schildmann, the nurse, back to her nurses' quarters at the infirmary when she arrives. She is not to be harmed or threatened but treated with all due respect. Do you understand me, Corporal?"

"Yes, sir."

Schlösser paused. He didn't know what to make of his putative daughter, Esmée Vallant. He was speechless. How in God's name could she betray him like this? Once French, always French. He had misjudged her.

"And in the meantime, I want all of Dr. Berglund's personal records brought to me. You will review those records, summarize them, and present them to me. My guess is that our Dr. Berglund has been very busy committing treason against the Führer. We'll be amazed but not surprised at what we find."

"What do I do with Esmée Vallant, Colonel?" asked Goten. "Does she go to the stockade, too?"

"Yes, she does. Jew rations for her, as well. Make sure there is no sunlight and no meat. One glass of water per day. No communication with any other prisoner. She's a troublemaker, and I want her out of circulation altogether. I also want her confession. Do what needs to be done. Hurt this Esmée Vallant if you must. We have to get to the bottom of how this happened." He was giving her up. Her run with him was at an end.

"Yes, Colonel," said Goten, snapping to. "Consider it done, sir."

"All right. Heil Hitler, gentlemen."

"Heil Hitler!"

The next day in his office, Schlösser summoned two junior officers.

"I want you to arrange a meeting of all prisoners—and all guards. I want a stage built where I can speak—a fine stage of new lumber. And I want a gallows."

"A gallows, Herr Colonel?" asked one of the captains.

"I am going to hang someone. Maybe two. We are going to have a spectacle."

"Is it for a holiday?"

"No. Make it one month from today. No more, no less. Don't fail me, gentlemen, understand?"

"Yes, sir!"

"Oh, one more design characteristic for my stage. A huge sign across the front. Make it say, 'Abandon Hope, You've Entered Here.'"

"Yes, Colonel!" cried the officers in unison.

"Good, now get out."

47

They came for her just before dawn when sleep was the deepest. One minute she was sleeping soundly, and in the next instant, she was on her back, on the floor of her small cubicle of a room, looking up at a man who poured the contents of her chamber pot into her face. The urine tasted salty and burned her eyes. She coughed and tried rolling to her side, but the man's arms held her pinned. He slapped her three times, back, forth, and back again.

"Who put you up to it?"

"I don't—I don't know what you mean!"

The man above her stood and kicked her with all the power he could generate in his foot. The toe of his boot caught her just below the pubis bone, and she all but passed out with the pain. She gasped and began sobbing.

"Get Colonel Schlösser," she cried. "He'll explain who I am."

"The Colonel says you're a traitor who should be shot. Is that the Colonel you mean?"

"Yes, no. I haven't done anything."

"Fräulein, we know you forged papers for Herman Rothstein. Just admit it. Once you tell us the truth, we can stop hurting you. Do you want us to hurt you again?"

She didn't respond so he again kicked Esmée, this time in the face. Her nose was shattered and began spraying blood everywhere. She was blinded but could feel her nightgown being torn away.

"You will talk. We will take you outside in the snow completely nude and leave you there for the crows until you tell us who asked you to forge the ID. Who did it? Who? Who?"

"It was—it was—"

She wouldn't say. It was her own sister who had come to her for the forged records. Claire was the one who'd actually come next door and told her of the plan to move Herman Rothstein. How could she say her sister's name to the Nazis? That just couldn't happen. So...she held her tongue.

They stood her up and marched her down the stairs of her dormitory complex, down a long sidewalk, and through a gate leading to the actual prison side of the camp. She saw the Men's Camp, the Family Camp, the Gypsy camp and beyond. Down to the far end of the path they made her travel, and she passed all five gas chambers/crematoria as she made her way to the Women's Camp. At the first set of barracks there, they unlocked the door and led her inside.

"See? It is warm in here. This is where you get to come when you talk. Now, back outside with you."

The wind was howling and snow blew sideways, horizontal to the earth as they led her down beyond the perimeter fence and out past the mass graves. There, at the end of the mass graves, she was manacled and chained to one of the hanging posts. They didn't raise her up on the post to hang her, however. They were just going to leave her there in the elements, nude and freezing, broken nose, maybe a broken hand where a jackboot had stomped it, crying and begging for mercy. "Please get Colonel Schlösser! He will tell you who I am!"

"Nonsense!" cried Goten. "Colonel Schlösser told us to bring you here and leave you to die. I'll be back in two hours. You can tell me then if you have a name for me. Goodbye, Esmée Vallant."

The men left her there with wind howling. She tried to shelter beside the thin pole they had chained her to. "Oh, Claire, please come to me. Please tell them!"

It wasn't two hours, but three. Finally Goten, wearing his heavy wool coat, cap and black gloves, and field marshal boots appeared to her out of the morning mist. He wasn't smiling. He was holding a steaming liquid, and she fixated on it. "For me?" she cried.

"This? This is my coffee. I'll give it to you for a name. You can hold it in your hands and feel its warmth for a name."

"I don't know the person who came to me. I don't have their name. Please believe me."

"Man or woman?"

"What?"

"Was it a man or a woman who came to you?"

"I—I—"

"Never mind. I'll return again in two hours. You will probably die this time from exposure, but we shall see. It doesn't matter to me. The grave is right behind you. We'll just unclip you and kick your body down into the hole. You're young, but the dead will welcome you. Goodbye, Esmée Vallant!"

Esmée maintained consciousness for another half-hour then at last succumbed to the mind-numbing, body-killing cold and passed out. Two hours later, Goten sent men to take her down and return her to the women's barracks. He had orders to obtain her confession, not to kill her. The other prisoners found a striped pajama top for her and trousers, and another gave up a pair of boots they'd been hoarding.

She came to and found herself among the working dead, prisoners whose lives were meted out a day at a time as they dug graves, transported dead bodies, and even went into the woods and felled trees and cut them up for firewood for the crematoria. The ovens ran around-the-clock so that duty was fairly common. Now they took Esmée and placed her on one of the wooden beds where two prisoners lay on either side of her and shared their body warmth. An hour later, the shaking was brought under control, and her tears could be explained to the others.

She was just warming up, feeling like she might not die from the cold, when they came for her again. It was again Corporal Goten. There, in front of the crowd gathered around her, he beat her with his swagger stick, a two-foot, leather-covered rod that bent easily and lent itself to whipping prisoners into submission. He hit her once, twice, then roughly hit her with his fist. "Names!" he cried. "Who told you to forge the name? Tell me and I will stop! Tell me and I will feed you! Tell me and I will give the barracks a meat ration tonight!"

She eventually passed out from the beating. It was clear to Corporal Goten that she wasn't going to talk. He went to Colonel Schlösser and told him of her resolve even in the face of the worst torture.

"I don't want her dead," said Schlösser. "Not yet. My stage is completed. One week until I have my hanging. After tonight, we will add another name to Esmée's as the featured entertainment."

"Yes, Herr Colonel."

Schlösser's eyes narrowed. "Bring me Dr. Berglund when he arrives back here. We shall interrogate him."

"Yes, Herr Colonel!"

48

"*A teraz na jutrzejszy raport pogodowy. W ciągu jednej nocy będzie dwadzieścia stopni poniżej zera.*"

"What is the wireless saying?" asked Claire as she came awake in the car. The car wireless was droning on in Polish, and she awoke to realize she was still in Poland, where in her dream, she was in France.

Dr. Berglund replied, "He's telling tomorrow's weather. Twenty below zero."

"What are those lights in the sky?"

"Those are the lights of Auschwitz. We are almost back. Now listen, if anyone asks anything, you didn't know who we were taking tonight. You were only doing your job, understand?"

"I understand."

"I don't want you caught up in this. You're the innocent worker who I pressed into service. Understand me? Don't try anything brave with these people, like telling the truth if they ask ques-

tions. That will only get you killed. Understand?" he asked
again.

"I understand."

"Good. Stay clear of what I've done here."

Claire meant to maintain her innocence, too. She had Rhonda to
take care of, and she had Esmée to watch over. She saw no need to
be caught up in the night's rescue mission as one of the complicit
ones. It would serve no purpose.

They drove on until the bright night sky above Auschwitz with its
hundreds of guard station lights and spotlights soon took over the
entire horizon before them. Claire saw all this and shivered even
though it was warm inside the van.

Then they were pulling up to the main entrance with its words
above the entrance, *Arbeit Macht Frei*—"Work Sets You Free"—
put there by the SS to fool new arrivals into thinking they had
come to a work camp, and that was the reason for the showers
upon arrival, to delouse and prepare for work after the long, dirty
journey by train. The guard station arm was lowered. Two guards
came up to Dr. Berglund's driver's window.

"Please exit, Doctor."

"What? Get out of my van?"

"Please, yes," said the huskier of the two. His finger was clearly on
the trigger of his automatic weapon. Dr. Berglund resignedly
opened his door and climbed out.

"What now?"

"The Colonel wants a word with you, Herr Doctor."

"The girl had nothing to do with this. She's an innocent nurse."

"She will be returned to her quarters. The Colonel has not asked to see her."

The doctor sighed and held out his hands as he'd seen a thousand other prisoners do. He was manacled and led away.

Claire watched all this in horror. It was over that fast. One minute he was with her and, in the next, he was being led away by the SS guards. She trembled from her head down to her toes out of fear for him. It was a helpless feeling that swept over her, the same feeling she'd had upon being taken captive after the night of the Commissioner for Jews attack in Paris. Totally helpless and without words, a good thing at this point, she was whisked back to the infirmary and told to return to her quarters, that she'd be back to work the next day. She headed upstairs with a heavy heart. The man who'd seduced her was under lock and key somewhere—she had no idea where—but she had a fairly good idea about how he was being treated, and it broke her heart to think on those things. She doubted she would ever see him again. Tears washed into her eyes as she lay down in her bed and cried herself into a fitful sleep.

When she awoke, she hated what he'd done to her in the van. But she loved him for all the other good he had brought to the horrible world of Auschwitz. She was conflicted. She found her ideas of right and wrong had been totally erased by the camp. She would allow anyone to do anything to her, no longer having either the strength or the will to resist. She thought about giving herself up to save the doctor because the patients needed him more than they needed her. But if she did, she would never see Lima again, and Lima needed her and she needed Lima. The little girl was her path back to good in the world. She needed her more than ever.

"Doctor," Colonel Schlösser was saying to the manacled, bruised, and battered Pietor Berglund the next morning, "I don't understand why you would risk everything for one patient. Yes, we've been through your personal effects and some of your infirmary records. We know what you've been doing down there. As of this morning, all Jews have been removed from your infirmary. Only our forces remain there. Your replacement will treat no more Jews ever again. That's how your efforts have turned out, then. Are you proud of what you've done here?"

"I have—have—nothing to say," Dr. Berglund managed to say through teeth that were broken and shattered from his beatings overnight. "You should just kill me now and be done with it. I beg you."

"Nonsense! We are having a public spectacle in one week, and you are now the starring attraction! You and your friend Esmée Vallant. Who made her forge the papers for Sergeant Manfred, Doctor? Was that you? Someone else? Tell us and you will receive water."

"I will tell you—nothing. Kill me and be done with it, please."

"Oh, we want the entire camp to watch you die. The other workers will see what betrayal costs in Auschwitz. You can be sure you will be the starring attraction in just one week, Doctor. Of course, by then you will be begging for death anyway. Corporal Goten, get this man out of my sight. Take him to the stockade and hurt him but do not kill him."

"Yes, mein Oberst," Goten replied.

"Off, now!"

49

Claire was allowed to visit Dr. Berglund twice. She was allowed to visit because Colonel Schlösser, relying on his familiarity with her, encouraged Claire to get Dr. Berglund to give up the names of everyone involved in the transfer of Herman Rothstein as Sergeant Helmut Manfred to Oświęcim Hospital. She said she would try, although she had no intention of doing any such thing. Especially since Esmée had helped, too. She had yet to see her sister and could only hope she was alive.

During the time of his incarceration, her heart was breaking. Here was a man who, she'd had to admit, she loved for his patients. It was her first feeling of love since Remy Schildmann. But, she knew, she didn't love him in a romantic sense. It was more a kind of human love for the good another imbues into life. It pained her to her core to think of him held in total darkness, freezing without adequate clothing and no heat, and given just enough food and water to sustain life.

The first time she saw him, two days after his arrest, she was shocked to find how much weight he had lost and shocked to find him blinded by the light in the visitors' room of the stockade. He was wearing thin cotton trousers, an undershirt, but no shoes. His skin was gray and his eyes rheumy and dilated. The prisoner and visitor weren't allowed to touch and wouldn't have anyway, given what even the slightest contact might have signaled to the German guard assigned to monitor the visit.

"Colonel Schlösser promises that if you'll give him the names of everyone involved he will commute your death sentence to life imprisonment."

Dr. Berglund's face brightened just for a moment, but then he laughed.

"Oh, my dear Claire, death would be so very welcome today, right now. I should be so much happier dead."

"Please," she whispered, "you're not the only one to think about. Think of staying alive until the Allies arrive and free the prisoners. You can have your life back when the war ends, Pietor. Please think about this."

"They're not going to allow me to live. I'm to be hanged as a public warning to other workers, Claire."

She forced the tears from her eyes as she didn't want him to see her crying. "There's no need. He said he will commute you, and I believe him. Please, Pietor. It's not so bad to give them my name. If you won't, then I will. Your patients need you!"

His face fell and his eyes closed. "Don't. Please promise. I will hang myself if you do, dear Claire."

"No, no, no, please don't talk like that! I won't, I promise. I'll say nothing."

The visit lasted only five minutes. She left the stockade feeling utterly discouraged by his words. He wanted to die. The doctor giving himself up for his patients in the fullest sense of the words.

That night, she went to bed and actually said a prayer, the first one since catechism. She prayed for his soul and for his peace.

It was time to let him go.

50

1 5 February 1944 and the dawn came without the sun. There was a low-hanging layer of storm clouds, blowing snow mixed with icy sleet, making walkways slippery. The morning was dark, never growing light, and the sky angry.

At seven a.m., several guards prepared Colonel Schlösser's stage for his speech and the executions that would follow. First, the prisoners had dug a wide fire pit in front of the stage, extending from corner to corner. Then they lit a fire down inside, out of the scoop of the winds. The fire pit would catch the hanged bodies once they were taken down and thrown from the stage. The entire area smelled of burning human flesh from the nearby crematoria, where the gassing and cremations continued around-the-clock day after day, week after week, and month after month.

At eight a.m., Dr. Berglund and Esmée were rousted from their stockade cells and marched out beyond the perimeter wire to the stage. They were forced up onto the stage and made to stand underneath the gallows crossbar. Both prisoners were wearing the striped cotton pajamas that all Auschwitz prisoners wore day in and day out. Esmée's eyes were clear, gray in the morning gloom, while the doctor's blue eyes were lackluster and resigned. No words were spoken, not even when the two prisoners stood side-by-side underneath the gallows. Esmée then turned her face to the sky and appeared to be silently praying. While the doctor, on the other hand, hung his head, staring at his feet, looking neither right nor left. Then a guard from the near side asked him to stand more upright. Hangman's nooses were fixed around their necks. Given a choice, Pietor Berglund would've thrown himself off the stage and hung himself, but the architecture and placement of nooses in relation to the front of the stage didn't allow for that. So he stood there, clad only in thin cotton, shaking from the sharp wind and bone-chilling damp, the noose around his neck, his hands tied behind him, now speaking softly to Esmée. She stood beside him, now weeping and praying wildly, almost out of control, begging anyone who came near for mercy. Of course, there was no mercy. She was Colonel Schlösser's prisoner, and mercy was out of the question at that point.

Claire had awoken at six a.m. that day and fell to praying as soon as her eyes opened. She prayed for Dr. Berglund's soul and for Esmée's soul, who she found out was to be hung, too. She prayed an intercessory prayer, seeking Divine intervention, for God to send his angels and save the doctor and her sister. But deep down she knew she was a non-believer. She had seen too much evil to ever allow room in her world for a loving God as described by the people in the world who yet believed. One hour in a concentration camp, she would say, and you would revise all of your beliefs for the rest of your lifetime. The speech was scheduled for ten a.m. and so, at nine-thirty, Claire told the other nurses that she was leaving to walk out to the stage.

Colonel Schlösser was beside himself. His dress tunic had a soiled spot above the stripes on its right sleeve, and that had put him into a rage. He cursed the laundress, cursed the other household help, and even told his wife he was sending her back to Germany, for she was "utterly and hopelessly useless to a commanding officer of the Third Reich." She was broken-hearted and called the twins to her side and tried to protect them from their father's ranting and lunatic raves. It wasn't the first time she'd ever seen him on fire, but it was the first time she'd ever seen it to this degree.

A number of important SS officials overseeing Auschwitz had been invited to the speech. The commander of the SS, *Reichsführer-SS* Heinrich Himmler, was the highest SS official with knowledge of Auschwitz and the function the camp served. Himmler was known to issue direct orders to the camp commander, bypassing all other chain of command, in response to his own directives. Himmler would also occasionally receive broad instructions from Adolf Hitler or Hermann Göring, which he would then interpret as he saw fit and transmit to the Auschwitz Camp Commander.

Below Himmler, the most senior operational SS commander involved with Auschwitz was *SS-Obergruppenführer* Oswald Pohl, who served as head of the SS Main Economics Office, known as the *SS-Wirtschafts-Verwaltungshauptamt* or SS-WVHA. Pohl's subordinate, SS-*Gruppenführer* Richard Glücks, served as the *Amtschef* (Department Chief) of the Concentration Camps Inspectorate, which was known as "Department D" within the WVHA. It was Glücks who was seen as the direct superior to the camp commandant of Auschwitz, SS-*Obersturmbannführer* Rudolf Höss. On the stage that day Pohl and Höss were expected, plus Schlösser and Pennske. So Colonel Schlösser thought himself entirely within his rights as second-in-command of the camp to demand that his uniform be spotless. He knew theirs would be, and he wouldn't settle for less. In fact, he couldn't afford to settle for less.

Wachbattalion personnel were absolutely required to be in attendance as it was their control over the camp that had come up short
when Dr. Berglund was allowed to escape "with his Jew," as the
memo stated, demanding their attendance.

At nine-thirty a.m., Schlösser and Pennske began their slow
amble, as they talked and discussed the camp, out beyond the wire
and up onto the stage. Across the back of the stage, the SS had
arranged a half dozen chairs in a semi-circle for the visiting brass
and for the two Colonels. As they arranged themselves, Schlösser
kept a sharp eye out for Claire, who was to bring her camera and
come photograph the occasion for the Reich newsmagazine. It was
one more way Schlösser meant to aggrandize himself and bring
more notice on his remarkable achievements as the SS officer who
actually managed the day-to-day camp activities.

Next came the audience, consisting of trusted camp workers. Most
of these would be lower-grade enlisted men of the Wehrmacht,
but a good number would also be Jews who had proven themselves capable and trustworthy in hands-on jobs at the camp,
including Jewish dentists responsible for removing the gold from
cadavers' teeth, the ladder men who piled the dead bodies on
ladders inside the gas chambers then ran them out one at a time to
the crematoria where they were thrown into the fire, firemen
responsible for the operations of the crematoria, woodworkers
from the forest crews, and other manual tradespeople that kept
the camp operating and slaying Jews and Gypsies by the thousands every day. Schlösser's whole point in making them watch
the hangings was to reinforce in them the notion of futility in
trying to help Jews escape such as Dr. Berglund and his aide
Esmée Vallant had done. Finally, Herman Rothstein himself, the
escaped Jewish locksmith, would be hanged as an example of
what happens to trustees who tried to escape. His agonies would
be long and terrible as he would be hung by a noose around his

bare chest and left hanging there in the elements long after everyone else had left until he died of exposure and starvation.

At 10 o'clock, Colonel Schlösser approached the podium and stepped up behind the lectern. Off to his left, just beyond the gallows, stood Claire with her camera. The Exakta camera didn't require the use of flashbulbs, but had its own built-in flash and so she could shoot an entire series of photos pausing only to wind her camera and advance the film to the next frame. She was set to do her job.

Colonel Schlösser began speaking.

"My fellow officers and soldiers, it is the Führer's wish that you attend here today for our teaching session, especially the prisoners among you. We are going to witness what happens to those who try to escape our camp. You are here as trusted servants of the Reich, and woe be to those who would attempt to defeat our laws and escape this place. Watch carefully, now."

Two SS guards approached the doctor and placed a black shroud over his head. Two others came from the right side and placed a black shroud over Esmée's head.

"Now," continued Schlösser as the color guard began a slow drum-roll from off to the right of the stage, "I am going to ask a final time if the third person involved in this escape attempt will come forward and identify himself, I will allow you to step into the shoes of either condemned prisoner here today and save their life by being hanged in their place. Does everyone understand my generous offer?"

Suddenly Claire was pierced through to her soul. She hadn't expected the offer. She could save Esmée by admitting her complicity. She would have to admit she was more than a dumb nurse lured along to help the doctor. Her mind raced. It was she, after all, who'd gone next door to the Admin offices and enlisted Esmée's help in forging papers to steal Herman Rothstein out of the camp. It was she who had helped Esmée choose the name of the SS sergeant, Helmut Manfred, to be used as the subject of the forgery, given his file photograph and the striking resemblance the Jew bore to the SS NCO. Wasn't it only right, then, that she would pay with her life for the fraud instead of Esmée paying with hers? The question beat inside her brain like the snare drums, hammering, hammering at her soul until she could stand it no longer. Taking a deep breath and allowing her camera to hang by its straps, she stepped forward. "I have something to say," she announced loudly and in a strong voice that rang out over the crowd.

Just as she spoke, she could hear Esmée shout, "Sister, no!"

"Please turn her loose, Colonel Schlösser!" cried Claire. "It should be my neck in the noose, not hers."

"Release the prisoner!" shouted Schlösser. "Release the woman."

It was an easy trade for the Colonel, much as he still loved the girl he had called "daughter." The noose was lifted from around her neck and the shroud removed. Claire began moving toward the gallows for her own death to occur. Just as she reached the gallows, a composition assembled itself before her. She touched her camera at that last moment, and using the waist-level viewfinder, snapped a final picture of the noose and of Esmée, who had just stepped forward toward the front of the stage.

Colonel Schlösser came around the lectern, stepped down from the podium, and crept up behind Esmée. Claire was struck with the understanding the German meant to prove he was as hard-hearted as the next SS officer by pushing a dear one from the stage into the fire. Suddenly, Schlösser moved behind Esmée, raising his arms—Esmée's body blocking his actual move from Claire's view —he seemed to push his one-time daughter off the front of the stage.

Claire, the professional photographer, was ready. Her camera, aimed the entire few moments at Esmée, tracked her and shot two fast frames as Esmée lurched forward and fell into the waiting fire below. She thrashed in its flames, making one final gesture upward with her arms as if supplicating her sister in her death. Her long cry of pain—her scream—made the blood run cold. The camera caught Schlösser pushing the manacled prisoner into the fire. For the moment, Schlösser was more focused on his putative daughter's struggle and death below than in watching Claire tear the roll of film from the camera, shove it into her pocket, and insert a second roll and begin firing off shots of the dais, the stage, the crowd, and the gallows, all in no particular order but taken to mimic the other, earlier shots she had taken in order to fool her captors into thinking they had obtained the one and only roll of film she had shot. In the press of the crowd around her on the stage, and in the confusion and terror of the moment, no one noticed. In the next moment, the Colonel threw the wooden lever and the wood floor beneath the doctor's feet fell away and he was hanged before everyone there. They were moments of frightening terror, confusion, and horror as the actual deaths were witnessed in near-field reality.

When it was over, Schlösser pointed at Claire and cried, "Tell us what you were saying! Tell us now!"

Claire, besides being shaken to her core, was aware that she had captured damning proof of a war crime against her sister. She went mute. Her only job now was to get the film out of Auschwitz. She refused to speak—at first. Then, suddenly, it came to her and she spoke up to deny she was about to say anything except that she would trade her life for Esmée's, that Esmée was really her sister and that she had been ready to die for her. She lied because she had to get the film out of the camp, the film containing the picture of Schlösser pushing a manacled prisoner into the fire alive. If she could preserve it and put it in the right hands, the film would eventually hang Schlösser, the war crime that it proved.

Evidently, the Colonel believed every word of Claire's denial of complicity. "I was crying out to take her place," shouted Claire. "I loved her"

"There was the family resemblance," he told Colonel Pennske over cognac that night. "I'd known all along that they were related."

"Does she live or die now?"

"It would be unfair to take her life. Whatever evidence of the fraud I might have eventually obtain died along with Esmée and Pietor. Their lips are sealed forever. The matter is closed. It must not be allowed to linger in the minds of the workers and the soldiers. Justice was quick, and it was complete. We are hugely short-handed on nurses so she will continue with her work at the infirmary. We are finished with the inquiry."

"Agreed. There is no evidence against the nurse. All nurses are on the Front anyway, so we cannot afford to lose even one if we can avoid it. Actually, I've thought all along she was just an unwitting tool used by that damnable doctor to help his pet Jew escape. He was making a point against the Reich, and he took the culpable one, Esmée Vallant, to the halls of death with him. Good work today. And did you get photographs of your success?"

"Yes, I demanded the film and camera from the photographer. She turned it over and was allowed to return to the infirmary. She's a good nurse and will help us in our effort to treat our soldiers."

"Excellent, Sigmund. Good day for you today."

"I'll know more when I see the actual pictures. But Berlin will be pleased."

"And the Führer."

"And the Führer."

51

T he Russians arrived in Auschwitz with enough advance notice to the Germans that more prisoners died while evidence of the camp itself was destroyed. First came the tanks up to the gates where they stopped momentarily and then drove up and over the wire. As they came, the remaining Jews shrank away, terrorized at what evil might be coming next. Other prisoners didn't move at all, however, as they were all but dead on their feet and unfeeling, doomed to spend what little time they had left as mute witnesses to hell.

Claire was in the infirmary when she first became aware the liberation was near. German doctors and nurses began fleeing. Many patients were abandoned to the arriving army to care for, while Claire simply stood, stunned, unsure what came next. Then she began dashing from critical patient to critical patient, helping and giving solace where she could, though she was greatly outnumbered and her skills sorely lacking.

Footsteps could be heard rushing everywhere outside as the Russian soldiers came pouring in. Then they appeared in the infirmary, talking in a language she'd never heard before, pointing out supplies and medicines that, she could only believe, they were going to take and use for themselves.

She was told to go to her room and stay there until further orders. The translator was a small German man, a prisoner of war, she guessed, or maybe a collaborator, she was never certain. But she did as she was told, taking special care to arrange her winter coat to go with her when she was released, as it contained all the photographic evidence of war crimes she could amass.

She was ready to accuse and prove war crimes. That was all that mattered to her from those first moments and beyond.

Two days later, the gates were opened, and she was free to go. Trains were coming and loading prisoners for journeys back to their homes and Claire joined them.

Three days later, she set foot in Paris at Gare du Nord train station. She broke into her parents' house—with the neighbors' approval —and was allowed to use the neighbors' phone. Calls to America followed—the neighbor had the phone number as he was watching the Vallants' home—and tears were shed. Then, at long last, she spoke to Lima. She was stunned to find the girl remembered her at all. After several moments, it came time to hang up. But first came the words that kept Claire alive and waiting to hear all those years at Auschwitz.

"Maman," said the girl. "I want you to come take me home."

52

1945, After Liberation

L eonard S. Kaplan, lead prosecutor for the American team, rolled down his shirtsleeves and prepared to meet with the witness named Claire Vallant. She was next in line among those waiting in his outer office for an interview. It was 1945, and the Allies were preparing their criminal prosecutions against the key Nazi perpetrators of war crimes committed against mankind in World War Two. Kaplan had come to Nuremberg from Washington, where he was senior partner at Cabot, Willow, Snipes, and Kaplan, an administrative and governmental law practice with close ties to the U.S. Government and its executive branch agencies. Kaplan was a tall six-five with a voice that rocked courtrooms and agency hearing rooms up and down the Potomac in his executive branch prosecutions of those individuals and companies that had run afoul of U.S. law. He had been selected by the War Department specifically to head up the American team's joint prosecution of Nazi war criminals for crimes against humanity. He buzzed his outer office and told the receptionist to send in Claire Vallant.

Minutes later, a slender, dark-haired woman with a quick smile took the proffered seat across Kaplan's small landscape of a desk. She was dressed in a stylish navy polka dot dress, low black heels, and wore just a smattering of cosmetics on her exhausted face. She carried a handbag she'd purchased in Paris with money given to her by her mother after the war when she was accumulating enough wardrobe to begin looking for a job and at the same time respond to the Nuremberg Prosecution's call for Auschwitz witnesses.

"Good afternoon, Mrs. Schildmann," said the attorney sonorously, "I'm Len Kaplan and I'm here in Germany to put German war criminals on the gallows. Thank you for coming."

Claire cleared her throat. "I'm Claire—Claire—Schildmann. Thank you for contacting me."

"We got your name off the Soviet roll as one of the prisoners at Auschwitz when the Soviets freed the camp. As I understand the file notation, you were a nurse there in the infirmary?"

"Yes, I was."

"Can you summarize for me what you observed during your captivity? Just a short paragraph will be enough."

"I was taken prisoner in April 1942, and remained in the concentration camp at Auschwitz until our liberation by the Soviets. While there, I tended to the medical needs of hundreds of patients, including members of the Waffen-SS, the Gestapo, the regular German army, and prisoners including Jews and Gypsies and political dissidents. I observed hundreds of injuries inflicted by the Germans on Jews as well as disease processes that regularly killed Jews from neglect and exposure. I personally observed savage attacks by German military personnel on prisoners, everything from beatings with dog whips to kicks in the head with jackboots to pistol whippings to shootings to knifings to everything else you've probably heard a hundred times by now from witnesses who've appeared here before me."

"Any attacks or actions you would personally consider war crimes? We're talking crimes against humanity here, specifically, inhumane attacks and murders so extraordinary that you knew upon observation fell outside the normal offensive and defensive efforts by soldiers engaged in war time?"

"Everything I saw was a war crime. But names of soldiers? Names of Jews? It's all a blur. Maybe with time—"

"Sure, sure, and take all the time you need, Ms. Schildmann. You'll probably meet with our team several times before the trials actually begin so there's no rush. I know some of what you've seen and experienced must have been so traumatic that maybe some of that is even blocked from memory right now. Those things might become clearer after some time passes. Now tell me, what is your present status?"

"As in employment?"

"Yes, and family, location."

"I'm working as a freelance photojournalist. I live in Paris with my parents, who have returned from America. I'm married, one child, a Lutheran and a member of the French Resistance, 2nd Battalion."

"Would you be able to meet with our legal assistants at this time?"

"What for?"

"They'll want to help categorize some of your potential testimony as well as discern what physical and documentary evidence you might be able to provide. Does that sound like something you can do today?"

"Yes. Where do I go?"

"Our office staff will accompany you to a different office as soon as you walk out of my office today. You'll be interviewed. It takes maybe fifteen minutes, tops."

"Sure, I can do that."

"Thank you."

Claire sat back and listened while Attorney Kaplan again spoke into his telephone handset and requested an interview staff member in his office. Then she left his office and was met just outside where she was led away.

When the door had closed behind her, Attorney Kaplan lifted the Dictaphone handset from his desk, pressed RECORD and began speaking, putting into a memo the other parts of their conversation:

"Witness Claire Schildmann appeared, a pleasant young woman in her early twenties, healthy-appearing, working as a photojournalist in Paris and able and willing to testify. Her knowledge is the standard Auschwitz package, including recitations of beatings and murders. She appears to have multiple first-hand knowledge of specific war crimes. Murders and brutality, medical operations and sterilization, withholding of medical care, inhumane food and clothing provisions. All war crimes. No names of victims or perpetrators except limited with either one or the other in any situation but never both at once. That is all."

Claire, upon leaving Kaplan's office, was met by a smiling American young lady and taken down a long hall to a large, open office with as many as thirty cubicles inside, many of them in use by workers interviewing other war crimes witnesses. Claire's handler found an open cubicle and they took seats inside.

"Now, said the young woman, my name is Naomi Gladstone. I work for the American War Crimes Commission. My specialty is legal assistance in the area of evidence-gathering. I'm here to ask about specific articles of evidence you might have in your possession or control that we might be able to use at trial. With me so far, Mrs. Schildmann?"

"I'm with you, yes."

"Now, let's begin with documents. Were you able to preserve any documentary evidence of any kind? We're talking about a diary, German camp records, medical records, recordings, photographs —anything like these?"

"No, I came away empty-handed." Claire's eyes clouded over at this point. She fought to hold back the tears as she didn't want the interviewer to think she was telling anything but the truth. She had her reasons for lying, but she resisted so she wasn't found out.

"Do you know where we might locate any items of the type I just mentioned?"

"No, I can't think of any locations?"

"If we asked you to come to Nuremberg and testify at trial, would that be possible?"

"Yes."

"Now, can you give me any specific dates when you witnessed German assaults or murders on Jews or other prisoners that were so horrible that they might be classified as crimes against humanity? I'm asking about egregious assaults, extreme or cruel methods of murder, death by hanging, death by burning, death in the gas chambers—did you witness any of these?"

"Yes, but I can't think of a single instance where I knew the name of the victim and the name of the soldier both so you could target a soldier with a specific victim. My first year I worked everywhere in the camp. After that, I worked mainly in the infirmary. We weren't exposed to Nazi treatment of prisoners for the most part, except we treated those who survived such things. But as far as witnessing them first-hand, not really."

"Were you personally subjected to any of these things?"

"No."

"Has anyone threatened you or your family if you testify or meet with us or tell your story in any way to anyone else?"

"No."

"All right, then, and you're sure no items of evidence?"

"No."

"All right, then. Is there anything else you'd like to add that I haven't asked about?"

"Not really."

"Well, thank you for coming today, Mrs. Schildmann. We'll definitely be in touch."

"You're welcome."

Claire was escorted out of the building where she caught a taxi in front of the Justice Palace and settled back for a ride to the airport.

"That wasn't so bad," she whispered to herself. "You made it through."

Claire stared out the taxi window, considering the whirlwind life she was living. She had returned to France on June 25, 1945. During the interim weeks, she devoted herself to the patients' repatriation. According to a September 16, 1945 article in *Le Monde*, *"Each day, this magnificent Frenchwoman makes the rounds, uplifting courage, giving hope where it is often but an illusion. The word 'holiness' comes to mind when one sees this grand sister of charity near these men and these women who are dying every day. She goes quietly about her work, always careful to avoid the spotlight and never giving interviews even when asked by this news organization."*

After touching down in Paris, she took a taxi to her parents' home at 25 Rue d'Arles in the Ninth Arrondissement. They had returned to France after the doctor was unable to obtain French documentation to support her application for hospital privileges in America. They couldn't afford to stay in New York and thus returned home. Lima and Claire had repatriated, of course, and the girl was thriving. The night Claire returned home from Nuremberg, the family was happy she was home; it had been a long day, Paris to Nuremberg and home again, flying time of about four hours, plus airport waiting at both ends, plus the Joint Task Force interviews.

"Claire," said her surgeon-mother, "what would you like for dinner tonight, darling?"

"Just light. Cheese and bread."

"Fish?"

"Fish is good."

"Darling," her mother said from the kitchen, "did they ask about Esmée?"

"Not specifically, no."

"Did they tell you anything about Esmée?"

"Definitely not."

"So we don't know any more about how she died than before today?"

"No, we still don't have the full story, Maman. Probably we never will." Claire swallowed hard to keep her feelings under control. It was just more than she was able to tell her mother, how Esmée had died. She was afraid the woman would curl up and die, strong though she was.

"That's heartbreaking," her mother said, coming into the dining room while wiping her hands on a dishcloth. "Would you like a nice glass of wine?"

"I don't think so. Perhaps some coffee would be good."

"Stay there, child. I'll get you a nice cup of coffee."

"No," said Claire, again taking up the thread of conversation she knew her mother wanted to re-visit, "we'll keep looking for news of how Esmée died. I know some people from the camp I can still ask. I'll do that."

"That would be a good thing," Dr. Vallant said. "A mother needs to know how her children die. At the very least." Her voice caught in her throat and Claire could hear the pain and suffering trapped inside the woman's soul as she cast about, looking for news of her youngest daughter. Claire's father, now retired from the design of automobiles, was every bit as vocal as her mother when it came to Esmée, except he went further, threatening to sue the German state for wrongful death in hopes of getting more information about Esmée's death. His wife, and daughter, Claire, reminded him at every turn how futile a lawsuit would be as the NSDAP and Third Reich no longer existed and thus could not be sued.

After bedtime, at two o'clock in the morning, M. Vallant came awake and then Dr. Vallant came awake too, alarmed by cries and sobs coming from Claire's room just down the hall from their own bedroom. They threw on robes and hurried to her door. Her mother didn't hesitate, entering Claire's room without knocking and finding her daughter sitting up in bed, a wild look on her face when her mother switched on the bedside lamp, and cries and tears issuing from her as she suffered from her demons. "Goodness," said the mother, "the dream is back again?"

"Yes, Maman, worse than ever."

"The one where you're being chased?"

"Yes, German soldiers are chasing me through a forest. They have done terrible things."

"Can you tell me?"

"It is 1941, near the village of Oświęcim—composed of Poles and Jews. Two young French sisters watch as trucks begin arriving, each loaded with some fifty Jews. Once unloaded, these Jews, mostly women and children, are marched toward a newly excavated ditch. They are beaten, forced to undress, and then led down into the ditch. A German policeman advances, upright, walking on…dead bodies, pistol in hand, and murders each Jew, one after the other, with a bullet in the back of the neck. Dressed in a white smock, the policeman takes breaks at regular intervals. During the breaks he drinks a small glass of liquor before returning to the ditch to kill another group. Over the course of an entire day, this policeman single-handedly murders the entire Jewish population of Senkivishka. Then the Germans leave after covering up the mass grave with dirt. The sisters watch as the dirt move for the next twenty-four hours. Then I wake up."

"Good God!" exclaimed her father. "Did you see this?"

"Not that I can recall." But it was Rhonda's story, the story she had confided in Claire late one night at the infirmary. Rhonda who swore she would do everything she could to see every last Nazi brought to justice if it took the rest of her life—which she knew it would.

"Was the other girl Esmée?"

"I don't think—I don't know. I only know a friend was one of the girls."

"Did you tell this dream to the Americans?"

"How could I, Maman? It's just a dream. I think."

"But it wasn't Esmée?"

"I'm not even sure, Maman. Please, don't. Let's all go back to sleep now. I'm sorry I woke you up again."

"Nonsense, precious child. We'll always come to you. And the dreams will lessen in intensity," said her mother. "You'll just have to trust me on that. But I've seen it in earlier cases of woundings back from the war before you. The memories will dim down."

"Thank you, then."

"Good night, darling girl."

"Night Maman, Papa."

Her mother switched off the lamp and everyone went back to bed and slept soundly the rest of the night. By the next morning, the interruption was forgotten and talk around the breakfast table was about everyone's plans for the day. Claire announced that she was joining other fighters from the 2nd Battalion that night for a reunion downtown.

After breakfast, they went their separate ways, Claire's mother to the hospital, her father to his den for reading, and Claire off into the bowels of Paris where she would find dispossessed survivors of the camps and work with them. Photographs would later be taken of the city and its efforts to recover from Nazi occupation and some of those photographs would find their way into news-magazines, papers, and wire services for distribution. She received small amounts of pay for her pictures but she was far short of self-supporting.

At night she would return to her room and check the shoe box at the top of her closet. Each night she would find her treasures: her grandmother's two pearl combs, her grandfather's gold pocket watch, Esmée's third grade class photo with the tallest girl in the back row barely peeking through the others—Esmée, and a small packet of cat fur from Kronos, the family's Siamese cat that adopted them in the freeze of January one year, as well as two baby teeth (whose, she no longer knew) and a votive from her grandmother's funeral. But there, in the midst of it all, was the most priceless possession of all: a single, undeveloped roll of 35mm film and a stack of photographs two inches thick. She kept the film tightly shut up inside the metal tin it was meant to be stored in, which was also the tin it originally came in when purchased. The threaded cap had never been unscrewed since the day in February 1944 that she witnessed Esmée being pushed by Colonel Sigmund Schlösser into a roaring blaze in the pit before his stage. Talk about a war crime! Throwing an unarmed, mana-cled prisoner into a bed of fire while alive? She had the bastard dead to rights, and she knew it. The only problem was, after weeks of snooping and asking questions of the Americans and Brits and French, it appeared Schlösser hadn't yet been arrested. Upon further inquiry, no one knew where he was. He had somehow escaped the sharp eye of the Allies. So what to do? Did she turn over his name as a war criminal and hope they find him? Or did she find him herself? Or did it even matter which? If the only thing she wanted was his death for the death of Pietor and Esmée, what difference did it make who did the killing? What difference did it make if the Allies hung him or Claire shot him? Or—better —burned him at the stake?

As long as he was dead, what did it matter to anyone—except maybe her, Claire—how he died?

But die he must.

In the meantime, she had the film just in case anyone ever asked why she killed him.

53

Her father, finishing with the morning paper, told her, "The Resistance, of all things, now operates out of an office two blocks from the Musée d'Orsay, on the Left Bank. They just opened."

Claire's eyes jerked up from her breakfast. "An office! But why on earth?"

He shrugged. "Evidently they are collecting stories. The story of the peoples' brave defense of France shall not be lost in history. It will be preserved and re-told. Also, there's the repatriation of those fighters taken away to prisons and camps. They now have a place to go and find families and friends and comrades in arms."

"I'll go there today," said Claire. "I'm leaving this minute."

"Maman," said Lima, now seven, almost eight, "take me with you, please."

"Not this time. But the Germans are gone; Maman will be back before long. I'll be safe and so will you. You stay here."

She went out into the garden where she kept her bike and unlocked the chain. Then she pushed open the gate with the nose of the front tire and rolled out into the street. Swinging her leg up over her bike she was struck by how light she suddenly felt and how bright the sunlight had become. Was that all it took, she wondered as she wheeled down the narrow sidewalk on her street? A spot of good news and she was a new person? She didn't dare question what she was feeling. Better to just feel it and ride along.

The Paris air brushed back her hair and fluttered her shirt around her arms as she rolled down a decline onto Pont des Arts, a bridge leading into the Louvre. It was the first week in October 1945 and the temperature was turning chilly so that, when she arrived at the offices of the Resistance, she hadn't even worked up a sweat. She hopped down from the bike, leaned it against the wall, and went inside. It was a large room curtained off into four equal sections by two curtains with an open desk up front that might have been for a receptionist. Claire waited, shifting foot to foot for a minute and then called out, "Anyone?"

There was no answer, so she called out again. "Hello? Anyone here?"

A female voice called back, "We heard you and we're coming!"

"Thank you."

A young woman maybe Claire's age brushed through the wide, gray-brown curtain. She wore her hair quite short and her sleeveless arms were quite muscular. She looked like she might have been a discus thrower on a track and field team. She came up to her side of the reception desk and sat down, indicating Claire should, too. Claire sat and crossed her legs. She was wearing shorts and a U.S. Army T-shirt that said ARMY across the chest. "I'm looking for some help."

"Sure, how can we help?"

"My name is Claire Schildmann. 2nd Battalion. Anything here for me?"

"One moment." Now the girl arose and disappeared back through the curtain. She returned maybe five minutes later carrying a 3x5 notecard. She handed it to Claire. "Remy says hello"—followed by an exclamation mark. "Leave a message with a number."

Without being asked, the girl slid a notecard and pen and ink across the desk. "Write away, Claire."

She wrote Remy a short note and included her parents' new phone number. Then she pushed the notecard back. The girl, without reading the notecard, stood and disappeared yet again through the curtain. This time when she returned, she was smiling. "I found one more note. It was poked deep inside your note slot." She handed Claire the notecard.

She scanned down. The notecard said, simply, "Sigmund Schlösser. Number 1445 Luttrichter Street, Cologne, Germany."

She was stunned. How in God's name would anyone ever know she was going to track down Colonel Schlösser? "Do you know who left this?" She asked the young woman.

"Oh, I couldn't possibly know. There are dozens of people through here every day. Sometimes more. I don't remember anyone's hand-writing."

Claire took both notes and placed one above the other. Each card contained the word "Number." She stopped and sucked in her breath. The words were printed exactly the same on the top card/bottom card.

"Same handwriting," said the receptionist, reading upside-down. "Sorry, I didn't mean to look."

"No, no, they are the same, right?" She turned the cards up so they were facing the girl. "Aren't they the exact same 'number'?"

"Definitely. Your Remy friend wrote them both. He knows you're looking for this Sigmund?"

That was quite far enough. Claire flipped the cards upright and slipped them into her waist pocket. "Thanks so much!" she called back as she went outside to her bike. She pulled her bike free and began walking it along rue de Amis toward a cafe. She needed to be alone and think.

She found a cafe a half block down and again propped her bike against a wall. The outside tables were all taken, so she went inside and ordered coffee and a *petit pain*. Then she found a tiny table along the right-hand wall.

Adding a dash of milk to her coffee, she allowed her mind to think about what she'd just learned. First, Remy was alive and around somewhere. Second, he somehow knew she was looking for Colonel Sigmund Schlösser. How in the world would he know that unless he was a mind reader?

That night, he called and got through to her at her parents' house. He was in Nuremberg but he was flying back to Paris that after-noon. They would meet later that night at a small cafe two blocks from her home. They decided it would be better for Lima if they met first and talked.

She was there at eight o'clock, the time he chose. When she walked in she was wearing a houndstooth skirt and jacket, a black silk top, and low-slung heels. *Soir de Paris* perfume had been applied to her arms and behind the ears. Her grandmother's pearls were around her neck. She wanted Remy to see her at her best; she had long played in her mind this meeting if it should ever happen. Most of all, she remembered one of their last times together, a time when she told him she loved him no matter what he'd done. She had regretted ever saying it: what was she thinking, setting herself up as judge and jury during the darkest days the world had ever known?

Then there he was, third table on the left, sidewalk. He was toying with his coffee cup until he saw her and then shot up and came toward her, arms outstretched. She moved against him and smelled the old cologne he always wore and, this time, the smooth face she loved. They hugged and patted then sat down.

"So, I found you," he started out by saying. "But first, I love you and always will. More than ever."

"My feelings haven't changed either, my love. Never will either. Why didn't you come looking for me?"

"I have a job in Nuremberg. I'm helping with the coming trials. But I knew my note would find you before long. I'm sorry I couldn't leave there."

"It's important work. I understand."

He grinned. "Hey, I've got a message for you."

Her heart jumped. Here it was. Now she would learn who knew she was looking for Sigmund Schlösser.

"Message from who?"

"Rhonda Maier. A nurse from Nice. You trained her at the Auschwitz infirmary. She says she wanted only to commit suicide over the death of her two boys. She says you worked with her and saved her life. Just before the liberation of the concentration camp she was conscripted to accompany the Colonel and his family to their secret location. Seemed like he wasn't well and needed a nurse."

"So that's what happened to our Rhonda. She just disappeared one night. We all thought they had come for her and gassed her because they had murdered her sons and wanted her silence. Instead she went with Schlösser."

"I know about the Colonel," Remy said. "I've been busy for three years helping put together cases against all the camp officers I could get information on. I have names, addresses, witnesses, photos and documents, in one case I even have a movie from Auschwitz, a movie made from a camera in a dictionary that someone dreamed up. Ingenious? But tell me what you know about the Colonel."

"The Allies haven't even located him. An assistant Kommandant that important, I have no idea why."

"Why don't they have him? Because he killed everyone who'd ever heard of him. That's what happened in all the camps when the Germans knew the Allies were coming. They killed everyone in the camps, burned up what they could of the camps, and made off with all the Jews' gold and diamonds and wealth they could carry. Didn't you see this?"

"I saw very little in the infirmary. We knew to stay with our patients and we wouldn't abandon them until the Soviets arrived. They had no one else looking out for them for two weeks during the transition. The Soviets then took me to the train to Paris. I didn't see much else. Or even care, to be honest. I only wanted to go home. I was exhausted, and I'd seen my sister murdered. There was—is—not much left of me but frayed nerves. But my story is common—no tears needed or asked."

"No tears shed, I can assure you. Everyone in France has a story."

"I know. Damn it all."

"Tell me about Lima."

"She asks about her Papa. She means you."

"Can I see her tonight?"

"Of course."

Remy continued, "I know about Sigmund Schlösser. Rhonda told me she saw him burn your sister alive. She says you were there on the stage. What can you tell me, can you testify?"

"The Allies have already been all over this with me. Yes, I can testify but no, I didn't tell them about the Colonel."

"Why not?"

"Because I don't want a conviction for him. A conviction is too good. I want him to burn like my little sister burned. An eye for an eye."

"My better angels say to talk you out of that."

"Then shut them up. There is Nuremberg justice and there is family justice. You know which one I want."

"I've given you his address. You have that?"

"I do."

"What are you going to do with it?"

"I'm going to go there and burn him up. I'm going to make a fire and put him in it."

"What about letting the Allies hang him? Your testimony would be enough."

"Probably not. From what you're saying, it would just be my word against his, especially if he killed everyone else who knew him. I'm afraid they would let him go or, worse, put him in prison where I couldn't get at him."

"True, either of those could happen after a trial where there were no witnesses but maybe one survivor. He would have a good lawyer."

"Then I will shoot him in the hallway. Something. He won't leave Nuremberg alive, I can promise you that."

"What are you thinking? You'll be allowed to leave after you kill him? What about Lima? What about me?"

"Leave it to me. They won't want me."

"That makes no sense. But I'll play along with it for a minute. Now, what if I said I'd help you?"

"You?"

"I haven't forgotten our daughter. I was responsible for the death of her parents. Now I've got to do whatever I can to help. She's uppermost in my mind right now. Now what do you say, Claire Vallant Schildmann? Do you want some Remy Schildmann help? Yes or no."

"Do you still know how to make bombs?"

"I do."

"Well, bombs are as good as fire for Schlösser. Yes, I want you along."

"Then count me in. One thing, though. I won't go to jail with you and I won't die for this. If those have to happen, it's on you, Claire."

"That's fair. Esmée was my sister, not yours."

"It's not just that. I have a daughter. And I have much work left to do. There are literally thousands of German war criminals I'm tracking. Schlösser is only one."

"All right, then. When can you leave?"

"Right now?" he said. "Can we leave right now before anything changes?"

She said, "Just let me call my Papa. I need to let them know I'll be away for a while."

"They'll worry."

"No, they're beyond worry. Now it's reality. Their horror has already come true, Remy, when Esmée died."

"It must be horrible."

"It is. And what of your father, Remy? What's happened to him?"

"He's been arrested and they're processing him."

"Goodness, was he—you know—"

"Yes, he was murdering Jews, I'm afraid. My dad's a Nazi through and through. Living in France and growing up here, it just never did click for me. Besides, I don't hate anybody. Except maybe the Nazis."

"Can you wait here while I call my Papa?"

"I'll be right here."

She went to the pay phone and dialed her home number. Sure enough, M. Vallant answered. "Hello?

"Papa, it's Claire."

"Are you all right? Do you need me to come get you?"

"No, Papa, but I won't be home for some time now. I have a new mission."

"Oh, I guessed. When you went to the Resistance offices today, I told your mother no good would come of it. What kind of mission?"

"I can't say, Papa. You're just going to have to trust me this time."

"You need to do what you need to do, Claire. I understand. But can I talk you out of it somehow? Is there another way to do your mission that we could help? Please think about Lima right now."

"I'm afraid not. Someday I'll tell you about it, Papa, but not now. It would be too painful. Lima will survive. I'll see to that."

"Then it's about Esmée."

She hesitated. "Yes, it's about Esmée. Trust me and say no more."

"All—all right."

"Thank you. We'll talk soon, Papa."

"Goodbye, Claire. Lima will be well. Godspeed."

"Goodbye, Papa."

She felt closer to him than ever before just then. Closer or maybe farther, because she couldn't tell the truth, couldn't tell him she was off to kill Esmée's murderer.

She returned to the table.

"All well?" he asked.

"All well, yes. Shall we go? How shall we travel? Train?"

"No need. I have my father's car since he was arrested. I've come up in the world, Claire."

"Indeed you have. All right. Let's go get our pound of flesh."

"The fire next time."

54

"My sources tell me that hundreds of thousands of Germans have immigrated to Argentina since just before the war to now," Remy told Claire as they set out on their journey to Germany. "This is why Argentina remained neutral during the war."

"Do you think Schlösser might be in Argentina?"

"Not at last count, he wasn't. But Argentine President Juan Peron has established ratlines, through ports in Spain and Italy to smuggle former SS officers and Nazi party members out of Europe."

"What about the Allies? They're just standing by and allowing this?"

"So far, it's working. Hundreds of Nazis are leaving Europe every week. My father was ready to go before he was arrested. Everything he owned had been sold and placed in Swiss banks but he tarried too long and the Resistance caught up to him."

"I know that Peron was taken with the ideologies of Benito Mussolini and Adolf Hitler while serving as a military attaché in Italy during the early years of World War II. What a horrible person."

"Now he's using those Nazis who have technical skills to help build his country, especially his army. It never ends, Claire."

"I've been told that French war criminals are getting passports issued by the International Red Cross stamped with Argentine tourist visas. This must be part of it."

"It is. So our search for Sigmund Schlösser must be done as fast as possible before he escapes from Germany. If he gets to Argentina, we have no contacts there, we know nothing about the country, and he probably dies an old man there, living off stolen gold teeth and diamonds."

"Then please, drive faster, Remy. That cannot be allowed to happen."

THE TRIP FROM PARIS TO COLOGNE WAS EXACTLY 501 KILOMETERS and should have taken just five hours, but then they had to add in additional wait periods for checkpoints and unexpected searches of their vehicle. All told, they were nine hours in the car, a late-model Mercedes Benz coupe.

The destination was Number 1445 Luttrichter Street in Cologne, Germany. The area was four kilometers west of the Deutzer Bridge across the Rhine, a very active shipping and import-export neighborhood in Cologne after the war.

Arriving just before six a.m., Claire and Remy decided to watch the house and see who came and went. It was a three-story, street-facing home sharing community walls with houses on either side —a fact which dismayed Claire as the architecture, coupled with respect for innocent families on either side, ruled out the use of bombs or fire on the dwelling itself. That left a much smaller target for the two Nazi-hunters.

Around eight a.m., just after Remy returned from a scouting session by foot, a young woman left the home and walked to the curb where she climbed into a parked car and drove off. Claire had no doubt: the young woman was one of the twins, either Nonna or Necci. "Interesting," Claire said to Remy, "the driver is probably not old enough to drive. That might tell us something about Schlösser's condition. Say he is too ill to go out for medicines or food he might be sending a daughter."

"Or it might be that he's already flown the coop and left behind his vehicle for the daughters."

"That doesn't work: he would take his kids with him to Argentina, wouldn't you think?"

"I don't know. How old are they?"

"Nonna and Necci were about nine when I began teaching them. Which would make them about twelve or thirteen now."

"Hmm. They would definitely go with their dad, then. Is he married? Was he?"

"To a very nice woman. Very quiet, very shy, Austrian lady who, I think, was probably repulsed by her husband's work and emotionally shut off. I always had the feeling she felt the surrounding horror very deeply. She would also cry a lot as I stumbled across her around the house fighting back tears for no reason other than the reality of her life. Which was way more than enough, obviously. I don't recall her name but I would definitely know her face if I saw her again."

"All right. I'm thinking we need to separate him from his family before we kill him," Remy said. "They sound like innocents to me."

"Yes, as far as that is possible, I suppose so."

"So we get him alone. Maybe go inside and drag him out at gunpoint?"

"Maybe. Let's watch the place for a day or two and see what we learn."

Remy nodded. "Agreed."

It was the second week in October 1945 and getting cold outside at night this far north in Germany. They ran the heater in the Mercedes but then began running low on petrol, so Remy switched off the ignition. "Can we sit closer together for body warmth?" he asked at ten a.m.

"Of course. I'll slide over."

She didn't take her eyes off the house, didn't look at her husband, but had she, she would have seen a smiling companion sitting close to her. It would have been obvious from the giddy look on his face that he felt the old feelings.

AT TEN-THIRTY ON THE FIFTEENTH OF OCTOBER 1945, REMY AND Claire witnessed Schlösser being carefully wheeled down the front porch steps, four in all, down to the sidewalk, by a man the size of a Volkswagen. He paused at the end of the sidewalk, opened the door to a beige Bentley automobile, and lifted

Schlösser bodily from the wheelchair and placed him on the backseat. He then collapsed the wheelchair and stowed it in the boot. The man then got behind the wheel and pulled away from the curb. Parked just four vehicles behind, Remy and Claire followed.

Up to the Neumarkt Circle they drove, until, coming back around the circle, the Bentley took a right on Zeppelin Street. Down two blocks and it pulled into a small parking area in front of a medical building. "He's going to see his doctor," Claire said. "We'll wait here until they come back out and then take him."

Remy reached and opened the glove box of his father's car. He retrieved a black Luger 9mm still in its patent leather holster. He removed the gun and worked the charging mechanism. "I've got this," he said. "You just press this trunk release here when I return to the car with him."

One hour later, the huge aide came bumping back down the stairs with Schlösser bundled in his wheelchair. He had a blanket over his legs and wore a heavy overcoat. He placed the old man on the back seat and took to arranging him. His collar was turned up. He wore an Austrian sheepherder's cap, which was pulled low on his head. To all the world he looked like any other old man seeking medical help for his ailments. But Claire knew better. She knew the man had been personally responsible for the day-to-day operations of a killing machine that had slaughtered a million human beings. He deserved what was about to befall him, times one-hundred, at least.

"Here I go," said Remy in a low, strong voice. "Pop the boot when you see us returning."

"Got it."

She watched, then, as Remy approached the old man on the sidewalk. Without hesitation he walked right up to the huge man, stuck the muzzle of the gun in his face, and demanded the Bentley's keys. He made the man open the Bentley's boot and climb inside and lie down. Then he slammed the lid, leaving the keys dangling from the lock. Then he slowly, almost nonchalantly, carried Schlösser over to the waiting Mercedes. Claire had popped the boot and was standing beside the open lid, waiting. She wanted Schlösser to see her face.

"Remember me, Herr Kommandant," she hissed. "Remember the sister of Esmée? The daughter you threw into the fire? Well, I'm here to take you on a ride. Are you ready for a ride, Herr Kommandant?"

He didn't look at all frightened, which was a letdown. Instead, his jaw tightened, and he seemed to accept that his time had come around at last. He was too old and perhaps too ill to resist.

It was inevitable, said his tight face and steady eyes.

Into the boot Remy lifted the man, rolling him onto his side. He then collapsed the wheelchair and worked it into the Mercedes' back seat.

She watched the lid close over him. Then she turned and spat on the ground. "Enough!"

55

W ith Remy in the driver's seat and Claire beside him, he turned to her.

"You have two choices. We can find a secluded spot on the Rhine River where no one will see you shoot him, or we can take him to Nuremberg to stand trial. Your call, my love."

She sat there, staring straight ahead, her fingers working along the seams of her houndstooth skirt. Could she shoot him? She wondered. Of course she could, she immediately knew. Shoot him in a heartbeat. But that would kill only him. Which left out the most important factor of all: the millions of Polish and Czech and German and French families who'd lost loved ones to Auschwitz, they wouldn't have the satisfaction of watching him die. They would never know, even, because Claire wouldn't be able to tell anyone.

"Drive," she finally said. "We're going to Nuremberg."

"As I knew we would," Remy smiled. He handed her the gun. "Take it and put it back."

Claire stowed the gun in the glove-box and sat back. "How long?"

"About five hours."

"Okay if I sleep?"

"Sleep away, my little bird. You've earned it."

"What about you, Remy?"

"I'm already planning your testimony for trial, Claire. You are going to put him away.

"One more thing. I have photographs."

He smiled again. "How could you not? You're a born photographer."

"They're terrible photographs."

"That's all right. I'll be there with you."

She reclined sideways in the seat, placing her head in Remy's lap on top of the old man's blanket from his wheelchair.

"I love you, Remy."

"I know you do, Claire. You always have."

"Do you still love me? Can you ever again?"

"Of course I love you. That never just goes away."

"Wake me up a half hour out. I want my makeup done right when we deliver him."

"You French girls."

"I know. Aren't we wonderful?"

"Nothing better. I know, I've looked all around. Give me a French girl named Claire any day."

"Good night, Remy. I'm exhausted."

"Sleep tight."

As they pulled into traffic, they heard a loud thump in the trunk.

She raised her head and yelled in the direction of the trunk, "Don't you dare die on me, you miserable old son-of-a-bitch!"

Then they were off.

56

One month later, Claire again appeared in the office of Leonard S. Kaplan, lead prosecutor for the American team. The tall attorney wore his usual three-piece suit that day, complete with a white shirt, collar pin, and club tie. His cufflinks were gold with the initial "K" and his right pinky ring was all diamond. On Claire, the irony of this Jewish attorney sending Nazis to the hangman's was not lost. She thought it the perfect final outcome for the struggle between victim and murderer.

"You're back again, Mrs. Schildmann. Has anything changed?"

"Yes, I've remembered the name of a war crimes victim and I can match her with Sigmund Schlösser as her murderer."

"Wonderful. And how do we prove this occurrence, I mean in addition to your testimony?"

"I have a photograph. I remembered it only recently."

Claire had finally felt recovered enough to accept a job. She was now working full-time for *Le Monde*, which was the most important newspaper in France after the war. Because the newspaper was as much or more about news analysis as it was raw news coverage, Claire had taken to writing editorial and opinion pieces, as well as the more common analysis pieces in her new, full-time employment. However, before she could let go entirely of World War II and its effect on her, she had to first testify against Colonel Sigmund Schlösser and his role at Auschwitz.

"I need to tell you," said Kaplan, "that you're the only war crimes eyewitness we've located to testify against Schlösser. Not only that, he's surrounded himself with a powerful team of lawyers who are going to make this prosecution very tenuous, at the least. We cannot afford to lose even one case, Claire, given the world opinion of our task here, so we're going to need to know from you exactly how we can best convict this man for his war crimes."

"There's my testimony," she said. "And there's the photograph, too."

"What would this other photograph be?"

She reached inside of her attaché case and removed a sheaf of 9x12 photographs, all black-and-whites. She placed these face up on the lawyer's desk, facing him. Ever so slowly, he began sliding them to the side, beginning with the top picture and working his way down. Then, halfway down, he came to the gallows picture.

It was the photograph of Schlösser shoving a manacled Esmée into a roaring inferno at her feet. One foot was clearly off the stage, and the other was just leaving the stage when the shutter on the camera released. The focus was perfect: Attorney Kaplan had never seen a better photograph of the murderer in the dozens he had pored over. He tapped a forefinger on the print. Then he looked up.

"You have the negative?"

"I do."

"Where is it?"

"In my bank box in Paris. I'm never giving it up so please don't ask."

It was true. After delivering Schlösser to the prison at Nuremberg, she had returned to Paris and stowed her negatives in a bank safe deposit box.

"I won't ask. We can take this nine-by-twelve and blow it up to 30x40 and mount it on a light cardboard, prop it in front of the judges, and convict this animal with this alone. Who is the girl?"

Claire fought back tears. "She's my sister, Esmée."

"Sweet Jesus. Your own sister? And you managed to take a picture?"

Claire shook her head. "I was the only one with a camera."

He smiled. It said it all, her comment.

"Just tell me this, Monsieur. Is it enough to see him hang?"

"It is."

"Can I watch him hang? Can I be there myself?"

"Ordinarily not. But as a member of the press, I don't see why not. Yes, I'll make sure that happens."

"And what about his lawyers? How will they try to win against this?"

"They will invariably try to get you to say the girl was committing suicide, and that Schlösser was reaching for her to try to save her."

"Total bullshit."

"I know. We'll overcome that. The trier-of-fact won't let it get by."

"And who is the trier-of-fact?"

"Rather than use a single judge and jury, the trial of high-ranking Nazi leaders will be conducted by a panel of four judges. The United States, Soviet Union, France and Great Britain will each supply a main judge. These four judges will find it was a war crime, not the act of a Good Samaritan bent on saving a young woman."

"I'll tell them my story. It's not a pretty one."

"Well, at least you survived, Claire."

"Did I?"

57

Naomi Gladstone again collected up Claire to work with her after her meeting with attorney Kaplan. They reviewed the photographs one-by-one and Naomi made her notes and affixed proper exhibit labels to the back of each one. The photographs included all of those taken of the experiments floor of the infirmary. These were difficult to look at and would require additional medical testimony as to what they portrayed.

"Now, Claire, your date of testimony will be January the twenty-eighth. Does that work for you?"

"Yes, it does."

"Do you need financial help to get here, stay over, and get back home?"

"No, I'm working."

"We can pay for your trip."

"I would like to pay my own way. That way no one could ask me if I've been paid to testify."

"Oh, my, you are much older than your age."

"I lived with the SS for three years. It will do that to a person."

"Let's talk about living with the SS. Can you give me a feel for your testimony? What it will be touching upon?"

"I can be asked anything about Auschwitz because I was there almost from the beginning to the end. I did everything there except gas people and burn bodies. The rest of it I did."

"You were the witness to many murders?"

"What? Next question, please."

"I'm sorry."

"Well, what do you think? I was at Auschwitz."

"I hate to make you even think about it. Maybe we should do this later."

"I think what will work best is if I tell my complete story one time through. I don't want to review it ahead of time. My mind refuses to think about it anymore. But I can get in front of a courtroom and make myself go over it without thinking at all. That will be best."

"Then that's what we'll do. Thank you for coming, Mrs. Schildmann."

58

At the Nuremberg War Crimes Trial, Claire Vallant Schildmann was called to testify by the French prosecutor. She gave the following testimony over the course of one entire day.

M. DUBOST: With the authorization of the Court, I should like to proceed with this part of the presentation of the French case by hearing a witness who, for more than three years, lived in German concentration camps.

[The witness, Mme VALLANT SCHILDMANN, took the stand.]

THE PRESIDENT: Would you stand up, please? Do you wish to swear the French oath? Will you tell us your name?

MADAME VALLANT (Witness): Claire Vallant Schildmann.

THE PRESIDENT: Will you repeat this oath after me: I swear that I will speak without hate or fear, that I will tell the truth, all the truth, nothing but the truth.

[The witness repeated the oath in French.]

THE PRESIDENT: Raise your right hand and say, "I swear."

MME VALLANT: I swear.

THE PRESIDENT: Please, will you sit down and speak slowly? Your name is?

MME VALLANT: Schildmann, Claire.

M. DUBOST: Is your name Madame Vallant Schildmann?

MME VALLANT: Yes.

M. DUBOST: Do you now go by Vallant for professional reasons?

MME VALLANT: That is how my readers know me.

M DUBOST: Let the record show we will refer throughout by the witness's maiden name, Vallant. You were born in Paris on 10 May 1922?

MME VALLANT: Yes.

M. DUBOST: And you are of French nationality, French born, and of parents who were of French nationality?

MME VALLANT: My mother is a German-born French citizen. My father is French.

M. DUBOST: Were you arrested and deported? Will you please give your testimony?

MME VALLANT: I was arrested on 9 February 1942 by Petain's French police, who handed me over to the German authorities after 6 weeks. I arrived on 20 March at Sante prison in the German quarter. I was questioned on 9 June 1942. At the end of my interrogation they wanted me to sign a statement which was not consistent with what I had said. I refused to sign it. The officer who had questioned me threatened me; and when I told him that I was not afraid of death nor of being shot, he said, "But we have at our disposal means for killing that are far worse than merely shooting." And the interpreter said to me, "You do not know what you have just done. You are going to leave for a concentration camp. One never comes back from there."

M. DUBOST: You were then taken to prison?

MME VALLANT: I was taken back to the Sante prison where I was placed in solitary confinement. However, I was able to communicate with my neighbors through the piping and the windows. I was in a cell next to that of Georges Politzer, the philosopher, and Jacques Solomon, physicist. Mr. Solomon is the son-in-law of Professor Langevin, a pupil of Curie, one of the first to study atomic disintegration.

Georges Politzer told me through the piping that during his interrogation, after having been tortured, he was asked whether he would write theoretical pamphlets for National Socialism. When he refused, he was told that he would be in the first train of hostages to be shot.

As for Jacques Solomon, he also was horribly tortured and then thrown into a dark cell and came out only on the day of his execution to say goodbye to his wife, who also was under arrest at the Sante. Helene Solomon told me in Romainville, where I found her when I left the Sante that when she went to her husband he moaned and said, "I cannot take you in my arms, because I can no longer move them."

Every time that the internees came back from their questioning one could hear moaning through the windows, and they all said that they could not make any movements.

Several times during the five months I spent at the Sante hostages were taken to be shot. When I left the Sante on 20 August 1942, I was taken to the Fortress of Romainville, which was a camp for hostages. There I was present on two occasions when they took hostages, on 21 August and 22 September. Among the hostages who were taken away were the husbands of the women who were with me and who left for Auschwitz. Most of them died there. These women, for the most part, had been arrested only because of the activity of their husbands. They themselves had done nothing.

M. DUBOST: Can you talk about the Revier?

MME VALLANT: To reach the Revier one had to go first to the roll call.

M. DUBOST: Would you please explain what the Revier was in the camp?

MME VALLANT: The Revier was the blocks where the sick were put. This place could not be given the name of hospital because it did not correspond in any way to our idea of a hospital.

To go there, one had first to obtain authorization from the block chief who seldom gave it. When it was finally granted we were led in columns to the infirmary where, no matter what weather, whether it snowed or rained, even if one had a temperature of 4000 centigrade—I'm exaggerating, obviously—one had to wait for several hours standing in a queue to be admitted. It frequently happened that patients died outside the door of the infirmary before they could get in. Moreover, lining up in front of the infirmary was dangerous because if the queue was too long the SS came along, picked up all the women who were waiting, and took them straight to Block Number 25.

M. DUBOST: That is to say, to the gas chamber?

MME VALLANT: That is to say to the gas chamber. That is why

very often the women preferred not to go to the Revier and they died at their work or at roll call.

The only advantage of the Revier was that as one was in bed, one did not have to go to roll call; but one lay in appalling conditions, four in a bed of less than 1 meter in width, each suffering from a different disease, so that anyone who came for leg sores would catch typhus or dysentery from neighbors. The straw mattresses were dirty, and they were changed only when absolutely rotten.

There were practically no medicines. Consequently the patients were left in their beds without any attention, without hygiene, and unwashed.

M. DUBOST: Was the Revier open to all the internees?

MME VALLANT: No. When we arrived Jewish women had not the right to be admitted. They were taken straight to the gas chamber.

M. DUBOST: Would you please tell us about the disinfection of the blocks?

MME VALLANT: From time to time, they disinfected the blocks with gas; but these disinfections were also the cause of many deaths because, while the blocks were being disinfected with gas, the prisoners were taken to the shower-baths. Their clothes were taken away from them to be steamed. The internees were left naked outside, waiting for their clothing to come back from the steaming, and then they were given back to them wet. Even those who were sick, who could barely stand on their feet, were sent to the showers. It is quite obvious that a great many of them died in the course of these proceedings. Those who could not move were washed all in the same bath during the disinfection.

M. DUBOST: How were you fed?

MME VALLANT: We had 200 grams of bread, three-quarters or

half a liter—it varied—of soup made from swedes, and a few grams of margarine or a slice of sausage in the evening, this daily.

M. DUBOST: Regardless of the work that was exacted from the internees?

MME VALLANT: Regardless of the work that was exacted from the internee. Some who had to work in the factory of the "Union," an ammunition factory where they made grenades and shells, received what was called a "Zulage," that is, a supplementary ration, when the amount of their production was satisfactory. Those internees had to go to roll call morning and night as we did, and they were at work twelve hours in the factory. They came back to the camp after the day's work, making the journey both ways on foot.

M. DUBOST: What was this "Union" factory?

MME VALLANT: It was an ammunition factory. I do not know to what company it belonged. It was called the "Union."

M. DUBOST: Will you tell us about experiments, if you witnessed any?

MME VALLANT: As to the experiments, I have seen in the Revier, because I was employed at the Revier, the queue of young Jewesses from Salonika who stood waiting in front of the X-ray room for sterilization. I also know that they performed castration operations in the men's camp. I have provided dozens of photographs of the experiments. I assume they've been passed to the court.

Concerning the experiments performed on women I am well informed, because my friend, Doctor Hade Hautval of Montbeliard, who has returned to France, worked for several months in that block nursing the patients; but she always refused to participate in those experiments. They sterilized women either by injections or by operation or with X-rays. I saw and knew several women who had been sterilized. There was a very high mortality rate among those operated upon. Fourteen Jewesses from France who refused to be sterilized were sent to a Strafarbeit kommando, that is, hard labor.

M. DUBOST: Did they come back from those kommandos?

MME VALLANT: Very seldom.

M. DUBOST: What was the aim of the SS?

MME VALLANT: Sterilization—they did not conceal it. They said that they were trying to find the best method for sterilizing to replace the native population in the occupied countries by Germans after one generation once they had made use of the inhabitants as slaves to work for them.

M. DUBOST: Can you tell us about the selections that were made at the beginning of winter?

MME VALLANT: Every year, towards the end of the autumn, they proceeded to make selections on a large scale in the Revier. The system appeared to work as follows—I say this because I noticed the fact for myself during the time I spent in Auschwitz. Others, who had stayed there even longer than I, had observed the same phenomenon.

In the spring, all through Europe, they rounded up men and women whom they sent to Auschwitz. They kept only those who were strong enough to work all through the summer. During that period naturally some died every day; but the strongest, those who had succeeded in holding out for six months, were so exhausted that they too had to go to the Revier. It was then in autumn that the large-scale selections were made, so as not to feed too many useless mouths during the winter. All the women who were too thin were sent to the gas chamber, as well as those who had a long, drawn-out illnesses.

M. DUBOST: The prisoners. What happened to their clothing and their luggage?

MME VALLANT: The non-Jews had to carry their own luggage and were billeted in separate blocks, but when the Jews arrived, they had to leave all their belongings on the platform. They were stripped before entering the gas chamber and all their clothes, as well as all their belongings, were taken over to large barracks and there sorted out by a Kommando named "Canada." Then everything was shipped to Germany: jewelry, fur coats, et cetera.

Since the Jewesses were sent to Auschwitz with their entire families and since they had been told that this was a sort of ghetto and were advised to bring all their goods and chattels along, they consequently brought considerable riches with them. As for the Jewesses from Salonika, I remember that on their arrival they were given picture postcards, bearing the post office address of "Waldsee," a place which did not exist; and a printed text to be sent to their families, stating, "We are doing very well here; we have work and we are well treated. We await your arrival." I myself saw the cards in question; and the Schreiberinnen, that is, the secretaries of the block, were instructed to distribute them among the internees in order to post them to their families. I know that whole families arrived as a result of these postcards.

M. DUBOST: Would you, Madame, please give us some details as to what you saw when you were about to leave the camp, and under what circumstances you left it?

MME VALLANT: We were in quarantine before leaving Auschwitz.

M. DUBOST: When was that?

MME VALLANT: We were in quarantine for two weeks.

M. DUBOST: These were all Frenchwomen from your convoy, who had survived?

MME VALLANT: Yes, all the surviving Frenchwomen of our convoy. We had heard from Jewesses who had arrived from France, in July 1944, that an intensive campaign had been carried out by the British Broadcasting Corporation in London, in connection with our convoy, mentioning Mal Politzer, Danielle Casanova, Helene Solomon-Langevin, and myself. As a result of this broadcast we knew that orders had been issued from Berlin to the effect that Frenchwomen should be transported under better conditions.

So we were placed in quarantine. This was a block situated opposite the camp and outside the barbed wire. I must say that it is to this quarantine that the 49 survivors owed their lives because at the end of four months there were only 52 of us. Therefore it is certain that we could not have survived 18 months of this regime had we not had these 10 months of quarantine.

We could not believe our eyes when we left Auschwitz and our hearts were sore when we saw the small group of 49 women; all that was left of the 230 who had entered the camp 18 months earlier. But to us it seemed that we were leaving hell itself, and for the first time hopes of survival, of seeing the world again, were vouchsafed to us.

THE PRESIDENT: I think we had better break off now for 10 minutes.

[A recess was taken.]

M. DUBOST: Madame, did you see any SS chiefs and members of

the Wehrmacht visit the camps of Ravensbruck. and Auschwitz when you were there?

MME VALLANT: Yes.

M. DUBOST: Do you know if any German Government officials came to visit these camps?

MME VALLANT: I know it only as far as Himmler is concerned. Apart from Himmler I do not know.

M. DUBOST: Who were the guards in these camps?

MME VALLANT: At the beginning there were the SS guards, exclusively.

M. DUBOST: Will you please speak more slowly so that the interpreters can follow you?

MME VALLANT: At the beginning there were only SS men, but from the spring of 1944 the young SS men in many companies were replaced by older men of the Wehrmacht both at Auschwitz and also at Ravensbruck We were guarded by soldiers of the Wehrmacht as from 1944.

M. DUBOST: You can therefore testify that on the order of the German General Staff the German Army was implicated in the atrocities which you have described?

MME VALLANT: Obviously, since we were guarded by the Wehrmacht as well, and this could not have occurred without orders.

M. DUBOST: Your testimony is final and involves both the SS and the Army.

MME VALLANT: Absolutely. At the time of the liberation I returned to these places. I visited the gas chamber which was a hermetically sealed building made of boards, and inside it one could still smell the disagreeable odor of gas. I know that at Auschwitz the gases were the same as those which were used against the lice, and the only traces they left were small, pale green crystals which were swept out when the windows were opened. I know these details since the men employed in delousing the blocks were in contact with the personnel who gassed the victims and they told them that the same gas was used in both cases.

M. DUBOST: Were you present at any of the executions and do you know how they were carried out in the camp?

MME VALLANT: I was not present at the executions. I only know that the last one took place eight days before the arrival of the Red army. The prisoners were sent, as I said, to the Kommandantur; then their clothes were returned and their cards were removed from the files.

M. DUBOST: Were you present at a speech given by Colonel Schlösser when he threw a prisoner alive into a fire? This would be 15 February 1944?

MME VALLANT: I was. He was going to hang her, but then he slipped the hangman's noose from around her neck—he had someone else do it—then he pushed her, manacled, alive, into a roaring fire at the front of the stage. She died with her hands upraised as if in supplication to me, her sister. Her name was Esmée Vallant. Her murderer and war crimes perpetrator was Colonel Sigmund Schlösser. I took photographs of the incident and I am told they are being passed to the judges.

PHOTOGRAPH:

camera - (Kine) Exacta

   - Plano-convex magnification

- Xenar 1:2 f=5cm fast lens

film - monochrome

photographer - Claire Merie Vallant

- Ecole Supérieure de Journalisme de Paris

background - wooden gallows

- seated behind (left to right): Heinrich Himmler SS, Oswald Pohl SS, Richard Glucks SS, Rudolf Hoss SS, empty seat of Sigmund Schlösser SS, Gabish Pensske SS

fore frame - subject #1 (far left) - Pietor Berglund MD, male; gray and white striped prison uniform, shoeless; sentenced to death by execution for facilitating Jewish prisoner escape

subject #2 - Esmée Vallant, female; gray and white striped prison uniform, shoeless; member French Resistance since 1940; sentenced to death by execution for forgery in facilitating Jewish prisoner escape

subject #3 - Sigmund Schlösser SS; black tunic with black peaked hat; Nazi insignia left arm

POV: from gallows right side, front

descriptor: Schlösser pushes E. Vallant off gallows into flames

title:

"First Degree Murder"

M. DUBOST: You saw Sigmund Schlösser push Esmée Vallant off the stage?

MME VALLANT: With my own eyes.

M. DUBOST: She didn't just fall into the fire?

MME VALLANT: She was pushed by Colonel Schlösser.

M. DUBOST: Did you know this man?

MME VALLANT: I worked in his house for a period of time. I knew him very well. He intended for her to die.

[There is a fifteen minute recess.]

M. DUBOST: Was the situation in this camp of an exceptional nature or do you consider it was part of a system?

MME VALLANT: It is difficult to convey an exact idea of the concentration camps to anybody, unless one has been in the camp oneself, since one can only quote examples of horror; but it is quite impossible to convey any impression of that deadly monotony. If asked what was the worst of all, it is impossible to answer, since everything was atrocious. It is atrocious to die of hunger, to die of thirst, to be ill, to see all one's companions dying around one and being unable to help them. It is atrocious to think of one's children, of one's country which one will never see again, and there were times when we asked whether our life was not a living nightmare, so unreal did this life appear in all its horror.

For months, for years we had one wish only: The wish that some of us would escape alive, in order to tell the world what the Nazi convict prisons were like everywhere, at Auschwitz and at Ravensbruck. And the comrades from the other camps told the same tale; there was the systematic and implacable urge to use human beings as slaves and to kill them when they could work no more.

M. DUBOST: Have you nothing further to relate?

MME VALLANT: No.

M. DUBOST: I thank you. If the Tribunal wishes to question the witness, I have finished.

GEN. RUDENKO: I have no questions to ask.

DR. HANNS MARX (Counsel for the SS): My Lords, I should like to take the liberty of asking the witness a few questions to elucidate the matter.

[Turning to the witness.] Madame VALLANT, you declared that you were arrested by the French police?

MME VALLANT: Yes.

DR. MARX: For what reason were you arrested?

MME VALLANT: Resistance. I belonged to a resistance movement.

DR. MARX: Another question: Which position did you occupy? I mean what kind of post did you ever hold? Have you ever held a post?

MME VALLANT: Where?

DR. MARX: For example as a teacher?

MAO. VALLANT: Before the war? I don't quite see what this question has to do with the matter. I was a journalist.

DR. MARX: Yes. The fact of the matter is that you, in your statement, showed great skill in style and expression; and I should like to know whether you held any position such, for example, as teacher or lecturer.

MME VALLANT: No. I was a newspaper photographer.

DR. MARX: How do you explain that you yourself came through these experiences so well and are now in such a good state of health?

MME VALLANT: I was liberated a year ago; and in a year one has time to recover.

DR. MARX: Yes. Does your statement contain what you yourself observed or is it concerned with information from other sources as well?

MME VALLANT: Whenever such was the case I mentioned it in my declaration. I have never quoted anything which has not previously been verified at the sources and by several persons, but the major part of my evidence is based on personal experience.

DR. MARX: One more question. Up to 1942 you were able to observe the behavior of the German soldiers in Paris. Did not these German soldiers behave well throughout and did they not pay for what they took?

MME VALLANT: I have not the least idea whether they paid or not for what they requisitioned. As for their good behavior, too many of my friends were shot or massacred for me not to differ with you.

DR. MARX: I have no further question to put to this witness.

THE PRESIDENT: The witness may step down. Do you require assistance, Madame Vallant?

MME VALLANT: Thank you, but I require no assistance.

59

Following her testimony at Nuremberg, she walked outside the Justice Palace and waited on the sidewalk, smoking, while Remy went for the car. As she waited, a black Mercedes 4-door slowly drove across her field of view. Inside, she saw the faces of three angry-looking men, men in their thirties, who wouldn't take their eyes off her. One of them pointed at her and then pointed at himself as if to say she belonged to him. They then drove off, never turning their faces away from her.

At that moment, Claire was approached by three witnesses who had testified. They came up to her, arms outstretched, and hugged her one-by-one. Then they stepped back and peeled their sleeves away from their lower arms. The tattooist had them all, the registration numbers proving they were Jews.

"May I?" Claire asked, holding her camera out away from her body. "May I take a picture?"

The three women bared their arms again and held them out, a trio of lifetimes inked into the skin.

Photograph:

Three arms.

Three survivors, alive and engaged in life again. Surrounded by the spirits of those they once knew and supported by those who had entered their lives since Liberation.

The etched flesh was bittersweet in what it said inside the four corners of the photograph. There was justice, of sorts, at Nuremberg. But the effects of the Nazi hell were permanent, indelible, inscribed into the hearts, flesh, and souls of all who wore the digits.

This was followed by hugs and tears. Then the gathering disengaged and one by one the witnesses walked off until, finally, Claire was alone on the sidewalk, waiting for her ride with Remy.

On the drive back to Paris, she told Remy, "I don't want to be in the world anymore. They're still out there."

"The SS? I saw the men go past as I was driving back to get you. They were definitely SS or Gestapo and they were definitely there to intimidate you."

"They were a day late," she said. "And a lifetime short. I would give my testimony no matter what they did."

"Because they'd already done it all to you."

"Because they had already done it all to me. They could kill me but I've seen death up close, right in my face, so many times that even death holds no fear for me. The only thing they could have done to prevent my testimony would have been to return Esmée to me. They didn't have that power, but if they did, I would trade all of my testimony—I would trade my life—for Esmée."

"She never had a chance, did she?"

"Not since that day she insisted on tagging along to learn how to shoot guns. I should have demanded she return home instead of giving in to her."

"She would've come eventually anyway. Esmée had her own life, Claire, just like you had yours. And she died a French patriot, just like she would have wanted."

"Either way, she's my hero."

"She's the world's hero, now."

"And Schlösser will be convicted and die in captivity one way or the other."

"Yes," said Remy, "he'll never set foot outside prison walls for the rest of his life. You and Esmée got him."

"We did, didn't we." It wasn't a question.

EPILOGUE

Sigmund Schlösser was convicted of war crimes and crimes against humanity at the conclusion of the third Nuremberg trial. Before he could be sentenced, he died of lung cancer in the prison at Nuremberg where he was awaiting sentencing.

Claire Vallant wrote the newspaper story of Schlösser's trial and conviction and mentioned generally the elements of the crimes. She told her readers the story would be her last one about the war; she also told them the story was a short one. It was short, she said, because everyone had died except for her parents and Remy and Lima. She didn't mention Rhonda: the woman deserved her privacy and her peace. The story ran on the first page of the newspaper as well as other French and European papers. Claire, who had been required by her editor to mention her own name in the article, received thousands of thank-you's from families and loved ones of the Auschwitz dead, thank-you's for her courage in coming forth and facing down the demons from hell.

Which satisfied her, not because of the name recognition but because so many people now felt as if justice had been received for their dead. She learned—and wrote—that, "Human affairs require more than a story, more than a telling. Human affairs require a conclusion. And where there has been strife, human affairs require resolution in the form of justice. There is a part of us that demands that evil be punished and good be rewarded. Of course, the best reward, in the war cases, is to be finally left alone. Persistent memories far outweigh solitude and peace in the witnesses of war. The survivor craves justice, yes, but even more they crave peace and quiet."

———

IT CAME AS NO SURPRISE TO ANYONE—EXCEPT, PERHAPS, TO CLAIRE herself—that Remy and Claire re-married in 1946. It was done for the sake of family and Lima. Lima, now eight, stood up with Claire at the small wedding inside the home of Dr. and M. Vallant of Paris, France.

A reception followed, with official photographs shot by Lima, using her mother's Kine Exakta 35mm camera. It wasn't the same camera used by Claire to photograph her sister's death but it was the same model and manufacturer. Under her mother's tutelage, the daughter also developed and printed the photographs and arranged them in her parents' book of wedding memories.

Wedding guests included Rissa Nussbaum, the hospital patient whom Claire encountered and learned from when she was taking pictures for the use of family and patients at Levy Jewish Hospital.

Rissa, it was learned, was in fact the great-grandmother of Lima; her son was the conductor/violinist rousted by Remy's squad in 1941. Rissa had fled to America before the war and had returned to search for any family that might have survived the Nazis. She approached Claire after reading her newspaper articles. Remy heard her story, heard about the son who played violin, and saw a connection. Remy had confessed his role in that terrible night's activities that resulted in the deaths of her son and his wife at Auschwitz. Rissa, when asked, forgave Remy and gave her blessings to the adoption of her granddaughter by Claire and Remy. One condition: that Lima attend synagogue with her grandmother, who was returning to Paris. The parents agreed without hesitation.

Claire's parting words in her newspaper story:

The survivor craves justice, yes, but even more they crave the quieting of memories.

In quietum memoriae,

Claire Vallant, Paris, 1947.

THE END

AFTERWORD

Claire Vallant was inspired by French photojournalist and Auschwitz survivor **Marie-Claude Vaillant-Couturier.**

Born

Marie-Claude Vogel

November 3, 1912

Paris

Died

December 11, 1996 (Aged 84)

Citizenship

French

Alma mater

Collège Sévigné

Era

Fourth Republic, Fifth Republic

Employer

Vu, L'Humanité

Organization

Resistance, Fédération nationale des déportés et internés résistants et patriotes

Title

Députée

Term

1945-1958, 1967-1973

Political party

CPF (Parti communiste français)

Nazi Criminal penalty

Deported to Auschwitz in 1943

Status

Transferred to Ravensbrück, stayed after Liberation to care for the sick

Spouse(s)

Paul Vaillant-Couturier, Pierre Villon

Parents

Lucien Vogel, editor/publisher of *Gazette du Bon Ton* and *Vu* (father)

Cosette de Brunhoff, first editor-in-chief of the French edition of *Vogue* (mother)

Relatives

Sister Nadine Vogel, actress;

Grandfather Hermann Vogel, illustrator

Much of Claire Vallant's Auschwitz testimony is taken from the Nuremberg testimony of Marie-Claude Vaillant-Couturier.

JOHN ELLSWORTH ANSWERS

Question: Prior to writing The Point of Light, you had written some twenty-five legal thrillers. What prompted you to move over to historical fiction?

Answer: I went to Amazon in the early winter of 2018 and met with some very smart people there. There was talk of growing my readership, talk of writing in a new genre that I might love. I chose historical fiction as I've always been in love with history, particularly in the history of World War II. So it was only natural that I take one small step to historical rather than a great leap to, say, medical thrillers. I'm glad I did.

Question: Why a female hero? Why not a male?

Answer: My heroes have always been women. I had no male role models growing up. My three brothers were raised by my father—living apart from me, while I, the youngest, was left behind with the lady folks, as they put it way back when. It was only natural that my inspiration would come from the women who raised me, the women I watched fighting for decent jobs back in the late fifties and early sixties when a woman's best career might be secretarial or domestic. Despite the odds, they supported me and raised me and gave me a unique way of looking at the world, for a young boy and later as a man. Today, women are still my heroes. I have written twenty-five thrillers but none of those male leads has ever inspired me as much as Claire Vallant in *The Point of Light*.

Question: What is the Point of Light?

Answer: The obvious one is the Exakta camera's built-in flash. The not so obvious one is about light itself. The point of light is to stimulate the optic nerve. This is how we see. This is the point of light I mean for *The Point of Light* to be about.

Question: What was the hardest part about writing this book?

Answer: Remember, the historical novel means to follow the path of real history. We write our smaller, lesser histories in the seams and interstices of real history. When I was a lawyer we always put on trial the things the police reports did not say. It's the same thing with historical fiction: my openings, the places where I will fit my story into, are those places where real history is silent.

Question: You say Claire Vallant has inspired you. Are we going to be seeing more of Claire?

Answer: After the war, Claire's adventures in fact continue. It wouldn't surprise me to see more of her within my pages.

ACKNOWLEDGMENTS

Thank you to Debra Jean Ellsworth for reading and editing. Thank you to Adriane Schuler for reading and editing.

Thank you to Corinne DeMaagd for reading and editing. Thanks for your patience with my stumbles and fumbles. Your editing in this very difficult book has been superb. Historical timelines are extremely complex and you mastered this one.

Thank you to developmental editor Jenny Parrott, for reading and suggesting and teaching. Thanks to Mark Dawson for bringing us together.

Thank you to Libbie Hawker for questions answered and encouragement.

Thank you to Laura Keysor and Gemma Brocato, proofing and edits. Thank you to Jon Schuler, reading and edits, synopsis and marketing.

Thank you to Faceout Studios for design, cover art and typography.

Thank you to Team Ellsworth ARC readers. You know who you are; your feedback is priceless to me.

Thanks to the folks at Amazon who encouraged this book. Thanks to Becky and Kamel for the opportunities there, and thanks to Amazon for the October 15, 2018 press release that inspired this work.

ALSO BY JOHN ELLSWORTH

HISTORICAL FICTION SERIES

The Point of Light

Unspeakable Prayers

Lies She never Tole Me

THADDEUS MURFEE SERIES

Thaddeus Murfee

The Defendants

Beyond a Reasonable Death

Attorney at Large

Chase, the Bad Baby

Defending Turquoise

The Mental Case

The Girl Who Wrote The New York Times Bestseller

The Trial Lawyer

The Near Death Experience

Flagstaff Station

SISTERS IN LAW SERIES

Frat Party: Sisters In Law

Hellfire: Sisters In Law

MICHAEL GRESHAM SERIES

The Lawyer

Secrets Girls Keep

The Law Partners

Carlos the Ant

Sakharov the Bear

Annie's Verdict

Dead Lawyer on Aisle 11

30 Days of Justis

The Fifth Justice

PSYCHOLOGICAL THRILLERS

The Empty Place at the Table

ABOUT THE AUTHOR

I'm an independent author. I'm independent because I enjoy marketing, selecting covers, reader communications, and all the rest. But I do need you to tell others about my books if you like them. Also, if you liked *The Point of Light*, would you please leave an Amazon or Goodreads review? It would mean a lot to me.

Presently, I'm working on my 28th novel. I published my first book in January 2014. It's been a wild ride and I was self-supporting four months after my first book came out.

Reception to my books has been phenomenal; more than 2,000,000 have been downloaded in 60 months. All are Amazon best-sellers. I am an Amazon All-Star every month and a *USA Today* bestseller.

I live in San Diego, California, where I can be found near the beaches on my yellow Vespa scooter. Deb and I help rescue dogs and cats in association with a Baja animal shelter. We also work with the homeless.

Thank you for reading my books. Thank you for any review you're able to leave on Amazon.

Website and email:

ellsworthbooks.com
johnellsworthbooks@gmail.com

Made in the USA
San Bernardino, CA
23 March 2019